PENUMBRA

SUSAN L. ALANDAR

Apropos Press

Book Cover by Miblart, adapted from original work by the author.

Published by Apropos Press

Print ISBN: 979-8-9900576-2-3

Penumbra:
a region of semi-shadow resulting
from the obstruction of light by an opaque object,
such as the corona around the moon during an eclipse.

A PENUMBRA IS THE SHADOW OF STOLEN LIGHT

"As flies to wanton boys are we to the gods."
—King Lear Act 4, Scene 1

CONTENTS

PROLOGUE

To my son, and all my descendants thereafter:

Nothing about our history will be remembered in a thousand years. All of our technology is gone, and all accounts with it. Without that underpinning of knowledge, memory will become myth, and only the gods will matter.

I was once just a man, albeit with genomic material that set me apart from the rest of humanity. I was genetically engineered with specific attributes and constraints meant for one purpose: to lead the survivors of Earth. Both the attributes and constraints have been magnified by the gods, for myself and all my descendants.

All of our humanity came grieving for a home lost, destroyed by our own ingratitude and arrogance. We found a new world, which we named Hiraeth.

This new world shone bright with promise when we found her. But Hiraeth is a living being, and knew what we had done to Earth. She feared us with good reason. Still, being merciful, she gave us survival.

Not without constraint. Having magic unknown to Earth, she constructed gods to control us.

The gods eclipsed the light of her promise.

One god has prophesied a great war will come in a thousand years. If he is disobeyed, the Prophecy War will end all of human existence.

Even Hiraeth's primary magic cannot break the magic of her gods once initiated. Mourning for us, she sought a way around prophecy.

One human soul had already cried out against the gods, against the injustice of freedom's loss. Hiraeth took that soul as her own, gave her immortality, and hid her within the god's prophecy. She alone, this Daughter of Prophecy, will remember who we were, and never change who she is.

After a thousand years, she may return to the people the freedom to choose their own destiny.

She may restore the light stolen by the gods.

Khandor
High King of Azlatan
Year 1

PART 1: THE HIGH KING

**IN THE REALM OF AZLATAN, YEAR 994,
ONE YEAR BEFORE THE PROPHECY WAR**

The Deities of Azlatan are thus:

*The God of Order is **Phaelon,** who guards the borders of our world; Phaelon's Nine Laws rule the races both Rioch and Duine.*

*The Goddess of Death and Justice is **Daimaine.** The High King commands her. She gave the bloodline of High Kings the gifts of Kingship. The High King rules all Dominions, subject only to Phaelon's Laws. Daimaine owns his soul.*

*The Goddess of Life and Mercy is **Liethe.** Her wisdom is beyond mortal ken. She gives the power of healing.*

*The Goddess of **Chaos** is unknown here, for she was exiled by Phaelon for a thousand years, and will bring war upon her return.*

—from the Annals of Azlatan

Chapter 1

Danon was too young for dissipation to have spoiled his darkly handsome face, but the temporary effects of a hangover were obvious.

He glared back at his reddened eyes in the mirror, and silently cursed the banging in his head and the aches in every other part of his anatomy. Still a little drunk, he winced at the added banging on the door of his room. "By all the gods," he bellowed, "stop the damned noise!"

"My apologies, Compatri." The nervous voice was muffled beyond the door. "You are needed in the common room."

Danon splashed his eyes with water from the bowl below the mirror, peered again at his dusky face and contrasting arctic blue (but still reddened) eyes and the tangled black hair that curled to the shoulders of his black uniform. The emerald star on the tall collar shamed him because it reminded him of his responsibilities.

He straightened, smoothing the leather tunic with a wry glance toward the bed he'd slept in...badly, and fully clothed...and finger-combed his hair while he crossed to the door.

When he yanked it open he glowered at the terrified young soldier who stood saluting him. "Why?" he demanded.

"There is a Tahmond," the soldier stuttered. "He has seized upon a young child, and the man with him claims he is your Bonded Duine and is asking for your help."

Varady.

The name and everything that came with it sobered him immediately. It reminded him why he'd come here, to the solitary inn boasted by the small town he'd left years before. Varady was the servant who had been more like a brother...his Duine, bonded to him by the Law of the God of Order. The man he had abandoned in shame and guilt.

Danon's liege had sent three soldiers with him for protection, knowing too well that the black-clad soldiers of his new army were often feared and distrusted. Danon had left his three unwanted companions to their own devices and retired to his room to drink away the misery of his own failures.

He vaguely remembered sending one of them to his family home, to summon Varady to meet him here the next morning. Apparently it was already the next morning, but something was wrong, and it involved a Tahmond...a priest of the god Phaelon.

A Tahmond, tacit enemy of his sworn liege, the High King of all the known world called Azlatan.

Danon pulled himself together, strapped on his sword, and gestured the soldier aside as he strode to the stairs.

He saw the Tahmond first, standing imperiously in vertically divided robes of black and white, his face painted with the same division. His hair was a halo of white. Chillingly, his eyes were white marbles, yet they saw with clarity.

The Tahmond was facing Varady. The Duine's pale fawn hair set him apart from the two dark Rioch soldiers who were the audience to the scene. A young boy clutched Varady's waist, his face buried against Varady's belly. Varady's hand was set protectively on the boy's shoulder.

"I told you to seize that child." The Tahmond spoke to the soldiers who flanked Varady and the boy. "He is the one we have been searching for, and must be brought to Phaelon's Temple."

"These men do not answer to you." Danon stopped at the foot of the stairs to confront the Tahmond. "They are soldiers of the High King, as am I."

The Tahmond's white eyes rolled to him. "Compatri. I know very well who you are. I was directed here to learn why the High King has sent a soldier of your importance to an insignificant town so far from his city. Now I know. It's because of this boy. I demand he be brought to the High Tahmond immediately."

"This boy?" Danon scowled. "Why do you think he should be brought anywhere?"

"Because I felt his power as soon as he entered the room. This is the Forbidden Child we have been searching for. He carries the shadow of the goddess Daimaine. It is as visible to me as your black uniform." The color black was sacred to Daimaine, and could only be worn by the High King and those sworn to him.

Danon's eyes flashed to the boy who had been barely four years of age the last time he had seen him...six years ago. He remembered his name was Jael. He was Duine, even though he had black hair, rare to his race.

"I am sure you are mistaken," Danon said carefully. "This boy has always been...odd. It's more likely you sense the problem that has always existed in his mind."

The Tahmond snorted his disbelief. "I demand he be brought to Phaelon's Temple."

Danon turned his attention back to the Tahmond. "The child is a subject of the High King, and will go nowhere except by order of the High King." His voice rang hard. "He will remain in my custody until I am ordered otherwise by my liege."

"I shall report this to the High Tahmond. You cannot deny the Law of Phaelon."

"There is no evidence regarding Phaelon's Law as it applies to this boy," Danon retorted. "Go back to Cabre. Make your report. The child stays with me."

The Tahmond drew himself up, furious. After a moment he wheeled, his black and white robes flaring, and left the room.

Danon turned to the soldiers. "Darin, leave immediately for Cabre, and go swiftly as you can. You must let the High King know what has transpired here, and that I await his command.

You other two, settle the bill with the innkeeper and go to the stables. Prepare the horses, including one for this Duine. We will be riding to my father's manor." As they all shot bewildered looks toward Jael, he snapped, "Now! Clear the room, and close the door behind you."

As they obeyed, he turned to face what he had most dreaded, and read with sinking heart the pain of betrayal in Varady's golden eyes.

Varady was tall, with the fair skin and hair common to the Duine race, but far more handsome than Danon. He was also, Danon knew, far more intelligent. He had always believed Varady should have been born Rioch, and not created a servant by virtue of his Duine heritage.

Varady had always known more about Azlatan, past and present, than the average citizen of either race. When he spoke he proved that was still true.

"I see by your uniform with its emerald star that you have become Compatri...the highest rank of Azlatan's new army, companion to the High King himself." Varady shook his head, looking down to stroke Jael's hair as the boy remained unmoving. "Six years I have waited for you, Danon. And all that time I thought you were in the Temple of Liethe, learning the magic of healing, and that's why you had no time to come home or even send word to us. What happened to your lifelong plans of returning as a healer to our village? Why and how did you instead become—this?"

"The story's too long to tell now," Danon began.

"I'm sure it is. And it's more urgent we start with what just occurred here. Whether or not Jael is who the Tahmond thinks he is, we need to get him to safety."

"He'll be safe with me until Khedran sends for him."

"You're actually going to turn him over to the High King?" Varady stared in disbelief. "Who have you become, Danon?"

"As you said. Compatri to the High King. Why did you bring Jael with you, Varady? I meant to talk to you alone."

"I didn't bring him purposely." Varady sank to one knee, framing Jael's face with his hands in an attempt to make the boy look into his eyes. "He followed me. I realized it when I was almost here, and had to bring him the rest of the way. He was fine, Danon, until we got here and he ran to this room. That Tahmond immediately blasted him with magic. Now he's retreated somewhere I can't reach."

"He's always been strange, as I told the Tahmond."

Varady gave up on communicating with Jael and stood to face Danon, his anger apparent. "Jael has spells, yes. But he's a good boy, an innocent child, and doesn't deserve being served up to those who would destroy him."

"The High King will not destroy him, Varady."

"How can you believe that? I know what the Tahmond was talking about. If the High King also believes Jael is the Forbidden Child, he has no choice. The prophecy is very clear. If a Forbidden Child is allowed to live, all Duine will rise up to kill all Rioch. Why would the King allow that to happen?"

"You have to know Khedran to understand he would not let it happen. Nor would he sacrifice an innocent child."

Varady's gaze sharpened. "What? It cannot be both ways. Do you think your High King is a god, like Phaelon?"

"Of course he is not a god. He is human."

"I've heard it said he is more Chaine than human." Varady's eyes swept down to the sword Danon wore. "That sword is forged of Chaine gold, and you wear it in the manner of a Chaine warrior. When you and I met a Chaine all those years ago, you denied she was human. Yet now you appear to have been trained by their methods."

"I was wrong," Danon sighed. "The Chaine people are human, as is the High King."

"I understand the High King was mentored all his life by their leader, the one they name simply The Chaine. Wasn't she the one we met that day? You were struck dumb as a fool when you saw her."

At that, Danon's mind flashed inexorably back to the day he'd turned around to the greatest shock of his young life, to face a woman unlike anyone or anything he had ever seen. The vision stood before him as tall as he was, with hair of fire and gold blooming wild about her face and shoulders. Her eyes were piercing grey-silver in a face exotic in its beauty, and her statuesque body was sheathed in leather armor filigreed with gold.

He'd been certain she was too beautiful to be human, and stunned speechless for several minutes.

Danon scowled at the memory, rubbing the ache between his eyes. "I didn't do any better the second time I met her. Shandiin is rather overwhelming. Varady, she's the main reason I'm here. I came because..."

He was interrupted by a knock on the door, and a soldier looked in. "The horses are ready."

His old home looked the same as it had six years ago.

Danon and his companions dismounted by the crumbling field-stone fence near the old stable. A worn path sloped away ahead of them, parting the deep grass beneath the ancient trees. The path led to an old stone manor where the entrance waited in shadow.

Jael remained in a state like sleepwalking, unaware of his sur-roundings but easily led by Varady's hand. Danon looked from the boy into the waiting eyes of his Duine. "Will you to take him to his mother, and not try to hide him somewhere?"

Varady stiffened in shock. "What, now you don't trust me?"

Danon sighed. "Of course I trust you. If there's anyone I have ever trusted, it is you. But you seem concerned about his safety and my intent, Varady. You must understand I have a responsi-bility to my liege. Khedran has searched for years for the child supposedly sired by his father. Is Jael's mother still here?"

Varady nodded grimly. "Mia will be in the kitchen. I will take Jael to her; she knows what to do when he has a spell like this.

Danon, I've known Mia for more than ten years. You and I were both barely sixteen when she came to help after your mother died. You can't possibly think she is King Allasar's secret mistress!"

Danon looked at the boy, at the black hair that made him different from the normally fair Duine. "We never knew who his father was," he pointed out, and sighed. "What I think isn't what matters. It's the business of the High King, and I serve him. Right now I have to go to my father, so I'm counting on you to take care of both Jael and Mia...and make sure they both remain safely under my father's roof." He shook his head at Varady's cold stare. "My allegiance to the King is sacred. I am trusting you to hold true on my behalf."

"My allegiance," Varady reminded him, "has always been to you, and is no less sacred than yours."

Danon winced at Varady's words, for he knew they were true. He watched him walk away with Jael in tow, circling the manor to enter through the kitchen instead of the front entrance.

"Take care of the horses," Danon said to the two waiting soldiers. "They don't have a stablemaster here, but there are plenty of stalls. I will go talk to my father, and secure our lodging." He patted the neck of his own white stallion. "Turn this one out in the paddock after you unsaddle him. He gets restless in a stall."

With that he turned to confront the man he had never been able to please, certain that things would be no different now.

The door was answered by the Duine who had served his father since before Danon was born. Farin hadn't changed much, only grown more grey and a little grimmer, and his shock on recognizing Danon was obvious.

"Is my father in?" Danon asked simply.

Farin nodded, nervously finding his wits. "Lord Landan is in his office."

"I can find my way. I have two companions. They are in the stable at the moment. Will you please arrange for each of us to have rooms ready?"

Farin's eyes swept him up and down. He swallowed. "Do they also wear the black?"

"Yes," Danon said patiently. "We are all soldiers of the High King, Farin."

With that he strode past, down the familiar hall to his father's office. Since the door was open, he simply stopped in the doorway and waited.

His father was bent over the papers on his desk. His hair had gone completely grey, Danon noted. But when the man lifted his head, he saw that his face was still made of stone, his dark eyes still piercing.

"Hello, Father."

Landan, Lord of Selagon Manor, stood up slowly as he surveyed the son who had been missing for six years. The son he had not bothered to inquire about, because he disapproved of his intent to become anything other than the next Lord of Selagon Manor.

Landan crossed his arms and met Danon's eyes coldly. "There was a stranger here, weeks back, all in black. I was told he belonged to the High King's army. But the Dominion Kings have always had their own armies. What does the High King need an army for, with none to dare challenge him? He has the power of the dark goddess Daimaine, and the Star Blade, and other powers that are his alone. There are strange tales of him; he is not like any High King before him...they call him the Black Wolf, for he is fearsome and possibly mad. He has been mentored all his life by that vile creature they call The Chaine."

Danon set aside his personal anger at his father's depiction of The Chaine; Shandiin had been his own mentor for more than five years. But his allegiance to his King required a response. "The rumors are wrong. Khedran is different than the High Kings before him, but he has need to be. He requires a central army for unity, and a new threat to Azlatan. The Dominion armies are useless, which was proven when his father was murdered within the walls of a Dominion King's castle."

"No army would have stopped that. Everyone knows Allasar was killed by the Duine Anzihi."

"Yes," Danon snapped. "He was killed by the enforcers, the ones charged with enforcing Phaelon's Law forbidding the mating of Rioch and Duine. Yet never—never in the entire history of Azlatan—had one dared touch a High King."

Landan dropped his arms, scowling. "If the stories are true, High King Allasar impregnated a Duine woman. The Duine Anzihi did what they believed necessary. What the High King did violated Phaelon's Law."

Danon shook his head. "Whether or not the tales are true, there has been instability within the Dominions ever since Allasar's murder. Is it any wonder his son seeks to remedy that for his realm, for all Azlatan? And that is why he is building an army, not for any of the nefarious rumors you may have heard."

Landan snorted. "You must believe that, since you have joined his army." He tapped his own collar, pointed at Danon's. "What is that star for?"

"It signifies my rank, which I am sure is of no interest to you. I find it necessary, Father, to intrude on your accommodations for some time. There are two soldiers with me, and we are awaiting word from the High King regarding an important matter."

For the first time Landan looked surprised. "Intrude? This is your home, Danon, though you have spurned it. I will ensure Farin and Mia have your accommodations ready. Is this important matter why you have come here at last?"

"No. It was time to let you know that I have given my life's allegiance to the High King, and to notify you of what you have already guessed...that I will not be returning as your heir." He paused, bit his lip. "Besides, Tahmond Law requires I be physically present to break the Bond of a Duine."

Landan gasped. "You go too far! Has this High King bewitched you? Do you suddenly hate all Duine, even the one who grew up with you, who lived for the day of his Bonding to you?" He was truly shocked into anger at his son's news.

"I do not hate the Duine."

"But what could Varady have done to displease you? He could not even be there to attend you, through no fault of his own. We thought you were at the Temple of Liethe, where Duine may not serve. Your allegiance to this strange High King has taken you too far, Danon. There is no need for you to break this Bond. And you, after all, have a responsibility to him!"

"Yes." Danon met his father's gaze and knew he would not be able to make him understand what it had taken years to accept himself. "A responsibility. The Duine are the responsibility of the Rioch, because their role is to serve us, and they are dependent on us. Even though we Rioch don't recognize it, acceptance of those things diminishes our own humanity. Those things also make the Duine less than they could be. It ties their identity and their purpose to someone other than themselves. It's wrong and it's unfair and when you see it clearly... it is heartbreaking."

He shook his head at his father's expression. "I did not expect you to understand. But I will no longer keep either myself or Varady in bondage."

"Varady loves you, Danon."

"Yes." He paused, thinking. "That is why it is so hard. I even drank myself blind because I dread telling him my decision. He won't understand any more than you do. Varady feels he has a lifelong claim to me because of the Bond sanctified by Phaelon. I have to reject that Bond, though I have always loved him. He is the only brother I have ever known."

That was all Varady overheard before he turned and walked away, as naturally silent as he had come.

CHAPTER 2

I t was nearly sundown before Danon went in search of
Varady. He'd been busy getting himself and his soldiers
settled in, and only felt an unease when he realized he had
unpacked without Varady's assistance; he'd learned very well
how to manage without a servant.

He knew the loyalty of his Duine. Varady should have
been nearby, awaiting his summons...no, his invitation. He and
Varady had never operated in the formal tradition of Rioch and
Duine.

Walking through the last golden light of day, Danon stopped
near the stable upon hearing a flurry of notes, a melody he
could not quite catch, then a run like a fall of silver. His breath
softened to silence. The flute's music rang on. It was like wind
and water, made by nature instead of man. His own white
stallion stood at the fence, straining toward the sound.

Both he and his horse shivered slightly when the music ended
abruptly. There was an afterimage of stars and harmony lost.
The horse snorted softly and wheeled away as though released
from some magic bridle.

"He's like ChanDethe," Varady said as he arrived by the fence
to join Danon. He had left his flute in the stable. His hair
was pale silk blowing about his face as he looked after the
stallion. "Do you remember the legend, Danon? ChanDethe is
the goddess Liethe's messenger. He is a small white cat she
carries, who can change into a great white horse or a great bird."

When Danon said nothing, Varady went on, his eyes still on the white stallion roaming the paddock. "He's nothing like the Selagon beasts, is he? He looks like he could really be ChanDethe in horse form."

"I named him that." Danon looked down, lifting a boot onto the lowest rail of the fence. "He's supposed to be a war-horse, but he's never really figured out the philosophy behind war. He loves to run, but has no temper at all. Nothing like the High King's other horses. So the name didn't stick. Everyone just called him my pet, so he's Pet."

"And I would gamble," Varady said softly, "that you are nothing like the King's other soldiers, either."

Danon leaned against the fence and turned his face to the man he had called brother. "You would win the bet. That's why they gave him to me. Hoping we would learn together, I guess."

"They?"

"The High King. And...a friend of his."

"Is the friend perhaps The Chaine, who you called Shandiin?"

Danon stilled at the question, guessing there was more to it. He studied Varady's profile, realizing Varady was no longer gazing at the stallion, but beyond the shallow valley cupping the small border town of Selagon. The bowl of the valley was already filling with blue shadow, though the sun still warmed the hill where they stood and gilded the crest of the far ridge. Varady's eyes lifted to a hunting bird scissoring upward from that line of light. Its wings stilled to a pointed crescent as it found the updraft from the Plains of Admech that lay outside of the known world of Azlatan.

He was still watching the bird when he spoke again. "When I met Shandiin all those years ago, she asked me a strange thing. She wanted to know if it was hard, being Duine. I told her no, because freedom isn't always necessary when there is love."

He finally lowered his head, turning to meet Danon's eyes. "She said love is dangerous when it keeps you in bondage. You have decided to no longer be in bondage."

"You overheard? Varady..."

Varady interrupted. "Tell me, Danon...is it true the Chaine even ride past the borders of Azlatan?"

Danon swallowed painfully. "I'm sorry you found out that way." When Varady only waited, he sighed. "The Chaine go where they please."

"They have entered the Plains of Admech, then. Yet the Tahmond have proclaimed that no mortal could pass there. Are the Chaine like the gods, Danon? I hear that they live far longer than we do, maybe even longer than the High Kings."

Danon wondered at Varady's train of thought, and a new anxiety edged his mind. "I believe the Chaine are mortal," he answered carefully.

"But that's impossible. You can't have it both ways. Either they are mortal, or they are not. Either they can cross into the Plain of Admech, or they cannot. Or could it be that the Tahmond are lying to us?"

"The Chaine are outside the jurisdiction of the Tahmond, Varady. They are immune to magic."

"Ah. Another paradox. We are taught that Phaelon gives his Tahmond rule over the natural order of our world. If the Chaine are outside the jurisdiction of the Tahmond, they would have to be from outside of our world...which I understand they are, yet no one speaks of that fact. Everyone believes Azlatan to be the only world."

"Varady..." Danon tried to interrupt, but Varady overrode him.

"...and aren't we taught that no paradox is possible within the natural order of things? So that makes all of this impossible. Or it is all a lie!"

With Varady's closing shout, they faced each other at last. Varady's face was a mask Danon could not read. "I'm sorry, Danon," Varady continued quietly. "Were you trying to say something?"

Danon couldn't answer.

Varady turned away again. "That puts everything in question, doesn't it? Like the whole idea behind our sacred Azlatan. Like the entire concept behind Duine serving the Rioch."

Danon looked away. "Yes."

"Don't falter now, Danon. You sounded so sure of yourself when you were talking to your father. You sounded very different from the man I knew, who only wanted to be a healer. Why did you give that up to become a soldier?"

"Because I failed at it." Danon's voice was flat. "I was unable to learn the magic, unable to use it. I had worked for it all my life, and I was a failure. That's why I stayed away. I was hiding from you, from my father, from Selagon." He sighed, and Varady waited until he continued.

"You mentioned Shandiin. She was there when I failed, and she is the reason I came back." Danon hesitated, shook his head, shoved a hand through his hair. "She is amazing, Varady. She gave me no pity when I failed my life's cause. Pity, I think, would have ruined me. Instead, she made me a soldier. She is a teacher of warfare, relentless, sometimes even brutal. She trained my mind, not just my body. Then she convinced me that hiding was wrong, that I should gather the courage to come back and tell the truth about who I am now. It took a while to accept, but I finally went to the High King and requested leave...and here I am."

Varady contemplated him knowingly. "I think Shandiin is far more to you than a teacher," he commented, and shrugged when Danon just looked away. "Well, at least you found something to replace the dream of healing. Something else to give your life to. Even if it means..." Varady's voice trailed off. He was unable to say it.

Danon, looked back, aching. "What are you going to do?"

"What does it matter to you?"

"That isn't fair. I was going to make provision..."

"You have no business making provision. You are casting me off. I am free!"

They stared at each other, both all too aware of this final paradox. No Duine, by virtue of his race, could truly be free. Not in Azlatan. Danon drew in a breath, thinking of the line of questions he'd been asked, remembering Varady's childhood fantasies. He felt nauseated. "You can't be meaning to leave Azlatan."

He shook his head before Varady could counter. "I take it back. You are right. I no longer have the right to tell you what you should not do, even out of concern—and I never realized until now how hard that could be. You would die out there, on the Admech. I know I cannot tell you not to go. I have given up that right. But I can beg you not to do this!"

Varady snorted in disdain. "I'm not going there so I can die. Do you think I am crazy enough to commit suicide?"

Danon shook his head. "I had some stupid idea that because you are different from most Duine, being unbonded would be easy for you. I didn't take the reality into account. I certainly never foresaw that you would go tromping across the border into the Plains of Admech, for whatever your reason!"

"Not just into the Plains." Varady gazed east, to adventure. "Through them. I want to find what is on the other side. I want to see the world outside of Azlatan, Danon. The legends that say the world itself is alive, a wonder far greater than the gods, and that it speaks to Prophecy's Daughter. Perhaps I shall be the first to discover who that is."

He laughed at Danon's astonished face, and placed his hand on his shoulder in the old way. "I am sorry for my bitterness. It was hard for me to understand all this. But I have decided that your intent was never to hurt me. I believe in you, Danon. You would never tie yourself to a star that did not have some noble purpose, even one my simple Duine mind can't comprehend." His golden eyes gleamed, but then his quick smile faded. "Still. It is your star you follow, and not mine."

"Yours may not even exist! How can you even consider..."

"Don't you remember the games we played as children, Danon? I always wanted to go to the Plains. I sang all the old legends.

And after you left, I sang them to Jael. He loves them as I do..." a shadow crossed his face. He looked at Danon sharply, then shook his head. "But no. Though I love him, I think Jael's fate is part of your star, and still none of mine."

Danon felt in that moment that Varady had already left, that Azlatan was far behind him.

Danon straightened and turned to him with hands lifted and open. "Please allow me one last thing. Please take Pet, and all his equipment. He is outfitted for a long journey, and I will replenish what few supplies I used on my way from Cabre."

"You cannot give a horse to a Duine..."

They both realized the truth in the same moment, and laughed, a bittersweet farewell to their old lives and the memories of the simpler rules they had broken as children.

CHAPTER 3

J ael was dreaming again of the lady in white, petting the white cat purring on her knee as she rocked on her cottage porch.

"I could see this place, but could never get here before." Jael scanned the fields beyond her cottage fence. The green prairie flowed unbroken to the horizon, a vast emptiness rivaled only by the open sky above. The small fenced-in cottage was the only ship in a sea of grass.

"I've been out there, walking forever in the grass." Jael shivered a little at the memory. "The dark lady is always behind me. I couldn't turn around and look...dreams are like that, sometimes. But I knew she was there."

Squeak, squeak went the chair. "Do you know who she is?"

"No." He squinted against the sunlight, thinking. "I never really thought about who she is before. She's always been around, like my shadow or something. Even when I'm awake." He looked up at the lady who wore a blindfold but could somehow see. Her hair was so white it seemed to have a light of its own. He thought her very beautiful, and very comforting.

"Have you seen Varady?" he asked her.

"Varady has a lot to do before you see him again."

He was disappointed. "I miss Varady."

"Lonesome, are you?"

"Varady was the only one who talked to me. Now that he's gone, it's like being out there." He nodded toward the eternal grass. "All alone."

He realized the light was dimming, as though the sun had gone behind a cloud, though there was neither sun nor cloud to be seen. "I am sorry you have to go," the lady told him gently. "Things are changing for you, Jael, but they will be better."

His eyes opened, and there was a fleeting feeling of loss, like the aftermath of Varady's music. Then the real world rushed back, and he felt a thing waiting like a gift to be remembered.

Jael scrambled to the end of his bed, throwing wide the window as though to let in the gift. It was the last month before Stareven, when summer began, and one of those high windy days that sets a child's heart free as the clouds chased through the sky. Rain-shadows walked the hills, followed by moments of glorious light. Jael raised his small face to the clean breeze.

The dream slipped away, but the lady's promise lingered after the memory.

He remembered the exciting news he had taken to bed the night before. He ducked back inside and dressed, scarcely taking time to wash from the bedside bowl before he was out the door and into the kitchen that was his mother's domain.

Morning sunlight glanced from scrubbed stone and metal pans. The fire in the great fireplace was banked low. Plants hung in profusion from the high rafters, sat on the open windowsills.

His mother, Mia, sat at a small table by a window, contemplating her hands on her mug, and did not hear him enter. He watched her for a moment with a warm feeling. Sunlight sang in the golden strands of her hair, and he saw for the first time that there was silver woven through. She seemed very small in that great room, and that surprised him too.

She looked up as he crossed to her, and her blue eyes brightened. "Morning bless, Jael."

"Morning bless, Mother." He allowed himself a ten-year-old's kiss on her cheek...his first attempt at a grownup reserve...then abandoned it and threw his arms around her. "Isn't it glorious?" he cried. "It's almost Stareven, and the High King is coming here, to Selagon! It's like one of Varady's songs come true!"

She hugged him back, a shadow on her face she would not let him see. There was only serenity in her eyes when he stood back, grinning widely. "Has Lord Danon said when the High King will be here?"

"He is still awaiting final word," she smiled. "You had best eat your breakfast."

He went obediently to the pot on the big woodstove, ladling a thick porridge into his waiting bowl. His chatter didn't cease while he added butter and sugar. "Farin says Lord Danon is Compatri, and that's the highest rank in the King's army!"

Farin was Bonded Duine to Danon's father, and too prone to gossip in Mia's opinion. She said nothing, smiling fixedly as Jael carried the bowl to the table. She knew that this Jael, this bright boy too often hidden behind a shadow, rarely gave her a chance to answer anyway.

"Maybe he's coming for our Stareven celebration," Jael went on as expected. "Do you think Varady will play his music..."

But he halted. He had stumbled against the memory of Varady's absence. "Why did he go?" It was a question he had repeated often.

"I don't know." She answered as she always did. She had not told Jael of the search for a Duine who had allegedly stolen his Rioch's horse. Danon had not pressed the issue and she had her own suspicions about it.

Varady had spoken to her before he disappeared, and warned her about the confrontation between Danon and a Tahmond. He hadn't asked her for the truth behind the Tahmond's accusation, but only relayed what he had seen and heard.

She had known then that someone would come for Jael. Someone more important than a Tahmond.

"It's okay." Jael's new response surprised her. "Varady has a lot of things to do now."

She looked at her son curiously as he spooned too much sugar into his porridge. He went on excitedly. "Farin says this High King's father got murdered!"

She took a quick breath. "Jael, your mind is like a butterfly. Stop now."

His spoon hovered in front of his mouth. "Farin says a Duine woman had a child by the old High King, and that's why he was murdered," he continued with gusto.

"I said stop! Farin is a terrible gossip and I do not want you repeating him, do you hear?"

His eyes widened with shock at her tone.

She gentled her voice, inwardly damning Farin. "The King's Messenger said the High King is traveling with a platoon of soldiers, and they weren't that far behind him. Now eat your breakfast, and then, if you like, you can go up by the road to watch for them."

"Can I really?" he shoveled in the last of his food, climbing down hastily to put his dish on the sideboard lest she relent. Mia watched him rush out the door, and her smile faded with his disappearance.

She rose stiffly and went to wash the dishes. Danon's father had been shocked at the messenger's news, most likely along with everyone in Selagon...except her.

She had waited, and now the waiting was nearly over, and she was afraid. Not for herself. She would stand tall, she promised herself...for the memory of her beloved High King Allasar, and for their son. Her fear was for Jael.

She began her routine duties, finding calmness in the use of her hands, and heard Danon and his father talking outside the kitchen door.

She stood very still, with the listening attitude of a hunted animal.

"Why is he coming here, Danon? No High King has ever come to this place!"

"Selagon will not be the first small town he has visited."

"Dominion King Handel should have some say in this." Landan sounded aggrieved. "Selagon is part of his Dominion. His Highness Khedran is bypassing the order of things."

Danon's sigh was audible. "Sometimes it is necessary, to get anything accomplished. I will see to my own breakfast, Father. No, don't call for Mia. She can serve me as well in the kitchen."

Mia stiffened as the kitchen door opened. She forced herself to turn slowly to face Danon. His expression caused her to take a deep, shaky breath.

For an instant she thought of him as he had looked more than ten years ago, when she had arrived here with the assignment to care for his dying mother. Barely past boyhood at sixteen, he had been more brother than Rioch to poor orphaned Varady, annoying his father with his collection of injured animals that he healed and released. How did that bright, kind teenager turn into this towering soldier, this black-clad Compatri with eyes of azure ice that had watched her so narrowly since his return?

Tired of duplicity, sorry for the change in his attitude toward her, she decided to face the truth now instead of waiting any longer.

"I know why he's coming, Lord Danon. Varady told me what happened. You saved Jael from a Tahmond who believes he is the Forbidden Child."

Danon frowned, then carefully closed the door behind him. "Mia, is there any chance this is true? That Jael is the child of High King Allasar?"

"Yes."

He blinked, and his expression changed to pity.

She had never expected pity. The straight line of her back rejected it.

"It's hard to believe," he said after a long moment. "I know Khedran, and a more honorable man has never lived. But his father forced himself on you, didn't he?"

"No. He did not. Some say I am a sorceress, that I put a spell on High King Allasar. Perhaps I did the same to you, so you could not see the truth."

"No." He spoke sharply. "I could never believe that, Mia. I know you too well." He saw her cold smile. "Of course, not as well as I thought. But I would stand for you. I refuse to believe there is evil magic in you."

She shook her head. "It wouldn't be wise to champion me. I have heard about your High King. He is called the Black Wolf, because he is cold and often merciless, unlike any High King before him. If you stand up for me, he would not appreciate it, and you could suffer at his hands along with Jael and me."

"No, Mia. Khedran is a fair and just King, whatever you have heard. But he has searched for you ever since the High Tahmond confirmed you existed, and that you were pregnant when Allasar sent you away. Can you blame him for wanting the truth, and to find his only living relative? He has not spoken of vengeance against you."

"Of course he wants vengeance. He does not have to speak of it. My people have walked softly for more than ten long years, waiting for his axe to fall. Phaelon's High Tahmond will demand it, and the Duine will ask for my blood, and Jael's, believing that our deaths will remove the threat of the High King's retribution...and more, if the god Phaelon's prophesied war is to be believed."

"What, that the Duine will rise up and kill all the Rioch if a Forbidden Child is allowed to live? No one really believes that."

"Do you think not? Allasar was murdered for part of that Law, so I am not so sure the rest of it will be denied." She crossed her arms. "Would you like your breakfast now, my Lord?"

It was a long way to the road for young Jael. He clambered over the last bit of rocky ground and entered the grove by the road. He halted to breathe in the cool air, to enjoy the green shadows and the flash of a stream. Then he crossed the water to peer past the trees to the empty road.

Seeing he had time, he returned to the stream and splashed his sweaty face, then stretched out on the bank. He knew he would hear any noise from the road, so he stared at the blue of the sky wheeling above the green leaves, the sun warming him on one side and shade cooling him on the other. He rejected loneliness, as he had all his short life, by opening to the living world around him.

Waiting for the transformation of peace, he found sleep instead.

He lay in the sea of grass that surrounded the familiar cottage, and became aware of the dark presence above him.

This time he would see her! He sat up, but the sky was bright and the looming figure was only a haloed shadow.

Black hair like a cloak covered the contours of her body, so long it tangled in the grass. He lifted his hands to shield his eyes, hoping to see her face. Blinking at the image, he realized that the figure was not a woman's after all, and the hair was in reality a cloak, and he awoke with a start to a black-clad stranger standing very near him.

Jael sat bolt upright, blinking hard, and saw the apparition become a soldier watering his horse.

Black horse, tall soldier with black cloak falling from shoulder to black boot heel, black clothing. No other color did he wear. Even the leather of his belt was black, and the hilt of the sword sheathed at his hip. His glossy fall of black hair brushed his shoulders.

He was, Jael thought as he gaped at the face in profile, beautiful.

When the stranger turned toward him, his eyes were an in-humanly brilliant emerald, and a flash of sun made them glow briefly. Jael felt a tug of memory from Varady's tales. Though it didn't fully come clear, and the eyes were very strange, he felt oddly comforted.

The man smiled down at him. "It appears I woke you. I was beginning to think you could sleep through the day."

"I was tired and waiting for the High King on the road. I saw you in my dream, only I thought you were the dark lady. Oh! You must be one of the King's soldiers, and I've missed him."

There was a glint of humor in the man's strangely jeweled eyes. "I'm with the soldiers, yes. But you haven't missed the King's grand entrance. I rode ahead. Good thing, too, or you might have slept through the whole affair."

The horse finished drinking and tugged at the reins to be allowed to graze. The soldier loosened the bit in consent and stroked the horse's arched neck in obvious affection.

Jael couldn't stop staring. "You and that horse are the most beautiful things I have ever seen," he said with a child's naive honesty.

The soldier arched an eyebrow, now openly amused. "Even in your dreams?" he teased.

Jael flushed with memories of taunts, disbelief, laughter. "I did see a dark lady, and a lady in white too! I have! People make fun. But a lot of my dreams come true. A lot!" He looked down, trembling.

He was stilled by a surprisingly gentle hand on his shoulder, and words spoken kindly. "What you think of yourself is far more important than what others think of you. Do not let their attitudes change what is true and strong inside yourself. It seems you have a gift they cannot see. That doesn't make your gift wrong, or them right."

They gazed at each other for a long moment, the boy struck silent by what had been offered.

But he didn't want the man to think him a braggart. "The gift may not be mine. This grove is consecrated to Phaelon, so perhaps the god sent it to me."

He could not understand why the hand abruptly dropped and the man turned back to his horse. He was only sorry the magical moment had passed, and unsure what he had done wrong.

"I dreamed of a very big place." He spoke lamely to the soldier's back. "The grass goes on forever, and it is very lonely."

The man looked back, seeming to consider. "Where would such a place be?"

"I don't know." Jael bit his lip. "Maybe near Cabre, the High King's City?" At the answering expression, hope fell. "I guess you would know. Maybe it's just a dream then."

"Maybe not. Maybe it's a place even the King hasn't seen yet."

"How could that be? The High King knows everything, doesn't he?"

The emerald eyes held laughter. "I am told only the gods know everything. I believe the High King is human, although I've heard that questioned. Perhaps with good reason." He turned back to replace the horse's bit. Jael felt he had been dismissed as a child. But he had so many questions!

"Please, Lord..."

All motion stilled. The stillness was so complete it was more obvious than a violent gesture. When the man turned back again, it was with deliberate care, his strange eyes hard on Jael's.

"You call me that? Are you Duine, then?"

Jael nodded. He realized it hurt to admit it, and he had never known that before. Tears threatened, and he swallowed hard.

Those vivid eyes searched him intently. "You certainly don't look it," the soldier said finally. A slow smile followed. "Nor act like it."

"My mother would shame me, my Lord." A great hurt throbbed in his throat.

The man frowned then, and finished adjusting his horse's bit, then swung easily to the saddle. Jael stood in silent misery, not having been dismissed.

The black stallion stepped lightly before him, and the dark stranger leaned down to tilt Jael's face upward. He studied him for a moment, then released him. "You may have a long wait until the King's arrival. I suggest you return home, and return just at dusk."

Jael blinked hard. "Thank you, Lord," he managed.

The soldier smiled and turned his black stallion down the hill.

Chapter 4

"It appears you will not have to wait in your roadside grove after all, Jael." Danon folded his newly received message absentmindedly. The messenger stood waiting, his bay horse blowing slightly from his run.

Jael, Mia, and Danon had been walking on the front lawn after dinner, while long shadows crept across the grass. Jael had been too full of excitement to wonder at Danon's constant companionship since his return from the grove.

The boy had been growing anxious that he was going to miss the King's arrival, not having been given permission yet to go. Danon had been watching the road and didn't seem surprised at the appearance of the messenger bearing the message.

"Isn't he coming after all?" Jael asked in disappointment.

"Oh yes," Danon replied. "But he is already at the inn and has requested we join him there."

"We?" Jael went pale. He had confessed his meeting with the soldier, but had felt reassured when Danon had not commented on his admission that the man hadn't known that he was Duine at first. Now, child that he was, he felt sure that his forwardness had been reported to the High King. He was both fearful and sad because he had thought the soldier kind.

Danon turned to the waiting messenger. "Remain here while they get ready. My horse will be brought around in a minute." He directed Jael and Mia inside and stopped with them just by the front door.

"Your best clothes," Mia told Jael. "You know where they are. Hurry and change."

The boy looked up at her, struck wordless, and ran for his room.

She spun on Danon, her face pale. "Who did he meet in that grove?" she demanded.

"You can guess as well as I. He frequently rides alone, especially when he wishes to think."

"Apparently he doesn't care to leave Jael in your guardianship any longer."

He read her anger, sighed. "Khedran is not a monster. He listens to reason, and will not bend to the demands of the High Tahmond regarding Jael. You can have faith in him."

"There are other things to consider besides your faith in your hero." Mia trembled as she reached for her cloak.

Jael's memory of the ride from his home was only a blur. Night had fallen by the time they arrived at the inn, Jael riding with Danon. When Danon dismounted and lifted him down, the boy's knees almost buckled when he tried to stand.

"Here now," Danon soothed. "No one is going to hurt you."

"Where is my mother?" Jael asked, for he had seen her leave in a carriage.

"She's already inside."

"I don't understand. What does the High King want with us? Is it because I was rude to the Rioch soldier? I thought he knew I didn't mean to be rude!"

"Quiet, Jael. It's nothing you've done, nor your fault." He took Jael's hand. "Anyone's fault but yours," Danon mumbled, leading him through the front door of the inn.

The room was warm and filled with light from the cavernous fireplace and the lanterns hanging from walls and rafters. It was also filled with black-clad soldiers, noisy ones, lined up at the long tables and filling their plates from heaping bowls and platters.

Danon kept a hand on the boy's shoulder. "This is Jael," he announced, sweeping the area with a warning look over Jael's head.

A nearby soldier wiped his greying moustache, glancing from Danon to the boy. Like Danon, he wore black with an emerald star on his tall collar. "Well now, Jael, your mother's apt to be busy awhile. Why don't you share a bite with us?"

Jael stared from the greying warrior to Danon. In his world, Duine did not sit at table with Rioch. Danon looked back reassuringly. "His name is Farbet, though he is getting too senile to properly introduce himself. The proper response to him is to say thank you."

Farbet snorted. "Don't let that green star fool you. He calls me senile, but I don't wear mine just to know when my clothes are right side out." A few of the soldiers thought this hilarious, and Jael relaxed as Farbet held out a hand to him. He even glanced around hopefully, looking for his friend from the grove.

"Is that really the boy?" he heard a soldier ask.

"Shut it off," Farbet warned. "Don't be confusing him with nonsense. It's bad enough getting dragged in here with this bunch."

"You mean he doesn't even know?" another soldier asked, and this time it was Danon whose glare stopped everything cold. He lifted Jael over the bench to sit by Farbet, who was filling an unwanted plate for him.

Danon reached past him for the plate Farbet had filled. The older soldier immediately replaced it with another and shoved a cup of milk at the boy. Jael picked it up to drink, not knowing what else to do.

"Bet you never thought you'd play nursemaid in this army," a soldier snickered at Farbet.

"Have been," was the growled response, "ever since you joined up."

"Has he already met the boy?" someone else asked through the resultant laughs.

"Yes. He came back from his ride today," another voice said, "and announced he had found his answer in a grove consecrated to Phaelon." There was disbelief expressed at this. "I know, I know!" the voice continued. "I asked him when he started looking for that kind of guidance, and he said, 'I never claimed to know everything.'"

Jael realized who they were talking about and put down his cup, looking eagerly for a familiar face. Just then a side door opened, and his cloaked soldier stepped in, bringing with him an eddy of cold night-wind.

He brought more than winter with his presence. Everyone in the room straightened in respectful acknowledgement of his entrance, even those with their back to the door.

But Jael was just a boy, too young for such distinctions. He was down and running before Danon could stop him. The familiar Rioch only laughed and waved Danon back. He swung Jael up from the floor as though he were a mere toddler.

Jael didn't even mind the indignity. "I'm so glad to see you! The High King has sent for me and my mother, and they took her somewhere without me!"

The man smiled. "She is quite safe, and you will see her very soon."

"I thought you were angry at me...oh!" Jael exclaimed as the soldier put him down and regarded him in question. "Because I forgot to give you the proper Duine salute, and I just did it again."

But his hand was caught before it touched his forehead, and the strange emerald eyes were grave. "Don't do it. No salute. You are not Duine. You are Rioch, Jael. Do you understand?"

There was a stunned silence in the room. Jael nodded dumbly, not understanding at all, and his hand was released.

"See that he gets something to eat, Danon," the man said over his head. "Make him comfortable." He turned on his heel, black cloak flaring, and left through an opposite door.

Jael peered up at Danon, who looked very thoughtful. Shrugging, the boy turned on his heel in imitation of his new friend and climbed up next to Farbet. "How did he know my name?" he asked, but no one answered his question.

Mia was schooled in the art of sitting still. She had been practicing that ability for some time now, waiting for the King's arrival.

She had expected him to be here, since he had sent for her, but she was left alone in this room, in a high-backed chair near the fireplace. She reflected that these last moments of waiting seemed longer than the years before, but she was determined to hold onto her courage. *Allasar's memory deserves the truth,* she thought. *It is time for me to be as brave as he was.*

The door opened and closed again as swiftly, and she was aware of his presence. It was a presence felt by all when a High King neared, part of his bloodline's magic.

But to Mia, it was a familiar presence, because she had loved his father. Because she would always love his father.

She came with dignity to her feet, touching fist to forehead to chest in proper Duine salute.

Khedran accepted the gesture wordlessly, barely glancing at her as he removed his cloak and threw it over a chair. He settled loosely into a big chair near Mia's, crossing his ankles to stretch his booted feet to the fire. Mia remained standing, as she had not been told to sit down. He was staring into the flames as though gathering his thoughts, and she used the moment to study him from lowered lashes.

She had seen him when he was just a boy, and thought him beautiful. Now she was stunned to realize he was far more handsome than even her beloved Allasar. He seemed stronger, as well, in face and form; much taller, as he had towered in that moment facing her. His strength was apparent in the swell of muscles beneath unadorned black shirt and breeches, exactly like those worn by his men but with no insignia of rank. That power was even more decided in his face, even the set of his lips.

He stirred finally and threw her a look sharp as a weapon. He had the strange emerald eyes of his bloodline, but she saw none of the kindness that had always been present in his father's. She fought down a chill of fear. But all he said was, "Please sit down, Mia. We have a lot to talk about."

She lowered herself to the edge of her seat. Facing the smoldering anger in that emerald gaze, she slid back fully and lifted her chin. "One thing I pray, Your Highness, that you understand my son is just as innocent as you are."

He scowled at her. "Do you think I would harm him?"

She didn't answer that. "Jael knows nothing about who he is, Your Highness. He thinks only that his father died before he was born."

"Which he did."

She swallowed. "I meant," she managed, "that he thinks his father was Duine. Please..."

"Let's get something straight, Mia. I will not harm my brother."

She sat back, startled by the invasive command voice of a High King. It wasn't hearing, exactly; the voice simply arrived between her ears. She had known Allasar to use it only in formal situations.

"I wasn't with my father when he died," Khedran continued in his normal quiet tone. "But he wrote me a letter because he knew what was going to happen. In it he told me not to avenge his death. You know I had the right. I could have hunted and destroyed the Duine Anzihi. None could have forsworn my vengeance...except my father. But he warned me against the instability that would bring to Azlatan. So...at his command, his killers have gone free."

Mia lowered her head and said sadly "Of course he thought of Azlatan at the end. Your father never failed his duty as High King." At Khedran's scornful gaze, she snapped, "I had nothing to do with his duty. He never failed his duty!" She lifted her chin in anger. "He was a good man, a great King, and brave. He knew very well we could be murdered if we didn't stay away from each other. We couldn't, so he made plans for your safety, and bowed to the inevitable." At Khedran's glower, she added coldly, "You don't understand. You are still young, Your Highness, and arrogant. You think you are stronger, better, that you would have done none of it."

His eyes narrowed, studying hers. "No. I wouldn't have done any of that."

"He planned for my safety too. Didn't you ever guess that was how I escaped?"

Khedran continued to study her for a long moment. Then he rose slowly and walked over to her. He leaned in to put his hands on the arms of her chair. Inches from her face, he spoke very quietly. "How can you be proud of what you did to my father? You are telling me he knew he would die...because of you. You challenge me with it, like spitting in my face. Are you a sorceress, Mia, to make a High King love you? Do you think you can bewitch *me*?"

His feral emerald eyes searched hers. *Allasar's eyes*, she thought in melting grief, but with that dangerous difference, and she understood in that moment why he was called the Black Wolf.

When she said nothing, he went on. "Perhaps you are not a very good witch. Perhaps I will have to make you work at it. Try to seduce me, Mia, or I will have you hung...as all of Azlatan demands I do."

"You don't have to know I'm a witch to hang me. Be done with it, Your Highness."

"Not until I know."

"You put yourself in terrible danger. If it's true I'm a witch, you open yourself to the same fate as your father."

He just smiled, and even that was terrifying.

She considered him for a long moment, this beautiful and perilous son of Allasar.

Like spitting in my face, he had said.

She understood, at least, his grief. And despite her fear, the familiar presence of a High King so near woke memory of Allasar, her great love. It made her heart ache.

She lifted her hand, and gently touched the heavy black silk of his hair, then drew close so that his stubbled cheek was warm against hers. He smelled faintly of soap and horses, and she smiled just a little, in memory.

"I would not bewitch you," she murmured softly. "Even if I could. I loved your father with all my heart. I would do nothing against his son."

He drew away at that, and she watched her own hand drop to her lap. "There was no sorcery." Her voice now was strong. "I loved him from the moment I first saw him. I know I am Duine...but you could never guess how little that had to do with it. Our love was never a shameful thing." Her gaze returned to his, anger renewed. "Sorcery you call it, and others say rape, because I am Duine. I say damn you all! It was nothing like that. He was the High King, and a man no woman of sense could not love. And he convinced me that I was worthy of him!"

He lifted an eyebrow at her naked challenge. "That you are Duine is of no matter to me, Mia. None of the High Kings have accepted the Law of Phaelon, the separation of races, though we have no power to change it. But my father was married. He'd given an oath to be true to his Queen. Violating that oath was wrong, impossible for a High King. It isn't in our nature. We are very different from our people, born that way out of necessity. Our standards ensure that our purpose cannot be corrupted."

"You know nothing of love, Khedran. I hear you are more Chaine than human, and the Chaine don't even have a word for love. Perhaps you are incapable of love."

His eyes narrowed on hers. "Perhaps. But it's apparent to me that you didn't understand my father, if you can't understand what he did was wrong for him. A wound to his soul."

Her shoulders slumped, and she sighed as she looked away. "I became aware of that after the fact. And he did explain the differences between himself and the rest of us. He told me that he respected and revered his people as we are, flawed and wonderfully human...but the Kings were created for the benefit of the people, not their own, and could not share those flaws. He was genuinely shocked at his ability to act on his love for me. He had never before had the inclination, much less the freedom, to make certain choices. But nevertheless, he always considered himself less than human."

She returned her gaze to his, to bravely challenge him again. "But I also know something else about your bloodline. I know you can tell if I am lying or not. Allasar could read people's emotions and so their truth, even though he truly hated the mutual intrusion that forced him to feel whatever they felt. He said it was both a gift and a curse shared by all the High Kings. So...I think you can simply answer your own questions by opening up to me. I invite you to do that."

He looked away. After a moment he asked, "Did you know anything about the plot to murder him?"

She realized from his hesitation that he didn't like his gift of empathy any more than Allasar had. "We both knew it was possible, but no...I knew nothing about when or how."

"How long did he suspect?"

She sighed. "From the beginning. Khedran, your father was neither bewitched nor a fool. He knew that eventually we would be caught, and he planned for many years for just that eventuality. He could not foresee where or when..."

"Years!"

She looked up at his exclamation, and saw his shock. "Yes. That is what I said. Years. Khedran, I am ...I am old enough to be your mother. I am...I could have..." she stopped herself.

"You could have been," he finished for her slowly, and she held her breath. "You were lovers that long, Mia? While even his High Queen...while my mother was still alive?"

"That long," she breathed. "I loved him that long, and I still do."

He turned away.

She thought, *I believe I just shattered his heart with that final proof of his father's immorality. As he sees it.*

After a few minutes he pulled his chair close, and sat down to face her. His eyes lost their fire as he studied her, and she knew he was using the gift that Allasar had called a curse.

Allasar had explained to her that forcing himself to lower his mental defensive block sickened him, sometimes physically, as the emotions of others bled into his. So she understood when his son drew back a little, and closed his eyes. It took him a long moment to regain himself.

He took a deep breath. "You do love him. You say he loved you, and I have to believe it because I can feel your faith. Also because I knew him, and know he had a great capacity for love. And...because he put his life at risk for you." He lowered his head. "But I still cannot understand how he broke his marriage vows, or how he could love two women."

She saw his pain, and saw now too the kindness that had been his father's. She didn't understand how he could change his personality into the savage wolf that she had glimpsed, but she found herself wishing she could help the man who faced her now. "Perhaps you can't understand because you have never loved. Love is more powerful than you could know, if you have never experienced it."

"Nonetheless, guard your heart," he murmured softly.

"What?"

He looked up, gave her a smile that didn't reach his eyes. "It's a warning that has been passed down since the beginning of my bloodline. Apparently my father didn't heed the warning."

It made no sense to her, so she addressed her real concern. "What will happen to Jael?" she asked. "You said you will not harm him, but if you give him to the Tahmond..."

"I'll do nothing of the kind. I have searched for him to protect him, Mia. The Tahmond consider him an abomination. I am taking both of you to Penumbra with me." At her surprised expression, he shook his head.

"I was angry at first, because I believed for so long you had somehow used magic on my father. Now I know differently. I know you loved him. I know my father loved you so deeply he gave up his life for you. You are the mother of my only living kin...my brother. I must respect that, for my father's sake if no other. Be at peace, Mia. I am your protector, even from the High Tahmond and the Duine Anzihi. You and Jael are safe as long as I rule."

Farbet looked up from his dinner to see the signal and nodded at Jael's questioning look. "He's ready for you now, boy. Chin up."

Jael looked at Danon, but he seemed distant, as he had since the man had passed through. Jael wiped his mouth and climbed down, walking to the far door, which was opened for him. He was increasingly anxious about his mother, and was glad to see her in a chair, waiting for him.

He hurled himself into her arms, and she released him reluctantly as he pulled back to look up at her. "Did you see the High King, Mother? Is everything all right now? Can we go home?"

She was very pale, he saw, even in the warm glow from the fireplace. But she managed a small smile and touched his hair in the old reassuring way. "I did," she answered his first question softly. "But we are not going home, Jael." She looked over his head at the man standing, arms crossed, behind him. "We are going to go to a new home."

"I don't understand. Where are we going, and why?" When she didn't answer, he turned to see who she was looking at.

Khedran dropped a hand to Jael's shoulder, but he spoke to Mia. "There is a room ready for you. Don't worry about Jael. He will be with me."

"No!" Jael cried but was gently held in place while Farbet escorted his mother from the room.

"But why?" Jael cried, pulling away. "I want—"

"Some of us," Khedran interrupted him, "have to start growing up while we are still very young. Can you do that, Jael?"

The boy swallowed hard and tried to stand as tall as he could. "Of course."

Khedran smiled. "Then rest assured, your mother is going with us. And you will get to see Cabre, and all the wonders of Azlatan."

Jael's eyes widened. "Is that what she meant? We're going to Cabre? With the High King? When? Where is he?"

He was answered by laughter, and a shake of the head. "Do you always ask this many questions at once?"

"I'm sorry. Mother taught me that Duine law says it isn't proper to be so curious, that we must accept and serve. I know you said I am not Duine, but..." he lowered his head, and felt again as yesterday that shameful stir of rebellion against his own blood. He had never been so confused.

"Think about it, Jael. Do you really believe it's wrong to be curious? Don't answer until you have thought, and answer me honestly, just as you did when you told me about your gift of foresight yesterday."

He thought of the sea of grass, of the lady in white who somehow gave him comfort. "I want to know where that place with grass is. I want to know so many things, Lord. There have always been so many questions, but I know there must be an answer to all of them, if only there were a way to get to them, if only I could...ask." He realized his fists were clenched. "Not silly questions either," he finished, rubbing his hands.

Khedran nodded. "So to be Duine means not to ask questions. But I have told you: you are not Duine. You can now ask all the questions you want."

There was a long silence. Then, "How can that be, Lord?"

"Don't call me Lord. You are Rioch. That term is not used among us."

Khedran turned, reaching for the sword on the mantel. It whispered metallically as it was drawn from its sheath, and a fog of light and stars erupted around him. Khedran smiled grimly as the boy's eyes widened on the magic sword known as the Star Blade.

Khedran reversed it and offered the hilt to the boy. "Trust me. It will do you no harm."

Jael took it, heavy in his two hands, stars sparkling before his eyes. Because of the stories Varady had shared, he knew that only those of the bloodline of the High Kings could hold that sword and live.

"I call you Lord," Jael said slowly, "because you gave me no other name to call you. Who are you?"

"I am called Khedran. I am the High King, Jael."

The boy stared hard at the Star Blade. Always a bright child, he remembered the gossip he had overheard about the reason for murder of a High King, and his mother's anger when he had repeated it. "I had heard it was a Duine woman who caused the murder of the old High King. Was it my mother? Did she cause the death of your father?"

"Your mother and my father made choices that ended in his death. But the only blame for his death lies with those who murdered him. And he wasn't just my father. He was also yours."

The blade trembled until Khedran put his big hand over Jael's small ones to steady it. He kneeled then, to face the boy at eye level. "He was ours. Welcome, little brother, to my world."

CHAPTER 5

The palace named Penumbra was the ancestral home of Azlatan's High Kings. The sea foamed at its back, icy waves shattering against the black cliff which was its foundation. Cabre, known as the King's City, spilled like flotsam at Penumbra's feet, but only one of the three entrances to its mighty towering mass came from the city. The other two ran along and above the sea's edge, the highest being the King's Way, an entrance few would dare to try.

Khedran made frequent use of the King's Way, although a misstep on that high stair could send a man plunging to his certain end. Jael, mounted on a black stallion in front of the King, peered over his shoulder at his brother's face in the stark moonlight, and saw no fear of the ride ahead.

The sea-wind tore at cloak and hair and mane. Grey clouds ghosted over the moon's bright face. Jael shivered against more than the wind.

"I should take the boy by the City Gate, Highness," he heard Danon say.

"No. I will take him up myself, and not have him subjected to those prying eyes." At a wave of the King's hand the soldiers were off. Khedran's arms tightened around Jael as he turned his stallion to the great stair. The horse snorted, flattening his ears, and began climbing.

Jael glimpsed moon-shattered water below and shivered despite himself.

"Afraid?" Khedran's laughing voice came over his head.

"No," Jael lied. "Just cold. Does the wind always blow here?"

"Like the scream of Chaos herself," Khedran replied. "In a storm the towers tremble with it. But Penumbra has stood for a thousand years, through the reign of all the six High Kings before me. There is no need to fear it will fall, Jael."

They passed soon between walls of black crystal, and Jael saw both moonlight and the glitter of stars within the castle walls. The wind's torment abated, Jael found interest in this, and Khedran seemed to sense the unasked question.

"Penumbra is built of Nightstone," he told the boy. "The stars it holds shine throughout the night, even if the sky is cloudy."

Then they were in the open again, and the wind seemed to stagger the King's mount for a moment. With lowered head, the stallion went on, and Jael shrank into his cloak and felt miserable again. The towers above were no longer of interest. He could no longer feel his nose. Through eyes blurred by wind he saw the glittering Bridle constellation rising over the sea, and almost whispered the Duine words against the power of Chaos it symbolized before he remembered, confused, that he was Rioch now.

The trip from Selagon had been long and wearying, after a departure from his mother that left him empty of understanding. She had told him she would have her own chambers in the palace, and that she had been promised he could visit her as often as he wished while the High King would ensure his education in the Temple of Liethe. But she looked at him with sadness before entering the shuttered coach which had borne her ahead of him to Cabre.

He had remained behind for a few days, close-quartered and guarded by Danon. The King's time in Selagon, he learned by careful listening, had been fruitful. He had heard Farbet brag that the Dominion King's subjects had flocked to the High King's banner, eager to join his glamorous new army. Jael had seen little of Khedran those days until he suddenly appeared, as though there had been no time between, to tell him they were ready to travel to Cabre, and the wonders they would see.

Those wonders had paled quickly, for Jael was used to neither riding nor the swift pace they set. All too soon he realized how alike one town was to the next, and the farmland between seemed to become more barren as they travelled. As they had neared Cabre, the day before, he had mentioned this, and Khedran explained Cabre's dependence on the tribute of the Dominions; the King's city and home were in Azlatan's least fertile sector. The Tahmond taught that this was for a purpose, Khedran explained. The King must always have care for his farthest lands.

"Hold on," Khedran warned as he tightened his grip, and Jael felt their mount gather himself and leap, terrifying him until he realized they had gained a flat promontory from which they could look down at the sea and the city curving around toward it. The wind had fallen.

Thousands of lights flickered like fireflies in the jumbled, man-made landscape below. Over the now distant sigh of the sea, he heard a rumble like faraway summer thunder.

"What is that sound?" he asked.

"Wheels," Khedran told him. "All night they roll, bringing things and people to the city for the next day of business. Cabre never sleeps. I allow most wheeled things to travel inside the city only at night, so that more agile traffic, and people on foot, can travel safely in the day. It has helped, but at night the noise goes on from dusk until dawn. In the day there is the noise of all the new construction I have ordered, though that is nearly done. I am glad of the height of Penumbra, away from all that."

Exhausted, Jael fought to stay awake, but was losing the battle as they approached the Tower Gate. A light flashed briefly from within, hurting his eyes, and then great dark doors were swinging wide. He got the impression of soldiers standing at attention, of warmth and a fire banked behind them, but of most immediate concern was the absence of wind and noise. They were inside, the doors were closed, and Khedran was dismounting. Jael swayed suddenly as the world spun. He was not aware when those strong arms caught him close.

He drifted awake after an unknown time to the sound of voices. His second awareness was of softness, and he moved his hands over the furs that swaddled him, at last pulling them down to blink over the edge at the ruddy glow of firelight.

He was in a curtained nook, bedded deep into warm furs. The curtains were not fully drawn, and he saw beyond a great cavernous room. Deep rugs covered the floor, and he could see art and weapons displayed on the stone walls. There was a fireplace as big as his nook at one end of the room; this and several lanterns were the source of light. Great fur-covered chairs were grouped to face the fire, but Khedran was standing at a table nearer him, peering down at something between his hands, which were braced against the dark wood tabletop.

"...no snow yet to close those entrances," he was saying, and lifted a hand to tap what Jael assumed must be a map. "Some sign of her return should have been seen long ago."

"Perhaps she has taken a different route," a strange voice answered, seeming unconcerned. Jael peered out curiously, but the stranger was outside his line of vision. "Besides, such as she could slip through your border defenses and onto your doorstep with no sign at all."

"Not with what she brings," Khedran growled, straightening, and paced over the rug to stare into the fire.

The stranger appeared at the table, and Jael was mildly surprised to see the light hair marking him...at least in Jael's mind...as Duine. A closer look revealed silver shot through the light brown hair and beard. The man stood straight and prideful, and looked older than the High King. He glanced briefly down at the map, then frowned slightly at Khedran's back.

"Khedran, we must discuss this alliance. There are rumblings from the people, and especially now from Phaelon's Temple."

Khedran turned back and stared at the man for a moment, then reached to a table where rested the Star Blade. He removed a small scroll from a drawer and handed it to the man. "Read it, Camion."

The man he addressed looked uncomfortable. "I know what it says. It's one of your secret missives from Khandor, the second High King, passed down through all the Kings to you. I have always been honored that you trusted me with it."

"Read it," Khedran repeated. "Aloud."

Frowning, Camion unrolled it and read in a careful voice.

Be wary of the High Tahmond, for he serves a god
who wants power over the people.
We came to a bright and living world
where freedom was expected,
but the gods have stolen its light, and it is my only hope that
the Daughter of Prophecy,
the one who speaks with the world, can bring it back.
Nevertheless, rule separately from the gods.
Lead your people to know they each have their own mind,
their own soul, and their own right to respect and be respected.

He didn't look up as he handed it back to the High King. "I gather that means we should not listen to rumblings from Phaelon's Temple."

"And beyond even that, I want to remind you of why the alliance was created. High King Allasar named The Chaine as the King's Defender because he trusted her. She had already given her oath and pledged her warriors to defend our bloodline. She was neutral to politics and had nothing to gain."

Camion sniffed derisively. "Except payment. You must not forget that. The Chaine are known for many things, but that one so well it is a common joke in the marketplace. It was not just for loyalty to your bloodline or rule, but I am sure a pledge of payment as well."

"Something that you, as Duine, could not understand has its own worth...because the Duine are always provided for by the

Rioch of Azlatan. But in this one case, there was no payment. Don't look so surprised. She gave an oath of loyalty and refused payment for the contract. You supported the contract with her, Camion, just as our fathers did. You knew that once accepted, the Chaine do not break oath nor dishonor a contract."

The Duine stiffened as though he had been insulted. "I supported the contract for a reason, and not all out of duty. I knew what she was capable of, as your Defender and your teacher of warrior ways. I feared for your safety also out of love."

Khedran looked away, then sighed. "I know, Camion. But you must understand—I don't think you ever appreciated fully what was asked of her."

"If I had, perhaps I would not have supported the asking."

Khedran gave him a mocking smile. "You are thinking again like a Duine," he said, but this time more gently. "It was a wiser move than even my father realized. The Chaine was sworn to protect me, but she saw the bigger picture, the whole truth, the fruit and not just the flower. My physical defense was only the flower. She was determined I would learn to think, to see and control the dangers that threatened me and my realm." He looked down at his fist, as though surprised to find it clenched. He flexed it, looking up. "The dangers that still threaten my realm. Dangers foreseen by the second High King. You have also read the other secret missive from Khandor."

Camion nodded. "I have been honored you would share that with me as well."

"Why wouldn't I? You are far more than a servant. I have trusted you all my life, Camion. But to the point, that message told me that I would have allies in the war that I believe is coming. I don't understand how Khandor could have foreseen it, but I am sure he was speaking of the Chaine people, who came here centuries after he was gone."

"That message also carried a warning. 'Nonetheless, guard your heart.'"

Khedran lifted his eyebrows. "Do you take that to mean I shouldn't trust their leader, The Chaine?"

"The warning is nearly a thousand years old, so it couldn't refer to her. But I think you honor her and her people too much."

"Is that so?"

Camion looked down at the map. "My opinion of course does not matter. But this continued alliance has the people worried. There are some who whisper it is she, and not you, who rules Azlatan."

"The whisperers want no change to Azlatan's course, and are in denial of its need. Many prefer the easy road, though it may lead to their own destruction."

Jael's stomach growled hugely, and he was so sure it would be heard that he twitched back the curtain as though just awakened.

Both men turned in his direction. "Morning bless," he said tentatively.

Khedran laughed. "He doesn't even know he has slept through one morning and is fast approaching another," he told his companion. "You'd best fetch Tari for his breakfast; he's bound to be ravenous. And have her send up enough for us too, Camion. It's been a long night."

The Duine did not smile, and Jael thought his eyes not totally friendly when he glanced at him before leaving.

Khedran turned to open the curtains at the windowed end-wall. Jael crept from his furs and stood blinking around the room. At the window the light was just turning to steel; at the opposite side of the room was a doorway through which he could see a massive carved bed that must be the King's own, though it did not look as if it had been slept in. These chambers were as large as all of Selagon Manor, he thought, looking up in awe at the high ceiling.

Khedran was drawing a table near the fireplace and arranging chairs like a common Duine. "You can bathe in there," he said cheerfully to Jael, nodding toward a door beside his nook.

Jael followed the nod and entered another large room that made no sense at all. It was hard, gleaming white, with a deep recess in the floor one could fall into! He saw no pitcher of water for washing, only his own puzzled reflection in a mirror above a tabletop, also recessed. He was still staring around when Khedran peered in.

"I hadn't thought." Khedran sounded dismayed. "It is all new to you, isn't it?"

Jael agreed and was shown the functions of various metal knobs. Khedran laughed at his amazement when water gushed from hidden pipes into the hole in the floor. Jael got in the bath while Khedran explained there were hot springs below the palace and pumps invented by their forbears, but for once all new information went over Jael's head. He was still too amazed, too awed by the High King and his change in circumstance and surroundings.

Soon he was alone again, up to his chin in warm soapy water and thoroughly enjoying the sensation. He drifted and thought about the conversation he had overheard, especially the mysterious woman the King had spoken of. The Chaine people he knew about, in a child's dubious way, though he had a surprisingly mature intellect and could usually sort fact from fable. The Chaine were outsiders, that was certain, with no ties to any of the conventions acceptable to respectable people. They were supposed to be unsurpassable warriors, large and quick and powerful. They honored no god. This was the part Jael found difficult to believe, for warriors without magic seemed vulnerable, yet their reputation was fearsome.

His daydreaming was interrupted by a sharp rap on the door, reminding him a meal was being served. He scrambled out hastily, drying on a great length of cloth almost as soft as the furs he had slept in, and dressed in the black shirt and breeches left out for him.

The table was now loaded with food, the aroma enough to make his mouth water. Despite this he hung back, shy now not of Khedran, but of the Duine who was already seated.

The Duine woman who must be Tari looked up from serving. He guessed her relation to the man named Camion by her light brown curls, though her dancing blue eyes were not nearly so fearful as her father's. She solved Jael's dilemma by guiding him with a firm hand on his shoulder to a chair next to Khedran, with the other hand placing before him a full plate. Realizing the men were already deep into another conversation, Jael attacked his breakfast. To him it was another amazement: an array of meats, cheeses, eggs, and fruits, with various sauces for dipping, and plenty of warm bread for finishing.

With the edge off his hunger, Jael began to listen, hopeful of hearing more about this mysterious Chaine who was apparently missing.

"You can't go riding off now," Camion was saying to Khedran, who appeared annoyed but remained silent, occasionally drinking from the cup Tari kept filled. "The wedding is to take place during the season. Already the aristocracy is arriving, and I look daily for the announcement that your bride is on the way."

Khedran looked pained. "That soon? I thought...oh, damn it all. There is much to be done other than this ratted wedding. I suppose it is too late to postpone?"

Camion's reaction was thinly veiled exasperation. "Your Highness, such a suggestion is, if I may say so, totally unacceptable even if possible!"

Khedran sighed. "Highness, is it? Why don't you just come out and say I'm being an ass?"

Camion looked appalled.

The High King leaned back, setting down his cup and running a hand through his heavy black mane. Jael saw weariness settle over his features and was surprised; he had begun to believe Khedran's energy was endless. "Of course you are right, Camion. Riding off at this point would incense every Dominion King in Azlatan, even those who still claim some loyalty. I suppose you have seen to all the arrangements? The proper escort through Cabre, and the dignitaries...yes, I am sure you have."

Camion, obviously uncomfortable, looked directly at Jael for the first time. "There is one matter..."

Khedran had seen the direction of Camion's gaze, and lifted an eyebrow. "I'm glad you thought of that. You must see that my brother has garb appropriate to all the ceremonies, and a Duine to serve his attendance."

Camion's face froze. He glared rather wildly at Khedran, back at Jael, then put down his own cup and rose stiffly. He saluted, fist to forehead to chest. "I shall do as bidden." He left abruptly.

Tari followed her father less abruptly and with a parting smile for Jael. When the door softly closed behind her, Jael and Khedran were alone.

Khedran turned to the boy. "Camion is my Bonded Duine," he explained. "He is very intelligent and well educated, and I trust him to see to many of the needs and details of my office. I do not believe in Phaelon's Law that made half of my people into servants to the other half...though this isn't something I can publicly challenge. It is instead something I simply ignore in personal practice."

Here Khedran halted, as though unsure how to continue. Then he sighed and looked at Jael with an expression of apology. "You were not properly introduced while he was here. I had a reason for that."

His voice was quiet, but Jael saw the same light in his eyes that his mother had glimpsed and feared. It softened only slightly as Khedran continued, "The lack of proper introduction, Jael, was meant as a careful rebuke to Camion, not an insult to you. He acknowledged you, and so by my command you, too, are his liege. It would have been more difficult if you had acknowledged him first."

"But I did not know!" Jael cried, ashamed.

"I depended on that. I waited for Camion to be the one to overstep the bounds of tradition. He acknowledged you. Once he did and was given notice in your presence to serve you, the sword was forged. He can no longer deny you."

Jael thought of the unwitting part he had played and did not like it. He understood the viewpoint of the Duine who served Khedran so faithfully.

He could also see his own. He had been an outcast his whole life and being told otherwise did not change the fact that he was still an outcast. This new life had currents he could not see or understand, and there was no haven in sight.

He looked up to see Khedran was watching him closely, as though awaiting an answer to an important question. He thought of the understanding offered to him in the Grove, and, perversely, of the dark lady who no longer stood behind him.

"I am too unlearned," he told Khedran. "My stupidity served you this time, but next time it could embarrass you. I need a teacher."

Khedran looked pleased, and a little surprised. "Yes. Well, I have plans for your education. You will receive lessons in the Temple of Liethe, and additionally here, from a Chaine mentor who may be best able to answer your many questions."

"Will I learn to fight like a Chaine?" Jael asked. "Danon said they are fierce."

Khedran laughed. "Perhaps not yet. I think we'll begin with a more rudimentary education. As for now...I'll send Tari in for you. Finish your breakfast and rest while you can." He was on his feet again, his mind as usual turning to the next matter to be addressed.

Jael found himself momentarily alone in the big room and looked around, still in wonder, but beginning to realize his new life was real. He smiled to himself, thinking of taking lessons from a Chaine.

CHAPTER 6

K hedran's bride was no happier about the upcoming wedding than he was. Nor was Princess Marre of the Dominion of Athea enjoying the company of snobbish nobility at her celebratory leave-taking party.

Trained to display only polite serenity at such formal events, she hid a wicked smile. The nobility were stepping aside skittishly as her personal guardian, a Chaine incongruous in worn and rugged leather, strode through them in their gems and velvet.

"Your watchdog is in a hurry." Sabar, the woman next to her, was also watching the Chaine divide the partygoers. "Going to speak to my father, I believe."

"Apparently," Marre agreed. She glanced toward Sabar's father and her own, the Dominion King of Athea, who stood arguing in a flower-bedecked corner. She flicked her eyes back to Sabar, the picture of a Lady's boredom in red silk and rubies, amused to have seen her friend's open appraisal of the Chaine's remarkably muscular body.

"I think he's terrifying." Deta was three years younger and innocent of any pretense. Marre had always liked Deta, though her own artists' eye considered Deta far prettier than herself. Deta's nose wasn't so frankly straight, or her lips as unfashionably full. "Why aren't you afraid of him?"

"Don't be a dolt." Sabar sniffed haughtily. "He's been with her since she was in the cradle. Phaelon only knows how much money Khedran's father must have paid to give his son's bride a lifetime bodyguard. I'm sure Marre notices him no more than she would the kitchen cat."

Marre's dark lashes dropped over her violet eyes, faintly tilted beneath her raven eyebrows. She seldom discussed her guardian with anyone, because of the common bigotry toward the Chaine. Sabar's attempt at blasé sophistication did not tempt her to break the habit. She was the only one who even recognized he had a name. To her he was Jhinn, not just a Chaine warrior.

"Your father looks very angry, Sabar," Deta observed.

"He thinks Marre's father too lax and believes the Dominion King should travel with a full troop and escort. Perhaps he has enlisted Marre's Chaine to help convince him."

"I've been to Cabre." Marre spoke in quiet defense of her father. "There was never any difficulty there or during the journey, Sabar."

"You have?" Deta was aghast. "Have you then met the High King, Marre?"

"Of course not," Sabar answered while Marre ignored them both. "The bride is never allowed to lay eyes on the High King until the wedding. That is the natural order of things. Marre was at the Temple of Liethe, but that was long ago, and things have changed."

"Changed how?" Deta asked.

Sabar glanced around, drew nearer, her dark hair braided with tiny rubies swinging over bare shoulders. "Things," she hissed. "Not just brigands and highwaymen, though there's a crop of those. But there are other things. From across the border."

"You're making it up." But Deta swallowed hard, and her pretty nose looked pinched. "Nothing can cross the border from the Admech. It is guarded by Phaelon's magic!"

"Then why is the High King raising his own army?" Sabar asked archly.

Marre saw Deta's frightened expression and remembered her manners. She smiled sternly at Sabar. "We're supposed to be having a party, not talking politics. There! The musicians are starting up again, and your partner is coming to collect you. Deta, I am sorry. We've scarcely had a chance to say good-bye."

The girl's eyes filled with ready tears. "Oh, we will miss you, Marre! It's exciting for you, I know, to meet your destiny. I hear that His Highness is terribly handsome, and to be High Queen...but I still can't believe you are leaving Athea forever, in the morning."

Self-contained Marre pulled the tearful girl to her and hugged her close. "No weeping. Just know I will miss you too, dear friend. Now go, and don't look back, or I'll cry too. We will meet again when you come to Cabre."

Deta nodded and was gone in a crush of pink silk. Sabar looked disgusted. "No tears from me, unless they were tears of envy." She bit her lip, having come closer to the truth than she had intended.

"I'll miss all of you," Marre responded.

"Ha. I've seen the High King, and even from a distance my heart fell at his feet. I doubt you'll miss any of us once you meet him."

Marre's lashes hid a hard gleam. "If you say so. You'll excuse me if I step out for a breath of fresh air."

Sabar watched curiously as the Princess of Athea passed beyond a velvet curtain. She thought she'd seen a touch of rebellion at the mention of Marre's betrothed, a most unexpected reaction from one so poised and proper.

Marre felt neither proper nor poised as she stood on the terrace of her father's palace in fashionable, terribly uncomfortable spike-heeled shoes. The stars gazed back at her unblinking, hard and cold as her future. The sky ruled by Daimaine reminded her of the colors she had lost with her art. Her hobby had been deemed unfit for a future Queen, so she'd given it up along with the freedom of her childhood.

She wished she had never been to Cabre, or any of the other places her father had taken her to ensure her education. There was no sense of wonder left to her, no anticipation. Her life was a map drawn by the uncreative hand of those before her, and it had left no room for her spirit. She knew no one else would understand her dread as she faced a life with a stranger, a life doing what was expected of her because of him.

"It is like a dream, finding a beautiful Princess alone in the starlight," a man's voice spoke from behind her.

Marre, startled, spun to look up into laughing eyes in a darkly handsome face. She glanced around, briefly shaken, for her Chaine guardian; saw he was nearby, unmoving but alert.

"Why Princess," the man continued in mock sorrow, "it doesn't appear that you remember me. I am devastated."

Memory sprang alive. "Pharmond!"

He looked delighted and bowed deeply. "I'm sure we'll only have a moment. They'll never allow the High King's betrothed any longer than that with a rapscallion like me."

Pharmond had always made her laugh. "How did you manage to get into the palace? My father will take you off by the ear, like he did when we were children."

He rubbed the threatened appendage ruefully. "How well I remember that. And seeing a Chaine berated for letting me near you was even more of a surprise. Um...where is your mighty shadow, anyway?"

"Near, as usual." She hid a smile at his apt description; Jhinn was just beyond the curtain. He was never far; she alone was aware of him most of the time, stealthy as he was. "Don't look so worried. He never minded us being together, unlike my father."

"Ah, but things have changed. We are no longer children." He looked at her in frank admiration, and she felt herself blushing. She was glad for the shadows that hid it but looked away anyway, plucking a flower from a trailing vine on the balustrade.

Pharmond brought back memories of an earlier and happier time. Her initial pleasure at his presence faded with memories of what had come since. She twirled the flower-stem between her fingers, noticing the petals were the color of blood in the starlight.

"Is it true you sold your family's home, Pharmond?" she asked.

"You have heard the rumors."

"They are almost legendary. And notorious," she added.

"And true," he finished, suddenly serious. "Tell me, Marre...does my breaking tradition bother you, when it is tradition that promised you from birth to a man you have never met?"

Her smile faded. Always aware of propriety, she turned and began a slow return to the ballroom. Dancers whirled by in a spangle of light and color, but the doorway was quiet enough for talk.

"Tradition is what it is, and I have accepted it," she said, under cover of the music. "But I heard that you turned your ancestral home into an inn, and hired Rioch to serve your patrons, turning out your family's Duine."

"All of them," he confirmed. "They refused to serve my paying customers."

At her look, he shrugged. "I was doing it for their good as well as my own. We all have to eat to live. I offered them the choice of serving at the inn or at the Temple of Liethe. They chose the latter."

"Of course they did. Weren't you brought to Council?"

He smiled brightly. "No. I sold the manor. They can't very well expect me to feed a herd of hungry Duine when I haven't a roof to call my own. I live in a rented space in Cabre now, while I work on the High King's oddly continual building projects."

Marre hadn't been aware of her father's approach, but he appeared at her side in time to hear Pharmond's speech, and he scowled. "By the time you sold your home, it was a flourishing business, and I hear you made a tidy profit from the sale."

"King Ardren," Pharmond bowed deeply. "I am honored to see you again."

"Not that you were invited," the Dominion King noted wryly. "I hear the Guild is threatening to take you to Council."

The music had halted, and they were drawing attention. Marre saw a certain individual heading toward them and felt a headache coming on. Rimon was Chief of the Builder's Guild; he never spoke in less than a bellow, and his eyes were angrily targeted on Pharmond.

Pharmond looked righteous. "I would of course obey any directive of the Council, but I don't fear it. High King Allasar long ago ruled in favor of competition with the Guilds."

"It cannot stand!" Rimon had arrived. Pharmond flinched visibly at the roar near his ear. "Making contract with the High King to build at a cost less than the Guild allows! Damn Chainish thing to do! Outside the natural order of things!"

The room had fallen quiet at Rimon's bellow. King Ardren signaled the musicians to play and turned back to Pharmond. "Is it true?" he asked. "You are working without Guild approval?"

Pharmond smiled. "Oh, but Your Majesty...High King Khedran did not require Guild approval for his building projects in Cabre, which have been numerous as well as lucrative...for me."

"Chaine law! Ruining business!" Rimon shouted. "The Tahmond should have prohibited it! High King Allasar should never have allowed them in!"

It was Marre's turn to flinch, knowing what would come, and it did. Ardren went purple with rage. "There will not be any disrespectful remark about any High King of Azlatan!"

This time the room and the music froze. Ardren's loyalty to the High King was fully known to his subjects and every other Dominion King. He had grieved at the death of Allasar as though it had been his own father's. His total and unquestioning support had helped smooth the way for the rule of Allasar's son.

Rimon realized his grave error. He glared balefully at Pharmond, as though it were his fault. "You undermine the Guild, which has served Azlatan loyally for all these centuries!"

Pharmond lifted an eyebrow. "Perhaps. But I gave honest work to those that the Guild set aside to keep their numbers low and their prices high."

"You have no respect for tradition!" Rimon bellowed.

"Perhaps not. But you had no respect for the workers you removed from your ranks without warning. They had families and Duine to support."

King Ardren stepped in. "Enough! This is supposed to be a celebration, Pharmond, not a political battle, and you were not invited. It's time you left."

Pharmond said no more but bowed respectfully to Marre and her father, and left with a last sad smile for his childhood love who was betrothed to a man she had never met.

Ardren laid a hand on Marre's shoulder. "Are you all right, my girl?"

"I don't think so, Father. I'm terribly tired, and—considering the trip tomorrow—would it be too rude if I left now, and went to bed?"

"Of course not. Run along, and I'll send up a Duine."

"Please don't. I am too tired even for a Duine." She felt as though only the stiff cage of her dress held her upright. She left the revelry swiftly, managing it unnoticed...almost a Chaine ability she had, Sabar had once remarked nastily.

Sound fell to a dim murmur behind her. The halls were empty, the household Duine probably gathered in the kitchen. Marre turned to the stairs and saw Jhinn, watching her with his usual impassive expression. He leaned back against the stair-railing with arms crossed against his expansive chest. His long auburn hair was tied back with leather and gold. The Chaine people loved gold, though it was not real gold, but the powerful metal called "Chaine gold" which had begun replacing iron and steel throughout Azlatan. His leather was worked with it, in a manner no Guild could match, and a heavy medallion hung from his neck.

Marre had done a painting of him once, in his leather and gold and forest green cloak. She had added no enhancement to that portrait. The strong lines of his face, the cool serenity of his blue eyes, were what she had captured. It was, she thought, her best work.

He had said two things about it: "May I have it?" and "Thank you." She'd never seen the painting since but remained joyful at the compliment.

He appeared relaxed. She knew nevertheless the deadly energy coiled in the long lines of his body. Remembering Sabar's "kitchen cat" comment, she almost smiled.

Pharmond's words were still ringing in her ears. "Did you see Pharmond out?" she asked, and Jhinn nodded.

"Did he speak to you?" she asked.

"Yes."

"Jhinn, do you remember when I was little, and my father sent Pharmond away? We were playing, but I can't remember what Pharmond did to make father so angry. Pharmond was always a ruffian, but he was not a bad boy."

"You were the only one who didn't think so."

She blinked. "What was it he did?"

"He struck you."

"But...why? And how could you let that happen?"

She thought she saw a flicker of amusement in the blue eyes. "Because you deserved it," he said, answering both of her questions.

Part of her wanted to be shocked. But suddenly she didn't want to hear any more. She started up the stairs, satin rustling.

And stopped, halfway up, to look down at him. "You are going with us, aren't you? To Cabre?"

"Of course."

She turned away from those watchful eyes. "I'm glad." She continued up to bed, refusing to think about the fact that his contract as her guardian would end when she married. He would be gone from her life, like her freedom.

Day two of the journey to Cabre was less than boring.

Dominion King Mikel seemed extremely nervous about something, Marre thought. And it wasn't about her Chaine guardian, who stood like a statue by the door, for Mikel had accepted his presence on previous visits, paying him scarcely more mind than the flock of soldiers who always attended the Dominion King.

Marre listened to her father making conversation and wondered if he was truly oblivious to the air of tension at Mikel's dinner-table. He'd told her he looked forward to this visit to their neighboring Dominion, especially since they might have to manage public inns for the rest of their journey. Marre's mother said she was unwell, however, and had asked for dinner in her room.

But Marre was beginning to believe they might have been better off at an inn after all. Mikel only pushed his food around his plate, very unlike himself. One of his chins trembled, she noticed, every time Ardren mentioned the High King.

Which was frequently. Marre wondered privately if her father was deaf to anything but the best reports from Cabre. Born with an intensely aware mind, she was skeptical of perfection.

But Mikel finally stepped over the line with the latest news, and her father reacted in shock. "What did you say?" he demanded.

Mikel became aware of the impact of his words and looked at Ardren apologetically. "Of course, I only heard it from a stranger passing through. It may be exaggerated. Khedran has always been rather unorthodox in his attitudes, but to claim a Duine as brother..."

"I've never heard of such a thing." Her father stared in disbelief. "Of course, it is exaggerated, or a bald lie. I think it only right if that witch-woman is to be brought to Council at last, but..." he waved the rest away but looked distraught.

Mikel blinked nervously. "Well...you'll be able to straighten it out soon enough." He turned to Marre, asking too brightly if she had seen Cabre recently.

"No." She welcomed the change of subject. "Not for years. I am told it has changed very much."

"That is true. It is cleaner, and the High King has extended the city with new construction, including a new garrison surrounding the outer city. Most of the buildings sit empty, including the barracks. His new army is stationed throughout Azlatan, and Penumbra's garrison can hold an entire Legion by itself. The city's new outer wall is sloped outward from the bottom for some reason only he knows. Wheeled transport is allowed only at night, so that the citizens can enjoy the streets by day. It is far safer as well." He frowned.

Ardren caught that. "Then why don't you seem pleased?" he asked.

"Because I cannot say the same for the countryside," Mikel told him. "I must admit I was surprised to see you traveling with such a small escort."

Ardren waved Mikel's concerns away. "There have always been highwaymen, and I've always traveled safely with my personal escort...and Marre, of course, has the Chaine."

"Things are not as they have always been." There was true fear in Mikel's eyes. "They may never be again, if the Forbidden Child is come."

Ardren stiffened. "The half-Duine boy you spoke of? Superstitious nonsense!"

"There are stories of his powers."

"You said you heard it from a stranger passing through," Marre heard herself say. "The story now doesn't seem so vague. Are you keeping something from us, Mikel?"

Her father stared at her in shock.

"I'm sorry, Father, to be blunt. But if we may be riding into a dangerous situation, I feel we have a right to know."

Mikel's jaws were working. At her words they stopped, as though he had decided something, and turned back to Ardren. "I know how you feel about the High King. I'm sorry it has to be me to give you bad tidings about him. I had hoped to avoid...but the Princess is quite right. You must know the truth." He took a deep breath, as though arming himself. "Khedran is a known madman, who doesn't sleep but rather prowls Penumbra like the Black Wolf he is called. And he has surrounded himself with misfits. I even hear..."

"Enough!" Ardren was on his feet and trembling with rage. "Marre, we will not remain under this traitor's roof another minute. Call the Duine and tell your mother we are leaving now!"

Marre didn't hesitate. The look of pleading she threw at Jhinn in passing was on behalf of her father. She knew his rage too well, and Mikel's honor was at stake if he continued his barrage. She saw Jhinn's nod of understanding and fled with relief to do her father's bidding.

Things always calm down when the Chaine stepped in, she thought, but she had not expected that outburst from Mikel. What kind of man was she going to marry? She realized how one-sided her image of High King Khedran had been, with only her father to paint the portrait.

The land grew more barren the farther they drew from Athea. Marre's mind whirled darkly, and her mother sickened before her eyes. Lathine did not complain, for she was a Queen. But the pounding and lurch of the coach were taking their toll. Her face was a mask of arthritic pain despite the pillows and blankets her Duine piled around her.

This day had started too early, the horses breasting a sea of mist in the paling dawn. They had paid for their beds at the inn the night before, and for once even her mother had been glad of the Chaine outside their door. Even so none of them had slept well, thinking of the stares of the men in the big common room below.

Marre had heard a surprising conversation between her father and Jhinn when they had arrived at the inn. Her father had apparently agreed it would be fitting for an escort from the High King to meet his bride's party on the road. A soldier on a swift mount had gone ahead of them to see to it.

If the Chaine had seen the need for help, Marre felt sure it was needed.

She saw her mother was sleeping among her pillows and drew back the curtains to peer out the carriage window. She had to rid her mind of this agony of thought or go mad.

Her father rode alongside the carriage on the great white stallion delivered to him from the High King just last Starfall. Not for the first time, Marre wondered at the magnificent beast. The horses of Athea were among the best in Azlatan, but none could match this steed. As Khedran had probably intended, her father planned to enter the stallion's blood into Athea's breeding program. Marre wondered again, watching the horse's dark almost slanted eyes, where Khedran had obtained such a creature.

A group of riders galloped toward them on the road, and her father reined in his mount as Jhinn drew alongside him. Jhinn was speaking almost hurriedly; she couldn't catch the words but felt the carriage sway to a stop. Her father turned to the escort riding behind and ordered them to the front.

A timid tug at her sleeve had Marre turning to her mother's frightened Duine. "Why are we stopping, Princess?"

Marre noted that her mother still slept and signaled the Duine to silence. She turned back to the window to see riders approaching in a cloud of dust. Her father's soldiers had drawn close, but she still had a clear view of the approaching riders as well as her father and Jhinn. She noted the Chaine's relaxed posture in the saddle, contradicted by the drawn sword held against his thigh.

She counted swiftly. At least twenty riders! Against their handful! Glancing again at Jhinn, she gave thanks for his presence; she knew he trained for this every day.

As the riders neared, she recognized the purple livery and crest of Dominion King Eleban. She remembered him as being overproud and overbearing with a brood of sons who warred with each other constantly. Though obviously envious of Athea's riches, he had treated them with respect in the past. Surely any fear was ungrounded. He would not dare attack the Dominion King of Athea—or the bride of the High King!

She saw Eleban himself as he halted his ugly bay in front of Ardren's mount, pointedly ignoring the Chaine. His men, however, watched the warrior sidelong. Jhinn, meanwhile, did not move but appraised them coolly.

"I found out by happenstance that you were within my borders," Eleban announced without preamble. "Does the Dominion King of Athea no longer welcome my hospitality?"

Her father chose not to take offense at the open challenge. "My wife is ill, Eleban. We travel swiftly, to reach the healers of Cabre without delay. We expect an escort from High King Khedran shortly, so the escort you have thoughtfully provided will not be necessary, though I thank you for it."

Hurray for you, Father, Marre thought while Eleban purpled.

"Khedran!" Eleban spat the word like an oath. "You give your daughter to a traitor, Athean King!" He pointed to the white stallion Ardren rode. "Has he purchased your loyalty with his gifts? Or perhaps you do not understand the danger he has sent creeping through Azlatan, with his sorcery and alliance with the Chaine?" Eleban glared openly now at the undisturbed Jhinn.

"Athea is a great distance from here," Ardren replied carefully. "I was not aware that you had a grievance against the High King. Has it been taken to Council?"

Eleban scowled. "Not yet. Not yet. It's more than a grievance, and he will answer to all of the Dominion Kings before it is done." He pointed at Jhinn, who gazed back dispassionately. "We must oust the evil Chaine! The High King was raised by The Chaine herself," he raged. "Now it is she, not the High King, who rules Azlatan. It is she who has brought despair on the Dominions by draining away its sons."

He urged his horse nearer to Ardren's. "Do you know where he came by this steed of Chaos you ride? Did you even question it? Neither did my own sons, lured into Khedran's black Legions by his promise of these horses. Nor did their sons."

Eleban gestured behind him, and Marre saw that the purple-clad riders were not young men; many were greybeards. They nodded in fierce agreement with Eleban's words.

"You see for yourself," Eleban concluded. "Khedran steals the young men of the Dominions and seeks to turn them against their fathers. Has any High King ever done such a thing? No! It is the enticement of The Chaine!"

Ardren looked concerned. "Do I have your permission to speak to the High King of this, Eleban?"

The Dominion King laughed shortly. "You ask my permission as though it is a quarrel that does not involve you. Go ahead, ask. But it will involve you, be assured. You have no sons of your own, but Athea does, and Khedran will take them too. You'll curse the day you accepted that white horse...and allowed that into your household!" Eleban threw a last withering look at Jhinn, and turned his horse as though to leave, but hesitated, looking back.

"Ask Khedran about it, if you dare. Ask him about the Duine half-breed he calls brother. His father allowed the Chaine into Azlatan, and then fathered the Forbidden Child, and Khedran protects them all. Ask him about it if you wish, and if you survive, tell me his answer upon your return!"

Marre watched them ride away, unaware of her fists clenched in her lap.

"Do not listen to them, Marre," her mother's soft voice came from behind her.

Marre looked back, surprised to see her mother sitting upright and fending off the attentions of her Duine. Lathine regarded her daughter with eyes fiercely bright in her pale face.

"As Queen you will hear rumors and rumors of rumors. There will be politics and policies and politicians, and stories to make your heart break. If you listen too well, it will be your undoing. As High Queen, you are one with the High King. You must keep the faith. Your only chance for happiness lies there."

Marre heard the wisdom in her mother's words, but looked away, because too many questions stirred in the dark recesses of her mind.

There was no question now of stopping for the night, even though Lathine remained in pain from her cramped position in the coach. Marre and the Duine did the best they could to make a bed for her on the floor of the coach, squeezing themselves into the corners. That soon became nearly unbearable. Marre learned something about physical pain: it blurred the pain in her mind.

They made a stop at dusk, to share food and stretch their legs. Lathine weakly dissented. She would not move from her makeshift bed, and only ate what her Duine could bully into her.

Marre saw how little she could help and climbed from the coach, her legs nearly buckling beneath her. She walked carefully in her hated but fashionably spike-heeled shoes and gazed around, waiting for circulation to return.

They had halted at the edge of a wood overlooking a river; she could see its silver sheen through the purple twilight. She moved away from the men seeing to the weary horses, and the sound of them was soon replaced by the twitter of birds settling into the branches above her head. She peered up at the first stars glittering through the boughs.

She crossed her arms for warmth, wishing she had remembered her cloak, and moved uphill to leave the trees. Glancing up the road, she was arrested by the sight of Jhinn, who stood at the hill's crest with his horse. The dying sun fired the red in his hair, and it struck her suddenly that only his habitual leather and the strange color of his hair would tell an observer that he was neither Duine nor Rioch, so not of her world. Somehow the thought made her uncomfortable, and she shook it off.

He was feeding his horse bites of an apple as he watched the road. It was as if, alone on that hill, the horse was his only friend, and she saw this as being symbolic of his long stay in Athea. That made her sad.

"He is a strange one, isn't he?" her father asked, stopping beside her. "I have to admit I am glad he's with us now, with the strange way the countryside is behaving. But Eleban was right in one thing, you know. How can we know what they think? I'll be glad to finally be rid of his presence when we are safe in Cabre. They are not like us, the Chaine. Their very existence challenges the natural order of things. The Tahmond ruled them as not even being human, which is why they didn't argue their immigration."

She frowned. How could living beings, any living beings, challenge the natural order? She could not perceive it as her father did, and his arrogance disappointed her. Yet even she had occasionally questioned Jhinn's cool detachment, his reliance on reason over emotion.

Uncomfortable, she turned away from her thoughts both mentally and physically, walking back into the deep shadows under the trees.

She did not see Jhinn suddenly mount his horse, peering toward the road ahead at oncoming riders. Nor did she see him glance swiftly back to the carriage and note her absence. He was ever aware of her exact presence and had known she was there with her father but moments before. She'd have been shocked at the nearly savage way he spun his horse in her direction.

Marre walked on, unaware, into the darkening woods. She paid no attention to rustling in the thick growth around her, being familiar with the night winds of Azlatan. Her feet followed a path, and she wondered dimly how such a path had come to be.

Shortly she stepped into a clearing where the stars brightened above her. She halted. Some sense told her of a wrongness. Nose wrinkling, she recognized woodsmoke, and peering across the starlit grey meadow saw darker objects scattered across its blankness. She recognized a camp and a campfire hastily doused. She recognized danger too late.

She was wrenched from her feet, her burly unseen attacker banding her ribs and smothering her face with a sweaty hand. Dimly she heard the screams of horses and men, the unmistakable sounds of battle. She kicked futilely at air, her back crushed against an armored chest, her head forced back against the man's shoulder. His fingers threatened to fracture the delicate bones of her face. There was a searing pain at the base of her neck, bones and nerves compressed to exquisite agony. She dangled helpless in the giant's grip, her feet kicking uselessly at his knees. Then the ground rushed to smash against her face while those massive hands engulfed her neck. Her ears roared; her eyes saw yellow lights in rings of darkness.

Then all sight and sound vanished.

Grief washed through her spirit like water through her bowels.

Death was here before she had lived.

She awoke to cold grass against her cheek. Stars wheeled overhead; at the corner of her vision shone the brighter aura of the rising moon. Beyond jagged spears of grass she saw the battle between a giant and her Chaine. She saw her valiant guardian fall under the giant's weight, and the giant's sword blurring with motion. She tried to cry out but could only retch. She managed to roll onto her back.

Hoofbeats like thunder neared on the path she had foolishly followed a lifetime ago. Above it came the crack of metal on bone, but the giant was not done. She watched him lifting the heavy sword, slashing downward again and again, as though he pounded the earth. But she knew it was Jhinn he destroyed.

Black riders with cloaks like wings beating in the wind passed around her. The King's soldiers arrived at last.

The giant scarce had time to turn before their leader was upon him. She heard metal ring on metal and thought for a moment the soldier was unhorsed; the giant seemed big enough to pound in the steed's head. But the rider wielded a sword surrounding him with cold starfire. Constellations glittered in its wake, and when the Star Blade fell, it was the giant who went down.

The rider began to dismount for the killing blow, but before his boot touched the earth Marre had struggled to her feet and found her ruined voice, barely loud enough to halt him. "Stop!"

The rider halted, turned in her direction. The others, still mounted, were still and silent, surprised by this ragged specter raised from the grass.

Marre straightened as best she could and walked to the one who stood waiting. "I claim right," she hissed at the tall man. In the sword's magic fog of starlight, his strange green eyes glowed like a wild thing's, and she thought she understood why he was called the Black Wolf. She looked away from her betrothed, to the enemy at her feet. The moon had risen to watch now, and its light was almost a glare on the blond giant's staring face. He lived yet, though the blood ran from him and drowned his lungs. She heard its gurgle and saw the sneer on his lips.

Things that cross the border, she thought. She knew this was not a creature of Azlatan, but something the Tahmond would not allow. She spared a glance for the sword that had brought the creature down and thought only the cold flame of Daimaine could have vanquished it.

She swayed momentarily, and another soldier dismounted as though to help her. Khedran lifted a gloved hand to stop him.

Gritting her teeth, Marre lifted her fashionable shoe and jammed the spiked heel into the giant's eye until she felt the splinter of bone into brain. She continued to grind it savagely as the enemy convulsed beneath her.

When it was done, she turned wordlessly and looked for Jhinn.

She found him lying half in a small running stream, his hair drifting on the current. She dragged him from the water and, on her knees, used the hem of her skirt to wash the blood from his face. She did not weep. She did not look at the mutilation of her lifelong guardian's body, but at the friend's face now forever still.

She knew that with this night her perception of the world was eternally changed.

"He was Chaine."

It was a comment, an observation, from the dark King who unnoticed had helped her move the body and who now stood behind her. She rocked back to stare up at him. "His name was Jhinn. He was my guardian, and my friend," she rasped. "He has been that since my birth, and I do not even know if he has anyone else who will care that he is dead. He was alone, yet no one really realized how alone—including me—because he seemed always to have what he needed, within himself."

She paused to swallow. Bitterness laced her ruined voice. "He was contracted, I know, to spend his life among strangers. But at least he had a choice. It was not made for him. He was, despite everything, the only free man I have ever really known. Only now do I know how much I envied him."

"You killed for him."

She shook her head. "I took vengeance, but I did it for myself, not just to honor Jhinn. That armored creature almost killed me. He almost took my life before I had a chance to know that it was my own. My own!"

Her eyes lifted defiantly to Khedran's. I know who you are, they said. I have given you my truth.

His chin lifted. "Princess," said the High King, "your life's choice is yours, as it was your Chaine's. It will not be made for you." His voice was as cold as the touch of the Deathqueen. Khedran turned on his heel and was gone from her.

PART 2: THE CHAINE

They came in the early reign of Allasar, the sixth High King: golden ships, sailing ships, like burning fragments of the sun on the far horizon. They came from the West, from where no mortal had passed in all the history of the world.

The people watched amazed the ships that ran before the wind, turning in to the bay edged by the King's City. The golden craft dropped anchor, and smaller boats were lowered from their sides. The gleam of gold also appeared on those that rode within them to the land. They all had hair like fire or autumn red, unlike either Rioch or Duine.

Powerful in stature, wearing leather chased with gold, they are the warriors called Chaine, who have no royalty but gave oath of friendship to the High Kings of Azlatan. They brought as gifts horses born of the wind, and to barter metal that cannot be broken.

Their leader came first, the one they called The Chaine. She strode out of the water taller than the men, with windblown hair of fire and gold. She dressed like her men in furs and leather with gold worked through. At her hip she wore a golden sword.

——From the Annals of Azlatan

CHAPTER 7

Danon was the only witness to the exchange between his King and Marre. He watched Khedran go from her, from the battlefield where a Chaine lay dead near Azlatan's unknown enemy. Danon could only guess the burden Khedran carried in this moment, and his heart bid him follow. But he knew better.

Grimly he turned his mind from the burdens a King must face alone, to the mundane tasks which were his. He knew he was no great soldier; despite the drilling he had received at Shandiin's ungentle hands, he believed he was the least of the warriors in Khedran's Black Guard. Danon had begun as a healer, and having received training in Chaine medicine, that single intent was now his only purpose.

He directed removal of the dead giant. His orders were followed gingerly, wary of the evil and the unknown, but Danon's swift scrutiny of the body had told him what he needed to know. This was a giant, yes, but a man, nonetheless.

Farbet grumbled. "Too bad he was allowed to die. We could have learned a lot from him."

Danon ignored this and turned his attention to the living.

Marre still knelt beside the fallen Chaine, unmoving since Khedran's abrupt departure. Her eyes were shadowed wells in her pale face. He noted terrible bruises on her throat, visible even in the moonlight.

He halted in front of her, gave himself to the dispassionate calm so much a part of The Chaine's training. He could not allow anger even in Khedran's defense, but it burned in his belly. This Princess had rejected the High King!

"I am a healer," he told her quietly.

"Then heal this man," she rasped.

"I cannot. He is gone, Princess."

"Then you are no healer. Liar!"

He drew a careful breath. "I am not of the Temple of Healers. I am not a Tahmond or Tahmine, who might be able to perform such a miracle with Liethe's help. I used the term only because it is more easily understood. I am only a physician."

She turned her bruised gaze to him. "So. A Chaine doctor. Another of Khedran's misfits."

His jaw tightened. "A moment past you were mourning this Chaine. I'm not ashamed of the training I have received from his people. Nor is the High King you so rudely dismissed."

He saw the pain of loss and confusion blur her features. She looked back down at her fallen guardian, and he watched her hand tremble on the bloodied auburn hair.

"I cannot help him," he told her more gently. "Nor could a Tahmine. The Chaine are immune to magic, living or dead. Khedran will see that his body is taken care of in the custom of his people. As you must know, Khedran was mentored from birth by their leader. I assure you of his respect for them." He held out a hand to her. "It's my job to help the living. Please…I would tend to your hurts, with your permission."

She refused his offer of help, standing stiffly. "I fear even Liethe could not help me this night."

But he sensed an iron will behind her grief, one equal to Khedran's own. He did not envy Khedran his promised bride.

Danon later hoped he never had to live through another night like this one. Seeing to the future High Queen had been his initial concern, but the battle had been violent if short, and there were others that needed him more. Khedran had requisitioned a homely farmhouse and there he had worked through the night, and it was nearly dawn before he had time for Marre again, to examine her hurts more thoroughly.

He looked a last time at Marre's poor bruised throat before drawing the bedclothes thoughtfully to her chin. She slept soundly from the draught he had ordered for her.

Danon was still amazed that she had denied her betrothal. Even the High King could not break the betrothal ordered by the god Phaelon. He shook his head, thinking of Khedran's impossible promise that she would be allowed a choice. She could no more refuse the duty of her birthright than he could.

But Khedran would challenge even the High Tahmond, he knew. His liege was a law unto himself, and liable to draw Phaelon's wrath upon them all.

Marre's mother slept in the next bed, and he was not sure she would survive the last leg of the trip to Cabre. She should not have come at all but, her Duine had told him tearfully, she had obeyed her husband's demand. Different than her daughter? Danon thought of Marre's fallen Chaine guardian and felt Marre had been as influenced as Khedran in her upbringing.

A farmhouse Duine came to watch over the sleeping women, along with a soldier to summon Danon to the High King. Shortly Danon was downstairs, entering the parlor where Khedran paced like the wolf he was often called, cloak flaring with each abrupt turn.

The drapes had been flung wide though it was not yet dawn. Khedran seemed oblivious to the rain-wind rattling the panes; the fireplace was not even lit.

"There you are," Khedran said as though he had waited hours. Danon, used to his ways, simply watched as Khedran strode to the lamplit, littered desk. The King glared down at papers that Danon knew were not the farmer's. He recognized the black and white seal of the Tahmond on an unwound scroll.

"The vulture already sent his message." Khedran tapped the scroll angrily. "The High Tahmond couldn't see the danger coming; apparently our enemies are as invisible to him as are the Chaine, so he gave no warning that the giant had crossed into Azlatan. Yet already he has questioned the worthiness of my bride. Why should Marre's misfortune make her unworthy? Her attacker was wrong, not she." He looked bitter. "Still, I don't know how he knew of her rape before I did."

"He is wrong," Danon denied. "She's bruised and battered, but has not been violated."

Khedran's eyebrows climbed. "So?" he asked in surprise. "How could he have made that mistake, I wonder."

Danon scowled stubbornly. "She is battered only above the waist, her clothing is intact...and her attacker still wore armor from neck to foot, so how could he have raped her? Her guardian was still fighting him when we arrived."

Khedran laughed softly at Danon's anger. "Now it's you defying the Tahmond. No, don't get defensive. I know that when you are certain of a thing, you are not wrong. Though it is a strange thing..." he looked momentarily bemused, then seemed to dismiss the matter.

He frowned down at the scroll on the desk. "While he natters over Marre's supposed misfortune, he doesn't mention the fact that invaders have crossed our borders. The borders that are supposed to be closed by Phaelon's magic!" He spat that like a curse, wheeling around again in the abrupt manner that he had. Khedran's brilliant mind changed direction as often as he paced. "Things are moving swiftly. Whether or not it was the Outsiders who destroyed the border wards set by Phaelon, it is now proven fact that they know that barrier is gone. And that they've come across. Openly, now, and armored."

Danon grimaced. Khedran had attempted to warn the Dominion Kings that the invaders they knew only as "Outsiders" were infiltrating Azlatan. It was almost impossible to convince them, and Danon could understand that. Before coming to Cabre and becoming one of the King's soldiers, even he would have been in denial that this could be true, as it had never happened in Azlatan's history.

He watched Khedran with renewed gladness that it was this man who was High King, for he was wise and more than unafraid. He had prepared for this, establishing an army and garrisons to defend his realm, although it had made him hated and feared by many of his own subjects.

But now they would have to believe. Khedran was right: war was coming. Khedran would at last be known as the hero he was, Danon thought, when it was seen that his efforts were Azlatan's hope.

"Not enough time!" Khedran was repeating, and Danon tried to untangle his weary mind, realizing he had slipped off into a daydream of easy victory while Khedran still faced the battle. "We're not ready. We need more troops on the border. Mounted troops." His voice trailed off and his attention flashed like a sword-point back to Danon. "That's why I need you."

"Me? My horse is gone," Danon said stupidly.

Khedran laughed outright. "I've heard the barracks teasing. I've been meaning to ask you about the Duine who stole one of our rare prizes, when we need each one so badly."

Danon flushed with guilt. He would not lie to his King...who would know it immediately anyway...but he hadn't been forthcoming about giving Pet away.

But Khedran had already turned back to the desk, sitting down to reach for a pen. "Your replacement mount won't do. I'll see that mine is made ready for you while you have breakfast. The High Tahmine is sending healers to take care of your patients, so you will be free to go."

Danon was adrift with weariness. The idea of riding Khedran's fractious black Chandar filled him with dread. "Where am I going?" he asked.

Khedran didn't look up. "To Ordhold. To find The Chaine. You'll have messages to deliver, one to her and one to Dominion King

Randmar." He reached for another paper, noticed Danon swaying slightly, and motioned for him to sit. "Better give yourself one of your own tonics," he frowned, but his voice was gentle...for Khedran. Danon sat gratefully, and Khedran studied him for a moment.

"Don't worry," Danon told him. "I'll get to Ordhold. Even on Chandar."

Khedran smiled faintly, and surprised Danon again with his infrequent gentleness. "I know you would never fail me. That's one reason I'd rather have you in Cabre, at my back during the next few weeks. But events have moved too quickly to have everything as I would like. The message I send I would entrust to no one else. The Chaine has been missing far too long, but sightings have come from Ordhold. Finding her and delivering these messages are your priorities. Do you understand?"

Danon felt humbled by the trust he had been given, and then proud. He met Khedran's strange emerald eyes for a long moment in pledge, wondering not for the first time at the confidence his King had in him. Ever since the first time...but no, this was no time for memories. Khedran had turned back, reassured, to his writing...and Danon must listen, for part of his message was verbal.

"I've been expecting The Chaine back daily," Khedran was saying. "She had planned to return long ago. My guess is she's run into trouble, but I have hope she is in Ordhold now."

"Where has she been?" Danon asked.

Khedran didn't hesitate to tell his Compatri the secret. "Across the border. If she's accomplished what she set out to do, we'll have the treasure that may save Azlatan. If not..." Khedran's pen halted, and his eyes lifted to Danon's with an unfamiliar expression. Danon recognized it belatedly as grief. "If not, she is dead. In that case all you can do is deliver my message to Dominion King Randmar, and speed back to me quickly as you can." He looked down at the page for a moment. Danon saw him visibly steel himself, and then the powerful King returned.

"Tell her everything that has happened," Khedran ordered. "Explain that the storm grows over Cabre, and there may be civil war. For Council will be called, Danon. By the Dominion Kings, not the Tahmond; the High Tahmond will wait for them before making his move to replace me. Phaelon's Law allows me to be tried only with the agreement of seven Dominion Kings in addition to himself and the High Tahmine." He looked up, caught the disbelief on Danon's face. "Don't be so foolish as to think this Outsider's attack will make him or the Dominion Kings listen to me. They do not want to believe we are invaded. They will search for every answer but the truth, because they want one that pleases them."

Danon shifted uncomfortably as Khedran slashed his bold signature at the bottom of a page, then rolled it and handed it unsealed to him. "This is for King Randmar. I bid you see that he gets it whether or not you find Shandiin. I need his horses, and I have no doubt that I will need his strong right arm, and I will need both sooner than I like. Randmar is steadfast in his loyalty, and can sway the rest of the Dominion Kings, but..." he shook his head.

"You truly expect a rebellion."

Khedran's smile was without mirth. "Not if I can help it. But as The Chaine says, you can only be sure of what you make sure."

That reminder of The Chaine brought back the shadow so unfamiliar on Khedran's proud features.

"Find her," was his final command.

A fool may accomplish what a wise man will not try.

Not even a Chaine saying, Danon thought; they don't credit fools so much. It was something Mia had told him long ago, while bandaging wounds suffered in a fall from a horse far too spirited for his skill.

And now I ride the King's warhorse, he thought, and I'm not exactly sure what that makes me.

At heart he thought he knew. If any man other than Khedran himself could find The Chaine, it was he...because only love or desperation would make a man chase the wind in hope of its capture. His own love for Khedran was, he thought, almost like that for the goddess Liethe, and almost like what he felt for Varady; he had never really understood it, though he suspected Khedran did. Khedran could command that from men, and knew it. But Danon's love for his King was all bound up, necessarily, with his love for Shandiin, and yet that was a separate thing, and there was the proof that he was a fool, for only a fool would love The Chaine.

Khedran had sent the right man, and he wondered if his King knew his secret.

The road was long and empty. Few travelled north, even in the warm months after Stareven. Danon shunned the sparse inns, and seldom allowed himself the luxury of a campfire. He travelled swiftly, in light and darkness, and was glad of the black warhorse he had at first dreaded. Chandar was northern born, of that secret line King Randmar nurtured in Ordhold, and he knew the road well. He was a king among horses. Danon cared for him at each stop, and Chandar guarded his sleep.

Not enough sleep. He tried dozing in the saddle, Chaine-fashion, but his mind drifted to memory instead of dreams. Finally, he let it be. Beneath an empty sky his mind went to years past, to the Temple of Healing, and awakening there to light as pure as a reflection in a child's eye. He remembered.

Liethe's Light came from no source that he could recognize. It was magic.

Awakening in the Liethe's Temple of Healing, he gathered himself as though for battle. He no longer tried to do as his teachers instructed. Open your mind and your heart, they told him.

He had tried. But the teaching and the magic were enigmas beyond his reach. He fought for the will to go on with the present but unreachable magic tearing at his sanity.

Each day was harder. So it took longer now, to sit up, to reach for the simple healer's robe upon the plain wooden chair, to pull it over his body and stare with dull surprise at his thinning wrists.

He looked up as the door opened, and a slender girl in a robe like his own stood within his chamber. The Light lived within her too, within the eyes that watched him with such concern. Somehow it felt right, seeing it shine within her.

He was glad it was her. Of all in this place, the young novice healer Rani was his only true friend. He sensed in her a purity that was missing even in the Tahmond and Tahmine who trained such novices as they.

"You look like despair," she told him. "It is wrong of you to treat yourself like this, Danon. It isn't the goddess Liethe that you battle. It is Chaos. Chaos left the mark of will and pride on the souls of mortals, so that it would not be easy to accept the Gifts of Liethe."

"No. The lack is in me, Rani. I've failed. I can close a wound – with thread; set a bone – with my two hands and a splint. But I can't heal. I'm a mechanic, Rani, not a healer. There is a lack. Perhaps I am more akin to Chaos."

"I won't listen to that stupid talk." She came to him, touched his arm shyly. "You are a healer. I know it. It's in your hands, and in your mind, and only a little bit away from your heart. You need to be needed, like all of us; it's a reason for life, the only reason for such as us. You need only to prove it to yourself. And Liethe will not let you give up without finding your proof. That's why I am here this morning."

He was puzzled and almost alarmed at her unfamiliar intensity. "What do you mean?" he asked.

"You are needed at the Altar. There is someone for you there. You must come with me."

"Rani, you can't play with someone's life. If you can't heal this one, call a Tahmine!"

She shook her head, sable hair swinging about her face. "No. He is for you. Come!"

She is fey, he thought. She is more than healer. She is like a High Tahmine; even the Tahmond who come here see it, and almost fear her.

She turned away at his nod, and he followed her, mind whirling with too many things. Healing had been his goal since the first crippled bird nestled in his childish grasp, but had he ever asked why? He had not thought about feeling "needed." His joy was in making broken things right and whole.

He passed an archway that vanished into airy height, and into the Chamber of Healing where the Light scintillated and the force of life sang like a choir, a harmony answered by his own spirit.

Hope returned. Maybe Rani was right. Maybe now...

But something felt wrong. It took him a moment to realize the huge chamber was empty, that only he and Rani were here. He looked at her in question, and she gestured toward the Altar itself.

A magic fountain rose from the center of the Chamber, and at its foaming crest lay the shadow of a man. As Danon neared, the fountain's crest ebbed like the tide going out, and he could peer through the liquid that was lighter than water, and see the man who lay within, now suspended just above the floor.

The sleeping face seemed made of marble. Fresh wounds marred it, still brimming with blood, for he lay in the sleep given by the Altar, where time does not move. The face was young and could have belonged to Danon himself. Rioch, handsome, aristocratic, with black hair blood-matted against his skull, blood soaking his black clothing.

"Sword wounds," Danon murmured. He glanced around the empty chamber. "Why isn't he attended?"

"He is a soldier of the High King." She gazed at him expectantly, as though he should understand.

He did not. Chilled, he looked back at the soldier. "His wounds are mortal. He needs a Healer, not a novice, certainly not me."

"The Healers gave him Liethe's sleep. They will do no more. He is a soldier of the High King." She shook her head as he still did not understand. "His soldiers belong to Daimaine, as does the King. The High Tahmond has warned the Healers of Liethe not to argue with the Deathqueen. She is, after all, Justice. She will decide in the balance should he live or die."

"Then why even bring him here? Surely there are others who could help, skilled with their hands, with medicines, if not magic."

"You. You healed by that method, before you even came to us."

It struck him then. "They don't know, do they? They don't know you brought me here. They intend for this man to die. Does the High King know that?"

Rani seemed to have shrunk. "I don't think so," she almost whispered. She raised her hands to cover her face, then dropped them and stood tall again. "It isn't the goddess." He heard true conviction return to her voice. "It is not Liethe who commands this unholy thing. I know it in my heart. It is Chaos, through the High Tahmond who has made a commandment that would end this man's life."

"Politics, you mean."

"Will you help him?" she pleaded.

"I can try. But my tools..."

A bag appeared from the folds of her robe. He recognized it as his own, taken from him upon his entrance to the Temple. He welcomed it as an old friend, something of himself returned to him. "Will we be disturbed?" he asked.

"No one will come near the Chamber until Daimaine has passed over."

Danon shuddered but knelt to his patient. He could almost feel the presence of the Deathqueen, but she did not tear away the gossamer magic that held the soldier in stasis.

That magic held back the bleeding while he worked. He did not realize that Liethe's Light was no longer visible to him. All withdrew from his consciousness except the task at hand. To rejoin muscle to muscle, knowing that it might not work again, but seeking life anyway. How much blood had the soldier lost, though? He could not replace blood. He could only hope.

He tied off the last stitch and finally stepped back, taking a tiny flask from his bag. Rani watched him in awe. "How did you learn to do that?" she asked.

"On lots of animals for a long time. Liethe's sleep is leaving him. When...if...he awakes you must give him this. It is not magic, but it will keep his heart beating until I return."

"What is it?"

He clenched his teeth. "It is Chaine medicine. It's his only chance, Rani."

He saw real fear in her eyes. Chaine. Unclean.

"It works!" He feared she wouldn't take it, guessing she would never have carried his bag, had she known it was within. "I bought it at great price, in Selagon. It once saved someone who would have died. There is enough left for him—if we hurry!"

She swallowed visibly. "Where are you going?"

"Rani, you said it yourself: Chaos works through the High Tahmond who sentenced this man to die. The High King must be told. I will go and bring help from Penumbra. You must stay, and get this medicine down his throat if you can, and keep him warm."

She looked at him hopelessly. "You cannot get to the King. Penumbra is guarded. They will never let you in. It is foolish—they might kill you if you try."

But she reached for the flask. He saw the courage it took for her to hold it.

"A fool may accomplish what a wise man will not try," he told her.

She'd been right; the Guards wouldn't let him in. But they hadn't expected a mad dash from a robed healer's apprentice; the element of surprise got him inside, where he ran like prey through the halls of Penumbra, the Guards like hounds at his heels.

He skidded to a halt at a dead end, then noticed a narrow stairway temporarily unguarded. His sandals slapped on bare stone as he bounded up, two steps at a time. Like a treed cat, he thought, finally seeing the closed door at the top, but it gave to his thrusting palm, and then he was in, whirling to slam home the inner bar.

There was a small thud behind him, metal on wood.

His back began to tingle, the place between his shoulder blades. *I must be dreaming*, he thought wildly. *I can't really be in the High King's palace with the Guards after me, and someone...something...behind me.*

He turned slowly. "Um," he said.

He saw the golden war-sword first, gleaming naked in the clear light through the open window of this small bedchamber. It lay on the low table by the single narrow bed, within easy reach of the room's inhabitant.

She regarded him calmly with level silver-grey eyes. For a long moment the tableau held: she, sitting on the edge of the bed with an elbow on a knee, chin propped on a fist, studying the young aristocrat in humble robe who had intruded; he frozen and wide-eyed at this lioness in her den.

Her shaggy hair was wildfire blooming over her sculpted shoulders. Her face was foreign somehow, achingly beautiful, with wide-planed cheekbones and jaw as strongly carved as her straight nose and modeled lips. Her sleeveless tunic was soft leather clinging to her strong curves, belted wide at the waist. Her long legs were also sheathed in leather filigreed with golden patterns, including her tall boots.

He remembered that he had met her briefly years before. Having never met a Chaine, and never a woman of such height and beauty, he'd been too shocked to believe she was even human. He'd been so overwhelmed by her he'd been unable to speak intelligibly.

He was no better now.

A scuffle outside the door, followed by fists pounding on wood, startled him back to reality. "Um," he said again.

"You already mentioned that," she pointed out. "And I think I remember you. Danon, isn't it? I'm pretty sure you told me the same thing the first time we met."

Muffled conversation behind the door. An unsure voice rising. "Queen Chaine! Are you in there?"

She did not respond, but remained with her fist supporting her chin as she studied Danon. A voice outside said, "I know I saw him come up here."

His eyes flicked to the sword, back to her. "Are you the Queen Chaine?" he asked.

"I hate being called that. My people don't have royalty. As leader I am called The Chaine."

Danon swallowed. "I have to see the High King. I don't see how you could be his lifelong Defender...you are not old enough!"

"Thanks for the compliment." She smiled while the assault on the door grew in volume. "Why do you want to see the King?"

"I need – look, are you really The Chaine?"

"I am called Shandiin. Pretend she's under the bed if that helps. I'll pretend you are really a Healer. You haven't answered my question."

He jumped at the sound of wood splintering behind him.

"I am a Healer." He spoke quickly, unsure where to start. "At least I was going to be, but..." he trailed off, searching for words.

"You have an unusual mind. Do you keep it all in one place?"

His mouth snapped shut. Wood cracked. "The High Tahmond is murdering the King's soldiers," he blurted, realizing immediately how unbelievable it sounded, heart plummeting as her expression hardened.

She stood up...and up, and up; he'd forgotten how tall she was...and he flinched at the sword she picked up.

"It's true," he added lamely.

"Move over."

He obeyed instantly. She strode past him to the door, considered the crack down its center, and shook her head. With her free hand she lifted the heavy bar, dropping it to dance back before the door crashed open and two soldiers spilled to the floor at her feet.

"Morning bless," she greeted them as she sheathed her sword at her hip. She glanced back at Danon. "Follow me."

Danon had never seen anyone go downstairs two at a time, and he was hard-pressed to follow with the robe hampering him. She demanded more details during the journey. Her long-legged stride continued down the hall to an inner courtyard, where men were seated to watch a pair engaged in combat in the center.

She halted briefly, then sat down on a stone bench as though to watch. He stared at her, at the seated soldiers, and at the two who circled each other warily. One was a tall muscular giant in only leather breeches, his red hair marking him as a Chaine. The other, he realized with some shock, was the High King himself.

He couldn't have explained why he thought so.

Khedran was also stripped to the waist, a powerfully condensed version of the Chaine he challenged. His long black hair was in disarray and his skin gleamed with sweat.

"Sit," The Chaine told Danon.

"We have to tell him..."

"Well, barge right in. Just don't get your head knocked off."

"Uh..."

"Sit."

"But I told you, Rani is–"

"Oh, jump up and down then. I don't care. It will only be a moment before one of them goes down and it's over."

Danon ground his teeth in frustration, watching the fight. The redhaired Chaine wrestler was a head taller than the tall King, and his arms seemed as big as Khedran's waist. The two circled each other warily, but the King's aura of confidence fairly filled the small courtyard. Danon flinched when the bigger man rushed. Khedran seemed to vanish beneath the towering bulk but reappeared standing while the Chaine landed with a jar that shook the ground.

Shandiin applauded politely. Khedran barely glanced in her direction, reaching to help his fallen opponent to his feet. A second later he was on his back, looking vaguely surprised while the Chaine got up unassisted.

Shandiin's laughter pealed. "Fool's throw!" she announced.

Khedran got up, grinning, and accepted the towel his friendly opponent handed him. His strangely brilliant emerald eyes flicked their way.

"This is Danon," Shandiin introduced. "He breaks into bedrooms with urgent news."

Khedran continued the drying process, lifting his eyebrows in question. Danon swallowed nervously. "I think...I thought...are you really the High King?" he heard himself say.

"That's the other thing." Shandiin rolled her eyes. "He's still waiting for the real me to crawl out from under my bed."

"I am not!" Danon's nervous temper finally broke, heedless of legendary presences. "You are the most rude, obnoxious woman I have ever met!"

Khedran's laughter led a diffident chorus from his men. Danon realized Shandiin was feigning shock, but her eyes held mirth.

"Wonderful," Khedran said. "Very perceptive of you, Danon. She is also sarcastic, cantankerous..."

"All right." Shandiin lifted her hands as though in surrender. "But I think you cheat at cards. Khedran, Danon has some important news for you. I shouldn't have baited him; he's right to be angry."

"You're a Healer?" Khedran asked him directly.

Danon shook his head. "No. And probably never, now, because the High Tahmond is ordering your soldiers' death instead of healing them." Having finally gathered his wits, he went on to explain what had happened.

Khedran turned to his men, who were already on their feet with weapons at hand. For the first time, Danon heard the command voice of a High King resonate between his ears. "Go, retrieve the injured soldier. And bring the girl Rani. She'll need our protection until we can get this straightened out with the High Tahmine."

Danon slumped with relief. The High Tahmine was equal in power to the High Tahmond, though she was growing old and wasn't often seen. She was the mortal hand of Liethe, even as the High King was Daimaine's. Only the High Tahmine had the awesome right to challenge the Deathqueen herself. That power was rarely used, for the Tahmine was wise, and knew that death was in most cases a natural thing.

The High Tahmond was feared. The High Tahmine was revered.

"So." As his soldiers left to obey his command, Khedran's normal voice held low fury. "My soldiers belong to Daimaine, do they? Well, so shall some others, before we are finished." His strange eyes held an unholy emerald fire, and Danon's mind flashed to rumors of madness.

But when his King turned those eyes to Danon, the fire gentled to a glow...and he felt his very soul became visible in their light.

"And who do you serve?" the High King asked him.

"Not Liethe, it seems," Danon replied. "Nor Daimaine, for my intent in life was to hold death apart." He looked at Shandiin, daring her to mock him. She only waited.

He stood to face his King. He had known the answer, he realized, the instant he had been asked. "I would serve only you, Your Highness. If you would have me."

Khedran smiled acceptance. He merely touched him in passing by, and a wondrous joy drove Danon to his knees. He belonged to the High King from that moment.

The soldier lived, not through his help after all, but because Rani had found the strength to test her belief to the full. It was she who gathered his soul from the Deathqueen. She said Liethe had seen no difference in this soldier from any of her children.

The High Tahmine did more than understand. Danon was not surprised to learn that the novice Rani was now of the Tahmine.

Danon's education in Khedran's service began and continued relentlessly. It battered his naivety into submission, for he was one of the men of Khedran's Black Guard now, and that meant he belonged to The Chaine for his training period.

Penumbra and later Ordhold became his home and his bat-tlefield, for he learned to hate, for a time, the burden that was The Chaine. The steel within her he could honor; her amusement hurt, and Shandiin, he found, was always amused. She used her laughter like a scalpel, cutting away the lack of critical thinking in her trainee even as he learned to cut damaged flesh.

For that was the miracle after all. She didn't believe him a failure. He learned Chaine medicine along with the art of war, and she never saw the incongruity in that.

CHAPTER 8

Danon looked up at clouds lowering to mantle the mountains into which he climbed, resigning himself to riding in the rain. The mountain weather was chancy, and he had known it could come to this. Yet he loved this untamed corner of Khedran's land and knew freedom in the wheeling wind. The sheer drop so near Chandar's careful hooves was a peril paid for by the awesome vista it revealed, the diamond flash of mountain lakes amid canyons and valleys dressed in forest green. Only frequent rain and deep snow could create such lushness. Everything, the Chaine claimed, has a price.

He felt an eagerness in his mount now that they had finally entered the mountains of Ordhold. This was Chandar's home. Here he had been foaled, and run the high pastures until his second year, when Khedran took him to hand. Weary though they both were from the long journey, man and steed alike drank renewed strength from the high country.

The threatened rain began in earnest, until Chandar's black mane streamed and rivulets shone silver on the rocky path. Danon rode on stubbornly, turning his mind to happier memories of this land as the rain thrummed around him. Here he had hunted and trained with Rioch and Chaine; he had lived from this land seemingly untouched by the boundaries of civilization, pristine and uncomplicated, as close to paradise as man can come.

Coming to know the hard folk of Ordhold, and Dominion King Randmar himself, had been an experience for Danon. Here was a different breed, who dealt with the harshest realities of nature as equals, and rarely turned to magic instead of their own minds and hands. Perhaps that was why they had no fear of the people called Chaine, who dealt with magic not at all. They had accepted even The Chaine herself, with the exiled High Prince of Azlatan, and made a home for them until the Prince became the King.

Learning to know them had also taught Danon about Khedran himself. Randmar's support was the surest stone in Azlatan's foundation, cemented by a respect Randmar would never give to a lesser man. Nor, Danon secretly believed, would Randmar have given over his Dominion to a High King unworthy of it. Such a thought approached heresy, for no Dominion King could claim separation from Penumbra. But Danon had learned more than even The Chaine could teach him, in Ordhold.

Chandar scrambled over a rock-fall and turned a corner that took their path beneath an overhang, offering some protection from the rain. Danon halted there at last, taking pity on the horse, and dismounted to wait for the squall to pass.

Chandar's black coat streamed, and steam rose from his hide. Danon took a blanket from his oilskin pack and dried him as best he could. The rain stopped while he cared for his charge, and when he turned to look out once more over the canyon the silence struck him more than the sight. The clouds had come to earth, ragged streamers even in the canyon below; the far mountains were no longer visible at all. His hopes sank, for he could not travel far in this. He had best get off the narrow trail and into the trees, and perhaps wait for morning.

He rode on between walls of stone to the valley floor and saw the first pines rising before him. But soon he rode in a silent world of pearl.

Chandar stepped lightly over good black earth, where Danon could see sprinkled the tiny starlike white flowers native to the highlands. Much beyond that he could not see, save the drifting fog and the blue-shadow forms of trees. All was suffused with silver. Even his hand on the reins seemed strangely pale to him.

For the first time in his journey, he began to feel uncomfortable. Once he thought he saw a shadow, large as a pony, slip away to his right. He remembered there were beasts here unheard of in the lower lands of Azlatan, wolves and bears. He shivered slightly, his free hand dropping to his sword.

In the same instant Chandar flung his head high, snorting a warning. Danon saw an edge of white in the great horse's eye. A large white body drifted past his right foot, and Danon almost jerked his boot from the stirrup before regaining control of his senses. The giant white cat reared to lay velvet paws against Chandar's shoulder. Danon looked into its golden eyes, the pupils round instead of slitted unlike most cats, and felt its deep purr of welcome. Chandar, far from alarmed, turned his head to whicker a soft greeting.

"'Lo, Majia." Danon laid his hand against soft white fur. Majia allowed the caress, then dropped silently to earth, watching him. Danon wondered at the intelligence in those brilliant eyes. The snowcats were companions to the northerners, never servants, but often acted as guide and guard on their travels through the ancient forests. Majia had favored Khedran. Danon was flattered and awed that the cat honored him as well.

Figures appeared among the trees, looming apparitions that sent a chill down his spine until the cat's human companions walked out of the fog. The first man was dressed in soft leather with a long sheepskin tunic, and a cap of fox-fur from which his own sable hair fell to his shoulders. He was bearded, like most of his people, and his eyes were the color of rich earth. Close to him walked his younger brother, dressed much the same, his eyes the green of summer moss. Danon knew them well, for they were King Randmar's sons.

"Jon," Danon hailed the elder, but his voice faltered, for the dark eyes were not friendly. He sensed then hostility from the whole group, though his swift glance showed several familiar faces. Brend, the younger Prince, appeared nervous, glancing from his brother to Danon.

"Compatri," Jon acknowledged, without the friendly use of his name. "Why are you here?"

Danon scowled. "Since when am I just Compatri to you, Jon? Is there no welcome for an old hunting partner?"

"Things have changed since you left Ordhold. If you hold allegiance yet to the High King, then I can no longer claim friendship."

Not here! Danon thought in disbelief. Not in Ordhold! If this place would not honor Khedran, then all could be lost.

Chandar sensed his disquiet and sidled; Danon checked him sharply even as he gazed at his former friends in dismay. "I don't understand. Ordhold is Khedran's second home. Many of you were like his brothers for the years of his exile. You, Brend...you hunted alongside him, and told me yourself the story of how he saved you from a pack of wolves."

The eyes of the younger prince dropped from his gaze, and Danon looked back at Jon. "Your father pledged his sword to Khedran in time of need. He pledged it on the blood of his own fathers! How could that pledge have been given lightly?"

"It was not given lightly, nor broken lightly." Jon's voice rumbled. "The Tahmond has spoken to me. A Forbidden Child has come forth. Phaelon's Law says if the Forbidden Child is allowed to live, Duine will rise up to kill all Rioch, and no magic can save them. The Tahmond says Khedran has taken in an abomination, the Forbidden Child, and to prevent the end of all of us they must both die."

They took him to the Dominion King of Ordhold, who was breakfasting at a table in the castle courtyard.

Danon was surprised to see Randmar's hair and beard were woven through with white; only his heavy brows remained dark, and the eyes that peered from beneath held an uncharacteristic weariness. Different, too, was his shape: Randmar had always been like the mighty oak raftering the courtyard, but now he was like a tree in winter, stripped of fuller covering so that his knotted bones were visible under hardened skin. He looked like a very sick man.

With this sad determination Danon looked at the two seated on either side of him. One was a Tahmond, vertically painted black and white with a halo of white hair. On the other side sat a woman dressed in the veil and gown of Liethe's service. Danon felt hope rise, just recognizing it. He knew the wisdom of the Tahmine, and still believed the Tahmond wrong in his interpretation of prophecy. Perhaps with her presence it would be possible to convince Randmar of that.

The Dominion King rose as he and Jon neared. His eyes were grave as he accepted Danon's formal bow. "I bring you warm greetings," Danon said carefully, "and a message from your High King."

Danon presented the flattened scroll he had carried next to his skin throughout his journey. Randmar saw it, but his hands remained at his sides. "Jon hasn't told you?" he asked. Danon saw a new uncertainty in the Dominion King.

"Jon told me." Danon stiffened his arm, refusing to lower the proffered letter. "I have heard one interpretation of Phaelon's Law. Perhaps in Khedran's words you may find another."

The Tahmond stood up at this, drawing his thin body erect. "Do not listen to him, Your Majesty." His voice was brittle as new ice. "What he offers is poison to you!"

Danon bit back a retort, locking Randmar's gaze with his own. He knew the integrity of this man, had heard Khedran speak of the comfort he had drawn from Randmar's strength during his exile here.

The Dominion King did not move, and Danon felt desperation slam his heart against his ribs. "You'd let even a condemned man tell his side." There was no pleading in his voice. He spoke for the High King, and none present must doubt it.

For that reason, too, he kept triumph from his face as Randmar slowly lifted his hand to the message.

It was struck from Danon's grasp before the gesture was finished, with a cry from the Tahmond who did it. "Think of your people!"

Danon looked down at the scroll on the floor, so missed the deep confusion in Randmar's face. He looked up at the Tahmond. "Are you so afraid of the words of the High King? Is your presumed truth so weak?"

"Words are always the weapon of Chaos," the Tahmond replied. "Chaos tricks men with words and willful pride. Your High King is a servant of Chaos, for he puts himself above the Law of Order, just as his father before him did! Allasar broke Phaelon's Law, bringing his seed to abomination. Khedran forgets his rule was given to him by the gods. He has boasted it is in his nature to rule, not in his office. He places himself above even what the goddess Daimaine has given him. And now he brings abomination into Penumbra and calls it 'brother'!"

The argument was too familiar to deter Danon, but he was surprised to hear the quote Khedran had made in his own presence: his nature to rule.

Then the Tahmine was standing, her head just at the level of Randmar's shoulder. She murmured something to the Dominion King, then turned to Danon, dropping her veil.

It was his friend Rani.

Her eyes warned him, so he did not speak her name. She looked past him to Jon. "Your father needs to rest," she told him in her quiet voice. "Please take him to his room. I will see that our guest is served."

"Guest!" the Tahmond cried. "He should be in shackles!"

Rani turned on him in reproach. "There has been no accusation against this man and no trial. Please go. King Randmar is upset enough and is still not well. He should rest until tonight."

The Tahmond looked as if to argue, but there was power in the Tahmine. "Until tonight then." He turned away. He was gone before Jon had guided his silent father through the doorway to his home.

Rani waved the hovering Duine away as Danon bent to pick up the unread letter. "Sit down," she told him, and he did. She served him food from the bowls on the table, like a Duine herself, as she gave him time to regain his composure.

"Are you unsure now of your High King?" she asked very quietly.

"No. I am not unsure of Khedran. All this talk of Phaelon's Law is disturbing, but I know the man he is. Randmar does, too."

"Yet even you cannot deny the words."

"Those things are not him. He is trying to save Azlatan from danger, but that danger is not a child. The Outsiders are crossing our borders, openly now." He looked at the message beside his plate. "That's what he wants Randmar to know. He needs the soldiers and the horses he was promised. Phaelon's border wards are no longer standing."

"I don't think he will get help from Ordhold." Rani sat beside him.

Danon ran his hands through his hair, anguished. "I can't believe this."

"I'm told your King is more Chaine than human." Rani's voice was distant. "He deals with a reality that too often forgets the gods."

He looked at her bitterly, remembering another time. "Some of us are more able to walk with the gods than others. You taught me that, if you recall."

"Yes. You replaced the goddess Liethe with your High King."

"Liethe is not stopping the Outsiders. Khedran is trying to!"

She bit her lip. "Despite the things I am told by others, I do not deny the High King. I believe in the ancient mantra. Like his forefathers, he is incorruptible. He is truth. The trust and honor of Azlatan live within him. But I seek my answers from Liethe. I will ask her help today and hope to have an answer by tonight." She drew in a breath and glanced around, ensuring their privacy. "The Chaine is here. In Randmar's dungeon beneath the castle."

He was too stunned to speak.

Tears sparkled on her dark lashes. "That's why I wanted to speak to you alone, without them guessing that I know you and might warn you. Jon had her put below several weeks ago when she arrived. Randmar doesn't know. But then Randmar's not really the King here, anymore."

Danon's fist tightened on the scroll. So Khedran had lost Ordhold. "I can't believe they have imprisoned The Chaine."

She was once again veiling her face, as though to hide the tears she fought. "Do nothing for now. Jon mustn't know I told you anything. Tonight will be the test, with Randmar present, and if..." she faltered, started over. "When you prove yourself, then you can speak out and demand her release. Then you can both leave Ordhold."

"What test?" he hissed as she rose to leave, but then he saw Jon returning, and his question died. Curiously, he noted Brend waiting nearby, and saw that Rani was going to him.

Soldiers escorted him to a pleasant room, and Danon heard the key turn in the lock as they left him. He was a prisoner.

He remembered his Chaine training. Patience. Calm.

He removed his clothing and bathed, then redressed and lay on the narrow bed with his hands clasped behind his head. Memories had held him in thrall during his journey here; now it was his imagination. The Chaine in a dungeon. Like caging a lioness, he thought. To battle melancholy, he had a childish daydream of rescuing her and riding away on Chandar. Varady would like that one, he thought.

But Varady was gone. Like Ordhold.

What kind of test?

It was full dark when Danon heard the key turn in the lock. He remained sitting with his boots crossed atop the bed. Jon looked in, scowling as his lantern revealed Danon so at ease.

"Come," Jon demanded. "They are waiting."

Danon got up slowly, stretching. "Who are 'they'?" he asked.

"You will see," Jon snapped.

Danon's bravado had worked. He sauntered out with his armed escort, feeling much braver than when he had come in.

They brought him to a heavily curtained room where Rani's robes glowed, like a candle in the torchlight, where she stood next to Randmar in a chair. The Tahmond stood in shadow on his other side.

Danon saw a tripod holding a single vessel, a silver chalice. He recognized it from his time in the Temple of Healing. It was an Altar Bowl. He remembered to make a formal bow to Randmar, who sat unmoving.

To his surprise it was the Tahmine who spoke first. "Compatri to the High King, we have been told that your Liege has given asylum to the Forbidden Child. Is it true that you know this child?"

Danon flicked a glance at the smug Tahmond. "Who is on trial here?" he asked.

"It isn't a trial," Rani said.

"Trial or test, call it what you will. What is it that you are trying to learn? I'm not even sure who you are accusing, Khedran or the child he has taken in. I might remind you of the teachings of your own goddess, Tahmine. Liethe's love and forgiveness are the altar of her honor. Would Khedran be so tried if he had slain an innocent child of ten years?"

There was a murmur from the soldiers in attendance. The Tahmond stepped forward in anger. "He uses Chaine words, twisting what is sacred. He desecrates the honor of Liethe. We speak of the Forbidden Child, an abomination!"

"A child. A boy who had nothing to do with his origin, who did not even know of it until the King came to claim him."

"A child grows to be a man," the Tahmond retorted. "Phaelon's prophecy of war cannot be denied."

"It is your own fanatic belief that creates a Forbidden Child. You are bringing Azlatan to civil war when now is the time we most need unity. The Outsiders are at our borders!"

"What is it you say?" Randmar spoke for the first time. Silence descended as he leaned forward, staring. "What is it you say?" he repeated.

"The Outsiders, Sire." Danon stood tall. "I've seen them myself. It's why I was sent to you. They have been infiltrating, but now they come openly. The High King is preparing for an invasion. He needs Ordhold. He needs your men, your horses, your valiant fighting spirit. While the Tahmond prattles of a child, Azlatan is at war!"

Randmar stood. Danon saw hope in the erect carriage, the return of vitality.

The Tahmond saw it too. "Chaine blaspheme on the sacred prophecies!"

"The Chaine is a friend of Azlatan," Danon retorted. "Haven't she and her people proved it, with the horses brought to Ordhold, with her own service to the High King? And for this — for this she lies underground, in some foul dungeon beneath this very castle!"

He felt Jon's grasp upon him, fought it off, but a heavy blow landed on his ear. He went to his knees, felt his arms being held behind him even as he fought to stay conscious.

Jon spoke to his father. "Even if what he says is true, it is Ordhold's borders we must protect, not Khedran's."

Randmar stared down at his son as though he'd never seen him before. Danon saw Rani move close to his side. "And what of The Chaine?" Randmar asked. "Is what he says true?"

"Yes," Jon admitted. "Yes! For Ordhold. Father, the Compatri still hasn't been tested. He gives you words, not proof. The Tahmond warned us that the coming of the Chaine has opened the way for the goddess Chaos."

"That makes no sense. And you did this without consulting me." Randmar was weaving strangely.

"You were ill, father."

Randmar finally allowed Rani to help him sit. "This isn't right. I do not like any of it."

Danon's hope faded with Randmar's flagging strength. He struggled, was surprised to feel his arms released. The Tahmond was there before he could regain his feet, demanding.

"Test him! Let the goddess decide who tells the truth! He knows this boy, by his own admission. Test him! The Light of Liethe will tell us if he has been near the Forbidden Child!"

Rani leaned over Randmar, her concern apparent. But at Jon's imperious gesture, she left his side and came forward.

She lifted the silver bowl from the tripod and held it out to Danon like a gift, lifting the lid. He saw the opalescent Light of Liethe brimming within. "Touch it," Rani said.

He lifted his hand and trailed his fingers through the familiar Light.

To his horror he saw the bloody path his hand left behind. He snatched his hand away, but the white Light had turned to red, and that glowing crimson spilled over the edge and onto the floor, running swiftly.

There were screams of terror.

He had one last glimpse of Rani before they took him. Her veil had fallen back, and as she stared at the scarlet pool in the bowl she still held, tears slid down her cheeks.

Behind her, Randmar had slumped in death to the foot of his throne.

Jon was King. Ordhold was lost.

Trussed hand and foot in a kneeling position, Danon was carried like so much meat to the lower warrens, the bitter taste of failure in his mouth. So much for Chaine planning and courage, he thought. But he didn't make a sound as he was hurled through the open dungeon door, landing hard on strawed stone. The door was slammed shut and his captors were gone, to return to the confusion in the castle above.

He lay there a moment, his nose pressed to cold stone and his knees beneath him, and felt depressed. There was movement to the side, and he rolled his eyes in that direction. His watery vision revealed a familiar leather boot, worked in a filigree of gold design, inches from his face.

"Oh no," he muttered.

The boot lifted to his shoulder, braced there, and shoved. He rocked onto his back, which placed his bound hands under his tailbone and his knees in the air. The position was no less uncomfortable – or dignified – than kneeling on his nose had been.

The Chaine surveyed him critically. She appeared unmarked by her imprisonment, other than the straw caught in her shaggy mane of sunset gold. The small room was well lit by the single wall-cresset; he could see flashes of the gold filigree in the soft leather she wore.

"What are you doing here?" There was a note of laughter in her voice. Knowing her, he wasn't surprised.

"I've come to rescue you," he snarled. She always draws out the worst in me, he thought. "Have hope, fair maid, for I have arrived."

She grinned in appreciation, stepping back as though for a better view. "You look very dashing. But how do you get on your horse?"

"Enough," he groaned. "Can you loosen these ropes?"

She knelt and rolled him onto his side, working the ropes from his numbing hands. "How did you ever let yourself get into this mess?" she asked as she freed him. "I had hoped you had learned something in all the time I spent with you."

"I don't see you leaping free on the mountain-tops. For that matter, I didn't see you overpowering my captors when they opened the door wide enough to let an army through. I think your reputation is much exaggerated."

"You weren't supposed to notice that. Try moving your fingers and toes. Your hands are purple."

He groaned at the fiery tingle of returning circulation, sitting up while she coiled the rope with a thoughtful expression. "What's going on up there?" she asked.

"I think Randmar is dead." Then, because it hurt: "Shandiin, I don't understand. They've turned against the High King and won't listen to reason."

She didn't look up from the rope, but frowned. "Magic and denial often win over reason."

"Don't tell me you believe this Tahmond."

"I only made a statement of fact. Tell me what happened."

He got up, walking around the cell gingerly to restore the feeling to his legs. As he walked, he tried to explain all that had happened since he had seen her last, even as Khedran had ordered him to do. She stopped him only once, when he told her of the dead Chaine that Marre had avenged.

"Jhinn is dead?" she questioned sadly, and Danon paused, sorry. But she waved him to go on and he knew she listened.

His tale slowed as he struggled to explain what had happened in Ordhold, among men he had called friends. When he came to the most puzzling part of all, the bloody light that had followed his fingers, he was sitting as she was, cross-legged in the straw. Their knees almost touched. He didn't realize his shoulders were forward, his head down as though in shame. He didn't see her sad regard, studying his bent head, and the look was gone when he looked up at last. He met only that level grey gaze that told him nothing at all.

"Could it be?" he asked her, and there was real pain in the question. "Could Jael really be what they say? He's a strange child, Shandiin, but he's still just a boy. I can't bring myself to believe there is evil in him. Or in his mother, despite everything. She was like a second mother to me."

"I can only tell you that they may be half right. No, Danon—no more questioning. Not here. I know you are torn. There will be far more pain, I'm afraid, before it's done. But I can't say any more here, where the walls may hide listeners."

Danon slumped. "I can't even warn Khedran about what's happened." He stopped suddenly, remembering. "He said you were bringing a treasure..."

She gave him a warning glance and he subsided, frustrated.

After a pause she asked, "Is Khedran all right?"

"I have no idea. How can anyone tell, with him? But he seemed very worried about you."

She looked away. "Are the Chaine I assigned guarding his door?"

"Yes, even when he threatens to kick them down the tower stairs. He really hates having them there. I'm not sure why he allows it."

"Because he promised me he would. You know how Allasar died."

There was a quick dancing flicker, and the wall-torch guttered out.

"Wonderful," Danon muttered in the darkness.

"Scared?"

"Quit baiting me. I'm not in the mood for it."

"Well, you might as well get some sleep. They've always brought a new torch with what breakfast they decide to deliver. There are two of us; perhaps we can overcome them."

"Sure," he said bitterly.

"Don't be so hopeless. This prison is not our destiny."

"Great. Another prophet. You aren't old enough...oh, wait. You are, you just hold your age well."

"Go to sleep, Danon. I'll wake you if anyone comes."

He lay down in the straw, knowing she would refuse to talk any longer by the tone of her voice. He was sure he wouldn't sleep, but he was wrong.

His eyes flew open at her touch, how much later he didn't know. He remained still because the pressure of her hand was a warning, then rose slowly to a sitting position as her hand fell away. She sat with her back against the wall, her face striped by moonlight that seemed to come through the dungeon bars.

Except it couldn't be moonlight. Not down here.

It took him a moment to recognize the special quality of that Light.

It gave Shandiin a pearly haloed quality as it came nearer. "Your Tahmine friend?" Shandiin wondered.

Danon didn't answer, but he didn't think it was Rani. The white Light washed through the bars, around the hinged door. They both rose as the door swung silently inward, and the Light began to retreat again.

"You go first." Shandiin gave him a nudge. "The Chaine don't deal in magic."

"Coward." But his own neck-hair was on end as he stalked stiffly through the open door. There he halted, Shandiin on his heels.

The Light had returned to its source, and the goddess Liethe stood waiting for them in the passage.

The Light was her veil and her gown, chasing itself through the pleats. Her eyes were hidden, blindfolded. In her arms was a small white cat.

She turned, gliding away down the hall.

Shandiin pushed him to follow. He did, quickening his step as he realized their guide was growing smaller ahead of them. Soon they were both running, their boots strangely silent on the stone floor. It was like a dream, but he knew he was awake.

This prison wasn't our destiny, he thought. She was right.

The vision vanished at the last turn in the passage. Sound returned with it, and the cold outside air.

Harshly whispered: "Danon!"

He turned to Shandiin, but she shook her head, the moonlit fire of her hair swinging around her shoulders.

"Danon!" Louder this time. Danon whirled at the added jingle of a horse's bridle. "It's me. Brend."

He came out of the shadows, then, leading three horses. Danon recognized Chandar with relief, and the paint horse who towered over even Chandar, ears flattened and eyes wild.

"Brend! How did you–"

"The Tahmine. Rani said you would be waiting at Randmar's escape route from the castle, and that I should bring the horses."

Danon swallowed. "Did you see anyone come out before us?"

"Only you two, running like Daimaine was on your heels."

Chandar squealed suddenly and struck back at the vicious stallion by his side. Shandiin swore and went to her horse's head, taking the reins from Brend. Her huge black and white paint tried to reach around her, ivory teeth open for Chandar's neck.

"Stop it!" she ordered, slapping him in the nose. Danon glimpsed the horse's other side as he backed away angrily, the white half of his face with the glass-blue eye. Shandiin grinned at them through bared teeth. "Isn't he just precious?"

Brend shook his head in wonder. "Jon will be glad to see that horse gone. We'd better mount up. We have only a little time before dawn. They'll know you're missing, and they'll be hunting for us."

"You're going, Brend?" Danon asked.

"With Jon as King of Ordhold? Yes." There was a momentary break in his voice, and Danon remembered Brend's father had died that night. But the young man stood strong. "Even the Tahmine sees strangeness in all this," he continued, "or she wouldn't have sent me. I ride with her now to the High King if no one else in Ordhold does. And Jon will know by my absence that my allegiance never changed."

Shandiin had subdued her mount and stood apart from them, watching in silence. Danon threw her a glance, and grasped Brend's gloved hand in his own. "Khedran will need every man. I think he will want to hear, too, that Randmar rallied at the last. I believe he would have answered Khedran's call."

A small silence fell, as though the Dominion King's spirit had touched them in passing. The moon had risen over the canyon, the silver sickle that was the Deathqueen's.

Brend saw it too. "The goddess Daimaine still honors the High King of Azlatan. There is hope."

Shandiin spoke at last. "There's another message for Khedran. From me."

"Aren't you returning to Cabre?"

"Not yet. There's the small matter of a treasure I had promised him. Tell him it comes by ship, and should arrive with the next full moon." She glanced at Danon. "The Compatri will be with me," she added.

Brend nodded thoughtfully, though he looked puzzled. "He will get your message, even if I have to ride my Liath to her knees." He patted his chestnut mare and handed Chandar's reins to Danon. The three mounted, Shandiin keeping her harlequin mount clear of Chandar's heels. Brend looked down at the baleful blue eye of The Chaine's steed. "What do you call him?" he asked curiously.

"Bastard, mostly. But his name is Windmaker, and yes, it's what you think."

Brend grinned and offered a salute to them both before turning his mount into the shadows.

Danon glared at Shandiin. "The Compatri will be with me," he mimicked in singsong. "What if I preferred to ride with Brend?"

"Then you'd have said so. Khedran will get the bad news better from Brend, and he'll know you and I are together." She grinned. "And you will have an adventure." She turned her mount, and he, muttering, sent Chandar alongside. Shandiin slapped her biting horse again.

They rode stirrup to stirrup at an easy walk, for they were at the far north end of the canyon and climbing. Danon guessed they would not have to worry about pursuit. The road south, which Brend took, would have been the logical route for them too. The ridge they climbed was rock; they would leave no trail.

"What treasure?" he demanded. She just smiled.

He sighed. "Where are we going, then?"

"North. The Everwinter Pass."

"I hope Brend put some warm underclothes on this horse."

"That horse would look funny in warm underclothes."

"Shandiin," he said, "you are rude, obnoxious—"

She grinned again. "I know. But you cheat at cards. Khedran taught you."

CHAPTER 9

There was no pursuit. They rode through the remainder of the night and most of the next day, climbing constantly into the range called Everwinter. As they rode, Danon told Shandiin more about the death of an "Outsider" at the heel of the High King's betrothed, and her subsequent attempt to break troth. He was still angry over Marre's disrespect, as he saw it, and felt sure the arranged marriage would go forward anyway.

Shandiin fell strangely silent for a time, and Danon gave up asking her questions after a few of her slow smiles.

The first patches of snow were on the ground when they stopped at last. The horses were tended first and tethered apart from each other. They built no fire, still being within reach of Jon's patrols, but took turns in their blankets beneath an overhang of rock.

They were riding again before the next dawn, still traveling on a path she seemed to know well. They were entering snow country. Shandiin's mood brightened with the sun rising in a crystal sky, but Danon refused to answer her easy banter. He was sulky, remembering too many events gone wrong, and angry that she would still not explain the purpose of this cold journey.

For it was cold. At this height, the snow never melted. Once she fell behind, and he rode a long time alone, Chandar following a trail as though he, too, had been here before. He was beginning to feel the loneliness of it when he heard the twang of Shandiin's bow, and the arrow singing overhead. A large bundle of feathers splattered the snow ahead him and she rode past his startled mount, dismounting to pick up the bird she had killed.

"Dinner!" she announced. "We'll have a fire this night, to cook." He had to smile at this, for the chill was settling into his bones. He was from the warm south, and cold had never agreed with him. She seemed to thrive on it.

Later he looked back to where she rode in her great cloak of white fur. She had given him her leather tunic, which was lined with wool, and he had found his heavy cloak in his pack. But he was still cold.

Her giant mount plodded behind Chandar with an expression of disgust. Feathers drifted about his neck as his rider plucked busily. Danon was surprised to hear his own laughter, and she looked up with an answering grin. "Dinner," she repeated. "Have you noticed our companion, Danon?"

His gaze followed her pointing arm to see the great white cat trotting easily in a ravine below their path, big paws like snowshoes on the white surface.

He felt comforted, as if it were a soldier of Ordhold not lost to his liege.

The path grew steeper, and Shandiin rode past him to take the lead again. He saw then that the clouds had returned and looked filled with snow. The day darkened until sunset wasn't even noticeable. He expected her to stop, but she didn't, and when she turned back in the saddle to study him in the deepening gloom, he set his jaw, refusing to show weakness.

"We're almost on the Pass," she called to him. "We don't dare get caught in the open with a storm coming."

He nodded his understanding as the first large snowflakes drifted to melt on Chandar's black mane. The snow soon began falling in earnest, and he sank deeper into his hooded cloak. The Chaine was no longer visible ahead of him, but his mount followed her by scent or sense, and Danon trusted him. Frequently the great white cat appeared at his stirrup as though verifying he was there.

Shortly the world was so dark he couldn't even see the lighter blur of his wool-gloved hands. The only sound was the muffled thud of hooves and the creak of cold leather, and the occasional rumble from his own stomach. Weariness settled over him like a living weight and he half-slept as he rode.

He was thus unaware when he rode out of the storm, and moon and stars glittered through the high clouds. The world was still, the air clear as ice. The world froze.

The cat woke him, unsheathing his claws because he did not wake at a gentler nudge. Danon blinked in surprise, seeing the cat vanish uphill. Looking back, it seemed he had come to the top of the world; the nearer mountain peaks were lower than his vantage. Starlight burst back at him from iced branches. Danon felt dizzy with the vast beauty below and above, where the constellation named The Bridle swung in cold glory.

He knew guilt as the horse trembled beneath him, breathing loudly from the labor of his uphill climb. He dismounted stiffly and almost fell, both legs numb with cold. Sweat was already crusting to ice on Chandar's coat. Danon gathered the reins feebly, knowing he could not let the horse stand so, and looked in vain for the vanished cat. The Chaine was only a dim memory at this moment.

Then he saw the square of light above. It seemed at first unreal, like a piece of sun-magic on this cold night. It took a moment to recognize it as a window with a light within. The window belonged to a structure built against the dark bulk of a great protecting cliff.

A door opened by the window, spilling golden light onto the snow. A shadow came out, and he realized it was her at last. He tried to lead Chandar, but she reached him quickly and took the reins, apparently in concern for the horse.

"We were lucky the storm broke, but he's almost done. It's only a little farther though, Danon. I got the fire lit for us. I'm glad of that cat! I saw him leading Chandar, and it gave me the chance to go ahead. I knew you'd need the fire."

She continued to chat, keeping him groggily aware as he staggered uphill, Chandar's hot breath on his neck. He didn't see her concerned gaze follow him as the door opened on glorious warmth. He stumbled in with Shandiin leading Chandar inside behind him.

The first thing he noticed in the strange round room was the great white cat, curled up on a giant hearth like a common tabby. Shandiin gave him a push toward the blazing fireplace. "Go, join Majia." He obeyed, almost falling into the pile of furs next to the cat.

He dimly saw Shandiin leading Chandar, whose coat steamed as ice melted in the sudden warmth, to a makeshift stall next to where her mount was already standing. That horse's divided face peered at him over the rough planking, reminding him of something. Black and white, he thought. Tahmond horse. He laughed, feeling oddly detached.

Danon vaguely heard the cat's complaint as Shandiin pulled a fur from beneath it to throw over him. The cat followed, purring loudly as it settled against his back. A new warmth settled over him, soft as dreams.

He slept.

He woke with the first edge of exhaustion gone. The fire's blaze had settled, darkening the room. He turned his head to find Shandiin nearby, cross-legged before the hearth. She had removed her white fur, but her hair cloaked her shoulders. Her face was in shadow, all save a wedge of light across her lips and the firm sculpture of her chin.

Who was she, this never-aging mortal? Caught in the familiarity of working (and fighting) with her, that question had been buried. But it had never been answered.

She leaned forward, her shaggy hair spilling over her shoulders, and added more wood to the fire. He saw in the new light that she had turned to watch him, and the old mockery had returned to her eyes. "You sleep like a child," she told him.

"That's because I'm just an innocent boy," he responded in kind, and sat up, pushing his dark hair from his eyes. His teeth felt furry and his beard was past the age of stubble, soft and itchy under his fingers. He noticed the cat crouched near Shandiin cracking a bone held between its paws. His own stomach growled.

She laughed, hearing it. "Dinner almost became breakfast. But it's still a few hours until dawn." He watched her rise easily to drag a pot from the fire, and ladle stew into a bowl that she handed to him. She remained sitting on her heels while he ate, propping chin on fists as was her habit. Even preoccupied with the very good stew, he thought she must have muscles of rubber.

"It seems you know Mia well," she said, apparently from nowhere.

Danon nodded, swallowed, looking up thoughtfully. "You must have known her once. She served in Penumbra when you knew King Allasar."

She looked away. "More stew?"

"I'll throw up if I eat more. Did you know her?" He wanted answers. Here, surely, there could be no hidden listeners.

She took the bowl from him, set it aside. Relaxing onto the floor, she crossed booted ankles and leaned back against the big cat. "Not very well. But I knew that she and Allasar were lovers."

He felt real shock, and must have shown it, for she laughed. "Don't tell me you believed it was rape. Oh, never mind. I'm sure you did, being you. I'll bet Mia didn't appreciate it if you told her that opinion, either. She never struck me as the type to want pity. Especially for something she felt no shame about. You seem to consider her like a mother, and children can rarely see their parents as human. Still, didn't it ever occur to you that she loved him?"

He remembered Mia's anger, which he had not understood. "No," he admitted. It was a long moment before he could lift his eyes to hers. She was watching him closely.

"Feeling betrayed, are you?" she asked softly. "Perhaps you preferred your assumption of violence, even though it made High King Allasar the villain of that worn-out scandal. Perhaps it never occurred to you...or anyone else, for that matter...that there was no villain involved."

He couldn't reply for a long time. She often forced him to battle his assumptions. The last time, it had been about his Bond with Varady. The pain of that loss remained.

He looked away while he gathered courage. "Do the Chaine ever love?" he asked her finally, flatly.

There was a personal need behind his question that he didn't want her to see. But he sensed her surprise, was aware when she sat up, hugging her knees to her chest. "I'm not sure I understand your question." Her voice was even. He wished that it had held some small hurt or insult, and for that reason plunged on relentlessly.

"You laugh. It's a weapon you use, I think. Even your anger is used carefully, to accomplish a purpose. You show little emotion otherwise. The Chaine are thought of as inhuman by a lot of people, and I believe that's why, more than any mystery surrounding your purpose in Azlatan."

"I see." Her voice remained level, waiting.

"I've never even heard you speak of Khedran with affection. Even though you have been his Defender since he was born. So, I don't see how you can sit there and pass judgment on whether Mia was a victim or a villain."

"I never claimed she was either one. I merely wondered if it had occurred to you that there may not have been any villain involved."

"You imply they may have loved each other," he retorted, "even though forbidden by Law and decency."

"Do you think they are both villains? Because they may have loved each other?"

"They had no right."

"Perhaps not."

He lifted his chin, glared. "Now you're just being Chainish. You're trying to lead me into a trap with words."

She tilted her head. "Who's trying to trap who, Danon?"

The question checked him sharply. He realized he was sweating, and his hands were clenched into fists. He looked at her now, locked eyes with her, and hers were brilliant silver in the firelight.

"I just wonder how you can know that Allasar and Mia loved each other–right or wrong–when you know nothing about what love is?"

There was a silent moment before she spoke. "Perhaps I don't."

"Then I am right, and you have never loved. Love is something beautiful, something...greater than the person who feels it. It is pure, incapable of dishonor. Can you agree with that?"

"No."

She met his eyes steadily. Danon felt like he'd been struck.

She sighed. "Danon, we can sit here and debate the meaning of love and life all night. In the end it will solve nothing. But I want you to listen to yourself and explain to me how it can be both ways. If love is beautiful, and greater than those who feel it –then how can it be that Allasar and Mia are evil for having loved? Perhaps, to make it simpler, you can simply attribute it to destiny. Perhaps the Forbidden Child is a prophecy that had to be fulfilled, and therefore both were mere puppets necessary to fulfill that prophecy. Does that make them evil?"

He saw the relentless logic in that. "Then Jael is the Forbidden Child? The Tahmond is right?"

"Maybe half right."

He looked up from miserable contemplation of his hands, wondering why he'd pushed so hard. Knowing why, refusing to admit it. He tried to focus on her words. "You said that once before. What do you mean?"

"Danon, I'm not sure if I should try to explain. And I'm very sorry if you think me completely uncaring. Especially as it relates to your High King."

"So you do care?"

"Maybe not in the way you mean. I...find him an ideal. He is
more than anyone I've ever known, and that's saying a lot. But
then, I understand him better than his people do. You may never
have seen him for himself; he rarely allows it. He has a depth of
understanding about people. It's...wisdom, quite frankly."

She shook her head, looked away. "It makes him sad, though
he'd never show it. He sees need in every person and understands
it's beyond anyone's ability to mend the dissonance in the human
spirit. It's in his nature to see it, to know he is different...not
completely human. He simply can't share the moral flaws the rest
of us have. It's not his choice. It's his nature."

She looked back, met Danon's eyes. "Like the other gifts of the
High Kings, it sets him apart from everyone, more curse than gift.
All of that makes him too different, Danon. He is always alone,
even in a crowd. Maybe more so."

He was stunned. "I never guessed any of that. But...you look up
to him, don't you? Just as I do."

He saw amusement return to her eyes. "Not the same, no. I am
an anarchist. I have never been and will never be the subject of a
King...and I have known more than one. No, don't ask about that;
I won't tell you." She turned to her pack, shoving the protesting cat
aside, and triumphantly produced a flask and two small cups. She
poured for them both, resettled in front of him with legs crossed.
"Let's talk about Mia and Allasar." She lifted her cup to her lips.

He followed suit, and the liquor warmed a path that needed it.

"Yuck," she said.

"It's not that bad. No more stalling, Shandiin. People think Jael
is the Forbidden Child. Tell me what you meant when you said
they are half right."

She took a deep breath. "Khedran doesn't know what I'm going
to tell you, Danon; I never had a way to tell him that wouldn't
tear him apart. The way of his bloodline...that lack of moral flaws,
that incorruptibility...I don't know if Khedran could accept the
truth about Allasar and Mia. His father loved both Rhiathe and
Mia completely. For years. Please don't ask again how I knew; it

doesn't matter. I found out when Mia became pregnant–the first time."

He stared. "What?"

"Mia and Queen Rhiathe were pregnant at the same time."

He stared harder. "And you're sure the child was Allasar's? That long ago?"

"Oh, yes. I'm quite sure, as he told me so."

It took him a moment to comprehend. "Rhiathe didn't suspect Allasar was the father?"

"She knew. In fact, she purposely put them together, knowing they were already in love and in misery, denying themselves. Hers was true love, because it was not selfish. She wanted the happiness of those she cared for...and she had the gift of foresight. She knew she would die in childbirth, leaving them both alone, so she put them together. She was an amazing woman, Rhiathe. One of the few friends I have ever held close."

He waited a long moment while she poked at the fire, showing no sign of continuing.

"Shandiin," he said warningly.

She looked at him almost hopelessly. He wanted in that moment to reach out and touch her face. *It isn't that she doesn't know sorrow,* he thought. *It's just that she refuses it. Just as she would refuse my touch, if I offered.* He did not offer.

She settled again, as though resigned, hugging her knees tightly to her chest.

"The night Khedran was born I saw the constellation called The Bridle turn red as blood. I knew then that the Forbidden Child had been born. You see, Mia had supposedly lost her child...her first child...in a fall down the tower stairs. The High Tahmine took care of her, and told us she had miscarried, but I realized that night it wasn't true. The red that you described, that you saw in Liethe's Altar Bowl when you were tested? It is the sign of the Forbidden Child."

She sighed. "It's not Jael. There is another brother, one born the same night as Khedran. I have no idea where that brother could be, but I know he poses mortal danger to your High King, and all of your people called Rioch. Phaelon's Prophecy is clear: 'If the Forbidden Child is allowed to live, Duine will rise up to kill all Rioch. No magic can save them.'"

She fell strangely silent, then, and would answer no more questions, finally snapping at him to give her some time before she said more. Danon could almost see her thinking, and awoke several times in the night to see her still awake, staring into the fire.

The next morning, she awakened him from spotty slumber, summoning him silently past the horses to the outside. The snow-cat had long since vanished on his own business.

Danon had thought their strange dwelling was high enough, on this Everwinter Pass they had found in a vanished snowstorm. Now she led him up the crowning peak where no horse could go. The sky was flushed with golden dawn, the earth still shadowed blue.

He saw her attain the summit, sunlight firing the floating strands of her unbound hair and the white fur cloak that she wore. She turned back to offer him a helping hand. The sun's face was too brilliant to bear, so he looked down at the wind-scoured rock as he drew beside her. He closed his eyes against the light and relished the clean smell that was the snow itself.

"Look," she demanded, and he opened his eyes.

They stood in a blue cathedral of sky. In the distance white peaks sparkled. Shandiin's pointing arm moved east, and he followed its line to what seemed to be a sea beyond a break in that distant mountain chain.

Then he recognized that the green-silver glimmer was a plain, the sea of grass far beyond the borders of the plateau that was Azlatan. He was gripped with wonder. The distant plain seemed to move on the tides of his straining vision.

"You are standing on the edge of the world you've always known," Shandiin told him. "I have been beyond. There is beauty there, Danon. Hope, and life. A whole world you never guessed existed. But a storm is gathering there, a storm building since the night The Bridle turned to blood. It is like the storm that builds even now, over Azlatan. I fear that the storms may meet. It's a strange world you live in, Danon."

He looked at her then, and saw the far distance reflected in her silver eyes.

"That I live in?" he repeated. "Who are you, Shandiin? What world do you Chaine come from, that you can travel between, and call us all strange? Why are you here?"

Her eyes stayed distant. "You ask questions when the answers are not important to the moment. We Chaine come from neither Azlatan, nor from those people you call the Outsiders. We gave an oath of alliance to the High Kings of Azlatan. Let that be all for now, Danon. We are the Chaine."

"You are different from your own people."

"So are you." She turned to look into his eyes. "You don't see your own true heart. But Khedran did, the day you met him. One of his gifts is empathy, the ability to know a person's spirit. It's why you are now Compatri."

She turned away again, lifting her arm to the west for him to follow. He blinked to see that beyond the Pass, which fell sharply to a broken jumble of hills and valleys cloaked in green, the sky was divided by a deeper blue that was the true sea. Faint broken silver was the sun on the waves, and a tiny fleck upon the horizon was a golden ship riding.

"You can't see our harbor from here," she told him. "We're still a short journey from the Chaine's northern hold. It's our only home now. We Chaine have journeyed outside of Azlatan for many of your generations, but Phaelon's Prophecy War has sent it's call even to us. The Chaine are coming home." Her arm fell at her side, and Danon knew she remembered one of her people would not be among those coming home.

She continued after a thoughtful silence. "We are gathering this last time, to fulfill an oath given to a High King long before your birth. We ride in defense of Azlatan." She sighed. "Too few of us to make the difference, I'm afraid. Even Khedran can't guess how great this storm will be."

"I don't understand," Danon complained. "The Forbidden is supposed to foreshadow the destruction of the Rioch of Azlatan. Why did your people promise to fight a war that isn't yours?"

She frowned at him. "This war, Danon, will impact your entire world. That's what I am trying to tell you. It's bigger than Rioch and Duine. You have lived your life thinking Azlatan is the whole world, but it is not."

She shook her head then. "I've already told you too much. We should just go, Danon. We have a journey ahead still." She turned to leave, but he stood and watched her start down the steep path, his mind ticking.

"Why did you bring me along?" he called to her retreating back. "Why did you tell me what even my King doesn't know? I think I've figured out everything but that."

She halted below him, looking up. The wind made a bright flag of her hair as she gazed back. Her silver eyes were deeply troubled, something he had never seen in her before.

He stepped down to join her, to gaze into those troubled eyes. "I think I understand now what you've been up to all these years. The crazy part is I didn't even know I believed in that Prophecy. Maybe that's everyone's problem in Azlatan. It's hard to believe you could be living in the days foretold so long ago. It's even hard to believe in the gods, unless you've been in the Temple, or..." he remembered a vision that had led them from a dungeon and shook his head. "There's magic all around us, but it has so little to do with just living. As soon as you're away from it, it seems like a dream. Or a nightmare. Except to the Chaine, maybe. Because you don't have magic. You don't even deal in emotions. You just see what must be done...and you do it."

He dropped his glance for a moment to her lips, set so firmly together. "You are more than an ally to Khedran. You were there even before his father's death. After that, you were the only person he could look up to. You taught him to operate on cold reason, not feelings. You tell me he is caring, but he rarely shows compassion, and never gives mercy to evil. But with all of that, his moral code...and yes, I know that part's inherent to his blood-line...controls him. That's evidenced by his refusal to sacrifice his little brother though it threatens his rule. So I understand why you have kept this secret. He will destroy the Forbidden Child to save his people... if he doesn't know the Forbidden Child is his brother."

She studied him, shook her head. "You don't think he would destroy the Forbidden Child if he knew he was his brother? He will always do what is necessary for his people, Danon. It's his only purpose." She looked away. "But it would tear him apart. That's why I have never told him. You have no idea what the Black Wolf keeps buried inside his own heart. At this point I'm not sure I do either."

"Buried? Are you telling me the Black Wolf is something he uses to suppress what he really feels?" When her lips tightened, he scowled. "I know what you said about him caring. But a lot of people think he doesn't have a heart."

She sighed. "Oh, Danon. He has a heart. I told you he has the gift of empathy, but it's a curse more often than gift. He has to have that wall of defense they call the Black Wolf. Without it he would feel every horror life gives to his people...the pain, the anger, the sorrow, any of the things that scorch the human soul. He has to call the Wolf, to keep his mind his own."

She stopped herself, looking down. After a moment she went on. "You asked me why I brought you on this journey. I will tell you now, although I have hesitated to give you destiny's unfair and terrible burden. I brought you to tell you about this secret, this thing only I knew, that I have kept hidden from Khedran. Because I won't be here when this Prophecy comes to its crisis. I can't be here for him. I can't tell you why. I have too many secrets I can't explain, Danon, but I'm sharing this part with you because I need your help. I can't be here when he will need most a friend who understands him...as I now know you do. He will need you, because the Black Wolf is bound to fail him at last, and it is my greatest hope that you will be able to help him when it does."

She lifted her head. "Remember that, when the time comes. Remember he is more than your King. He is also a man with a bright spirit that this Prophecy War may well destroy even if it's won. He will need the strength of a friend, and you are his chosen Compatri. I know you love him more than your own self, and I believe destiny's web has given you a far greater mission than you realize."

Her eyes held his, and he saw in hers what could only be grief. "Danon...Khedran's only purpose is to save everyone else. You may be the one who can save him."

She looked away then, into that vast distance, and he saw her swallow. "Now...we have a long trip ahead of us, and I will not talk about this again. I ask that all of this remain between us, because you are my friend, too, and I trust you to do what I can't."

He was stunned to see tears escape her eyes as she turned to walk away, and in that moment wished he had only ever known her coldness and her laughter after all.

CHAPTER 10

Wind had scoured the heights, but snow was still a heavy mantle on the lower ramparts of the Pass. The horses waded through chest-high drifts. For once even Shandiin's mount was too involved with the work to misbehave.

Danon looked back once to see their night's shelter in daylight for the first time. From this distance he could see it had once been the corner tower of an ancient fortress. What he had thought a cliff was a wall higher than ten men; there was a weathered suggestion of crenelations at the top. There was only rubble where there had once been other towers to guard this northern pass into Azlatan.

Their frozen world was silent. He felt the long passing of ages in this place, built by men so long ago it was no longer a memory.

"It was called Khaibara." Shandiin spoke from beside him. "It was named after the mountains that your people left behind on their exodus to Azlatan a thousand years ago."

"That exodus is a myth, isn't it? Like the one about a living world Prophecy's Daughter talks to? But this...this fortification is real. Why haven't I heard of it? Such a place must have been the pride of Azlatan before it fell. And how did it fall? Does Khedran know about it?"

"Khedran knows. I brought him here a long time ago, to show him what was lost to Azlatan and his bloodline. Khaibara was built in the beginning of time in this land, not by magic, but by the hands of men. The few stories remaining say that the second High King himself designed it and directed its building.

"In that beginning, Danon, men hadn't forgotten that there is a world beyond your borders. Even the Tahmond, who harbor old stories others ignore, have grown forgetful. But your ancestors knew better than to trust to magic alone. The enemies of Azlatan may wield magic, too, and if the strength of the Tahmonds and Tahmine should fail against it, then only the brave hearts of lesser mortals will stand between Azlatan and its enemies."

"Then Khaibara was built against what is coming now. How did it fall, Shandiin, before its time had come?"

"Just that. Time, Danon, can level mountains. Khedran spent many long hours here, pondering the changes wrought by time. If the great walls of Khaibara could crumble under time's slow power, what of the hearts and minds of mortals? Mortals could have kept these walls standing, Danon, even as mortals built them. But time and peace are the enemies of strength."

Danon looked back at the ancient fortress one last time, blinked, and turned away from the sad remnant of greatness.

The drop from the Everwinter Pass was sudden, and the horses spent much of it snow-sliding on their haunches. Danon and Shandiin frequently dismounted to help them down steeper passages, some filled with drifts from the previous night's storm. The sky held clear, and as the sun rode higher in its great vault Danon's eyes became mere slits in his cold-reddened face.

He halted finally, listening to Chandar breathe like a bellows in the unearthly silence. The great stallion stood in snow to his chest and could go no further.

Danon peered about, realizing he was lost in so much bright light, sky and snow no longer separated. If Shandiin were near, he could not see her. He was going snow-blind.

"Shandiin?" he couldn't call loudly. She had warned him of avalanches from the overladen Pass. There was no answer in the white silence.

Chandar snorted, trying to back up in his trough of snow. Danon stopped him, worried for Khedran's beloved horse. He heard a low growl behind him, stiffened before realizing it was the snowcat. "Majia!" he exclaimed in glad surprise as it glided by. "I thought you'd gone back."

"It is unusual," came Shandiin's answering drawl. "First time I've seen one of them leave Ordhold. Danon, why are you trying to quarter into a drift instead of around it? Chandar's stuck!"

"Where are you?" Danon turned toward her voice, blinking at nothing.

"Uh-oh. Can't you see?"

"No," he admitted.

"Here. Let me help you down, and put this scarf over your eyes before it gets worse."

He slipped from the saddle, and was surprised when she seemed to lift him free of the snow that trapped Chandar; he was confused enough not to question what should have been impossible. Then he groped for the scarf she offered. Her hand closed over his wrist. "It is bad. Hold on while I do it for you."

Relieving darkness, soft warmth over his cheeks and ears. He felt her nearness, as she tied the fabric securely. "Sorry," he muttered, ashamed of being weak in front of her.

"You are a bother, aren't you? Getting in trouble, asking questions. I'll bet you were a real plague to your father. Curious, rebellious creature."

He had to smile even in his predicament, remembering many scoldings and his yearning for freedom from his father's narrow world. "How did you guess that?"

"Easy," her voice was offhand, but he felt her brush his hair back from his forehead.

She moved away and he heard Chandar's snort and her responding croon. "Snow's fallen in behind him," she told Danon.

"I'll have to dig him out enough to turn around. He'll hurt himself trying to back up."

"He's all right, isn't he?"

"Sure. Just too smart to fight this trap you got him into. Dumb horse would follow you anywhere."

"He's not dumb."

"Nope. Just loyal. You've stolen the affection of the King's horse, Danon. C'mon, cat...help me dig!"

The sounds following ended with Chandar's final desperate plunge from his snowy trap, and his triumphant neigh answered nearby from Shandiin's painted horse. Shandiin laughed at this. "I do believe old Windmaker got lonesome all by himself. All right, Danon, we can go on now. You just missed the turning, and it gets easier farther down. We can all take a rest. We will be out of the snow by nightfall."

She took his arm and the reins of both horses and led them through the snow. "Is Majia still here?" he asked.

"Yep."

"You said they never leave Ordhold."

"Cats generally go where they please."

"Kind of like the Chaine." Danon grinned under his blindfold, realizing the snow was less deep on the path she guided him to. "But I was wondering about the Ordhold part. We've left Ordhold?"

"Thought you knew that. Khaibara is on the border of Azlatan."

"That means I am outside of Azlatan."

He could almost feel her appraising glance. "Think you'll survive?"

"It's just a strange thought is all." He was remembering another wanderer, who had crossed the border far to the south of here. *Varady,* he thought, *are you still alive out there?*

Lunch was cold and brief. She allowed him to remove the blindfold while he ate in the shadows. His vision cleared but she folded the scarf thickly to tie as a sunshade above his eyes, plastering black mud below them to reduce glare from his own cheeks. She followed suit for herself and tied on her own headband so that her hair was a fall of copper fire from gold-chased leather. He wondered again at her people, who had such strange-colored hair.

"Now we ride," she said. "We're almost at timber line. It will be easier there."

Danon swung onto Chandar with a sigh for the tired horse, and another for himself. Even Shandiin's steed was too tired to snipe at the black stallion striding at his shoulder. Only the cat and The Chaine seemed tireless. Danon bit back any complaint, remembering too well her scathing comments during his training.

He was glad of the trees when they reached timberline. Shandiin caught him staring up at the smoky blue pines and grinned back at him over Windmaker's painted rump.

"They're the same as the trees in Azlatan," she told him. "There will be some below that you won't be familiar with, only because they are indigenous to the far north. Nothing you won't feel comfortable with."

"Has Khedran ever been where we are going?"

"No. This is our stronghold. He doesn't belong with the anarchist Chaine." Her teasing smile had vanished.

Danon clucked softly to Chandar, and the black flattened his ears but moved up alongside the paint. Shandiin looked straight ahead, as though ignoring him.

"Look," he said. "Maybe you misunderstood me, up there on the top of the world. I like what you've done. Let anyone else complain that Khedran's not human. I don't believe them. He just thinks, that's all. I figure you may have saved the whole world by teaching him your ways."

She shrugged. "I understand the concerns of your fellow countrymen, Danon. We've kept ourselves disassociated from anything to do with your people's beliefs. They distrust the Chaine enough, as it is."

Leaving the mountain's eternal winter behind, they descended into a canyon where autumn had come into full glory. It was later in the season than Danon had realized.

The horses scarcely made a sound in the thick carpet of old leaves. A mist rose with the sun, so they swam through a veiling sea. The trees were purple shadows until the sun pierced their upper boughs, and Danon exclaimed at sudden beauty.

Trunk and limbs were golden, and the leaves a deep copper veined with scarlet. The sun slanted through to the forest floor and a faint scent like cinnamon rose up. Cinnamon and wet earth and...he sniffed the air eagerly...the distant tang of the sea.

"There is nothing like this in Azlatan," Danon called to Shandiin, who rode ahead.

She turned back in her saddle. "Of course not. Azlatan's borders don't reach far enough to the north, the only place these trees grow. The leaves have turned as all leaves will in autumn, but the glitter on each trunk is its own resin, which dries like a coat of amber. That stays through winter, which you call Starfall, and the summer of your Stareven, when the whole place is gold and emerald. The wood of the golden trees is almost as strong as the metal you call Chaine gold. It's what we use to build our ships."

Danon gazed around in awe, wondering what other marvels lay outside his known world. Chandar had quickened his step, and his ears were pricked so they nearly touched at the tips.

Shandiin noticed this, grinning. "Maybe he's warmed up enough for a short run? I'd like to get over this next hill."

"He's had less rest than your evil horse," Danon retorted. "But he can still leave him behind!" He lifted the reins, asking instead of demanding, and the black answered with a sudden burst of speed between the trees. Shandiin kicked her big mount to follow.

Chandar warmed quickly to the uphill work, leaving a whirl of cinnamon-leaves in his wake. Danon could hear the painted horse blowing loudly as he fell behind. He still demanded no race but left a balancing tension on the reins and let Chandar set his own pace. The stallion flicked his ears back, flattened them, and flew over the hillcrest like a deer, checking himself only slightly for the downhill plunge. The Chaine's horse was outrun.

Danon thought he heard Shandiin call him back and grinned to himself. He wouldn't let Chandar hurt himself, but it felt good to be ahead of her–if just this once!

A fallen log made an easy hurdle, and a clear swathe opened invitingly ahead of them. Danon tugged at the reins, but Chandar ducked his head, pleading for more freedom. Danon was still undecided when the snowcat shot past them.

Chandar veered, startled, even as the cat whirled on him with a feline scream. The black stallion sat back on his haunches, striking out like the warhorse he was, while Danon's head rocked on his neck, and he clamped his legs to the saddle.

Majia crouched bristling out of Chandar's reined reach, his eyes blazing gold. His growl was a rumble of warning, and the big horse trembled at the treachery of his old friend.

Stunned, Danon's hand fell to his sword even as he pulled Chandar back. As he reached, something whistled past his ear, and a feathered shaft sprang from the tree beside him.

"Don't move," A woman's voice warned from the trees.

Danon obeyed, his only movement to tighten the reins in another warning to Chandar. The warhorse stood drawn together, balanced to spin on his hocks.

"I said don't move." The voice pinned Danon for that instant. "Have no doubt the next arrow will be for you."

He heard with sinking heart the oncoming hoofbeats of Shandiin's racing mount.

"Stop them! Block the path!" came the voice again, obviously warning others ahead of him.

A touch of his heel spun Chandar broadside while he yelled warning to Shandiin, "Go back! It's a trap!" and dismounted with a leap that took him between the trees.

His attacker was where he had anticipated, her chestnut hair swinging as she spun to meet his flanking attack. He was only marginally quicker because she was encumbered with the longbow while he catapulted the remaining yard, knocking her down by sheer momentum.

Bereft of her weapon, he found he had hold of a fury as certain as a cat's, and felt his breath explode when she managed to lever him into a tree. He spun from her path and bore her down again, this time ensuring she landed face down and sprawled beneath him.

In that position she felt no more substantial than a child, though his bruised ribs knew better. "Shandiin!" he summoned breath to yell. "Over here!"

He felt all the fighting tension drain from his hostage. "Damn it," she muttered.

Then he saw the others, stepping from the trees. Not armed with unwieldy long-range weapons, these, but with swords at the ready. Chaine men. Three of them.

Danon rose slowly, releasing the girl, and saw Shandiin join them, nodding to the men who sheathed their swords. "Damn it," he echoed the girl, and she sat up.

"Good fight!" She grinned at him. Her headband was leather and gold, and her eyes a wide honest brown. She had the slender, coltish look of youth in leather pants and furred jerkin.

Shandiin was glaring at the girl. "He bested you. You should have waited for these men. Danon, I see you have met Shajii. These are Roinn, Jaihann, and Djarr." The men nodded politely, seeming unsurprised at their leader's sudden appearance.

Majia strolled up to join the party, purring as he brushed against Danon as though in apology. "He saved your life," Shajii told him. "I was a little quick..."

"Too quick," Shandiin snapped, the sting in her voice causing the girl to wince. "You should apologize."

"No," Danon denied. "She couldn't have known I was not an enemy."

Shandiin just arched an eyebrow, and turned with the men to disappear toward the road. Shajii came lithely to her feet, swept leaves from her clothing, and extended a friendly hand. "Come.

We have something to make your ribs feel better. You look like you've journeyed long and hard to get here for such a rough welcome. I'll have to make it up to you, especially since she," and here Shajii tossed her red hair to emphasize the word, "seems to think you are worth apologizing to." She gave him a friendly punch in the arm that unbalanced him.

"Are all Chaine women like that?" he asked dryly, rubbing his arm.

She raised pale eyebrows. "Like The Chaine?" she questioned, clearly misunderstanding him. "Not at all. She has this sense of responsibility that never leaves her alone."

"And you don't?"

She shrugged. "I should have let you go by. The men would have stopped you more safely, since there were more of them. Shandiin claims I am too impetuous."

"I see. Well, you Chaine aren't known for being impetuous."

She gave him an arch look. "We Chaine," she said, "aren't known for much of anything good, in Azlatan. She says we have to be careful there." Shajii cocked her head. "How come she brought you along? You're a Rioch, aren't you?"

He nodded to the second question. "You'll have to ask her," he replied to the first.

As they reached the road Shandiin was already mounted, leaning low in the saddle in rapt conversation with the man she'd named as Roinn. She didn't glance toward Danon. Chandar stood with his muzzle close to the snowcat, who had apparently made friends again all around. The big horse nickered at Danon as he took the reins.

"He's beautiful," Shajii proclaimed. "I can't understand how you could just abandon him like that. The longbow can easily kill a horse."

"You had no reason to shoot at him once I was off."

She looked at him in approval. "A Rioch can think!"

Danon grimaced. "Now you sound like her. Contrary to what she may have taught you, young lady, the Chaine are not the only people with a mind."

He mounted while she mouthed "young lady?" and stomped away, returning with two horses. She mounted one, Roinn the other, and they turned off to follow Shandiin.

The girl dropped her mare alongside him. She indicated Chandar. "Is he yours?"

"No. He belongs to the High King."

Her mouth snapped shut and she looked at him speculatively. He noticed her pale eyelashes were so thick her eyes had none of the naked look familiar in some of the red-haired Chaine. He grinned at his own interest in such a small detail. She was only the second Chaine female he had ever met. He found her fascinating, though she lacked Shandiin's cool maturity.

Since she remained silent after his response, he returned his interest to his surroundings. Freshly cut stumps appeared alongside the road. Only when they had topped another hill did he realize how many there were and begin to be curious. Curiosity turned to near alarm as they skirted a rocky cliff and he saw a wide path denuded of all trees; even the stumps were gone, stacked in a pile to one side. A hill crowned only with covering grass rose ahead of them.

He checked his mount, frowning.

"Does such destruction bother you?" Shajii asked.

He eyed the stumps, like teeth pulled from the wounded earth, and then saw that the holes had been filled in. "It does. I have always been uncomfortable with that which should be whole but is not. I can see there is planning here..."

"Yes. We Chaine know balance is always necessary. We don't take from the land unless there is need, and we always repay. There is a sapling in nurture for every tree we have taken. They will be planted in the spring, when they will flourish."

He nodded, but she forestalled his next question.

"First you must rest," she told him. "Our need was great, to do this to the forest we love, but Shandiin will know when the time is come to explain it to you."

He thought he guessed the answer when they topped the hill.

The other side fell away to the beach, gleaming like white salt in the sun, and the blue sea rising to the blue sky. The harbor was a great bite taken out of the land. There were buildings within the untouched forest upon the headland.

Never was a view more breathtaking, even from the height of the Everwinter. But it was the ships that stopped his eye.

Chaine ships. Golden ships.

They rode easily upon the sapphire waves, their great sails furled in sleep, but the flow and curve of every line bespoke life. They were creatures waiting to awake to the dance of wave and wind, tethered restlessly even now.

A fleet of them. He tried to count but lost his numbers amid the dazzle of sea and sun and gold.

"Are there so many of you Chaine?" he wondered aloud.

"Our numbers have grown. I was born here, and there are others. But our ships are not just to carry us, but our treasure."

She looked down on them, her dark eyes full of gold. Khedran's treasure!

Danon looked back from the golden ships to the barren swathe from which they had been born, to the great canyon at the end of that road, for he knew now that it was a road from canyon to sea.

"What is that treasure?" he asked. "What treasure requires such a highway, such ships?"

Her laughter was sun on surf, and she whirled her little mare away gaily. "You don't trick me so easily. If Shandiin hasn't told you, I won't. Come!" and she urged her mount to a canter atop the hillcrest, toward the inhabited forest he had glimpsed upon the headland.

He let Chandar follow, the sea-wind in his hair and the sun in his eyes. But he turned back once more before entering beneath the boughs of bronze and amber, to look on the sea and the golden ships of the Chaine.

CHAPTER 11

B uildings rambled between the trees that stood tall around them. The Chaine built to live with nature, not shut themselves away from it.

Among the trees, friendly paths like deer-trails connected homes and businesses alike. Everywhere was evidence of commerce: each home had a shop, many whose industry was evidenced by its products frankly displayed. Azlatan looked askance at the mercenary Chaine, who were focused on work and profits. Their settlement was proof there was no indolent class among their ranks...from what Shajii had said, their leader least of all.

He saw no sign of Shandiin. For that matter, the place seemed deserted, with evidence of work abandoned mid-task. He questioned Shajii as they entered a clearing that housed the stables, where Chandar snorted loudly at the pastured Chaine horses.

"I imagine they've all gone to the Hall," she responded, dismounting. "The Chaine will want our immediate report on the ships' progress." She glanced at him sidelong. "Along with other things. I will find someone to tend your horse."

Danon dismounted stiffly, feeling weariness return like a mantle. It appeared he was not needed at her meeting. He tried to ignore his bruised feeling; he thought they had grown close, in their travels. She had even said they were friends.

Well, she was a leader with duties, like his liege. So...he should have known better.

Aloud, he said "Don't bother. No one's touching Chandar but me, and right now he needs plenty of touching." He slapped the black's shoulder, raising dust to prove his point.

They entered the stable, where Danon was surprised when Chandar gave a rolling neigh that shattered the silence. It was quickly answered by a human "Yeow!" and an equine whinny, and Windmaker's familiar black and white face appeared over a stall door, long ears upright. Danon grinned as a human face popped up beneath it, an elf with carrot-colored hair bristling and face almost as red with anger.

"The brute stepped on me!" the elf complained to Shajii, and then his eyes lit suspiciously on Danon, who had placed a warning hand over Chandar's quivering nostrils.

"Good day," Danon inclined his head graciously. "Is the box stall next to Windmaker available for my horse? It seems these two have become friendly on the long trail."

"Does he bite?" the urchin demanded.

Shajii giggled, drawing a new glare. "Don't worry, Dinn. Danon, here, will take care of his own horse, and I will help if he allows. How did you end up with Windmaker?"

Dinn howled anew at his charge's latest abuse – it appeared the paint horse was now standing on his foot. He clubbed him away and shot fury at Shajii's laughter. "Just lucky, that's me. She will be charged extra for this." He disappeared again, ostensibly to continue grooming his leader's steed.

Danon's eyebrows climbed. "Shandiin pays?"

She looked at him curiously. "Of course. She'll pay for Chandar, too, since you are her guest." She deposited her saddle on a rack and led him to the loosebox next to Windmaker's.

The stable was roofed high, with its own skylight sifting sun onto the clean deep straw. Danon surveyed the roomy stall with satisfaction as he led Chandar within, giving saddle and bridle to Shajii's waiting hands. Chandar went straight to the watering-trough, which Danon realized in amazement welled with clear bubbling water. Running water! He was inspecting it...it had both an in and out flow, in a stable, yet!...when Shajii came back with brushes and rags.

The two worked in companionable silence, till Chandar's coat was returned to black silk and his feet were cleaned and oiled and his long tail combed out to sweep the sweet straw. Dinn appeared then, with a warm bran mash which Danon had requested. He inspected it before offering it to the horse, ignoring Dinn's astonished laughter.

"I hope Windmaker received the same attention," Danon said coldly as he closed the stall door behind him at last.

"I didn't eat his food for him," Dinn snorted, earning him a slap on the ear from Shajii. Danon realized he was about the same age as the girl, just shorter.

"Stop it," she admonished. "You know the Rioch treat their horses like pets. Shandiin is almost as bad. And I'll bet you sleep in the stall with yours!"

"That's different!"

"It's always different when it's your horse," said Shajii, and smiled at Danon's laughter. "Are you ready to go, Lord Danon?"

"Go where?" he asked.

"Now it's your turn to get taken care of," Shajii said. She dropped coins into Dinn's waiting palm, and Danon followed her out into the autumn afternoon.

They followed a path that wandered uphill toward glints of glass in the trees high above. Soon he could make out a long, windowed construction built partway into the hillside. It was surrounded by a covered porch, and a steep narrow stair lifted from path to door.

Inside he found a long hall bright with afternoon sun on stone-tiled floors. It was flanked with long trestle-tables, each covered with a white cloth and bearing brass bowls of autumn leaves and late-blooming mums. A long unlit fireplace covered the other wall, built of brown and sandy stone with great copper pots hung above the mantel. The room was warm, and Danon looked up in admiration at the skylight, which focused heat as well as light into the room.

He was distracted by a new entrance and startled to realize he was not the only Rioch in this northern settlement. There was no mistaking the typical patrician features of a countryman, though the man's hair was faded to old cotton around his weathered face. He wore the loosely belted robe of a scholar.

"Tarfon," Shajii acknowledged with coolness in her voice. "This is Compatri Danon, formerly of Selagon and now right sword to your own High King."

Danon inclined his head. The old man's eyes were like grey ice.

"Is my mother in the kitchen?" Shajii asked abruptly, and at Tarfon's nod turned back briefly to Danon. "Tarfon will show you your room and bath," she told him. Gone was her laughter and coltish youth, replaced by cool Chaine grace. "One of us will bring you your dinner, in a little while." She turned without smiling and walked away. Danon's puzzled gaze followed her.

"She is very beautiful," Tarfon agreed to Danon's apparent thoughts. "As all Chaine women are beautiful, with their hair like burning fire. Savage women, neither of the dark Rioch nor fair Duine, and cold as the blades they wield. Be warned, Compatri. They aren't for the likes of us."

Danon felt both disgust and unease. Even though Tarfon had read him wrong, the words echoed precariously within his own mind. He regarded the old man as coldly as Shajii had. "You're no mind-reader," he told him flatly. "I was just thinking how obvious it is that she does not like you."

Tarfon smiled viciously, revealing long yellow teeth. "Of course not. None of them do. The Chaine do not like anyone outside of their clan; they feel they are superior to us, and they don't like anyone who has guessed that simple truth, which they hide so well...in Azlatan."

"What are you doing here, then?"

"Studying them. And waiting on the guests of this inn, like some unbound Duine. The beasts require it of me, for room and board."

Danon quirked an eyebrow. "Perhaps you had best show me to my room, then. To earn your supper?"

He received an angry glare. "It is not a laughing matter," Tarfon stated haughtily.

"Then perhaps you'll just direct me. I'm not used to being served by a scholar, anyway."

"I am not just a scholar!" This time the oldster fairly thundered at him, and Danon rubbed his temple in wonder that the Chaine put up with him at all. "I am Tahmond, more than those who remain in the defiled Temple while they allow these blasphemers to remain in Azlatan. I determined that truth is needed, the truth about these–these abominations, and once I find proof that they are, indeed, agents of Chaos–"

"How long have you been here," Danon interrupted the tirade, "looking for this proof?"

"Thirty years," the old man said proudly.

"Tarfon," Danon sighed, "please show me to my room."

After bathing and dressing in new clothes provided by his host, Dannon contemplated what to do next. His stomach cried for food even as his body ached for sleep, and he stood a moment in indecision, wondering if perhaps Shandiin could be in the dining hall, and if he should go and see.

There was a sharp rap at the door and Tarfon came in with a covered platter. He set it down with a clang, while Danon steeled himself against the unwelcome intrusion.

"You didn't tell me *she* had returned," Tarfon accused.

"The Chaine?" Danon guessed. *Does everyone talk about her like that?*

"The Chaine, yes! Chaos incarnate! She says the ships leave tomorrow. Will you go with them?"

Danon realized the old man was agitated beyond bearing; he had dropped the tray out of weakness as well as anger. His hands fluttered and his face was a peculiar shade of grey. Danon stepped forward in concern, grasping the man's thin shoulders firmly.

"Still yourself," he commanded quietly. "Here. Sit and drink this water. I'll tell you what little I know, but you must be still. You're too old for this excitement, Tarfon."

The old man obeyed, though Danon had to help steady the cup to his lips, and it chattered against his teeth anyway. Tarfon wept tears of gratitude for his simple assistance. "It's been so long since I have heard a word of kindness. You don't know..."

"Shh. Quiet, Tarfon." Danon noted the blue lips and fingernails and looked around for his cache of medicines.

Still in the stable. *Damn.*

He was on his feet and at the door in a smooth rush, yelling loudly for Shajii. He was about to head to the stairs when a door opened across from his and she peered out in surprise, hair dripping and body swathed in a towel.

"My saddlebags!" he demanded. "The old man's having a heart failure. I need the saddlebags, now!"

She didn't hesitate or question but left hurriedly to pass on the word.

He turned back to his room. Tarfon gasped in pain. "Don't leave me!"

"I won't." The aged body was weightless in his arms, swung gently from chair to bed, where he scarcely dented the white coverlet. "Breathe, Tarfon. I am a physician. I have sent for medicine."

"Please! You must listen..." bony fingers grasped at his shirt, the other hand drawing something from his cloak. "Take this. It is for the High Tahmond. I know I can trust you to deliver it safely."

Danon took the scroll, thinking only of his missing medicine. "You must try to relax. Breathe deeply."

When his medicine bag arrived, thrust over his shoulder, he took no time for thanks but ripped it open to find and unstopper the vial containing what would give the gift of sleep and, hopefully, stop the wild gyrations of Tarfon's ancient heart. "Water!" he ordered, and the cup appeared swiftly. The contents of the vial were added, and he slipped an arm around the man's thin neck and began lifting it to the blue lips.

The old man struggled in his extremity, and Shandiin leaned in to help. Tarfon's eyes widened in horror.

"Get back!" Danon ordered, recognizing the old man's true fear of her.

"I'll help." Shajii knelt at the other side of the bed, the towel slipping to reveal much of a small but shapely bosom. Tarfon's eyes rolled, but there was no fright when they fell upon the girl. Shajii helped Danon steady him, and the liquid trickled messily, but was swallowed.

The results were almost immediate. Pale blue eyes rolled up, then closed and bellows breathing slowed to a peaceful pace. Danon watched critically as color began to return to the age-riven face and let escape a long sigh of his own relief.

He looked at Shajii, who gazed back wide-eyed. He motioned for her to pull up her towel and she did so, blushing deeply. "We're lucky the sight of you didn't finish him off," Danon grinned. "He's a lascivious old goat, if I don't miss my guess."

Her eyes flicked behind him, and he remembered Shandiin with a start. He began to pick up his scattered medicines. "Thanks," he said over his shoulder. "Did you bring it up yourself?"

"Found it in the stable on the way back," she replied. "First time you ever left it behind. Must have had something on your mind."

He turned then, saw her standing with her back against the door, arms crossed. The sun from the skylight painted autumn in her hair. For once she didn't look amused.

He glanced at Shajii and felt anger. Did Shandiin believe him vile enough to take advantage of a child? For so Shajii seemed to him in The Chaine's golden presence. Shandiin was dirty, weary with a burden perhaps only Khedran could understand, but still...The Chaine.

"Nothing on my mind," he told her curtly, "but the end of a long ride, and food and rest. I'll have to postpone the rest, it seems. Tarfon here will have to be watched closely."

"I can do it," Shajii offered.

"No," Shandiin told her. "You can't. Come with me, Shajii." The girl's eyes widened at the brusque order. Shandiin's departure was abrupt.

"Go on," Danon told the girl. "There's food; Tarfon brought it. I'll be fine."

She nodded distractedly and left. So young, Danon mused. But she had that special strength of her people; she would grow, perhaps, into another Shandiin.

Well, almost.

He sighed over the cold food but ate ravenously, checked his patient again, and settled into a chair beside the bed, thoughtful. He examined Tarfon frequently while the sun slanted to evening and the sounds of a large gathering came to him from the dining hall.

It seemed he had been forgotten again. He was so weary that the hurt loomed larger than it should.

He tried to shake it off, got up to light the fireplace and a lantern. Warmth had fled with the sun, and he covered Tarfon with a blanket he found folded beside the bed. The forgotten scroll rolled off as he did so.

He picked it up and sat down once more to his lonely vigil, glancing up once at the high window where the stars blazed, bright even through the reflected light from the fire. He was tired, but his mind raced in circles, and finally he leaned to the lantern, unrolled the scroll, and began to read.

He decided, glancing through to later passages, that Tarfon was quite delusional, having come to the conclusion that Shandiin was truly the goddess Chaos. Danon could only shake his head at the convoluted designs the old man had built to prove his theory, and lost interest in his ramblings.

Shandiin came in later, and stood for a long moment looking down at him where he slept in the chair. His hair was loose over his forehead, and the scroll hung from lax fingers. Shandiin removed it gently and glanced through it. Then she re-rolled it and leaned forward to touch Danon lightly on the shoulder.

She stepped back quickly, for he was up before he was awake, checking his patient. He sank back down, running his fingers through the dark disarray of his hair.

"Did it again," he said in disgust. "Can't even stay awake to watch a patient. Why did you come back, Shandiin? Checking up on me?"

She sighed and dropped the heavy scroll on his lap. He started almost guiltily at the sight of it.

"No," she said. "Haven't you learned yet you don't need a shepherd? Today you defeated a warrior–"

"Who, Shajii?"

"Don't doubt for a moment that Shajii is a warrior. Did you think she's a child? She's the same age as the woman betrothed to Khedran. She is Chaine, and we have a longer lifespan than most; the appearance and eagerness of youth is longer as well. You not only bested her, but you also rightfully rebuked me twice, and then saved this man's life. When are you going to stop apologizing for yourself?"

"Quit being kind. It's unlike you."

He was sorry immediately but set his teeth against apology. She said nothing.

He could see the slow rise and fall of Tarfon's thin chest. "Thirty years. Thirty years, he said, without a word of kindness. He cried when I tried to help him."

He looked back at her then. She stood against the wall, slumped uncharacteristically in weariness. She still wore the stained leather from Ordhold. Her eyes gleamed in the firelight, unreadable.

"Why?" Danon asked her. "He's a filthy old man, half crazy, as disgusting to me as he must be to you. Yet he is a human being, and his work," he fingered the scroll that despised the Chaine, wanting to tear it to shreds, "his early work shows he had a mind, once. A good mind, capable of reason and understanding." He swallowed. "You let him stay among you for thirty years. Why? It should have been apparent years ago that he needed more than the Chaine could give. He was going mad, among you who understand nothing of.... of..."

"Of love? Of being human?" She slapped his own words back to him. He flinched but challenged her with his silence. She sighed. "He was Tahmond. Failed Tahmond, Danon, even as you failed as a healer in the Temple of Liethe. He didn't find the answer in his Temple, either. You're right; he was capable of reason. It's our belief that reason is inherent to any rational, healthy human. But he was Tahmond, and unable to discard Tahmond beliefs. Reason is like fire; it can consume the flimsy kindling of irrational belief... and sometimes all it leaves is ashes. You often fight the very battle Tarfon fought, Danon, and at the same danger to yourself. Should we bar you, then, from the infection of reason? Send you back to the Temple of Liethe, with orders not to think, but only to accept?"

"Enough." Danon was on his feet, looking down at her in her slumped position against the wall. She stared back, unmoving. Her still face revealed nothing of the anger he had heard in her voice.

"I have had enough," he continued, "of your lecturing, your condescending, patronizing, and wholly foul judgement of those who disagree with your way of doing things. Simple humanity was all I was talking about, Shandiin. Simple kindness to an old man!"

"Even one who believes I am the evil Chaos, and seeks to destroy me?"

He drew breath sharply at that, then expelled it. "Even that. You let him exist in a world of loneliness until the only thing left to him was insane anger. If you truly believed he was an enemy, you should have just killed him, cleanly and swiftly, as in battle."

Her shoulders dropped even further. "Perhaps you are right." She looked over at the sleeping figure. "But he wasn't always that way. It's hard to take the life of one weaker than yourself. Especially when he was at first a reasoning man. His search for some evidence against us came long after he arrived, Danon. He was brilliant once. His intelligence was a threat to the High Tahmond. This was his exile. They threw him out."

She bent to pick up the scroll Danon had again dropped in his anger. "Perhaps you can see what I mean, in early passages. He searched then for truth, not realizing the danger to himself."

Danon accepted the scroll, scowling. She started toward the door, paused with her hand on the latch. She spoke without turning around.

"A few days ago, on the Everwinter, you had a different opinion of the Chaine, and what I have done."

"Shandiin..."

She turned at her name, silencing him with the cold challenge of her eyes. "Already reason and magic war within you, Danon. Who will I be? Friend? Or Chaos?"

"What do you care what I decide?" he flung back.

She closed her eyes at that, as though too weary to respond. "You are being childish and unkind, Danon, things of which I know you do not approve. And you are not thinking, of which I do not approve. We are both too tired to continue this conversation. I believe I will go to bed. It will be dawn in a few short hours, and you are facing your first journey by sea. I will send someone to watch Tarfon. Good night."

He knew she had made her own attempt at reconciliation. Once he would have accepted this gratefully. Now his hurt feelings fused his anger.

"Send Shajii," he said to her back.

She stiffened. When she turned around once more, he was sorry to see the return of pain. It was etched deeply over her strong fine face.

"I won't send Shajii. I called her out earlier to give the news to her and her mother." Shandiin swallowed, opened the door. "Your Princess Marre's Jhinn was Shajii's father," she told him, before it closed behind her.

The painting of Jhinn was small, almost too small for the vibrant colors it contained. Yet Danon, who had never met the living man, felt with a heart-stopping certainty: this man could not be dead.

He was immortal. He was the essence of health, vitality, self-containment. In those stern features was captured the ideal, the elemental Chaine.

Danon released the painting almost reluctantly to waiting hands and wondered. It revealed the man, and it revealed the artist.

"Marre?" he questioned. "Princess Marre of Athea painted this?"

"Yes," said Jainn, wife of Jhinn, mother of Shajii. "Jhinn was very proud of it. You must understand. He was under contract as her guardian, and so was nearly always with her, from the day of her birth. Marre was as much his daughter as Shajii, whom he knew only on brief visits."

The words were spoken without anger, and Danon sighed for one more of the many things beyond his understanding.

They were briefly alone in the dining hall, golden dawn in the skylight above them. The room filled with light like a crystal cup, and Danon wondered vaguely if the effect was real or part of his sleepless condition. Sleep had come only briefly, even though his patient slept now under the watchful eye of Danon's own Chaine physician teacher.

Jainn's dark eyes were faintly reddened from weeping, but she turned to replace the painting on its shelf with quiet composure. She was tall, and her skin was a clear smooth fawn blushed with rose, her long hair the deep red of good wine. It hung past her slender waist, which was belted by a wide green sash. He thought of what he had learned in reading Tarfon's scroll, that the Chaine did not marry, but bonded with love and respect in a union called *amharen*. Jainn, like her *amharen*, dressed in green and gold, leather and wool.

This woman is a warrior, like all the Chaine. Yet her steel is sheathed in velvet. She is a woman, and soft as needed. Far different from Shandiin's rough and sharp-edged grandeur.

"More food?" she asked him politely.

"No, thank you. May I ask if you will be sailing with us to Azlatan?"

She began to clear the table. "I hadn't planned to, before. Jhinn was coming home once Marre was in Cabre. But now there hardly seems reason to stay."

"Certainly you're going." Shajii entered with cheeks reddened by the cold outside. She seemed excited, untouched by sorrow for a father whose memories were mostly missing. Yet Danon had begun to know the Chaine, and he saw the way her hand lingered for a moment on her mother's shoulder. "We need you, Mother. You know Shandiin has asked that as many go as can. And surely you don't want to stay behind in boredom, just waiting for our return."

Jainn arched an auburn eyebrow at her daughter. "So speaks youth. Shajii, I should have never allowed you to go so early to warrior-training, and then enter the competitions. You are entirely too eager for battle, having had only a taste and not the full feast."

Shajii shrugged, then turned to Danon. "Shandiin has Chandar ready for you to ride, and she's straining at the bit –"

"I think you have her mixed up with my horse," Danon grinned.

"Now you sound like her! C'mon, she's waiting. You too, Mother."

"Not I. I think I had best sail to Azlatan, at least to keep an eye on you. Which means I have packing to do."

Shajii rushed Danon into the morning sun, down the tall stairs to where Shandiin waited, not looking as impatient as Shajii had described. There were many riders mounted, but The Chaine stood with Chandar at Windmaker's head, engaged once more in conversation with Roinn.

At Danon's approach the man turned away as though to mount, but Danon caught his swift appraising glance as he did so. Roinn's eyes were as grey as his leader's, cold and level, and his dark red hair was bound by a leather headband. Danon recognized the same unbending strength described in Marre's painting. He realized the man had never spoken to him, and he sensed a rivalry. *Amharen* of Shandiin? According to Tarfon's writing, that term was as close to marriage as the Chaine ever came. Danon was still too puzzled by the concept to guess, but there was a leaden feeling in his gut as he surveyed the powerful and handsome man.

Shandiin smiled and handed him Chandar's reins as though their deep-night argument had never happened. "You finally get to see Khedran's treasure. Let's ride!"

He kept Chandar at Windmaker's shoulder, aware of Roinn who fell in behind them with Shajii. The rest of the Chaine riders followed in a long column from the settlement, and no one spoke as they galloped up to the hill's crest. From there Danon saw a ship drawn close to shore. A long ramp led from its opened side to the shallow water, and many more Chaine waved with an air of celebration as they passed.

Shandiin glanced across at Danon, her eyes laughing, cloaked in sun and wind. "Have you guessed yet?"

"I'm afraid to," he smiled back. He was glad she had set down her burden and her anger, glad that they were once again friends. "You'd accuse me of making assumptions."

They started up the wide road to the canyon, and it was then that Danon sensed a change in Chandar. The black stallion was set against the bit, his ears pricked, and Danon had to check him sharply. After that he ran with ears flattened and head tucked down in anger. Danon saw sweat spring out on the great bowed neck, until he gleamed like black oil.

"Follow me," Shandiin commanded Danon, frowning briefly at his mount. She turned her paint aside abruptly, lifting her arm in signal to the column of following riders.

They broke apart smoothly to each side of the road, and Danon wheeled with Shandiin, still fighting with Chandar while a great roar went up from the Chaine warriors like a victory cry.

An answering chorus came from the canyon, where more riders waited. Then came a sound like rolling thunder, shaking the very earth. Danon looked to the canyon's mouth, where the sun had just cleared the great enclosing cliffs.

The horses sprang from shadow onto that golden road, a surf of tossing manes and shining coats and rolling eyes, plunging and squealing as they were driven from the canyon to the Chaine who made a living fence along the road to keep them in. Danon's heart leapt for the beauty of that wild herd, while Shandiin's laughter was lost beneath their thunder and her eyes gleamed at a vision of untold wealth. More than iron muscles and strong backs, these horses carried the wind as their heritage, fire as their blood. Chandar called to them, and Danon controlled him without thinking as he sorted out individuals. A mare of honey gold raced by with the wild grace of a deer. That one alone was worth all Selagon, yet there were so very many, and Danon's eyes blurred with tears at the glory of them.

"They are from another world, Danon. I told you I had been there." She turned to Roinn, who rode up to her on his steady grey. "Follow them down. Hold them on the beach; it will take hours to load all the ships, and they will be impatient."

Roinn nodded and wheeled his horse, and Shandiin looked up-canyon. Her smile faded.

"There," she breathed, and Danon followed her gaze.

He blinked away the dust as the last of the herd thundered by. For a moment he saw only the blue shadows of the cliffs, and then the horse moving through them.

This horse came alone at a springing trot that carried his enormous frame over the ground as swiftly as mortal horse could run. Danon gasped at the sheer size of him, and when he moved into the sun...there to pause, surveying them with haughty grandeur...Danon felt dizzy, gazing upon a legend come to earth.

He dwarfed any mortal horse. He was so white he blazed. His mane swirled profusely about his head and shoulders, and his tail bannered over his hindquarters to spill down onto the ground.

His wide-slanted eyes seemed made of flame. He looked upon Chandar, and Danon felt Chandar tremble, and the High King's black warhorse bowed his head to his own king.

"He's like a god," Danon stammered. "He's the steed of Chaos!"

Shandiin shook back her hair. "We journeyed a long time together, he and I, for these are his descendants that we brought, and they obey him. Even Chandar knows him, though he was not born upon his plains or his mountains, far away to the East. You of Azlatan would name him as you did, the steed of Chaos. But to those of that other world, the people of the plains and the eastern mountains, he is known as the Gift of the Sunqueen, because that goddess, who you call only Chaos, gave his descendants to them. He is ChanDethe. They say their prophesied Deliverer will stop the enemies who have always hounded them, riding one of his offspring with the same name."

Danon stared, and the mythical stallion watched Shandiin with eyes as intelligent as any human's. Chaine and horse seemed to communicate for a long moment. For an instant he saw a small black mark under the long forelock as the great creature turned, and then he was gone.

Danon swallowed his awe. "So the other people also have a prophecy," he said. "But why would they give up their horses for us, Shandiin?"

"It is part of their prophecy that ChanDethe would take the Shalmira away when their Deliverer appears...and there will be a great war." She sighed. "Prophecies are always a two-edged sword, traps for the unwary."

"The Shalmira? Is that what the horses are called? Where..."

She waved his words aside. "Their story is too long to tell now." She looked bleak. "Damn magic! Damn prophecies! Riddle within riddle. At least Khedran will have the horses, and not have to mourn Ordhold's."

"He'll have the horses, but not the men of Ordhold."

"True. We have to hope that Khedran's Black Guard and the Chaine will be enough."

"He has ten Legions now. He's worked hard in your absence, Shandiin, while the Dominion Kings rant that he is stealing their young men for some nefarious purpose. They won't believe his warnings that the border wards are down, that Azlatan is open to invasion. And when he took Jael into Penumbra, it gave the High Tahmond fuel to make him even more unpopular. He's fighting a war before the real thing even comes."

Shandiin looked grim. "Yes. He's been caught in that maelstrom his whole life, and it will only get worse. And he's probably still fighting the nightmares, too." At Danon's look, she added. "He's had them since he was sixteen. Won't talk about it, but he gets little sleep because of it."

Danon scowled. "Jael," he muttered. "I remember now. Jael has dreams, too."

Her eyes pinned him like grey steel, and he stammered a little. "He always had dreams. But we didn't think about it much. He was crippled in other ways, not always present. Sometimes he seemed to live somewhere else, some shadow world. When that became public knowledge, it gave the High Tahmond more ammunition to use against Khedran."

Shandiin's mount sidled beneath her, impatient. She checked him automatically, her eyes remaining on Danon. "And the High Tahmond has far too much influence on some Dominion Kings. They are fools. Because no matter what they think, Khedran is the greatest weapon and the only hope this world has."

Now her eyes held lightning. "The Black Wolf is inhuman by weaker standards, but he was not made for the weak. I'm getting my people and these horses there for his command, but he must convince the Dominion Kings the storm is coming. The Prophecy War is nearly upon us."

PART 3: THE HIGH QUEEN

The High King is the Gift to Azlatan.
He of the emerald eyes and power in his being
commands the goddess Daimaine,
who gave him the Gifts of his rule.
He is known by the magic of his presence
and his voice that is always heard.
He is incorruptible. He is truth.
The trust and honor of Azlatan live within him.
Daimaine is the goddess of Justice
and rules at his right hand.
The High Queen,
chosen by the God of Order Phaelon,
rules at his left.

—Mantra for the High King,
from the Annals of Azlatan

CHAPTER 12

Danon had departed in search of Shandiin at Khedran's order, but his patients from the battle with the Outsiders remained sleeping in the old farmhouse the King had requisitioned for their care.

Marre's sleep was deep and dreamless, born of medicine and the weariness of inner warfare. She slept unaware of her surroundings, of the old Duine who watched at her bedside, or the soldier who had guarded just inside her door since Danon had gone.

The Duine drooped at last, unable to remain alert even in the face of high royalty come to her household. Farbet watched in sympathy as the old woman started up suddenly at a sharp rap on the door; he turned in annoyance to raise the bar and scold any soldier so inconsiderate.

He opened the door, changed expression quickly, saluted.

"How is she?" Khedran asked.

"Still asleep, Highness." Farbet stepped aside for the King's entrance, frowning as the old Duine dropped to her knees and saluted, touching her forehead and then her chest. "The old one here is tired to the bone," he added. "She says there is no one else to spell her."

Khedran shook his head, and helped the old woman rise from her knees. "Dawn is breaking," he told her. "Tahmine healers will be here shortly, and Farbet will watch over the Princess until then. Go, and get what rest is left to you."

The Duine was awestruck. "Thank you for your kindness, your Lord Highness." She was gone with speed surprising for one so old.

Khedran's mind was far distant from a Duine's awe. "The vultures are gathering, Farbet." There were lines of weariness on the High King's face; Farbet knew he'd had less sleep than the creaky old Duine. "Another army has camped near Cabre in the last day. The Dominion Kings find the upcoming wedding a good excuse to surround Cabre with their own men."

Farbet scowled. "When they realize an attack of the Outsiders..."

Khedran's laugh was short and harsh. "I understand why you would hope they would see the truth. Unfortunately, our enemy is too cunning. He knows the weaknesses of men who have lived so long in peace and comfort, and do not wish for change. I'll have the Temple healers use magic to preserve the giant's body for display, but I doubt that one Outsider's armor will convince the Dominion Kings we are being invaded." He turned back to the window, and Farbet knew he was thinking aloud when he went on. "So strange, this attack on the Princess. Only one of that band was in armor that would mark him alien to Azlatan. Yet the others...all of them dead, and some by their own hand...must have been Outsiders as well."

Khedran began his habitual pacing while Farbet watched thoughtfully. "It was the one in armor who attacked her," he continued. "He was a giant, able to overcome even a Chaine. Why didn't he attack with his allies? Why was it so important to attack or murder the future High Queen?"

Khedran paused at last, his hands clasped behind his back as he regarded Marre's still form. "Then I have immediate word from the Tahmond that she has been violated, when Danon swears she has not. It's all very strange, Farbet. There is magic here, evil magic."

"It's as though the enemy sees our movements," Farbet agreed uneasily. "As though this was planned as an act against you, Highness."

Khedran nodded thoughtfully. After a moment he resumed pacing. "It would be a way to undermine me, to make me a King without a Queen. It's never happened, you know, that a High King has not wed the bride chosen for him." He looked back at Marre. "The Tahmond may hope it would make me the last of my bloodline. Perhaps...at her choice...I already am. That would suit the High Tahmond very well."

He turned slowly, met his loyal soldier's shocked eyes. "In any event she is in danger, and must be guarded. Farbet, you served my father, as your own father served before you. As Compatri I have only you, and Danon, and I need you both, but... I have sent him on a necessary journey for me, and now I must ask you to be Master of the new Queen's Guard. You will choose the most trustworthy for your Legion. You will be charged with the duty to defend Princess Marre...if necessary, to lay down your life for her."

"As I would for you," Farbet answered quietly.

Their eyes met in a warrior's silent understanding, and Khedran relaxed at last, with a loud sigh. He did not thank Farbet, but honored him by accepting his pledge, knowing it forever safe.

Khedran left then, to meet the dawn and the one he had known would come. He stood alone by the sagging open gate outside the old farmhouse. Before him lay the road to his city, paved only with dawn-gilded dust. He heard the bells of Liethe's carriage, and a smile momentarily softened the grim lines of his face, though his green-jeweled eyes never lost their brooding.

Then it was there, upon the road. The carriage bearing the High Tahmine seemed created of pearl and opal, and was drawn by horses of the same color, with eyes the color of the sky. By magic bred, the only sound they made came from the delicate bells on their harness, flashing like diamonds through the drifting veils of their manes.

They floated past him, needing no driver to guide their silent pace, and halted so the carriage door was exactly in his reach. He opened it and bowed his head to the one mortal he would give that obeisance.

Two of her Sisters alighted first, slender beneath their floating opalescent veils.

One of the Sisters whispered "I beg of you not to tire her, Your Highness. She should not have come."

He nodded understanding, and stepped forward to offer his young strength to the High Tahmine. She was like a sparrow in his arms, no more weight or substance. He set her on the ground like the fragile vessel she appeared to be, but she remained upright and drew back her veil to peer up with bright birdlike gaze. Her spirit remained bright, but Khedran realized sadly that her mortal body failed at last, living more in the twilight of Daimaine's cold borders than under the bright sun of day. He knew that she would cross over when her replacement was found, and that he would lose his most powerful ally with her passing. Closer to his heart, he would lose the foster mother he had always loved. His own had died in childbirth.

She smiled and her face pleated with wrinkles. "You were a beautiful child." Her voice was like reeds in the wind. "You are even more beautiful as a man."

"Are you going blind, Mother?"

"I see your smile. I see more than anyone thinks I do." She took his arm with her claw-like hand, openly admiring the hard muscles beneath the black leather. "The beauty of the High Kings is necessary to ensure the people pay attention to their wisdom. Isn't there a place to sit, you liege of Daimaine?" There was nothing querulous in her voice.

He glanced at the Sisters as they went to care for the wounded, and then helped the High Tahmine with unpracticed gentleness to the homely small garden set away from road and house. A wooden bench waited near the overgrown path, where it caught the sun's early rays. He helped her to it, and she arranged her gown and veils closer around her, as though cold even in the sun. "Don't tower over me," she commanded. "Sit down. Are you certain we are alone?"

The garden clearing could hide no listeners. "Quite," he said, lowering to sit at her feet after settling his black cloak over her shoulders. She smiled at this, and on him, cross legged before her like a young boy awaiting a story. Even so relaxed, he was like the great black wolf he was often named. Khedran was a different man in her presence, she being so close to his heart, but the good Tahmine never underestimated him.

"You have heard from the Tahmond?" she asked.

"Yes. At which time I knew you would follow. I am guessing you know what his message was?"

"He is a fool," she announced complacently.

Her dimming eyes did not see the imperceptible release of tension in his long frame, but she sensed it. "You believed she was violated?" she asked sharply.

"The young physician said not. I still don't understand the lie."

"It may have been a mistake. The insufferable High Tahmond is a man without wisdom. He thinks only a body may be violated, not understanding that a mind can be raped as well. Now, tell me what happened. All of it."

He obeyed. He did not spare himself the ignominy of Marre's rejection, or the fact that he had allowed her the death coup as though she had been a soldier in his ranks. The Tahmine said nothing while he spoke, but her gaze sharpened at this, and she studied him carefully.

"It was a strange deed for a maiden," he finished. "But I saw her rage, which perhaps you understand better than I. She never faltered but destroyed him like an insect under her heel."

"That doesn't surprise me. Even women other than your Chaine warriors are often capable of violence, a fact few men realize. I am surprised by your reaction. I do believe you were impressed."

He shrugged. "I admire courage. In man, woman or beast."

She eyed him for a moment, then straightened as though against the heavy burden of his warm cloak on her thin shoulders. The sun had ridden to the level of the house windows, which blazed it back at them through the trees, and she could hear the distant business of soldiers readying for travel.

"Your bride must come with me, Khedran. To heal in the Temple of Liethe, until the wedding. There can be no question of taint upon her if she comes to you from the Temple."

"She may choose not to come to the wedding at all. I gave her that choice."

"You know she will, you arrogant young stallion, or you wouldn't be so complacent about it. Just stay away until I send for you. It seems you already have the ability to irritate her, which I might even find reasonable, but I'll help her to see that her place is in Penumbra."

He changed the subject abruptly. "Even if you didn't see what the Tahmond saw, you had to know something. That's why I knew you would come. Are the Outsiders as invisible to you as they seem to be to them?"

"The Outsiders are like clouds or shadows, too insubstantial for Tahmond magic or even mine. Not invisible, like the Chaine, but nearly so. I think the High King may know more than I about that." Her face turned meaningfully toward the distant soldiers. "My Temple leaves that to the power of Penumbra, and the strong hand of the dark goddess. No, I come to aid your bride, and to warn you that the same cloud hangs now in the north."

"Ordhold?" he asked sharply.

"One of my Sisters walks under that cloud. I may send Liethe's carriage for her soon. I worry about her there."

He rose in agitation at her news, to gaze north as though he could see across the long leagues to the land of his youth's exile. "Did you see my messenger on the northern road? I sent my Compatri, Danon, to find The Chaine and bring her home."

She peered up at him. "I find it odd that you would speak of your home as hers. She is not one of your subjects, Khedran." When he said nothing, she added, "Your Compatri isn't visible even on the outskirts of Ordhold's new shadow."

He sighed, seeming to dismiss it as out of his hands, and turned back to her in apology. "You are weary. I will have Princess Marre brought to your carriage. I thank you for your help, Mother."

"Then perhaps you would grant a boon?"

His eyebrows lifted. "What boon can I grant the High Tahmine?"

"There is another in Penumbra I would like to see. The one which, I am told, you call your brother."

"Why? To see if the legends are true? He's only a child, Mother, and I will not comply if the High Tahmond demands he be tested."

"A test may prove nothing," she said mildly.

"Then why?" he asked.

She looked away. "I fear for him in Penumbra, Khedran. As you said, he is only a child."

"He is under my protection."

Her eyes flickered. "He has a shadow at his shoulder. The same one that dogs your heels. I fear for you both...in Penumbra."

He scowled. "I have no shadow at my heels or anywhere else. Penumbra is the stronghold of my bloodline, given to the first High King by Daimaine herself. There can be no danger there."

"Nevertheless," she sighed, looking suddenly even older. "There is a shadow on you both."

The King's city of Cabre lay tumbled within its walls, high houses crouching over steep crooked streets. Its boundaries stretched for leagues along the rocky shore, foundations climbing over natural rock. In the reign of the seventh and current High King, the landward boundary had been greatly extended by a second great outer wall and garrison, and new dwellings were added constantly, though they seemed unnecessary to the puzzled citizenry.

Penumbra rose dark and stunning from Cabre's sea-south corner. Far to the north, on the opposite corner bounded by the cliffs that marched to the great Rammorth Range, softly gleamed the Temple of Liethe.

Liethe's Temple was part of the cliffs themselves, built into the natural terraces like a giant's stairway from the city. While Penumbra loomed like a dark guardian to the south, the Temple rose with grace and beauty to the north.

The Tahmond Temple squatted within the city itself. It's roof of hammered silver shone like a star among lesser structures. It lay precisely between the halls that gave honor to Daimaine and Liethe, an intentional balance binding those to mortal earth.

In the first flush of dawn the citizens of Cabre awakened to the pearling chimes of Liethe, which held hope and yearning for the promise of each coming day. But in the evening Penumbra answered with the darker bells of Daimaine, as purple twilight settled over sea and city. Silence fell afterwards, a time of meditation and reflection on the deeds of the day and the mortal dark of falling night.

Marre heard the dark bells when she awoke in a high chamber within the Temple of Liethe. She was alone, though as she lay upon the soft bed, she felt she had been watched over. She had no idea how long she had been there.

Still half in a healing trance she rested and listened to the dark tolling bells of Penumbra. In her mind the Star Blade sang again, and a proud High King turned at her call. He had allowed her the right to destroy her enemy and accepted her defiance when she had been prepared for fury.

She pushed away the memory.

Rising, she went to the open window as the last deep tones of the bells drifted into night. The sky changed from deep sapphire to clear amethyst where it met the jeweled plain of the sea. The first stars blossomed silver, and they too had their earthly reflection: even from here she could see Penumbra, its dark towers like a ladder into darkness, its own unknown constellations shifting across its walls. Her eyes fastened upon it, dark-starred against the purple, and she was scarcely aware of the great city between.

The night became black and silver. Daimaine had reclaimed the world.

Jhinn's face rose before her again, not in life but in death. She shuddered, more afraid than she had been that terrible night. Her hand went of its own volition to the pale cloak left beside her bed. Flinging it over her shoulders, she fled to the door with no conscious thought.

She halted in the unfamiliar hallway, pulling the hood over her hair. Opalescent Light drifted around her, reminding her finally of the gentle voice and hands of the High Tahmine, who seemed to carry that magic Light within herself. Marre's heart reached for that comfort as a child to its mother. She would find her. The Mother would banish the haunting faces.

The hall outside her chamber door was short, leading to a flight of steep winding stairs. Marre went down them slowly, the pearled light guiding her bare feet on the cold stone.

She halted twice in amazement at the length of the stair. She realized she had been isolated in the highest chamber of the Temple. Left in safety, she thought. Safe except for her own ghosts, who followed her even here.

The third time she stopped with head tilted, listening. The softest sound had come to her over her noiseless descent. It became the sound of weeping. Not a wailing cry, but muffled despair. Not one voice, but many.

She stood with the open door visible below her, ready to turn and flee back upward. But she was drawn almost against her will, still afraid yet called by the unknown sorrow in those voices.

At the foot of that interminable stair, she saw a pillared cavern. Even the pale magic Light did not reveal its distant walls; the room seemed as unending as the sky. She saw men crowded upon the vast stone floor between the forest of pillars. The weeping came from these. Nearer, it took on a cadence, a measured chant that wove a spell around her mind. Wordlessly it sang despair, and loneliness, and loss. Marre clung to the stone beside the narrow door and listened, staring, feeling a return to the dark place she had escaped by her will. Fear bound her in icy chains. She felt her heart, like a caged bird beating against her ribs.

With a mighty effort, as though the cold chains of fear were physically present upon her body, she drew back into shadow and battled the wild panic in her breast.

Duine. She gave them a name, a reality to cling to. They are only the Duine, she thought. They are the homeless ones, who come to the Temple for mercy. They have nothing to do with me. I am of the Rioch, and of royal lineage. I am neither homeless nor lost.

Am I?

She bowed her head. To her relief the wordless song fell away, like a sigh. She dared open her eyes, was startled to see a hand just within the door, on the floor scant inches from her shadowed feet.

The hand belonged to a man. It was spread wide, to support the weight of its owner, who had pushed himself to a half-sitting position with his back to her. His head was turned to a companion she could not see. By some trick of light she could see clearly the tendons rayed from the strong wrist, and a strange drawing on its back. The drawing depicted the familiar constellation called The Bridle.

"How long?" Its owner was asking his unseen companion. "How long must we hide in these pale caves?"

"Be glad of the Light," was the low response. "Better pale than darkness, and we're fed and safe until it's time to take action."

"I await that as eagerly as you, brother. But I come from the south, not the dark cold north. I miss the sun."

"Patience. We gave an oath. We've been called for a purpose."

Marre drew back carefully, her bare feet silent on bare stone. But at these last words she hesitated at the foot of the stairs, frowning.

That hesitation was her undoing. The man chose that moment to turn and saw her there. He rose swiftly and she froze as he came toward her.

She drew the hood closer about her face so that her eyes were in shadow as he stopped next to her. She watched without understanding as he bowed deeply, then realized he had taken her for one of the Temple's novice Sisters, draped in white.

"Your Sister has already arrived," he told her. "Do you look to join her?"

She nodded. She would feel safe, with one of the Tahmine. Her stomach contracted with fear as he turned to lead her into that vast room, but there was nothing to do but follow.

The Duine within had laid down as though to sleep, many without even a cloak between them and the cold floor. She and her guide threaded their way between them. She saw no women or children, but only men in this underground world. A few snored openly. She felt herself in a nightmare. *They are only Duine*, she reminded herself. *There is no reason to feel threatened.*

After a time...as in a dream, she could not guess how long...she noticed that the Light was brighter, as though nearing some source. She dared to lift her eyes from the carpet of humanity and saw ahead one of the Tahmine, bright in her opalescent veils.

The lambent figure rose from a kneeling position, turning to Marre's guide. "Your brother will rest well now," Marre heard her say to him. "He sleeps Liethe's sleep, and his wounds are mending. But I beg you speak of peace to your people. It does not honor Liethe to fight within her Temple."

Marre's eyes dropped almost involuntarily to her guide's hand, which he fisted while he said humbly, "I will speak to them. It is not the way to thank the goddess for her hospitality."

The Tahmine seemed to notice Marre for the first time. "Your Sister came seeking you," he explained, "so I brought her."

The Tahmine eyed her. "I don't think it's me she seeks."

"The High Tahmine." Marre spoke quickly. "I must see her right away. Please, Sister."

"You have come to the wrong place. There are only Duine here."

"So many!" Marre looked around her and shivered. "Has Liethe called them?"

At this the man looked at her sharply, as though he could pierce the shadow under her hood.

The Sister lifted her chin. "The goddess would not so unbalance the natural order. This is the fault of a changing world, the unnatural changes wrought by those they call the Chaine, and men weak to the will of Chaos. The old values are failing, Princess of Athea. These are the harmless ones, whose Rioch no longer honor the rightful ways."

Marre drew back at the words and tone, and the Tahmine looked apologetic. "Forgive me, Princess. It's not my place nor my need to place blame, but only to serve these unfortunate people who cannot help themselves."

Marre realized the man next to her was staring and felt a return of pride with her revealed identity. She let the hood fall back from her face, determined to shed fear with its shadow. "These are all men. Are there others, Sister?"

"The Temple has many levels. Women and children are sheltered elsewhere."

"Why are you here?" the man asked Marre suddenly.

The Tahmine turned on him, while Marre stood astonished by his boldness. "She is here at the invitation of the High Tahmine," the Sister scolded. "To rest and heal, like you and these others. The Temple is home to all Liethe's children. Come now, Princess. These people need their rest."

Marre lifted a hand. "To the High Tahmine," she reminded.

The Sister halted momentarily, then drew Marre away. "I cannot." She spoke in a low voice, meant only for Marre's ears. "You should not be here. There was a Sister assigned—it is her cloak you wear, I think. I must find her. We must not alarm these." She indicated the Duine. "The High Tahmine is very ill. The Temple is disturbed enough. Please return to your chambers."

Marre hesitated, looking back at the man who had questioned her so boldly. She remembered the words: "We have been called for a purpose." She thought of the symbol on his hand.

All was silent as she and the Sister moved back through the sea of sleeping Duine.

CHAPTER 13

Ardren, Dominion King of Athea, was miserable.

His daughter had vanished within the Temple of Liethe, beyond his reach; his wife lay abed, and did not speak, though the Healers told him her pain was gone. He hated this miserable city, without comfort or friend or family or his own wide green lands. And now he looked at his High King and blinked in further misery, without understanding.

Khedran stared back implacably.

"Forgive me," Ardren said. "Never has my loyalty to the High King been questioned. But I must question your understanding of this situation, though I would not dishonor you."

Khedran chuckled softly, a sound Ardren found chilling. He stiffened himself against it, as he had against this barren room just off the sacred Temple of Daimaine. Though the rest of the palace known as Penumbra was quite beautiful, he had thought of Marre with sadness upon entering here, disliking the fact she would have to live anywhere near this cold austerity. The tall western window was undraped, the fireplace unlit, the furniture stark...what there was of it. The room was as grey as the sounding sea beneath the open window.

"That was well and carefully spoken," Khedran said. "But...King Ardren, can you truly separate my words and actions from my person? I find that an admirable defense for maintaining sanity in an insane world." He leaned forward in his chair, until scant distance separated them. "I understand the situation very well," he went on, his voice now as hard as the stone walls. "I am not a popular High King. I am far different from my ancestors because I have to be. I seek survival of my people, which too many are unable or unwilling to realize is threatened."

"No!" Ardren cried. "It is a Duine Anzihi trick! Please, you must realize that. Phaelon would not allow such an event to happen. It cannot be invaders from outside of Azlatan."

Khedran leaned back, sighed wearily. "The Duine Anzihi are no longer a power in this land. They were defeated when I returned from exile, and haven't been seen since. You search for a known enemy, King Ardren, because you fear the unknown. I can understand that. The darkness ahead is a fearsome thing. Yet it must be faced."

"The High Tahmond would warn us."

"The High Tahmond is blind. Even the High Tahmine is blind to the Outsiders, but she, being both wise and honorable, has admitted it. He, being who he is, will not."

"Then why hasn't the High Tahmine come forward?" Ardren didn't realize there was a note of triumph in his own voice, until he saw Khedran's strange eyes narrow in warning.

"She is ill. The Sisters have sent word that she is resting, and she is old beyond mortal years. But I know her. She will find a way, even if she must fight the Deathqueen herself. She will come forward."

Ardren chewed his lip in confused apprehension, his spirit torn. Khedran turned his head to stare into the empty fireplace. His profile in the cold light was made of marble. Ardren thought again of his daughter and felt a delicate sadness.

"I am glad you requested this audience," Khedran continued after a moment. "It's a mark of your integrity that you come to me with your doubts, rather than listen to those gathering around Cabre. It's no wonder you speak of a Duine Anzihi plot, for Azlatan was changed by them. My father's death was the end of an age,

King Ardren. It was a good age, a secure and peaceful one for served and servant."

He turned his emerald gaze back to the Dominion King. "It has ended. My people yearn for a time that is gone, denying that its ending was written in the blood of a High King. The Duine Anzihi were his murderers, yet they are not the danger that we are facing now. Can't you see that?"

"No," Ardren whispered honestly.

Silence, one beat. "You have seen the body of the giant who attacked your daughter?" Khedran asked.

Ardren shivered. "How could I miss it? You have it on display like–like a hunting trophy!–in the sacred temple of Daimaine."

Khedran's smile was cold. "Can you think of a more fitting place?"

"Yes!" Ardren found his courage, his inner turmoil turned to outrage. And a step beyond that: betrayal. "Yes," he repeated, breathing heavily. "Buried. Decently buried and gone. It is carrion, nothing more, and only brings disgust and dishonor to Penumbra, Daimaine's Temple."

"Tread carefully," Khedran warned softly. "Penumbra is my home, and I am the Tahmond of the goddess Daimaine."

"As all High Kings have been. But never before..."

"Never before," Khedran interrupted, "has a High King faced an invasion of Outsiders."

"Unproved, I tell you!"

Khedran made no response this time but stared back silently. Ardren stiffened at the shockingly brilliant emerald fire in the High King's eyes.

It banked to a simmering feral glow, and he realized he had met the Black Wolf.

"Did the others ask you to come?" Khedran demanded.

"Others? If you mean the Dominion Kings, the answer is no. I came on my own accord, as you said, out of my own loyalty to your office and because my daughter..."

"But they have approached you," Khedran interrupted again. "And you have been among them."

Ardren now knew seeping dread. "Yes," he admitted.

"Give me their message."

"I told them I would bear no messages." Ardren hated the tremor in his own voice and swallowed. "I told them that their complaints should be brought to you for resolution."

"Tell me their complaints."

Ardren felt a disunion of loyalties, a division in his spirit. But he responded to his High King. "They do not like the creation of your army. They feel you are stealing the young sons of Azlatan who should serve their own Dominions. They believe you fill your coffers with crops and supplies more useful in their own lands. Quite frankly, Your Highness, many are concerned about your garrisons within the Dominions, though I have personally found they ease the administration of Athea."

"But you see their point."

Ardren blinked. "Yes."

"Continue."

At this, outrage returned. "The half-Duine boy. You defy the High Tahmond himself, keeping him here!"

"They are all fools," Khedran said coolly, "nattering over a broken bowl, while their house burns around their ears. I thank you for coming to me, Ardren. But I had hoped that you, at least, could understand the enormity of what is happening at our borders."

He is insufferable, Ardren decided. He is arrogant and willful as Chaos. Perhaps he is mad, as many think. Ah, my poor daughter!

He rose at Khedran's dismissal to leave the cold grey room, Marre's phantom on his heels.

The Annals of Azlatan said that there was somewhere in the world a likeness of each of the gods, so that they might be known to anyone wise enough to behold them. The location of such likenesses remained unknown for two of the four. But since all mortals must recognize Daimaine through Death, or perhaps even through Justice, her image was there for all to see. It stood within the depths of Penumbra itself, in the Temple of Daimaine, where the sun never came. It was the heart and core of Penumbra, and here the Nightstone lived always, constellations wheeling across the walls and arches of that enormous chamber that also served as the command hall of the High King.

Daimaine's statue stood seven times higher than a man, with the stars brightening as they climbed her height, until at last they blossomed to silver flame within the black glass of her hair. Her face was living moonlight, so terribly beautiful that men looked away after one frantic glance, and for long moments after bore the afterimage of her sign: the blazing sickle she wore upon her forehead, both moon and scythe of souls.

A man stood dwarfed at the base of her towering Nightstone statue. He was not gazing at her, however, but at the magically preserved corpse laid like a sacrifice at her feet. He seemed mesmerized by the dead giant's mutilated face, by the strange armor.

The watcher was Bannon, Dominion King of Tesna. His was a small Dominion upon Azlatan's eastern border. It was a rather poor Dominion, and this was only his second visit to Cabre. He did not pretend that he had come to celebrate a wedding.

He turned at the distant sound of an arrival, his narrow face alert. Bannon was not a handsome man, with drooping eyes set to the sides of his head and his mouth an unhappy short line beneath a bladed nose. But there was intelligence in his dark eyes, and he straightened as a lightless door opened and a tall man came through, visible in the starfire and moonlight gracing this fearful hall.

Bannon recognized the wolflike walk and plain black garb of the High King. More than that, there was his Gift-given aura of presence. He needed no crown or scepter.

Khedran stood for a long moment, looking up at the Deathqueen's terrible beauty as few men could dare. There was an angry defiance in his stance that Bannon found puzzling and even uncomfortable to watch. Nevertheless, he made up his mind to speak. The Dominion King cleared his throat and spoke softly, knowing his voice would carry in this silent place of stone. "I see our enemy here. I wish those outside the city's walls could see as clearly."

Khedran's gaze fell from Daimaine's unearthly beauty to find a subject far less beautiful than most. Bannon bowed deeply, recognizing what a chasm he had dragged his King across.

"Bannon!" Khedran exclaimed, and the Dominion King was surprised to hear the warmth in the voice that spoke it. Khedran strode toward him with a glad welcome upon his face.

Bannon answered his handclasp with bushy eyebrows upraised. "I am honored by your memory, Your Highness. We met but once."

"When I ascended to rule seven years ago. But others have spoken highly of you... including my father. And I do not quickly forget a friend. Even at my ascension, not all the Dominion Kings were friendly."

"You make swift judgments."

"I have to." A brief shadow crossed Khedran's face. "I find, occasionally, that I am wrong." He straightened. "I received your message. You said you had important news for me."

Bannon looked back at the Outsider's corpse. "I heard about him when I arrived this morning, and had the message sent right away. The idiot who told me didn't believe the evidence of his own eyes. It amazes me how people pick and choose what parts of history they want to believe in. The existence of the Outsiders is clearly documented in the Annals as those Phaelon did not allow into Azlatan, who serve the goddess Chaos. This is not the first Outsider I have seen." He turned back to Khedran. "There is more to my story. I would rather not continue it in here."

Khedran nodded in understanding, and led him from the Temple.

They went through three doors, none of which would open at the same time in order to protect the darkness of Daimaine's

Temple. Each door was guarded and handled with precision. Khedran never broke stride. The last door opened upon the chamber where Ardren had held his frustrating audience.

Here Khedran crossed and lifted his hand to the opposite wall. The cold grey stone opened soundlessly to a sunlit corridor beyond. Khedran smiled at Bannon's surprise. "This Sacristy is as much Daimaine's as the Temple. It is left as austere as Justice must be, for that reason. Your journey and your message are arduous enough. We will find a warmer part of Penumbra to talk."

"Thank you." Bannon moved into the wide corridor, noting the narrow west windows that stretched its distant length. Peering out as he fell into step with Khedran, he saw the sea so near it roared against the outer wall and lapped at the window-ledges. "Is this the lowest level of the palace?" he asked loudly over the sea-thunder.

"Yes," Khedran called back. "Sometimes the tide almost overflows into this corridor. The stair called the King's Way climbs above us to my own quarters in the west tower. But we won't have that far to climb."

The hall was long, and full of the sea-smell unfamiliar to Bannon. His long shanks easily matched Khedran's stride, though he slouched a little as though it were wrong to be taller than the High King. He pictured them together in his mind's eye, as he had a habit of doing: the awkward stork, and the hunting wolf.

He was very aware of the restless strength of the man he walked beside. He was still surprised at the friendliness, more so as he recalled Khedran's earlier mood as he gazed at Daimaine's statue. Bannon studied people, now finding his High King the most fascinating of all subjects. He recalled rumors of madness, and a pet wolf he had thought tamed, which had killed his best hunting-dog. *Was that madness, or nature?*

They left a stairway to enter a walled garden. Plants climbed in green profusion, jeweled with bright flowers. A single great tree provided a high verdant roof over a pond where golden fish darted. The very air swam with green light. "Is this magic?" Bannon asked in delight, looking around.

Khedran smiled at his reaction. "Not at all. It used to be open to the sky, but there is now a roof of green glass above the branches. It's my favorite place when the day is grey."

Bannon thought of the dark and terrifying glory below them, felt glad of this more earthly and understandable beauty. He thought again of the defiance he had witnessed earlier when the High King had looked up at Daimaine's statue. "I like this room. There is less need to feel humble here, isn't there? I'm guessing this is your design."

Khedran looked surprised, then laughed openly. Bannon wondered at this swift mood change. *Either he is truly mad*, he thought, *or he simply revels in his wolfhood.*

The High King was still chuckling when he answered. "Yes, it is. And I have never been accused of humility. Nor has anyone but The Chaine ever analyzed me so openly before."

"Forgive my forwardness, Your Highness."

"No, I won't. I enjoy plain speaking; I was raised on it. You surprised me, is all. The Chaine and her sharp tongue have been away too long. Come, there's a table and seating here. You have had a long journey. You must be tired, and most probably hungry waiting for me all day."

Bannon gladly lowered himself to the bench flanking the simple stone table. Khedran had vanished at his own mention of food, and Bannon awaited his return with some amusement and a warmth he recognized as pleasure. He had a newfound admiration for his King. He meditated on this. *I loved my pet wolf, too,* he remembered.

So he refused to be surprised when Khedran set down a tray filled with food and took the bench across from him. "There's even some wine," Khedran said, placing a pitcher by the tray.

"What, no rare hummingbird's tongues to eat?"

"Those are only for our stoutest warriors," Khedran smiled at the jest. "Our hummingbirds are big as horses, and their tongues are the heaviest part of them. Like some Dominion Kings I know. Let's eat, and I will hear your tale."

"It may sound unbelievable," Bannon noted, and there was silence as they both munched, Khedran feeding morsels to a small ginger cat that appeared from the shrubbery. Bannon knew he was being given time to collect his thoughts, which had indeed become scattered by new discoveries.

"I remember your return to Cabre very well," he began, as Khedran continued feeding the cat. "There was some dissension when you took leadership, because you immediately revoked some laws made during your absence, and reinstated others."

"The ones they call Chaine laws," Khedran recalled.

"Yes. The Guilds in Tesna still complain about them, although I have seen an improvement in their wares since competition was introduced. Some of the new methods of making things...methods sold to them by the Chaine...have made their lives easier."

"Was the price abominable?" Khedran asked in amusement.

"Of course. The Chaine aren't noted for humility either, are they? Anyway, the subject of my story has more to do with a law I thought you had revoked."

Khedran looked up, waiting.

"There had been a two-year drought during your absence," Bannon continued. "It hit several of the Dominions very hard, including mine, and my neighbor's. The stores of Cabre were used to alleviate the shortage of crops in several Dominions."

"A shortage I still question." Khedran frowned. "Your Tesna had reserves enough, as I recall, and never took advantage of the High Tahmond's generous offer from my treasury."

"Oh, the shortage was real enough in some Dominions. Druna, which neighbors my Tesna, was hard hit. I saw this with some surprise, as I had considered Dominion King Rebran to be a prudent man. But I get ahead of my story."

Khedran was finally beginning to show some impatience. "If you're leading up to the revocation of 'surplus' distribution, you are correct in thinking I stopped the practice immediately. The stores are there for a purpose which no High King has ever had to explain to his subjects. Neither shall I."

Bannon used that opening to share one of the insidious rumors that disturbed him. "Some of those who are camped outside your city have quoted you as saying the people are there to support you, not you the people."

The emerald eyes narrowed. "Hummingbird tongues," he reminded.

"Your point is well taken. Anyway, I saw the danger...eating being a mortal habit, and eating for free being a habit almost as hard to break. But I do not think your ruling had the effect you thought it did. Once the supply lines were opened, I don't believe all of them were cut."

"Who was taking supplies?"

"Duine Anzihi."

Khedran blinked. "Proof?"

"The word of a dead Dominion King. Rebran told me he had discovered a cache a week before he was killed."

"By the Duine Anzihi?"

"Yes. Along with others, who dress like Daimaine's dead guest."

Khedran frowned. "Let me make sure I understand you. First, you believe the Duine Anzihi have been siphoning supplies from the Dominions."

"Hindsight being clearest, I believe that was Rebran's original problem, as he seemed as puzzled by the shortage as I."

"So, you believe the Duine Anzihi had been stealing supplies for some time... and that they are somehow in collusion with the Outsiders. What made you suspect them?"

"Several things. Among them: I have no Bonded Duine, unlike my friend King Rebran, and so manage my own affairs. Therefore, I had no shortage. But Rebran was a hunter, a sportsman, with a trusted Bonded Duine and little patience for details."

"I hear no facts."

"True. But the drought and its aftermath frightened him a little. He watched his reserves closely for a time. A longer time, apparently, than his Duine thought he would. Another shortage developed after Stareven harvest. Suspicious, Rebran let his Duine believe he had left to hunt and doubled back to follow him instead. He found his supplies at the end of that ride."

"What made him distrust his own Bonded Duine?"

Bannon drew a piece of parchment from his tunic, set it down between them. On it was drawn the lines of stars depicting The Bridle constellation.

"His Duine had this mark on his hand. Rebran told me he had seen it before and was troubled to see it on the hand of his own Duine. He told me he was sure it was the sign of the Duine Anzihi. Have you seen it before, Your Highness?"

"Once." Khedran straightened; his jeweled eyes held rage, and a painful memory. "It was on the knife that killed my father. Tell me about the connection to the Outsiders."

Bannon nodded, troubled. "As you may have gathered, Rebran and I were friends. He came to me when he discovered his Duine's secret. Rebran was not a man used to duplicity. I will admit his continued surveillance was my idea, based on the symbol's strange existence. He was unsure how to proceed.

"I knew, Your Highness, that you had to be told. But first I wanted to see this cache for myself. That was my undoing. Rebran and I rode together, with a small band of soldiers, to view the scene. Too few soldiers. The Outsiders were there ahead of us, depleting the Duine Anzihi stores on their own behalf. I was wounded early in what must have been a short battle and left for dead beneath my horse. I crawled out when I regained consciousness and found everything gone and my soldiers killed."

"What became of the Duine?"

"His body was next to the man he had betrayed, his knife buried in his own belly. Out of grief, I expect. They had grown up together."

"Were any of the Outsiders killed?"

"Yes. I left their bodies to rot in the cave where the stores had been hidden."

Khedran's fist was clenched next to the drawing. "Did any of them share the same symbol as the Duine?"

"Yes. There were three, wearing the same armor as the corpse in your Temple."

"Dark or fair? The one below is as blond as any Duine."

"You didn't look closely enough, Your Highness. I found the same mystery in the cave. The hair is light, but it is not the natural color. It's been altered. I believe if you remove his garb, you will find his body hair is quite dark."

Khedran stared without comprehension for a moment, then took a deep breath as though drawing himself back to calm. "So. Would a Rioch bleach his hair to look like a Duine, and don the armor of an Outsider? A mystery, Bannon. More than one. I had thought the Duine Anzihi vanished." He looked down at the parchment. "Yet this proves me wrong."

Bannon was silent, waiting.

Khedran continued after a moment's thought. "The Dominion Kings will view this as proof of a Duine Anzihi resurrection. That's what they're claiming already, even without your new evidence. Bannon, is there any proof at all... besides the symbol...to show they are doing this for the Outsiders? The Rioch provide for the Duine. Hiding food and supplies for those who would invade Azlatan hardly makes sense. By all the gods, even I find that hard to believe!"

"I wish I had more evidence for you."

Khedran leaned back. "You obviously passed through the camps of the Dominion Kings on your way in to Cabre. Some of them hope to bring me before Phaelon, Bannon."

"Yes. I was approached by Eleban, the fool. But they must convince both the High Tahmond and the High Tahmine that they have just cause before they can bring a High King to Council. And Phaelon's Law requires that seven Dominion Kings also agree before a High King can be brought to Council. There is a lot of complaining, Your Highness, but none but Eleban are insane enough to consider doing that. And they would certainly not do it before you have an heir."

Khedran looked surprised, then thoughtful. "Of course. If I die without an heir, the bloodline dies with me. That would play havoc with their beliefs about the natural order of Azlatan, would it not?"

Bannon looked uncomfortable. "Quite. Won't the Tahmond know as soon as the Queen is impregnated? If certain Dominion Kings have their way, your son would not be defended by The Chaine."

"I'm sure The Chaine and her people would die shortly after I do, if those certain Dominion Kings have their way. She, of course, would have other plans," he added grimly.

"You mentioned she has been gone a long time. Perhaps..."

"No. She's no coward, Bannon, and she does not break oath. She's on a journey on my behalf, and if she doesn't return, it will be because she is..." Bannon watched curiously at the King's momentary hesitation, followed by a shake of his head. "It would be because she cannot," Khedran finished. "At least now I know I have some time, that they won't attempt to call Council until after the wedding."

"Which is when? Everyone is waiting for the announcement now that your bride has arrived."

Khedran hesitated, then sighed. "The Princess of Athea is presently a guest of the High Tahmine."

Bannon was sure there was more to tell but was too wise to ask. "I hear the High Tahmine is ill," he said instead. "They can't call Council without her, either."

"Or her replacement," Khedran confirmed. "She's very old. Bannon, I've troubled you after your long journey, but I have more questions. Then I hope you will allow me to order a room for you, here in Penumbra."

"I am honored." *Wouldn't turn that down*, he thought. *Things are too interesting!* "I will of course be at your disposal should you need me, though I have brought no army, nor do I have one to send for. The garrison you established in Tesna has taken care of what military needs I have."

"Bannon, did you tell your garrison commander about the Outsiders?"

"I did. Commander Tyran happens to be my nephew, trained by your Black Guard, and returned to us even smarter than when he left. He's a good man, and I can be objective about relatives. Under the circumstances he entrusted me to deliver this message and awaits your command in that regard. Meantime he has secured the cache and its evidence, strengthened the border patrol, and ordered his men to silence to avoid a panic."

"Excellent. Do you know where the Outsiders could have crossed the border?"

"Tyran said he has an idea about that."

"Your border has already been compromised. Tyran needs more men, seasoned soldiers. Damn it all!"

"I've seen many of your Black Guard here in Cabre. Haven't you any to spare him?"

Khedran looked bitter. "He already has my best. All the border garrisons have my best, but they are stretched too thin, because I do not have the horses needed for reinforcements. In addition, many of Cabre's troops are green, called in with their training incomplete–thanks to the Dominion Kings who surround us, who have left their own lands empty except for my Guard. Damn them! If the Outsiders should cross now, in any numbers..."

Bannon paled, realizing how many things Khedran juggled, and the danger should he drop even one. Khedran saw his reaction and gave him his grim smile. "We can only hope the Outsiders don't guess the situation."

"Surely the Dominion Kings would not attack Cabre," Bannon exclaimed. "You have no need to defend your city. Even if the troops are on foot or green, couldn't they be sent to reinforce your border garrisons?"

Khedran shook his head. "Don't be so sure of Cabre's safety," he warned. "Those Dominion soldiers are not camped out there for mere show. But I would take the chance, except for one thing. You saw the Outsider. Taller and more powerful than a Chaine, no matter what race he really is. The armor he wears weighs more than a normal man could carry. He defeated a Chaine and could easily take on several of my unmounted soldiers at once. The horses are the key, Bannon. There aren't enough for a third of my Legions. And far less of those are trained for war." Khedran was on his feet now and pacing in a way that Bannon guessed was characteristic.

"Is there nothing we can do?" Bannon asked.

"There's still Ordhold. I hope. Bannon, I'll have you seen to your room now. You will rest, and then I will accept your offer of help. I need you near me, to watch and listen, and advise. I juggle too much; I fear a slip. You give me hope."

"You honor me deeply." Bannon watched Khedran's prowling a moment. "My King...do you ever rest? There are rumors that you even walk at night, in your sleep."

Khedran glanced up, lifted an eyebrow. "Hummingbird tongues," he reminded. "Please, let's find your room."

Chapter 14

The sky was dark iron, lowering over Cabre like a sieging army while the real armies swelled around her walls. The city people scurried about in their furs, trying to continue business as usual while rumors ran like sewage from street to street.

There was silence from Phaelon's Temple. The High Tahmine was ill, perhaps dying, and no replacement had been named. A witch and the prophesied Forbidden Child lived in Penumbra, and the High King was possibly quite mad. No wonder the wedding, awaited these many years, was silently delayed while the storm gathered.

Marre stood at her window in the Temple of Liethe, and watched the clouds shred themselves upon the highest towers of Penumbra. Her adventure of the night before had her very uneasy, like a dream that wouldn't fade. Her ghosts haunted her still, and one of them lived in that palace.

A young novice came in with a tray, saying "I brought your breakfast, knowing how awfully long you've been asleep." The smell of fresh bread made Marre's mouth water.

"You're right. It must be two days since I have eaten."

"Far longer than that, Princess. I've watched over you this last turn of the moon."

"That cannot be! We weren't a day's ride from Cabre when...when..."

The girl blinked at her. "You were hurt, and you slept and slept, and the Sisters said Liethe had touched you or I would have thought you dead. But you healed!"

Marre realized her throat didn't hurt, and she knew there were other injuries which she no longer felt. She was whole and strong, save for memories too near to be a month old.

"A mirror," she demanded.

"Over there, Princess." The novice continued laying out breakfast while she watched Marre askance.

Marre saw her hair in disarray, tumbling free over the pale shoulders of her nightclothes. But her throat and face were unblemished, her slim body straight and unhurt. Further, her face reflected none of her inner torment. In fact, it glowed with health, and even the persistent dark circles under her eyes were gone.

She snapped at the novice. "I want to see one of the Tahmine. Now!"

"Now? But..."

"You heard me." Marre swung around to glare at the girl, her hair settling like a dark cloud over her shoulders. "A month! They had no right. Call them now."

The novice fled, and Marre's fury was unchanged by the fear on the child's face.

Jhinn has been gone from me for a month. She flew from that thought to the next. *It must be Starfall by now. And has Khedran known for a month that I lay bewitched?* For so it seemed to her, that she had been entranced against her will, and lost a month of her life.

She found herself eying the laden table. Muttering to herself, she picked up a small wedge of cheese. Moments later she was sitting to do full justice to the simple feast spread there.

The novice didn't return until she was finished, and the Tahmine with her eyed the empty plates with satisfaction. "I trust you feel better now," was her greeting.

"My hunger is gone, but not my anger. How dare you..."

"We did not," the Tahmine interrupted gently. "It was the choice of Liethe, Princess, and no mortal. We were as surprised as you must be."

Marre heard the ring of truth, and subsided. The full stomach helped too. Nor could she believe the gentle Sisters could commit an act so vile as to hold her hostage for a month.

"Could you do nothing?" she asked. The Tahmine merely shook her head.

"What about my parents? Are they well? My mother was ill."

"All is well with them. They could not come to see you, because those under special care are in areas of the Temple closed to all but the Tahmine. The High Tahmine had left clear instructions for your treatment before she fell ill, and that meant leaving you to Liethe's care. But your parents have been kept aware of your condition. Would you like to see them?"

"Not right this minute. Has...has there been word from the High King?" *Has he asked about me?* she thought with burning cheeks.

"There has been nothing from Penumbra," the Sister replied. "I assume that His Highness, like the Sisters, waits for some sign from the High Tahmine. It has been a most difficult time."

"For whom? For the Temple, or all Cabre? There was talk of Council."

The Sister threw a glance at the novice, who had eyes like saucers. "We do not have the time, nor is it our place, to listen to rumor. We serve Liethe. That is all."

Marre turned away with an exclamation. *Why do I care?* She asked herself. *He freed me, there in the cold moonlight. But Father would never allow me home. I belong to the Temple, now, and the affairs of the world don't matter. I am safe here. I will ask asylum, and I will never have to leave.*

She realized she was shivering. "I'd like to have my clothes brought to me. I must go. I must see the High Tahmine."

The Sister signaled the novice to fetch the garments. She was watching Marre with concern. "I will take you. But you must understand she will probably be sleeping. Are you sure you want to go now?" This last as Marre pushed at her hair with trembling hands. Marre nodded, her mind racing.

She dressed quickly in the gown brought to her, unaware of color or fit, and didn't bother to bind her long hair. The Tahmine led Marre down the stairs. Marre realized shortly that she had passed several doors in her strange journey the night before and found new reason to wonder at herself.

The Sister turned off, and again Marre entered the Light that pervaded the Temple. They were in a corridor, and then there were more stairs, and another landing below, showing only the plain grey light of the stormy day.

There was a man in black waiting on the landing.

Marre felt her heart thud once, savagely, before she recognized him for what he was not. But she had halted her descent in that moment, and the Tahmine looked back at her questioningly.

Marre didn't move, still staring at the soldier.

He wore the black of Khedran's Guard, but with an emerald star and sickle moon at his shoulder. His cape was lined with green satin. His hair and beard were iron and old silver, but it was the uniform that she read, and the emblem.

"That arrogant bastard."

"Princess?"

"The High King dares too much. The Master of the Queen's Guard has always been the Queen's choice. It is an honor for the warrior who accepts, and he serves for life, whether hers or his. Rhiathe's Guard Master was honorably discharged at her death, and it isn't Khedran's place to choose mine!"

The Tahmine followed her gaze, but chose to ignore her words. "He seems to be a kind man. He has a room here on the main floor and has helped the Sisters with simple tasks here. It must be a lonely vigil, but his only complaint has been that he is not allowed upstairs to watch over you."

"As though I need to be watched over in Liethe's Temple! He is not my guardian, Sister, but my captor. I thought I was given free choice, by his Liege and King, but apparently Khedran is not a man of his word. Either I go to him, or I am not to be allowed to leave this prison. There is no choice in that bargain."

Marre saw the Sister's shock even through the veil. "I'm sorry," she quickly recanted her unintended insult. "To you this is home. I do not have your calling. I just realized...I could not bear it, to be cloistered here."

The Tahmine made a graceful motion, as though to brush that aside. "Yet apparently you would refuse your destined title as well. What is it you do want, Princess?"

Marre's throat hurt. She saw Jhinn again, in moon and shadow, and remembered a dying flame that was her own spirit.

"To live my life," she managed. "Freely, as I wish, not as...as some destiny would have me live it. Freedom is being able to choose."

The Tahmine studied her as though trying to understand. "There are those of us who would disagree. What do you do with such freedom once you have it? Without destiny or duty to give you purpose, what is there to live for?"

Marre thought again of Jhinn. "One could choose one's duty."

The Sister made no reply to this, but started down the stairs again, and Marre followed. She saw the soldier look up as they neared, and snap to swift attention as he recognized her.

She strode by, unheeding. Only at the edge of her vision did she glimpse alert blue eyes that gave the lie to the grey in his mane, eyes rayed not by age, but by sun or laughter. She refused to acknowledge him.

She hung back as they neared the chamber of the High Tahmine.

What is here? What is that presence?

Her steps faltered. There was a Shadow here, instead of Light. *No one else feels it.* "Stop."

The Tahmine turned back at the faint plea. "Is something wrong, Princess?"

"I shouldn't bother her now," Marre heard herself say. She was being warned from this place by something she could not see, could not fight. "She will be sleeping. I'm sorry, Sister..."

Weakness washed through her. The Tahmine gave her a steadying shoulder, helped her to a long bench down the hall where she sank, sick and dizzy.

A heavy warmth slid over her shoulders. Green satin against her skin, the lining of her Guard's black cloak. She did not look up. His boots were within vision of her lowered head. Shining boots, but worn. A true soldier's footwear.

"Thank you, sir." It was the Tahmine who spoke to the soldier. Marre raised neither head nor voice. "Will you be so kind, please, as to go out and guard the door? I want no interruptions for a few moments, while I care for the Princess. She rose too swiftly, I think, from her sickbed."

The boots moved away. Marre looked up slowly, to see the Tahmine had thrown back her veils and was watching her steadily.

"That was not a spell of sickness," the Tahmine said, "but something else, wasn't it? I don't wonder at your troubled mind. I cannot believe that Liethe would want you sacrificed on the King's dark altar."

Marre stared.

The Sister continued, placing a cool hand over Marre's in comfort. "You question your destiny. So would I if destiny would mate me to evil. But don't you see? You have been freed. You have only to accept what is given you."

"I'm not sure I understand you, Sister."

"There will be no wedding, of course. You will not have to choose between the Temple and Penumbra. It is the only explanation for what has happened...the sleep given to you by Liethe, and the silence of the High Tahmine. Both delay the wedding. The gods move in their own courses, Princess, and their intent is obvious. The Black Wolf will fall."

"The Black Wolf." Marre repeated it slowly, like a lesson. She withdrew her hand from the Tahmine's. "Isn't that what they call Khedran? How will he fall?"

"Only Phaelon knows. We wait, while the Dominion Kings gather their armies outside the walls of Cabre. The Wolf will be the last of his bloodline, Princess. His father cast off Phaelon's Law, and even Daimaine must read the judgement this time, as Khedran has brought the fruit of evil into her own house."

Marre shook her head. Never in history had the Sisters of Liethe spoken against a High King. This was incomprehensible. She thought again of the unknown presence guarding the door of the High Tahmine.

"Daimaine?" she wondered aloud, thinking of the mysterious Shadow.

"Daimaine has returned to Penumbra, after these thousand years of peace." The Tahmine's voice was soft, but the words struck Marre like cold steel. "Khedran has been seen within his halls, battling the darkness himself while Cabre sleeps. Some believe him mad, struggling with his own dark dreams; possibly it is no other than the Deathqueen that he fights. Daimaine gives to the High King this final honor, to try to win him from Chaos in these last days. Yet even she must bow to the will of Phaelon in the end. We know what the outcome must be. Even the Tahmond are silent. We watch and wait."

They have forgotten something, Marre thought suddenly. *So had I.*

"The Outsiders!" she cried. "While you all watch and wait, and the Dominion Kings gather around Cabre, what is being done about the Outsiders?"

"There are none, of course. Phaelon gave Azlatan to us, promising..."

"But I was attacked by one of them!"

"Please, Princess, you must calm yourself. All is not as it seems. Khedran sees too well the end of his reign and seeks to convince us of an enemy who does not exist. He is protecting himself."

"I was attacked by one of them, I tell you. If not for my Chaine guardian, I would have been killed."

"What better evidence for Khedran to offer, than the life of his promised bride? And since you did not die, he seeks to keep you prisoner here, as you said yourself."

Is that why he freed me? She was seeing him again, turning away from her, cold as the moonlight on Jhinn's dead body. *Am I useless to him, living? Is that why he let me destroy my attacker, who might have told us where he came from...*

She moaned, and buried her face in her hands, suspended by shock and disbelief. This end to her despised destiny she had never foreseen. She tried to calm her shattered mind.

No. I should be happy. I will be free. Free to live my own life at last.... if there is a life. If there is an Azlatan, without a High King to lead it. What then, when the Black Wolf has fallen?

She had only her own fear for answer.

"They will not wait much longer," Bannon reported sadly. "The Dominion Kings believe you are purposely delaying the wedding. There are murmurs that the direct bloodline is tainted, because of Allasar, and perhaps it is time to install one of your distant relatives in your place."

Khedran did not answer him immediately. Yet Bannon was sure his King had heard, so he remained silently waiting.

If Khedran was a man who could be pitied, Bannon thought, *I would do so now. But you do not pity a force of nature, a power as elemental as storm or stone.* That, he had learned, was the spirit of Khedran. He had come to know his King well in these last weeks. Knowing any man well normally meant knowing his weaknesses, but Bannon had yet to find any, and suspected this was a sin for which Khedran's enemies would never forgive him.

If Bannon's report had disturbed the High King, Khedran didn't show it. He sat very still in his chair by the fireplace, fully dressed despite the early hour of Bannon's appearance. The firelight was a soft diffusion in the black velvet of his hair, his brilliant eyes shaded by lowered lashes. Khedran studied the fire, as though he could find answers in the flames. His hands rested precisely on the chair-arms, unmoving as the stern line of his lips.

"They know you are staying with me in Penumbra," Khedran said finally. "If they offered such a plot in your presence, it was not murmured. Do not seek to spare me, Bannon. They have challenged. Were there Tahmond who heard?"

"Yes. The High Tahmond himself."

"Who is their choice for my replacement?"

"It's still undecided, of course. But the consensus rests with Ardren of Athea."

Bannon was surprised to see a flinch, a movement of self-reproach. It puzzled him, that Khedran would even ask the question. He did not believe there was room in Khedran for defeat, for thoughts of who would follow if he fell.

Khedran looked up, caught the question in Bannon's eyes. The High King smiled faintly, as though in self-mockery. "Marre's father," he explained. "My staunchest supporter, until recently. I was too harsh with him. He was not ready for rumors of war. Your appraisal?"

"Ardren is a good man. Even in the face of what he must consider overwhelming evidence against you he doesn't forget his long loyalty to you. He is unsure."

Khedran lifted an eyebrow. "Does that make him a good man? Or a fool?"

It was Bannon's turn to flinch. Khedran's cold Chaine logic occasionally disturbed even him, who considered himself reasonable. "It gives us some measure of added time," he said finally. "Ardren gives them no flag to rally to. They will hesitate a fraction longer, to see what is next. Have you had word from Ordhold?"

"None. Nor from the High Tahmine."

Bannon scowled. "The High Tahmond was silent at the meeting, did no more than give his blessing to the gathering. Yet even that is ominous, Your Highness. Perhaps we should go to the Tahmine..."

"No."

Bannon's mouth snapped shut.

"If I approach the High Tahmine now, it will be taken for what it would be, a sign of desperation. She would have come forth, by now, if she could. Going to her is not the answer."

"You're so sure of her." If Khedran knew no desperation, Bannon was becoming acquainted with it. "What could be holding her back, Khedran? She promised delivery of your bride. An announcement now, of the wedding, would halt them that much longer."

"For what purpose?" Khedran asked.

Bannon subsided.

"I must assume," Khedran continued, "that Ordhold is not coming, nor the horses that would make a force of my fledgling army. So, what purpose would it serve to delay, Bannon? I won't beg for stolen hours, like a convicted criminal facing death. Nor will I allow the Dominion Kings to make me a victim before their stupidity makes victims of them. This invasion must be stopped before it has taken over Azlatan. I will call Council myself."

"No!" Bannon cried. "Without the High Tahmine you would fail Council. They have already decided without a trial, like all ignorant men. There is no reason among them, Khedran. If you must act now, use Daimaine. The High Tahmond claims you are no longer in favor with her, so you can't call on her. Prove it's not true."

Khedran shook his head. "He knows that no High King will use Daimaine against his people, and twists that knowledge into a lie. I alone know how dangerous she is, Bannon...and she has become more so, not less, in my own lifetime."

"But you do have the power to call on the Deathqueen to deal with them. This is not a time for mercy."

"It's not a matter of mercy, Bannon, but of right and wrong. Yes, at my behest the Deathqueen would take them. But I destroy only evil. They are not evil. They are just human, with human flaws and failures. Conceited and petty and foolish, perhaps, but not evil."

"What is evil, your Highness, if it isn't turning against your own High King?"

"Rebellion isn't evil. Forcing them to obedience through fear or violence would be evil. I am not a tyrant."

At Bannon's look of dismay, Khedran sighed. "Bannon, my own father forewarned me of this duty, in his last letter to me. I remember every word. He said I must have faith in myself even when my people turn against me, because my duty is to save them all."

Bannon sat back, understanding the power of the father's words to his son. "Your Highness...what if they use violence against you, as some are insane enough to suggest?"

"To push them to that point would be just as wrong, because I would then have to defend myself...with the same result as using force in the first place. They are my people, Bannon. My duty is to save them, not to harm them. I must call Council, and find a way to help them see reason with the facts as they stand."

"You know what they will demand of you." Bannon met Khedran's calm gaze with desperate sadness. "Without the High Tahmine to defend you, the High Tahmond and seven Dominion Kings could decree you have violated the ethics of your rule. The High Tahmond would call Phaelon's destruction on you. You would die!"

"Possibly," Khedran agreed, and Bannon's heart broke.

"Your Highness...please reconsider. They will call you Chaos if you continue this path."

"They will be alive to call me nothing if I do not. This must be resolved, or Azlatan will fall. Go to bed, Bannon. Shoulder your own burdens, not mine."

Bannon rose automatically at the dismissal, but he trembled. He hesitated, recognizing his own fear, swallowed hard. "Your

Highness," he said formally, knowing this the bravest thing he'd ever done. "Love creates its own burden."

Khedran's eyes closed briefly, as though he had been struck. When he recovered and looked at Bannon, his eyes were dark, without the emerald light they normally held.

"Love gives no claim to my life or its burdens, Bannon. I do not accept any love that demands less of me than I do of myself. Nor would you offer it, if you would only think."

"My King, love is a matter of the heart, and not the mind."

"A fallacy I will not argue with you, for I do not want to accept that you listen after all to hummingbird tongues. Beasts love without mind, not men. Will you disillusion me so sadly?"

Bannon hesitated, wounded. "I don't understand your Chaine beliefs," he said finally. "Isn't it true they have no word for love?"

"No, it is not true. They have a greater word for love. It is *amhara.* It combines 'love' with 'respect,' for there can be no true love without respect. It is also a word of gratitude, for it addresses our connection to the world and everything in it." He sighed. "Bannon...I know you are cautious of me; I wish you were not. You may speak openly to me. I spoke before out of frustration, not anger at you."

Bannon sat down slowly, accepting this challenge with his native curiosity springing sharply to life. There was some quiet satisfaction in Khedran's watching eyes, the only hint of expression on the High King's handsome face.

"You are far too different from other men," Bannon said recklessly. "You separate yourself by your office and refuse even an expression of concern born of love for you."

Khedran smiled in acknowledgment of Bannon's truth. "And you, alone of all men I have known born in this land, my land...you, I believe, could come closest to understanding why."

"But I don't understand, Khedran. Oh yes, your separation is more than comprehensible to me; you are High King and must be careful of dangerous connections. Yet does that mean you must repel any benevolent emotion?"

"Yes. It does. I cannot allow emotion to prevent me from doing what I must do."

"So, you must not allow love to ease your path," Bannon said sadly.

"*Amhara* is not meant to ease my path. It requires me to do what I must for the safety of my people."

CHAPTER 15

Marre had come nightly to the chamber of the High Tahmine, only to have that strange Shadow fall upon her, leaving her unable to knock. But this time she saw the door open, though her hand had not moved from her side.

She blinked at the figure revealed to her. Thought, for a moment, she faced the High Tahmine herself.

The woman was an aura of white light, white hair spilling haloed about her, eyes covered in a blindfold. She held a cat in her arms. The cat bristled, peering past Marre, and spat.

One slim hand calmed the feline, then lifted as though admonishing someone just behind Marre. Marre felt the immediate change like a shower of cool water. The Shadow that had held her in thrall had withdrawn at that one gesture, not in fear, but in quiet anger. Marre shuddered in its aftermath.

Then the white lady turned away from the door, and Marre flung herself after her, terrified of abandonment in that cold and shadowed hallway.

A moment later she stood bewildered in a closed room. Had the door never been open at all? Where had the lady in white gone?

This was no magic Temple room, but an ordinary bedchamber. A fire burned brightly in the hearth, and softer lamplight filled the corners. A large bed draped in ordinary fabric dominated the room. A chair beside it held a sleeping occupant, fully dressed in the robes of a Sister. Marre recognized the same unwaking sleep that inhabited the novice in her own chamber.

She moved unchallenged to the larger bed and looked down at last on the High Tahmine.

She saw two things: this was not the strange figure who had let her in, and the High Tahmine was alert and watching her with glittering bright eyes.

She was lost in the immensity of that bed, fragile as yellowed paper that would crumble at a touch. Only her eyes were alive.

"Marre of Athea," the Tahmine said in a voice dry as dead leaves. "You have come at last. I had begun to believe you would not."

"I couldn't come before, Mother. There is a Shadow, that none could see but me. But you know about that, I think."

The bright eyes flickered. "Yes. I have been its prisoner, these last weeks. You must have a great hidden power of your own, to have come past it. I can breathe at last; it is gone!"

"It wasn't I who sent it away. Didn't you see her, at the door? There was a lady in white. She glowed like white fire. She let me in and sent it away."

The Tahmine clutched briefly at her coverlet, then relaxed. She smiled, and Marre saw an echo of beauty, lost years past counting. "You have been honored, I think, as no Sister of this Temple could claim. I believe you saw Liethe."

Marre shivered. "I wanted none of that honor, though I am grateful. I've been as much a prisoner as you...or your sleeping Sister, over there...and I have been a pawn of this evil magic. I only want to be free of it! Can you understand that?"

The Tahmine sighed, closed her eyes briefly. "Yes," she said, "I can. Once, Marre of Athea, I had a name, and a life I could call my own, until Liethe came and claimed it as hers. Destiny is a kind of death, for certain spirits."

"You have regretted being High Tahmine?"

Again that strange, lovely smile. "No. But I understand those certain spirits. There are so few of us, you know. All else are like children, and that is why we need the gods."

Marre scowled and saw laughter in the old eyes. "Such foolishness," the Tahmine told her. "I know you, Marre of Athea, better than you know yourself. I have watched you grow up, a process still uncompleted, that will never be completed until you stop rebelling long enough to see what you are rebelling against."

Marre dared to sit on the side of the bed. "How have you watched me?"

"We of the Temple have our ways. Be assured the Tahmond have watched you also. Our magic eyes extend to the borders of Azlatan and see all save that which is not of Azlatan. The Chaine, and the Outsiders."

Marre took a deep breath. "So, the Outsiders do exist."

"Of course. One almost killed you. But you pluck at so many questions, Marre. What is it you really want to know?"

"You may know better than I. Why did you call me to you?"

"Ah, you saw that trap quickly. You will make an excellent High Queen."

"My destiny," Marre said bitterly. "Even you say destiny is a kind of death."

"But you have an advantage I did not. It is not a goddess who will command your heart, but a handsome man with a mind and heart of his own."

"Is that supposed to be a better choice?"

The Tahmine laughed. "That is up to you. Can you manage a handsome man with a mind and heart?"

Marre was taken aback. "Tell me then. What do you think I am rebelling against? I had believed it was against a destiny that would narrow my life to one choice, and that is no choice. I realized it most fully when that Outsider would have taken the life I never yet have been able to live."

"Haven't you? And what is it you planned to do with your life, if you could free yourself of destiny? You are a child, Marre, who has yet to learn what life is. You chase it like something just out of sight, something you can catch and hold if everyone will just leave you alone."

Marre looked down. "I knew a certain spirit. He walked in strength, every day of his life. No one told him how to live. He chose."

"Your guardian Chaine. Khedran told me about him. I have seen the influence he had on you, though my magic never revealed the man himself. Were you in love with him, Marre? He sacrificed his life for you."

"No." Marre shook her head. "My love for him was nothing like that. I admired him, because he fulfilled a duty which he had chosen to accept. And...his death was no sacrifice. He lost a battle he had meant to win. A sacrifice is made willingly. His death was a horror, an injustice, as good lost to evil will always be."

"You have come far, to see the difference between sacrifice and duty. Choice is inherent to duty. If duty is denied, a soldier will be a coward, and a merchant will be a thief."

"And a High King will be a tyrant," Marre added viciously.

"He is not a tyrant, though he appears to the envious to be an arrogant man." The Tahmine smiled complacently. "He is proud and willful, and has good reason to be both. He is also more beautiful than you, if you don't mind the truth. You could never settle for anything less."

Marre stared, shocked.

"What, you still haven't admitted it to yourself? You have admitted you loved your Chaine guardian, even if you were not in love with him. Is the High King less than he? Think it through. But for now, listen to me: If you believe as I do that the Outsiders are evil, then you have found your duty no matter what personal decision you may make about the Black Wolf. I need your help, on his behalf. The Dominion Kings, or even Khedran himself, will call Council soon. Khedran will be brought before Phaelon without the High Tahmine to stand with him. Can you understand the danger in that, with the Outsiders invading our borders?"

Marre sat back, her mind spinning.

The Tahmine went on, plucking nervously at her blanket. "The Duine are filling our lower warrens like a slow flood, for some purpose I cannot comprehend. The Dominion Kings, and even my Sisters, are influenced by the same Shadow you and I have known. I believe madness entered Phaelon's Temple long ago. Khedran is called the Black Wolf, but his own people will pull him down and eat him because the prophecies have been tangled. I am helpless in their net."

Marre placed her hand over the Tahmine's, more to still their nervous movement than in comfort. "What can I do?"

"I am useless to him, Marre. I am too old, and Daimaine has touched me already."

"Is she the Shadow, Tahmine?"

"No. Don't you see that is why I am afraid? Daimaine is Justice, and Death a fairer face than youth can understand. The Shadow is another, and possibly as strong!...though you saw Liethe warn it off, for a little while. I believe the Shadow is linked somehow with the Outsiders."

"Then we are lost," Marre said bitterly, "And the battle is up to the gods."

"No! The High King is our hope. Only he can battle the Shadow that took us. Those of his bloodline cannot be corrupted. He is our only hope," she repeated, "because he is the truth in a world of lies. The Tahmonds have lied about our history for a thousand years while the Kings have stood true, keeping the influence of the gods separate from their duty of leadership. They have quietly ensured that the people retain their right to their own minds, to their own respect, to their own belief in their own destiny."

The Tahmine lifted a clawlike hand to touch Marre's. "Believe nothing the High Tahmond says, Marre. Liethe has always stood for the High King, and I believe in this one. But now, when he needs me most, I cannot go to him. I cling to this side of life only by the grace of Liethe's Law, which says I cannot die until my replacement is found. It is my replacement who must stand beside Khedran. The Shadow has defeated me. I have not been able to send for her, as I should have long ago, and it is now nearly too late."

"Then tell me which of the Sisters your replacement is, and I will bring her to you."

"That is what I ask of you. But it will not be easy. She was in Ordhold, and escaped there only just in time, for the Shadow has taken that land. She has traveled hard, with a Prince who brought her along to his exile. But the Shadow has followed her, always seeking to keep her from me and from Khedran, and it has stolen her strength even as it took mine. She is near now, in the camp of the Dominion Kings outside of Cabre. Her companion, the Prince of Ordhold, has been stricken with the Shadow's sickness of the mind and cannot come further. She is nearly lost to us, Marre. She must be released from the Shadow."

"You think Khedran can release her?"

"Yes. The Shadow is made of corruption, and has overtaken too many of the Dominion Kings, and some of my own Sisters. But the High King is incorruptible. He can stand against it. He is the only one who can save her from the Shadow."

Marre bowed her head, thinking. She didn't yet understand the many currents of magic and politics whirling through Azlatan, but clarity had come to her own role in her own mind. She felt her own spirit burn higher. "They call you the Healer of Healers," she told the High Tahmine. "Yet you have used no magic on me."

"It's all gone, I'm afraid. And you don't need it, for you have a courageous heart. I am glad, because my beloved son...did you know I fostered the High King, after his mother died in childbirth?...oh, Marre, he deserves so much. He deserves a High Queen as strong as he is." The Tahmine smiled. "I warn you he will not be easy. Khedran is proud and willful, and untamed by love. But he already respects you, and that is a mere step away from love, for him."

Marre's eyes held a challenge. "I will require his respect," she said. "But love...that's another matter, isn't it?"

The soldier was there. He was always there when Marre came to that part of the Temple where he was allowed, waiting for her.

She walked up to him openly, watching his surprise turn to question as her eyes raked his strong, black-uniformed body and the emerald symbol of the High Queen's Guard, lifting finally to his iron and silver hair. So obvious was her measure of him, as a man would measure another man, that his blue eyes were rife with wry amusement. She came barely to his shoulder.

"You have been assigned to me," she told him coolly, "without my request or approval. Or was my approval a condition of your appointment?"

"No," he replied honestly, adding quickly, "Your Highness."

"Your name, please. And your rank, before Khedran had the audacity to promote you to my service."

"Farbet of Cabre. Compatri to the High King."

One beat. "Oh." She allowed herself the merest trace of a smile. "Perhaps not as audacious as I believed, then. You claim no Dominion, but only the King's City?"

"I served his father. As did my father before me. As," he added, "I now serve you."

"You understand why I ask."

He nodded. "The circumstances are unusual. Otherwise, your Guard would have been your choice, as is proper."

"You have a noble heritage of service. Were you given any choice in the change of liege from King to Queen?"

The soldier called Farbet regarded her for a long moment. All amusement left his eyes. "I accepted his request with honor. I will remain in your service until after the wedding, because of these unusual circumstances. Then you will take your place as High Queen, and if I have not served you well, you may order my dismissal."

"To return to Khedran?"

"I would not return to my King so dishonored. He would break my sword and order my exile."

She was not surprised. She measured the man again, putting aside all memory of a former guardian who could never be replaced. Respecting his heritage of service as well as his confidence, she revised her estimate of his body from stocky to burly, just as the youth in his eyes gave lie to the grey of his hair.

Her eyes paused on the sword he wore, registered its make and the way that he wore it. She smiled to herself. It was Chaine. Her trust fell into place like a key smoothly into its lock.

"I must see the High King immediately," she told him.

Was that relief in his eyes? "I will send a messenger, Highness."

"No. You must understand, Farbet. I must go to him. I have a message from the High Tahmine. The fate of Azlatan may rest on it."

"In that case," he answered...she had counted one breath, no more..."I shall need to summon a carriage, and an armed Guard."

She glanced again at his sword. "You look capable of guarding me alone. In fact, you must. You are sworn to my service, and I will trust no other. My message is too important. I also have reason to believe there may be treachery within this very Temple. With that in mind, how can I trust any unknown soldier? If even the Sisters can be corrupted –"

He raised a hand swiftly, halting her words while his eyes swept the empty hallway where they stood. "We will leave immediately, Highness, but we must do it without the whole city being aware."

"We need two horses and an extra uniform for me. Perhaps a heavy cloak to make it less obvious."

His smile was almost savage, as though he had found treasure. "Yes," he said gruffly, with more respect than any polite honorific. "Follow me."

The Tahmine had assigned him chambers of his own on the ground floor. He went ahead, making her wait once around a corner while he vanished briefly. He came back with a caution of silence before he hustled her into his room.

Once there he handed her an extra uniform and turned his back. She took a deep breath and slipped out of her gown, pulling the black tunic on in a flurry of embarrassment. It came nearly to her knees.

She looked around, sat on the bed to begin pulling on the black breeches, stumbled upright again. The pants, pulled up beneath the long tunic, came just below her breasts. "Farbet," she pled in despair, "do you have a belt?"

He turned slowly to regard her. She stood with flushed cheeks under his expressionless gaze, arms crossed to keep the pants up, nothing but toes and fingertips visible against the black swaddle.

"If you laugh," she said with an attempt at haughtiness, "I'll break your sword myself."

"Of course," he replied evenly, so like Jhinn it made her heart ache. But she caught the glimmer in his eye and the curve beneath his mustache and found with human relief that he was not her dour Chaine at all.

The belt was produced, cut, and altered before she buckled it to her slim waist. This bloused the overlarge tunic but secured the breeches.

Farbet eyed the sleeves, set to pinning them up.

"You seem quite good at this sort of thing," she remarked.

"A soldier learns to do many things." He gave her black leather gloves while he reached for boots.

He glanced at her diminutive feet, set to stuffing the toes of the boots, then motioned her to sit down and put them on. The extra material in the pants was shoved into the boot tops.

He watched as she stood and walked a few steps, then draped a spare black cloak over her shoulders and raised the hood to cover her hair. "It's raining out; you'll pass, and I'll be dressed the same. I assume you can ride?"

She nodded. Swinging his own cloak over his shoulders, he led her to the hallway.

She tried to match his long soldier's strides in the impossible boots, her heart pounding, realizing she was more excited than nervous. She had purpose: she was finally acting, not just existing.

She straightened her shoulders under the cloak, and then they stood outside, atop the broad fan of Temple stairs.

The air was wet and cold and intoxicating. It carried the tang of wet earth and salt sea. She raised her face beneath the hood to the grey sky and felt the rain on her cheeks like a kiss. Oh beautiful, her spirit sang, released from a strange imprisonment; for a moment she drank the world and was happy.

Then she brought her attention back to the more immediate need.

She and Farbet were only two of many cloaked figures at the top of the Temple stairs, though their black uniforms drew sidelong glances from citizens intent on their own business. The city proper began at the foot of the steps. Pedestrians, equestrians and the occasional carriage splashed through the rain-wet streets where puddles gleamed like broken shards of mirror.

She looked at Farbet; assured, he started down the stairs.

He broke a path for her through the crowd. She stayed close to his back and kept her head down, watching rainwater slap around her giant boots.

The crowd parted with alacrity for the High King's Legion Master and his follower. They trotted across a narrow street and a carriage rolled too near, sheeting water over them both. Farbet uttered a low curse but did not turn to check on her. *He's performing as the officer with a raw recruit,* she thought wryly, wading over the curb in his wake.

When he turned into a less-traveled side street she risked a peek at the close-crowded houses they passed. This was her first glimpse of a residential section of Cabre. The brick houses were tall and narrow with pointed roofs and tiny windows tucked under the overhang. All the windows were thin and tall, shutters open to the grey-metal light. Steep narrow yards wore grass like green skirts. Marre could see the warm glow of lamplight in many of the windows they passed and felt a rightness about it. This was life, not as she had known it or ever would, but she found it comforting.

She had fallen behind Farbet in her dreaming and saw him waiting for her. She ran to catch up and almost lost her hood, slid to a halt pulling it around her face, peering up at him with wide lavender eyes. He looked very stern, and when he turned in to the stable yard, she stayed close.

"Wait here," he said abruptly in the yard. She scarcely looked up from her wet boots, reminding herself severely of her purpose, and very aware that many strangers were around her. She saw no other soldiers and guessed Khedran had never before had occasion to station one of his men at the Temple of Liethe. More, the steeds of Liethe needed no stable that mortal horses might share, so this was a public stable.

The rain regained strength as she waited. She shrank within her hood as it thrummed around her, watching drops jump frantically on the stones of the stable yard to rise in a white foam. The thrum filled her head until she startled at the unexpected touch on her elbow.

Farbet offered wet leather reins. She glanced at the bay gelding on the other end, who stood with head down and ears flattened against the downpour. She pulled the reins over that unhappy head and lifted her clumsy boot to the stirrup.

The saddle was cold and wet. She grimaced, readjusted her cloak, turned her mount after Farbet's. He motioned her alongside, leaned in to be heard over the rain.

"Stay beside me. If the way is narrow, ride behind, but close as you can." She nodded in understanding.

Farbet kicked his horse to a trot, daring no quicker gait in the rain. Marre urged her mount alongside and found the bay's gait bone-jarring. She endured it in silence.

The rain did not abate. The streets were streams rising past the horses' fetlocks, deeper in places. Marre glimpsed huddled forms in doorways as they passed, realizing the rain had cleared some traffic for them. Where it did not, Farbet rode boldly through as the King's emissary, and Marre followed his example as best she could.

She lost track of their route, losing interest in her surroundings as rain turned to wet slashes of sleet. It was no great difficulty to keep her head down when they halted at a gate. Farbet exchanged incomprehensible shouts with the soldiers who guarded it. When the gate opened her horse went through without urging. Release from the wet pounding was joy for both Marre and her mount.

She dared a peek, found herself in a long stone hall ending in a wet courtyard: Penumbra's flanking army garrison. Farbet dismounted and stepped to her knee, reaching up for her.

"You're drunk," he warned her in a quick undertone. "I've brought you in for discipline. No one will speak to you or expect answer. Fall!"

She let go all holds, obeying with such faithfulness they both nearly fell to the stones. He cursed with frank reality, hauling her upright in a grip of iron. "Take care of the horses!" he commanded a Guard who came running, and half-carried her through a recessed door.

Head down, hanging over his arm like a sack of meal, all she could see was rough wooden planking under his feet, but she was aware of lamp and firelight, and many male voices that fell away at their entrance. "As you were," Farbet ordered gruffly, and dumped her ungracefully into a chair where she bowed head into knees as though sick unto death. *A barracks,* she thought wildly. *I ask to see the High King and he brings me to a barracks full of soldiers.*

"Leave this one alone," Farbet told them. "He's got troubles you won't care to share." There was some snickering, quickly stifled as Farbet growled at them. "I was told the High King is on his way here?"

"He's due soon," someone replied, sounding curious.

"I'm sure word has gone ahead that you are here," another voice added. "Has something happened at the Temple, Sir?"

Farbet grunted and there were no more impertinent questions. A moment later Marre felt a mug of hot liquid pressed into her gloved hands. "Drink this," Farbet ordered. She took it gratefully, hands trembling with cold and reaction, and sipped the bitter stuff beneath her hood.

In so doing she realized she could see dimly through the loose weave of the cloth, and her cheeks burned. It was a barracks all right, narrow cots spaced down the long room with a fireplace at either end, and soldiers in various stages of undress. Marre averted her eyes.

The door slammed open. Soldiers leaped to attention – the one nearest, she realized dimly, with his britches hobbling his ankles.

Khedran's low voice was somehow familiar; she recognized that as part of the Gift of his bloodline, but it held a resonance personal to her, so it took a moment to understand what he was saying.

"...all of you ready to ride, immediately. King Bannon has reported the arrival of a rider from Ordhold in the Dominion Kings' camp. Be prepared to fight if they will not release him. Ordhold has fallen, it seems to some dark sorcery attributed to me."

Marre hunched as the soldiers went into motion. She sensed rather than saw Khedran approach, saw a shadow that was Farbet step between her and the High King.

"I'll assume there's a reason you are not at your post." Khedran's voice was quiet as he spoke to Farbet, but it rang cold.

"There is. Highness, please have them wait outside a moment."

Another voice, tenor after Khedran's low tones, and unfamiliar to her: "Must I wait outside also? It's miserable out there."

Khedran answered. "You can stay a moment, Bannon. Though I imagine your reasons have to do with curiosity rather than rain." He added orders to his officers, and the room began to clear.

"You ride into great danger," Farbet said very quietly, "if the news you have is true."

Bannon spoke up coolly. "It is true! I saw the rider's arrival and heard his rather disconnected tale. The man from Ordhold is sick or insane, and so is the woman who arrived with him. I've tried to talk Khedran out of this mad ride, but he won't listen to me. The camps are like an anthill attacked by wasps, and far more dangerous."

"Ordhold is part of my realm," Khedran reminded them both tightly. "This may be the news I've waited for. I must learn the truth, and quickly. Why are you here, Farbet?"

"I bring a message," Farbet said pointedly, "for the High King only."

"Your message wears very large boots," Bannon commented, "for such a small person."

There was a brief silence, during which Marre felt eyes upon her. "I think you had better explain," Khedran said.

The room was cleared of soldiers. Marre made her decision swiftly.

She straightened, throwing the hood back from her long fall of hair. "You'd both better go," she said, looking at Farbet. "I have to speak to the King quickly, before he leaves. The High Tahmine knows of this rider. It's why I'm here."

Farbet bowed, eyes gleaming, and obeyed. Marre glimpsed Bannon's long curious face before the door closed behind them.

She was alone with Khedran.

She stood as he dropped the bar across the door and turned to her. The simple fluid motion captured her artist's eye, and she felt her heart sledge against the cage of her ribs. His black cloak fell in a straight line from left shoulder to boot-heel, flung back from the right to free his sword-arm; his sword was sheathed against the long line of hip and thigh. Suddenly time stood still, and she saw with new clarity.

He was an absolutely stunning man, as she had been told so often. But he was more than that. It was his spirit she saw, filling him like wine sparkling through a crystal glass. She realized this was what she had searched for and found missing all her life. Her world came alive at last.

Despite everything she had hated about her betrothal, she fell in love with him in that instant.

Her own will served her. She did not move; her face remained at rest. But his strange and beautiful emerald eyes nearly ruined her. They were too full of living; they were eyes meant to perceive and command. The cold stillness within them did not truly seem to belong to him. It took her a moment to recall that he was a King who stood alone and faced civil war, and the Shadow, and an end to his life and all his bloodline.

Her own rage was his victory over her. This pure flame that was Khedran should never have to face such loss.

But her voice held strong and level. "The High Tahmine has sent me to you. You have already gained half of her message. I give you the other half. The woman who rides with the man from Ordhold is the next High Tahmine. She is under some magic spell sent by the Outsiders. You must find her so she can take her place in the Temple."

She wished she could read his expression as he regarded her coolly. "Do you doubt me?" she demanded.

"I was just wondering about her long silence. And yours."

"I just learned of it. The same magic I spoke of has attacked me, and the High Tahmine herself, inside the Temple. She calls the magic a Shadow. The Tahmine believes you have power over it, and can free the new High Tahmine from it."

He was frankly puzzled, now. "A power I know nothing about over a Shadow I cannot see. Thank you for the message, Princess Marre. I'll look for your mysterious new Tahmine, in Eleban's camp."

"I'm going with you."

She hadn't known it was her intent until the words were out, and then she knew it had to be. Something was wrong. There was some purpose in Khedran that she sensed as dangerous to him.

He lifted a hand, palm up. "Why? If you ride with me, assumptions will be made. The same assumptions you denied were true, when last we spoke."

She lifted her chin against that captivating emerald gaze. "For Azlatan. The Outsiders are evil. They will destroy us, if we cannot defeat this magic and make our own people see the danger."

"Spoken like a High Queen. Have I been chosen, then...as the lesser of evils?"

She remembered her intent to require his respect. "It appears necessary." Her voice was cool and flat.

He studied her for a moment while she held her breath. Then he simply nodded, stepping to a soldier's open footlocker to toss a pair of boots in her direction. "Bannon will find these less amusing. I believe this uniform will fit you better, as well. You will ride as one of the Black Guard, but openly. I'll wait with the others."

Chapter 16

The rain had stopped. The setting sun slanted through the city, burning through the storm-shadows. Marre glanced down at the white shoulder of the horse she now rode, remnant rainwater pooling beneath his feet. Her hair swung free across her shoulders, and she rode proudly between Farbet and Khedran, Bannon and Khedran's amazed Guard lined behind them.

There was strength in Marre, despite her small frame. Bannon watched her and recognized a pride to match Khedran's, untamed and dangerous. He thought of traps and benevolent emotions and planned to watch events unfold with great interest.

The sun sank behind them, and Penumbra's dark bells tolled through the murky twilight as they passed through the great gates of Cabre. On the outer plain, the world rose around them like a great black bowl. The sky was another dark bowl, placed rim to rim. Campfires were like red stars fallen to earth.

This is a different world, Marre thought. *Beasts hunt here, and they are men.*

Torchlight approached, making silhouettes of the men who surrounded them. "The Black Wolf is not welcome here," growled a voice through the darkness.

The Star Blade sang free of its sheath. Khedran's mount half-reared, startled by the fog of starlight that appeared around him, filled with silver fire-blossoms that illuminated without burning. All knew Daimaine's Gifted sword, a reminder that he could summon the Deathqueen herself.

Khedran controlled his black charger with easy grace. False courage was lost in the cold light of the Star Blade, and the men who were revealed by it fell silent as the High King turned his mount slowly, resting the dazzling sword atop the stallion's arched neck. The King's strange eyes glowed like green fire in that light, another fearful sight.

"The Black Wolf is among you." Khedran's command voice sounded within the minds of his watchers. "Do any in this pack wish to offer challenge?"

There was no answer, though several people stepped back. Marre's eyes searched the crowd for a familiar face. Torchlight grew stronger as more torches appeared, red fire battling the silver aura that surrounded Khedran.

He sheathed the sword wordlessly, disdainfully. "I seek Ardren, King of Athea," he announced.

"I am here."

Marre's father stepped from the crowd, a thin upright figure.

Khedran nodded to him, cold respect. "You have received a rider from Ordhold. With a companion. I have come for them."

Ardren glanced toward Bannon, who gazed back unflinching. "We expected you, Your Highness." There was no welcome in his voice. "So did the High Tahmond, who arrived ahead of you. He is with the Prince now."

"Prince Jon?" Khedran asked.

"I believe the Prince of Ordhold is named Brend. He says Ordhold has fallen. Not to any invading army of Outsiders, but to sorcery. The High Tahmond says there are questions to be answered."

"For once he is right. Take me to him."

"You may not take your Black Guard with you. The High Tahmond says you have hidden too long behind the wall of your army. You must come alone."

Marre saw Khedran's grim smile, saw him move to dismount...saw Bannon lean as though to stop him, then check himself with a gesture of dismay.

Marre kicked free of her stirrups, ducked under her horse's neck, and arrived beside Khedran even as he stepped to the ground. He looked down at her with a lifted eyebrow.

"Marre!" Ardren cried with surprise. "You…"

She spun to her father, full of fury. Words came to her, words she had once despised, and now flung as a weapon. *"'Daimaine rules at the right hand of the High King, and his Queen at the left,'"* she quoted the old verse. "Do not try to deny me entrance, Father." She glimpsed torchlight on naked blade: Farbet's. "Nor my Guard. Did the Tahmond have anything to say about denying entrance to the Master of the Queen's Guard?"

Ardren stared at her. "You don't have to do this. I thought you safely in the Temple. I was going to come to you, to tell you to come home. To Athea."

"You are far too late. Destiny found me, and I have chosen to marry the High King. Proudly, as you taught me."

"You're going to marry him, knowing…"

"Knowing he battles an enemy that almost destroyed all of us, on the road to Cabre. Or have you managed to forget that, Father? These are the same soldiers who rescued us, that night. These soldiers, whom you refuse entrance now. But not to me. I, and my Guard, and Dominion King Bannon, will enter with the High King."

Ardren stepped back from her, his mouth working wordlessly. She faced him with the full determination of her intent, and after a long moment he spun on his heel and walked away.

Khedran flipped his reins to one of his officers with a brief "Wait." Then the four of them followed Ardren. The crowd was a blur of torchlight and shadow, and even with Farbet walking behind like a great bear and the Black Wolf at her side, Marre felt vulnerable. *He should not have accepted that maxim,* she thought. *There is too much danger here.*

They came to a tent, no temporary dwelling but an elaborate structure with carved posts holding a doorway of silken draperies.

Guards stood at the entrance, and Ardren strode past them, with a murmured command she could not hear.

Marre glimpsed movement too near Khedran, glanced sharply toward it. She got an impression of white hair and slim limbs, and the apparition was gone. But she felt uneasy, with a familiar dread she could not place.

Then they were inside the tent, where lamplight lay golden on rich tapestries and furs, as luxurious as any she had seen in Athea.

The High Tahmond was there. He sat in a silver chair, like a statue beside a burning brazier, painted and robed half-black, half-white, his hair like cotton and his eyes like pearls. Marre shivered at the sight of those eyes. They were blind but moved with the precision of the sighted. As they passed over her, she drew nearer to Farbet. Then the eyes found their target: Khedran.

Khedran seemed unaware of the power of those white eyes. He was measuring the confines of the tent and its occupants: Ardren, who gazed at his daughter; Eleban, regarding the Tahmond with satisfaction; and the other Dominion Kings who entered quietly, nerves obvious.

The Tahmond's face was unreadable behind the covering paint. But it did not turn away from Khedran. Marre looked away from that harlequin mask to see Khedran's gaze had dropped to the couch beside the Tahmond's throne, where lay a young man like a sacrifice on an altar. Marre thought he was dead.

She felt the return of her nightmare. The Shadow was here, and it had done more than take that young man. It had touched everyone who had gathered in this rebellious camp.

"The young Prince sleeps," the High Tahmond said to Khedran. "He lives under a corner of the Shadow, and you brought the rest of it with you when you entered."

Marre saw Khedran glance toward her as though in question. She struggled to speak, to warn him of the Shadow he could not feel. Her tongue swelled against her teeth, and she began to choke. She was choking, and Jhinn would die if she could not warn him...

It was Farbet who saved her this time, with a roar like the bear he resembled. He tore her attacker from her, flinging the body aside to catch Marre, who swayed into his arms with eyes staring at the girl thrown and crouching like an animal against the couch. A blade gleamed in her hand, but it wasn't the knife Marre saw. It was the eyes, lightning glowing in the dark. It was the cold fury of the Shadow.

There was movement, a tide of sound around her, but Marre was scarcely aware of it. She saw Khedran drop to one knee, capturing the girl's knife-hand. For just a second longer Marre felt the Shadow, then it left the young woman crouched there, and the knife had fallen to the floor.

"Rani." Marre tried to make sense of the single word Khedran spoke, of the fact that he was on his knee to a Duine. Inanely, Marre thought: *That is wrong. The High King kneels to no one but his Queen.*

"Rani," Khedran repeated. He caught both the girl's hands, as though to get her attention. "What's happened to you? Your hair has gone white. You look very ill."

Not Duine, Marre realized. *She's young, but her hair has turned white because of the Shadow.*

She is not old, but she is not young anymore. She is Tahmine.

Shocked murmurs filled the room. The Dominion Kings recognized her now, even as Marre had. Rani did not need Liethe's veils for recognition, any more than the old woman who waited for her in the Temple. Her love of Liethe shone from within.

Khedran stood, drawing Rani up beside him. She looked up at the High King as though bedazzled, then turned and saw Brend on the couch, and went to him with a cry. "Prince Brend! Oh, thank the goddess, he lives. He rescued me from Ordhold, Your Highness, but the Shadow followed us here, and nearly took us both. He can be healed now, in the Temple of Liethe." She looked back at the High King. "King Randmar has died," she told him. "There is some sorcery that has overtaken Prince Jon, and Ordhold lies in its Shadow."

"You are Tahmine," the High Tahmond spoke from his throne. "Yes, you have been under a Shadow, as has the Prince. Do you understand the meaning of this?"

Rani turned to him, frowning. "I do not. I know only that I have returned from a strange dark place. I was lost in Shadow, and it was the High King who brought me back."

"Such spells are easily broken," the Tahmond intoned, "by the sorcerer who directed their casting. He does not call upon his goddess, but uses sorcery. Daimaine will not protect him, because his father sullied the bloodline of the High Kings, and brought upon us the Forbidden Child."

Rani looked stricken. A hum of many voices rose through the gathering, then fell away again. Khedran's eyes remained on Rani for a moment, as though expecting her to say something. Marre's heart sank when the Tahmine remained silent. This was to have been Khedran's new hope, the new Mother of Healers!

It was Bannon who broke, nearly seizing the Tahmine in his extremity. "You know it isn't true. Tell them!"

Rani stared up at the Dominion King, her face a study in wild confusion. "Only Liethe knows. No answer has been given to me."

The Tahmond struck his staff upon the floor. "Then I call upon those who will stand up for Council. The High King must face Phaelon."

"No!" Bannon shouted. "Azlatan is in danger! Can't you see the evidence? You had a Tahmine among you that you believed to be a Duine. What kind of power is that? A Dominion King faithful to the High King dies, the new Dominion King turns heretic, and Ordhold is lost. Would you see such destruction in your own Dominion? The danger is from outside our borders. I have told you that and I will say it again. I have seen it. We face the Outsiders. We face Chaos herself. Chaos has entered here!"

"As the prophecy warned us," the Tahmond interrupted smoothly. "Upon the birth of the Forbidden Child, seed of Rioch and Duine, which this sorcerer has taken into Penumbra."

Bannon spun on him with fists clenched. "Why are you only talking about part of the prophecy? What about the part saying Phaelon's protection of Azlatan's borders will end? What about the Prophecy War?"

"The wards still protect the borders." The Tahmond spoke smugly. "There will be no war. Phaelon is a merciful God."

"So you claim only part of the prophecy is true? And you are the only one who can say which part of it is and is not?"

Bannon flicked a dismissive hand and turned away to address the Dominion Kings. "It is time for each of you to search your own heart and mind. You know that in all our history our High King has always been pure and true in the care of his people. The first High King even gave his own life so that his son could lead us safely into Azlatan. Now we are threatened with an invasion of the followers of Chaos, yet this double-talking, power-seeking Tahmond dares to call Council against the King who has just proven his power over this dark sorcery that bewitched even a Tahmine. He seeks to call Council...to test...yes, to *destroy* the true, the last High King!"

Only Bannon knew his reason for his choice of words, but Marre felt a cold fear of new prophecy in the silence that followed. Her eyes darted to Khedran, who had watched Bannon speak without expression, as though bemused. Not once had he spoken in defense of himself. Marre knew with dreadful certainty that he would not. He allowed Bannon this battle as an honor that was due the loyal Dominion King. Khedran had made his decision long before this moment.

Khedran looked around to see faces now confused, now hostile, now full of dismay. He smiled, that mocking smile Marre already knew, and shook his head faintly as he looked down at the High Tahmond on his painted throne.

"It is I who call Council," he said quietly.

The throng roared. Rani's head lifted. Marre thought she looked agonized, thinking that Khedran was giving himself up like some noble sacrifice.

"No!" Ardren stepped between them, looking from one to the other desperately. "This can't be necessary."

"But it is." Khedran lifted a hand for silence, and when silence came, he continued quietly. "This civil strife must pass. There is no time for it. We must unite our Dominions before the Outsiders come openly in numbers we cannot predict. My duty requires we unite, so I will face Council for that purpose."

He looked over at Marre then, and she saw there no sacrifice, but the eyes of a conqueror. "For Azlatan," he said while his gaze held hers, "I have made a choice between evils."

Her vision blurred with tears.

Ardren wouldn't give up. "No! We cannot chance the death of our High King!"

Khedran turned to him respectfully. "Then what would you suggest, King Ardren of Athea?"

"It is the half-Duine who has caused all this. Simply give him to the Tahmond. The High Tahmonds also have protected Azlatan for a thousand years. Give the High Tahmond the boy, and everything will return to normal."

There were murmurs of agreement.

Khedran's face went to stone, and he turned on the Dominion Kings in scorn. "You believe everything will return to normal? Use your minds. I have been accused of sorcery. Ordhold has gone down to an unnamed enemy. An Outsider, Azlatan's enemy in hiding, sought to murder the woman betrothed to be High Queen. You cry of a threat in the army I have created for your protection, and accuse me of the worst kind of treachery for its purpose. Despite all of that, you believe everything will return to normal if I sacrifice an innocent child to the Tahmond who accuses me, and whose power to protect Azlatan vanished when his border wards did, nearly thirty years ago!"

The High Tahmond was immediately on his feet.

"Lies! He lies about the border wards! And he does not respect the power of his own goddess, since he will not call on her even now. He knows that she will not protect him, because his father sullied the bloodline of High Kings. His power is over, I say!"

Khedran did not deign to respond, but his obvious fury was so powerful even the Tahmond drew back. Those emerald eyes swept the room like a weapon. "I have called for Council." Even his voice was deadly. "A countering demand has been made by the Dominion King of Athea, and I have denied it. If there is another demand to be made before seven of you step forward in judgment, let it be made now."

Bannon cried out, "We cannot be ruled by a Tahmond! You must have an heir!"

Khedran turned to him. "Are you making a demand, King Bannon of Tesna?"

Bannon looked anguished. "You must name your heir. Everyone here knows that if convicted the Tahmond will see that you are destroyed by Phaelon. There must be a High King to follow you. You must name him."

"I protest that demand!" cried Dominion King Eleban. "His denial of it would mean nothing. There are others here related to his bloodline. The Tahmond can name the new High King from among them, or an entirely different one, if he chooses. Do let this one be the last of his bloodline. We must have a new High King we can trust and..."

Khedran's laughter cut Eleban's speech short and shocked even Marre, coming so soon after his fury. Eleban drew back as though he stood too near a menace of madness.

"So, you do see the importance of that, Eleban?" Khedran asked through his laughter. "You admit that Azlatan needs to be united behind a High King?"

"I think I understand that better than you!"

"I see." Khedran's laughter stilled to a smile, but his eyes remained feral. "I assume it couldn't be just anyone. If not of my blood, then at least one of you...a Dominion King."

"Yes! But not the traitor Bannon."

Khedran shrugged. "Very well. This demand is not denied. In case judgment is called, in case I should fail that judgment and die, I will now name my heir from among the Dominion Kings." Khedran turned to the Tahmond, who looked as stunned as he could behind his harlequin paint. "The Tahmond can approve my choice. Is that acceptable...or is it your intent to rule in place of a High King?" he demanded pointedly.

The Tahmond's fury was apparent, but he was trapped. "Subject to my approval," he agreed after a moment. "But you will still face Council."

"Of course. Then my choice is Ardren, of Athea."

Marre heard shouts of approval through the roaring in her own ears. Only the sight of Khedran standing unbroken kept her standing, while her heart quaked.

"I witness and approve," said the Tahmond, and Khedran smiled.

"Long live the King," he said, and drew the Star Blade.

It blazed from black to white in that enclosed space, like all the fires of the night sky had gathered on its blade. Men fell back from it, as men had always fallen back.

All but one.

That one laughed, and flipped his sword end for end, catching the cold flame of the blade in his bare hand. Khedran held it out to the Dominion King, and Ardren cowered from the black hilt.

"Take it," Marre challenged. "Take it, Father, and be the High King of Azlatan."

"You know I cannot!" Ardren exclaimed. "No mortal may hold the Star Blade unless chosen by Daimaine."

"Or someone sure enough not to fear Daimaine's choice," Marre said cruelly. "Is there no one here? No one who would claim the Star Blade?" She turned as she spoke, searing them all with her contempt.

Their answer was silence.

So, they had all forgotten, in the thousand years of peace in Azlatan, the meaning of the sword that was Daimaine's: it embodied the rule of the High Kings. A deadly cold had fallen over all of them, the cold that heralded the coming of the Deathqueen. The Tahmond's assurances that Khedran would not call upon his goddess, that she would not protect him, were suddenly meaningless.

"You are all fools," Marre said through that cold presence from which even the Tahmond shrank. "Fools and cowards. You dare to invoke the wrath of Daimaine by challenging her High King to Council, yet not one of you is man enough to face the goddess of Justice! Why? Is it because you know in your heart that Justice is not with you? You have blinded yourselves, searching for answers in lies and cowardly theories, because you are afraid of the truth."

Marre had stepped away from Farbet, addressing the throng. Now she turned back to Khedran. Wary, he watched her come to him.

She halted so near she had to throw back her head to look into his face, yet in that moment she seemed tall. "There has been enough of this," she told him. "With honor and courage you have faced fools, but you cannot win. You cannot battle fools with reason they refuse to see. So, I provide the alternative. Perhaps it is the destiny that I have always dreaded, but now it is my choice." Her eyes met his emerald gaze with an intensity almost painful. "You may hate me for it. But it is the answer that will save your life, and your life is necessary because your people need you."

She lifted her hands and saw him recoil in startled understanding. The crowded room rumbled with the same knowledge, Ardren's cry above the rest.

"It is I who claim Azlatan," she shouted above the mob's noise. "Daughter of Ardren, Marre of Athea, I claim right to rule as High Queen of Azlatan!"

And she laid her hands upon the silver fire of the Star Blade.

Khedran's eyes remained locked on hers as she did it. She knew it was the greatest arrogance of all, believing so completely in what she did that the possibility of death did not matter. She intended to save the High King. If Daimaine did not accept that, she held only contempt for the world she left behind, and scorn

for the goddess who took her from it. She took the Blade and held
to it even as the pale fire of Death burned through to her brain.

Chapter 17

arre opened her eyes to silver flame. She could only sense Khedran's presence behind it.

I didn't know, was her next thought. *Such power! What have you given me? And why?*

When Daimaine answered, every person in Azlatan heard her voice, a torrent of vicious cold pouring into ears and failing hearts. *"These worthless mortals refuse to believe that Azlatan's borders have fallen and war is on their doorstep. Despite this, my beloved King is merciful, and will not call on me to do what must be done. I know that you, Marre of Athea, are not so merciful. Therefore, I have given this power to you. You are now, by my word, the ruling High Queen of Azlatan. Give me leave to smite all those who rebel against him."*

Marre's fury held as her vision cleared, and her eyes narrowed at the Deathqueen's words. She whirled to face the mob of terrified men. "Shall I?" she snarled at them. "Shall I command Daimaine to kill you all?"

Her only answer came from the High King himself.

"Please, Marre, don't do this. My purpose has been to save our people, not to harm them."

With his words she felt the remainder of the mysterious Shadow fall away. Its meddlesome impact on the Dominion Kings, including her own father, vanished with it.

But she continued to survey their terrified faces, and sneered at them. "Did you hear him? Do you realize what you have almost done? He has always stood between you and danger. You were about to destroy your own savior. I will not forgive you, but I will honor your High King, and let you live."

"So be it." Daimaine's chilling voice sang now for her alone, and Marre sensed her cold disappointment. *"I will leave this power with you, to do as you see fit. You may rule with him or over him. But never forget, mortal woman, that he will always belong to me!"*

She shuddered as that deadly presence faded, for Khedran's sake. She turned back to see he still watched her closely. His expression became grim as she lifted the Star Blade from his hands and stepped away from him.

Stars glimmered from the dark sweep of her hair. The sword lay within her grasp like the scepter it truly was, now as familiar as her own fingers curved round its hilt. A web of silver fire had fallen upon the black of her clothing. Her cloak crawled with runes splintered from moonlight. Her witnesses fell to their knees before her.

All but four, who remained standing.

Khedran, at her back, waiting.

Bannon, frozen beside them.

Rani, who stood guard over the fallen Prince of Ordhold.

And the High Tahmond, who stood heedless now of his carved chair, his white eyes staring wide upon her.

"Go." Still furious, she commanded the Tahmond with the awful resonance of the Deathqueen's voice. "If you value your life, you will use your magic to confirm to the people of this realm that the goddess Daimaine has united Azlatan. *Go!*"

The High Tahmond fled her, fled a living magic even he could not face.

She turned to Rani next, and another voice entered her mind, this one warmly familiar.

You have met two goddesses now. Beware of Daimaine's power. You are in greater danger than you know. Remember why you went to Khedran.

I remember, she told the old Tahmine. *Daimaine awaits you. Did I earn his respect, Mother?*

The response held a sigh. *Yes. But he may never forgive you.*

Then I will laugh at his weakness, Marre replied coldly, and knew by Rani's expression that she had heard that strange exchange of minds.

"You will go to the Temple," Marre said to Rani. "Take Prince Brend, for he will require healing even though the Shadow is gone from him. You are the next High Tahmine." Marre heard a distant chime and knew Liethe's Carriage had already been sent. "May you be as worthy as the Mother you follow."

Rani looked behind Marre to Khedran's burning presence. Marre stiffened at the pity in the Tahmine's lovely face.

She relaxed when Rani's eyes were as quickly averted. Khedran had accepted none of it.

Marre swung to Bannon, who was helping Farbet to his feet. The latter seemed to be in a state of shock.

Bannon met her gaze. "It seems you have brought my warning to truth. Hail to the first ruling High Queen, Chosen of Daimaine."

She heard animosity behind his carefully chosen words, loyalty to the man he thought she had supplanted.

"Do not misunderstand. Khedran is not and will not be the last High King."

Like Rani, Bannon looked to the man behind her. "He might have something to say about that."

Marre shook her head, and spoke from the knowledge the goddess gave her. "Our purpose is achieved. Azlatan is united. The Chaine ships will arrive in the morning with the horses promised to Khedran for his army."

"Your army, now," Bannon reminded her.

Marre stared, then whirled to follow his gaze...behind her.

Khedran had not moved from where he had stood when she took the Star Blade from him. He had been watching Bannon. His glowing emerald eyes, guarded and narrow, moved reluctantly back to Marre.

She forced her voice to be steady and spoke loudly for the benefit of the Dominion Kings, who were still afraid to look directly at the power which had come among them.

"The Black Guard remains in the command of the High King. His army was created to defend Azlatan. For that purpose it will ride, before the setting of tomorrow's sun. Khedran remains High King, by my word, and as my Consort." She lifted the Blade and it glowed anew. "Farbet and the Black Guard will go with us now to Penumbra. Bannon will lead the Dominion Kings to Penumbra at dawn."

"I hear and obey," Bannon said.

She lowered the pale flame of the Star Blade, and walked out in her Gifted glory, leaving Khedran to follow. She did not look back.

She had always heard of the King's Way, the glassy black stair above Penumbra's sea. The ascent was made in silence, Daimaine's magic lighting their path. Her mount breasted the dark wind in obedience rather than courage. Her Gifted power was beyond his equine understanding, yet he sensed it, as all Azlatan did.

Dawn was still far away. Daimaine's power swept the dark land swiftly, assisted by Tahmond and Tahmine magic. Even the sea heard the whisper of change.

Khedran rode beside her, silent as he had been since leaving the camp of the Dominion Kings. He had remained silent even at the foot of the Way, when she had given orders to the Queen's Guard, and sent them on strange errands through the darkness. Without question he rode with her up the cliffs to Penumbra, while the moon rode high above. Marre's mind ran once more over her orders and the events they would cause. Assured there was no more she could do until dawn, she allowed the presence of Khedran, never forgotten, to fully occupy her mind.

They topped the stair, and he checked his mount alongside hers at Penumbra's tower gate. They both dismounted as the gate opened, spilling light over them.

She left her horse with a soldier who flinched from the evidence of her new power, starting up the narrow stair that same power told her led to Khedran's chambers. She smiled slightly when she heard a low murmur of voices behind her, Khedran's soothing over the broken tones of his men.

A true King cannot relinquish leadership, she thought. *He could not leave a demoralized rabble behind him. His rule is in his nature, not his office.*

Penumbra embraced her. She stepped into the furred and golden light of Khedran's chambers, halting to listen to its welcome and share its memories. Penumbra clamored around her.

She pushed aside in disdain the various concerns of the many occupants of the palace, Duine and Rioch, who had yet to understand the apparent usurping of their Liege.

She sought the lonely traces of a woman somewhere within the walls of Penumbra, a woman she sensed as a kindred spirit. The woman was here twice, both past and present, but still belonged to the past. Marre didn't fully understand this, but knew she would find her along with the boy Khedran called brother.

But not now. The door closed behind her. Khedran had entered, and they were alone. She turned to face him, the Star Blade still in her hand.

He faced her warily still, his back to the door, waiting. She felt the thrum of power in her veins, and with it the temptation to invade his mind, to pierce the thoughts behind those cold emerald eyes.

He sensed it. She knew by the quick diamond-flare of his nostrils, for he let no expression give him away. Only that reflex he could not control, like an animal scenting danger.

She studied his stance and was reminded of her lethal Chaine guardian. She lifted the Star Blade slightly.

"You must know why I took this from you. Azlatan could not remain divided. They would have killed you. And you are badly needed."

"Did Daimaine tell you that?"

"She didn't have to. I know you are needed. And you are still the High King."

"By your word. But not, Your Highness, as your Consort."

It was as though he had struck her, a blow that robbed her of breath. Her cheeks flamed with humiliation, followed swiftly by fury.

She wanted to unleash the power that would drive him to his knees and rob him of the pride he wore like a mantle. Daimaine responded to that desire with cruel joy, and the Star Blade flared with a brilliance that forced him to avert his face.

That single involuntary movement was all that stopped her.

"You fear me." She spoke coldly, without mercy, as he had spoken to her. Aligned still with Daimaine, she allowed herself a dangerous exaltation in her power over him. It was like strong drink warming her belly and her breasts, frankly sexual. "You are afraid of my power, aren't you?"

He returned his gaze to her, those glowing eyes narrowed against the bright flame of the Blade. "Daimaine's power spills from you like blood from a wound. I'm not a fool, Marre."

"No, but you hate this power as much as you fear it." She lowered the Blade and smiled. She had in that moment realized his greatest fear and his greatest courage. "Magic, alone of all things, can break your will and your spirit, and make you less than you are. You would prefer death, wouldn't you?"

She was answered by clear, wordless fury.

She turned away and saw herself for the first time in an unexpected mirror.

An aura of pale flame edged her form. Stars glittered through her dark hair, starfire from her eyes. She hated Daimaine in that moment, for what had been done to her...and so also to the man she loved.

Reason and magic, she remembered. *They cannot exist to-gether.*

And now he is one, and I am the other.

Her anger fed on itself till she was nearly blinded by her own light.

"Daimaine warned me." She spoke to her reflection, and the King behind her. "You belong to her. There is no release for either of us, in life or in death."

She turned back to him. "This is her Justice, Khedran. She would not let you confront Phaelon. This is what we traded, for Azlatan."

Bannon rode through the first blue light of dawn. The Dominion Kings of Azlatan followed him, united at last by the power of a justice they had known as surely as they would someday know death. Marre had accomplished this thing, he thought, using the Deathqueen's whip to lash them; he had no doubt that the woman who was now High Queen would have allowed Khedran's enemies to be struck down. Only the plea of the High King had stopped her.

He sighed heavily and shifted in his cold saddle. Daimaine's intervention had been the one thing to make them face the truth of the Outsiders. Even the High Tahmond could not deny the evidence of Marre's gift of power. He wondered if the Dominion Kings had been influenced by some insidious magic that had brought them to the point of rebellion, and if the Tahmond had been behind it.

Some half-forgotten memory tugged at him, a line of lore found in his dusty wandering through the ancient writings, the hobby of a curious and solitary man. *Two-sided gifts*, he thought. *Twice-edged blades. A gift from the gods is never free.*

Khedran, he thought, can even you have the strength for this? That woman will devour you with her power. Perhaps better, after all, that you had died in confrontation with Phaelon.

He could not see the path his horse followed, though the dawn had brought full light. He wiped away the tears that blinded him and rode a sad victory into Cabre.

Even those who had slept that night awoke knowing that change had come upon them.

There came the sound of steel-shod hooves ringing on the paved streets of Cabre. Yet no sound of riders, no voice of man, was heard above that slow multitudinous march.

The people went to their windows and looked out on a new age.

The banners of the Dominions moved through the streets, bright in the new sun. Yet no fanfare of trumpets heralded that parade of royalty.

The High Tahmond walked among them, assisted only by his silver Staff of Power, his blind eyes seeing the path more clearly than the men who rode as slowly as he walked.

And along their road stood a fence of dark sentinels. The Queen's Guard.

Every step of pavement used by the Dominion Kings was guarded by them. The entire Legion had been dispatched by their new High Queen, and her display of force was set with grim purpose. Marre had not forgiven the Dominion Kings their rebellion against Penumbra. Her own father saw the black wall fencing their march and stared straight ahead with a sharp knife of fear in his belly.

Yet still more wonders awaited.

Penumbra itself had come to life. It did not fade with the sun, as it had always faded in the greater light of day. It blazed in sapphire glory, embraced by stars.

Daimaine had awakened.

And after more than thirty years, the golden ships of the Chaine had returned to the harbor.

Marre hadn't slept. She had passed the night in meditation, alone.

It had begun thus: Stunned wonder.

I dismissed him. I treated him like a Duine. No...like less than a Duine, for there is honor in the departure of a loyal servant.

She had stood at the open window and watched the clouds ride over the sea, scattering stars around them. The moon soared free above, brilliant as Marre's cold hands upon the windowsill.

I dismissed him. I could summon him as simply, and he would have no choice but to obey. He is mine, while he lives.

In all the ways that do not matter.

By my word. Not as my Consort.

Yes, by the all the gods! Even that, if I willed it. I feel Daimaine's power singing in my veins. With it I could bend his heart and his mind to me, until he could not draw breath for need of me. Khedran, the Black Wolf, High King of Azlatan...mine!

And he knows it.

Ah, he does not guess in what way I would bend him. Nor would it matter. That I have the power at all, that I could take from him his will, which is his self...that is enough to earn his hatred. Didn't I know this about him, even at our first meeting?

I have lived surrounded by fools who could not see me for what I am, but only as fodder for destiny. Before Khedran, only Jhinn gave me hope that we mortals could be more than silly children.

But now hope has become truth. It lives in Khedran's eyes, in his spirit.

I love him. He is more than worthy of my love. What shall I do?

She spun from the window, stared at the room which had been Khedran's, which was now hers.

The Star Blade lay where she had placed it. She saw it, suddenly, as it had appeared in Khedran's hand, when he had defied the

Dominion Kings...was it only this same night?...and saw him, the image of a will unbroken, a man unconquered.

Love was a word too weak for what she felt. She smiled, alone there in her high tower.

She knew now why she had dismissed him.

She would exile him rather than give in to that insidious power that would destroy his will...and therefore this thing she felt, this thing beyond love.

She made her vow to him.

If you break, if you become less than you are, it will not be by this power. No matter how angry you make me, your spirit will remain your own until your death gives it to Daimaine. This, my King, I promise.

Not just for you. For myself.

She had battled the seductive power of the dark goddess, and won.

Finally at peace, she met the dawn alone.

CHAPTER 18

Shandiin stood at the bow of her lead ship, her hands tight on the rail while the dawn wind whipped her hair around her shoulders. Her eyes were on the nearing shore, and the midnight towers of Penumbra with its glittering stars.

"Something's happened," Danon said from beside her. "I've never seen Penumbra like that in the daytime. And I think...those are soldiers of the Black Guard lined up on the beach."

"Daimaine is awake," she murmured.

"What do you..."

"Hush, Danon. Please. Go away and let me think."

She knew he shared her concern, and that he added concern for her to his worries. She couldn't care. Her mind was whirling, and she had to sort it out before she took a step onto that beach. She had to consider every possibility, and not let emotions tangle her mind.

Where was he? What if he...

Shut up, she told herself.

She had been gone almost two years. Danon had explained Khedran was facing a civil war. Why did his soldiers wait on that beach? Had there been a rebellion?

Seeing Penumbra awake in daylight terrified her. Had he, despite all her warnings, gone to Daimaine for help?

She knew Daimaine's restrictions. She was the only person living who fully knew the truth about Daimaine.

Too many secrets, she thought. *The weight of them grows heavier every day.*

When Daimaine had given Khedran's bloodline the gift of Kingship, the goddess had intended to keep her power over the people. Khalen, later named the first High King, had bargained that away. Daimaine had relinquished her power in return for his living sacrifice. Because of that, she could do no harm to the people without the permission of a High King.

But Daimaine was tricky. And she would make a second bargain if asked. She would gladly take another King away from this world, to be a slave within her separate reality.

Had Khedran sought to save his people from civil war and from prophecy by giving himself to her?

The ship was slowing, its sails flapping loudly as they turned into the wind. She hardly noticed as her eyes searched that line of black-clad soldiers.

Roinn appeared beside her. "We've dropped anchor."

She began to answer, stopped when she saw the High King.

Khedran walked through the ranks of his army, and then alone to the edge of the water, where he waited. He was dressed in black, as they all were, but even from this distance she knew it was him. She knew his height, his stride, his stance.

Tension drained from her. Her worst fear had not come to pass.

She turned to Roinn. "The horses can swim in from here. I don't need a boat. I'll ride Chandar out, then you can release the others. I must go to the High King and find out what's going on. Take command, Roinn."

She went below to where Chandar was held for her, and rode the stallion down the floating ramp into the water. The horse swam strong to the reef that shelved the beach. As soon as he got his footing, she slid off and waded in her resined boots through the shallow water, watching him go to his beloved master as the rest of the horses began catching up and passing her by. She smiled at the reunion of horse and man, and remembered when Khedran, a boy of sixteen, had fallen in love with the newborn foal, a gift from his father.

Only two years later, Khedran had stepped confidently into his role as the autonomous leader of Azlatan. Her guidance and the murder of his father had forged him, in terrible pain and perfect intent, into exactly what he needed to be...a strong and fierce High King, unlike any before him. Because of this, and because he wore the black sacred to Daimaine and he had the reflective eyes of a wild animal, his people in fear and respect had named him the Black Wolf.

She alone knew his truth. Behind the eyes of the Wolf, his love for his people was what drove him. The science of a lost world called Earth had engineered his ancestors with the sole purpose of creating an incorruptible leader for its survivors. The magic of Hiraeth had only magnified that purpose.

She had waited a thousand years for the time of prophecy, when she could at last leave, freeing the people of this world from its false gods.

But the Kings were necessary for the greater good. Their inborn purpose would never allow them to truly be free.

She shook off the sadness of that knowledge.

Looking around now at the crowd of horses and men surrounding her, she remembered nearly forty years before, when she had come to find Khedran's father, High King Allasar, waiting alone on this same beach. She'd known a flash of hope, on seeing him there. She had momentarily hoped him to be someone she had met briefly, a dark stranger from another world who had given her portents and warnings and a sense of wonder.

Of course, Allasar had not been him.

She had only seen that dark stranger once since coming to the world of Hiraeth. He had come to give her a final warning that she tried to heed even though she was sick of puzzles and prophecies. They were what had trapped her, her own truths hidden, for a thousand years.

As she neared the beach, Khedran was laughing at Chandar's playful greeting. When he turned to see her stride out of the water, she glimpsed his heartfelt joy upon seeing her there.

In that unguarded instant, saw also his love for her.

She lost her breath and almost had to stop walking.

Why did he seem so familiar to her, as if she had known him a thousand years ago? How could she know with such certainty that his spirit was far older than his body...that he was at least as old as she?

No, she told herself. *It can't be. He's just familiar because you have known him all his life, and you've been away from him for so long. It's just a trick of your mind.*

That had to be it. She reminded herself her mission was to leave him, leave his world, so that she could take the damned gods with her. She had lived a thousand years on a world not her own, with leaving as her only goal.

She reminded herself of that now, with every step toward him.

He watched her come to him, his emerald eyes now carefully unreadable, as was his habit. The sea-breeze danced through his black hair, blowing it about his handsome face. She saw there the shadows of fatigue nearing exhaustion.

Curse words flew through her mind. He was on the edge of implosion, she could tell, with weight on his shoulders he could share with no one. If she thought she'd glimpsed some hidden love for her, it was only part of the burden he carried, and, she felt sure, the part least important.

And it could never be.

"Sorry I'm late," she began as she neared him, as though she'd been gone only hours rather than years. "I brought your horses, and your Compatri. He took good care of Chandar." She stopped to take in the horses passing by as they came out of the sea, the soldiers who took them, the crowd behind them, the dazzling towers of Penumbra.

She turned back to find him watching her instead of what she had brought to him.

He said, "The Tahmine Rani told me Jon is now King of Ord-hold, and that he held you imprisoned."

"Yes. He had Danon thrown in with me. But we're both here now."

"Jon will pay for it. He'll pay for all of it, in time." But briefly again, his truth slipped through. The warmth in his gaze belied the chill in his words. "I thought I had lost you, Shandiin."

She turned away from him then, from what could never be. "Walk with me," she told him. "Tell me what has happened here."

He gestured to a soldier to take Chandar, and they walked together to Penumbra.

Marre watched from the balcony. She alone guessed what was coming, having gleaned it from some unknown place where Daimaine's magic lived.

She turned from the sea and the golden ships of the Chaine, and she alone in all that city gazed to the east, while the horses came out of the western sea. Gold and bay and white and grey they came, more beautiful than the jeweled waters from which they climbed, shaking wet diamonds over the men who waited in awe.

There is a world beyond our borders, Marre thought. *A world from which these steeds of war have come to us.*

For each soldier there was a mount, who came willingly and full of knowing, to blow the hot breath of being upon their Chosen.

These are the Sacred Ones, the Shalmira, bred beneath a desert sun far from this place.

Each man in that bright morning spoke the name of the steed which had been given him and laid a hand upon his spirited beauty...not in ownership, but in a partnership which would not be broken while either lived.

For today. They have been bred and born for this moment, this place.

Marre stretched the power Daimaine had given her, but could not see how the Chaine had become their bearers. She only knew that it was for a purpose.

The Forbidden Child will soon be known. The Outsiders are a dark storm crowding the borders of Azlatan, driven by a power even greater than that which has been given to me.

She turned back to the scene below, as the treasured horses were led away one by one to their new home. The stables had been built for them as part of the High King's mysterious new constructions in Cabre.

The silence of morning was gone. Marre heard celebration, as even the Dominion Kings gave joyful homage to the miracle they had witnessed.

Unity at last, she thought. *It will be needed. Let them celebrate, before the Shadow comes upon us all.*

She searched for the one among the many, the one who mattered to her as no one else ever could. She found him easily, for he stood at the water's edge with a black stallion who bowed his great neck to his master. A tall woman in tawny leather stood with him, her hair of fire and gold blowing about her shoulders.

The two did not touch but turned in unison to walk to Penumbra. Marre watched them come, her eyes narrowed on the legendary warrior known as The Chaine. She realized there were questions even her new power could not answer.

But she knew this: *The time of Prophecy has come. This, then, is the beginning of the end of a thousand years.*

PART 4: GIFT OF THE SUNQUEEN

ON THE PLAIN OF ADMECH, AZLATAN YEAR 994, ONE YEAR BEFORE THE PROPHECY WAR

*As the mortals crossed from Admech into Azlatan,
the God Phaelon closed and warded the border behind them.
Any mortal who would neither rule as Rioch
nor serve as Duine,
would wander always in the wilderness beyond the border
with no god but Chaos for comfort.
Phaelon's face was turned from them, and they were no longer
called either Rioch or Duine,
but only Outsiders.*

—–from the Annals of Azlatan

CHAPTER 19

As a child, Varady had tried to see the end of the world.

He had clung, dizzy, to the edge of the cliff that was Azlatan's eastern border, and peered over it until his senses wheeled and he felt he was falling into the sky. Though terrified, he looked.

His courage had brought him the miracle of wonder, and a thirst for knowledge.

Peering at the distant horizon, he realized a vision of unending distant clouds was in fact snow-ridden mountains. Real mountains in a real world outside of Azlatan.

Between and below, the Plain of Admech seemed as far away as the sky. He had dreamed that someday he would find a way down.

His someday had come. He and the horse nicknamed Pet followed an ancient road down from Azlatan, a road no one else had traveled in a thousand years.

The Plain had been featureless from above, flattened by the limits of vision. Varady found the reality near the border slashed by ravines, tumbled with rocks.

When his first night outside of Azlatan arrived, a strange apparition appeared to him.

Varady thought at first that he dreamed. Pet walked patiently beneath him. They traveled the floor of a deep ravine which cut away from the west, and it was dark between its walls. The sky was a pale trail of diamond-dust above, the stars of The Bridle now only a brighter glow at its eastern end. Varady had grown drowsy in the darkness. He blinked at the apparition ahead and halted his mount.

Pet blew softly as though in question, unconcerned.

It was a cat. A small white cat, strangely luminous in the darkness.

He was amazed at a legend come true. This had to be the cat form of ChanDethe, Liethe's messenger! Varady watched it drift away past a turn in the ravine. He quickly urged Pet to follow, trotting around the rocky wall.

The sun came up.

The cat led them from the ravine onto the steppes. There was no shadow on that plain, nowhere to hide. Pet walked knee deep in the pale stiff green grass, and Varady rode toward an unbroken horizon.

He looked back once and saw the looming cliff that was Azlatan's eastern border. He thought it strange that it looked foreboding from below. He shivered a little, turning away from it.

He rode into the rising sun, following the path the cat had given him.

He lost track of time. The sun rode before him in the morning, behind him in the evening, and baked him so brown Danon wouldn't have known him.

He shed his cloak, and then his shirt, and left breeches only to protect him from the saddle's chafe. The sun burned moisture from him as it tanned his body, and bleached his hair almost white, many shades lighter than his skin. The hair grew past his shoulders, and he tore a strip from his useless shirt to make a headband to keep it from his eyes. He rode and walked and hunted beasts of the grass with his bare hands and grew strong and hard as a Chaine warrior of legend.

One day he found himself climbing a hill, and he was so used to walking the flat steppe that he stumbled. Pet nudged him to get up, but he lay on his back a long time, staring at the cloudless sky. The stallion snorted as a person might shrug, and fell to grazing.

Varady was waking up.

Mindless, he thought. *I have been as mindless as sky or earth; the horse has more sense than I. I think I was bewitched, in the beginning, and I welcomed it because I was weary with the ways of Duine and Rioch. But I am a man, and this hill tells me that part of my journey is nearly over, so I must return to thinking like a man.*

He rolled onto his flat belly and looked through the stiff blades of grass at the stallion who grazed a few lengths away. Pet was snow white, his mane and tail like spun sugar trailing in the sun. He was beautiful as myth, but his ribs showed. The grass was not enough for him on this journey, and water was scarce.

Varady licked the salt of blood from his cracked lips. He was glad he had spared the horse, walking instead of riding. Danon's saddle was lost, vanished somewhere behind them on the prairie.

He got up and climbed to the top of the hill.

More hills. They looked like snow, but they were sand.

Varady raised his eyes from the dunes and saw a bright jagged line hanging over the horizon. He began to smile.

He stepped into the desert, his eyes on the distant mountains of his dreams.

The sand was hard going, a pale tide that dragged at his feet. The sun watched him all day and rolled down the sky to send his shadow streaming ahead of him.

The cat he had named ChanDethe came back that night, walking before him over the dunes. It did not tread sand, but passed above. It stayed just beyond him and his mount, and so led him to solid ground again.

Rich grass bent beneath his feet, the kind he had known in a world he could barely remember.

He fell.

The grass was cool. He slept.

He dreamed of horses running. Their thunder rumbled in the earth. He awoke and heard it, waking, where his ear pressed down. His body felt it, a low echo in his bones. The moon shed a blanket of light that could not muffle the earth's drumming.

Varady's eyes flew open, and he scrambled upright. He was barely in time to catch Pet's trailing reins. The horse tugged, denied his wish to join the distant herd, and shook his head in anger.

Varady tied the reins around his wrist, and Pet swung to face north, ears pitched forward. He stood like a statue save for the constant flare of his square nostrils. Moonlight shattered in his eyes. The horse recognized what Varady had only dreamed. He was bewitched.

A cold night wind channeled the grass. A sound like silver followed it. He and Pet stood together until fire sprang in the east, and dawn was come.

Pet moved at last, with a low whinny of loss. He turned to his master with a look Varady found eerie. It was a look of recognition, of intelligent acceptance of his lot and his duty. It was a look of sadness.

Varady was sure they were going to die here.

He didn't know how long it had been, only that there was no strength left in either of them, man or beast, to continue their journey. Varady untied the reins from his wrist, flung away Pet's bridle, freeing him. But the horse stayed with him. Their bond was forged of more than leather, now.

The sun came to ride Varady's back. He lay face down, but light pulsed red behind his eyelids, even when he dozed. Sometimes awareness returned, so bright it hurt. He could wish then for a return of the enchantment that had kept pain away, realizing he had lived in a dream throughout his journey, and that the dream was now gone.

He thought fleetingly of Jael. There was something he should understand. He dozed.

Varady didn't know that Pet moved with the sun, always between his master and that burning sphere. The horse's shadow was the only shade he had throughout that day. The stallion guarded in the only way he could and gazed always east, with an attitude of waiting. A white horse of Azlatan would have died beneath that desert sun. But Pet's heritage was born of it. His forefathers had known this desert.

At last Varady woke fully, consciousness sharp as a blade in his guts. The sun rode his back. The ground was hard. There was dust in his throat, and he tried to spit and couldn't. He lay face down, but light ran red behind his eyelids. There was no escape from the heat.

His horse screamed shrilly above him. Varady rolled over to see the stallion standing over him, ears flattened in rage.

His warhorse was guarding him. Varady tried to crawl, and the horse moved to stand squarely between him and an intruder.

"Hold," a voice commanded. "Stop!"

Pet leaped, and Varady rolled away from flying dirt. He heard the collision of horses, the thud of hooves striking dirt and stone. He pushed himself to a sitting position.

The chestnut mare Pet challenged was not fighting. She spun, turning shoulder and haunch to Pet's desperate strikes, as though understanding the stallion's weakened condition.

Pet's valor could not pass this simple defense. Varady saw him stagger, turning, his great heart stronger than his poor body. He would kill himself, fighting an uncontested battle.

"Stop him!" the mare's rider called. Varady realized it was a woman, and realized she had been speaking to Pet, as though to reason with him. Now she pled with the man. "My horse will not fight a Shalmira!"

The word meant nothing to him, but Varady couldn't bear to watch his horse struggling, and he called to him.

Pet dropped back, uncertain. "Come," Varady called.

The stallion snorted, turning from the enemy who would not fight, confused and trembling. Varady lifted his arms to him, and Pet came on unsteady legs, pushing his head down with a soft whicker of worry.

"It's all right," Varady whispered to the wide dark eyes. "Rest, my friend." Pet breathed into his hands, and swung round to stand beside him, obedient but still wary. Varady turned back to the woman.

She was dismounting. Varady stood, though the world tended to turn beneath him. He leaned on his horse.

"That's far enough," he warned.

The young woman halted her path toward him, straight as the spear she carried upright in one hand. Her eyes moved from him to his horse, and she sank slowly to one knee, her back straight, the spear braced between earth and her extended arm.

She was all long angles, and very tall. Her bare arms were brown, as was the long throat rising from a simple buckskin tunic, and her eyes were dark. Only her hair was darker. It was glossy black, braided in a heavy rope over one shoulder.

She studied him as carefully as he did her. She saw a powerful man with long hair bleached by the sun to sand and silver. His eyes were deep gold. She saw male beauty that caused her nostrils to flare.

"I am Stormwing," she told him. "My horse is Inzrah, of the Shalmira." Her large eyes moved from him to Pet, as though expecting a similar introduction.

She is dark, but she is not a Rioch of Azlatan, Varady reminded himself with some effort. *Yet I cannot believe she is an evil Outsider.*

"I am Varady."

She nodded, waiting. He glanced at Pet, remembering that she had introduced her horse, remembering also Danon's chosen name for the horse nicknamed Pet. "My horse is ChanDethe."

He saw shock widen her eyes. The spear trembled in her tightened grip.

Too late he remembered that the mythical ChanDethe had more than one form, and one had been the horse stolen by the goddess Chaos. He eyed the spear, wondering if he could throw himself aside before it pierced his heart.

The spear lowered, and he stared at it lying on the ground with Stormwing alongside it, her forehead touching the earth in obeisance. "I am unworthy of this honor." She spoke into the dirt. "Yet I will serve, Lord Varady, as the Sunqueen asked."

He gaped at her, looked at Pet as though for direction, and tried to pull his failing wits together. "Perhaps, uh...Stormwing, perhaps some water, for me and for my horse? That's the only service I need."

She was up before he could finish, running to her horse to pull down a waterskin. He could hear the liquid sloshing within as she ran back, and weakly slid to sit on the ground, reaching for it with almost unbearable thirst.

She handed it down, open, and then cried out as he upended it to pour the precious stuff down his throat, the metal taste of it so exquisite it spasmed the muscles of his throat. She snatched it from him, splashing him, then fell to her knees as he tried to wrestle it back, spilling wet glory over them both. Pet added his own desperation, long head reaching for the waterskin. Varady was shocked when she slapped the horse away, almost sobbing. It was that action which brought him to his senses. He stilled, gasping.

"You'll be sick!" he realized she had been repeating this over and over. Tears washed the dust from her hollow cheeks. "You can't drink so fast!"

He released the waterskin to her, his stomach already cramping.

Her eyes lifted to his, spangled with tears. "I am so sorry!"

He waved her away, sickness rising, and vomited the cool water. She held his head, crooning, while it gushed even from his nose. He managed the smaller sips she offered, then blacked out again.

He woke strong in the twilight, and sat up with eyes seeking the woman. She stood in the purple dusk beside the white glimmer that was his horse. She held a skin of water wide open for him, but the stallion only sniffed it politely, lowering his head to graze instead. The horse had recovered. He saw laughter in the tilt of her head as she turned toward him. As soon as she saw him watching she stilled.

He lifted a hand, beckoning. "One more drink, please?" He was sorry for her apparent fear of him. "With all my thanks."

She came to him almost timidly, kneeling with simple grace to offer him a brimming cup. He took it with both hands and watched her over the rim as he drank. Her hands rested neatly on her long thighs in their buckskin breeches, but her body leaned back just a little as though she must somehow keep her distance.

He set the cup aside carefully. "I thank you again, Stormwing. I believe you saved my life, and that of my horse."

"The Sunqueen willed it," she replied softly.

He drew up his knees, laced his fingers over them, bracing. "Who is the Sunqueen?"

Her eyes widened. "Where are you from, Lord Varady?"

He winced. "Not Lord. Just Varady. I come from the west. Beyond the sand, and the grass...and farther. From Azlatan."

"I have never heard of this place. And you have never heard of the Sunqueen. It is a mystery, Lord...just Varady...that you could cross the places you describe, and live. It is a greater mystery that you come riding on a Shalmira unknown to us, for they are all known to us. They are..." the slim hands lifted momentarily, winging apart in search of a word. They fell back to her thighs, defeated. "They are the Shalmira. That yours bears the name of the Sunqueen's Gift, the father of all Shalmira, but is from somewhere distant..." she paused.

Puzzled, he waited.

She drew breath, small bosom rising under buckskin. "We have a prophecy," she explained, "that a stranger will come to Deliver us, and we will follow him—we and the Shalmira—and defeat our enemies."

Her explanation brought more questions than answers. Varady shook his head. "I am a stranger, but I don't think I am who you are looking for. I beg your patience, Stormwing. Who is the Sunqueen?"

Her brow furrowed. "Our goddess. The Bearer of Gifts. The Sunqueen."

He was stunned. "Four gods," he whispered. "Liethe, of Life and Love. Daimaine, of Justice and Death. Phaelon, the God of Order..."

"We do not speak of him," she said primly.

He blanched. "The Sunqueen is the fourth god?"

"Did you not know of her, in your land?"

"I do not recall the name. We call her something else." *Chaos, he thought. We call her Chaos. She is the enemy of Phaelon. Must I believe that? I am in a different world now.* "Tell me, Stormwing...what are your people called?"

"We are the Sundancers, who honor the Gift of the Sunqueen."

"Meaning the horses? The Shalmira?"

She nodded gravely. "But the Gift of the Sunqueen is many, and the greatest is yet unknown. Perhaps it is you, Varady."

He looked away. "I don't suppose you would understand, if I told you I hope you are wrong."

"Oh, but I would!"

He looked back in surprise. Her eyes were troubled. "The Sunqueen warned us. The Gifts of the Gods are always two-edged, a knife easily turned in mortal hand. Like the Sun is bright and brings the good earth to grow...and hot, to burn it."

"And the Shalmira?"

"We love them." Her hands turned over, palms up. "They leave us."

Her gaze moved north, somewhere behind him. Varady remembered horses running, running, through a black and silver night. He shivered. "I almost lost my horse to them, in the night."

She looked toward the horses. "He stayed. So now you are his Chosen, and you will remain together. Many were not so lucky as you and I."

He wasn't sure he understood that, either. Apparently a Shalmira was more than just a horse. *And how did Danon get one?* But the sadness on her face led him away from this line of questioning.

He had never heard of the Sundancers, but he shuddered at their beliefs. *Do they worship Chaos?* He swallowed again, trying to remember the ancient annals which, he'd been taught, were more truth than legends. "Stormwing, have you ever heard of the Outsiders?"

She rose lightly to her feet, looking down at him from her slim height. Her face had gone cold. He remembered the spear.

"Yes. They are our enemies, thieves of children, murderers of souls."

His body relaxed. Her description, at least, showed her not one of them. "They are enemies also, in my homeland," he reassured her.

She relaxed as well and turned away to go to her saddle-pack. Her horse grazed, free but watchful, some distance away. The chestnut's white-blazed head and stockings were bright in the deepening dusk.

"How did you know I am not an Outsider?" he called after Stormwing.

She glanced over her shoulder. "A Shalmira accepts no evil master." She pulled a package from her bag. "If it were not for yours, you would be dead. From a distance you look very like one of them."

They ate dried meat, which Stormwing explained was made from the flesh of wild deer. He learned that the Sundancers grew no crops, but hunted meat with bow and arrow, harvesting other food from the land. They travelled lightly while following the Shalmira herd and protecting them and themselves from the Outsiders. Those evil ones came from the south, and took children they made slaves, and occasionally stole a Shalmira. A missing mare, in fact, was Stormwing's reason for riding so far west. She said they often found the stolen horses dead, killed by the furious Outsiders who could never tame them.

Varady found the meat both tough and spicy, but his stomach was grateful. Strength returned with wonderful speed, and he spared a moment of thanks for the protection of Liethe, who had unaccountably sent her white cat to lead him.

He wondered if Liethe had anything to do with the mysterious Sunqueen.

After they finished eating, Stormwing told him to ride her horse, knowing his would follow as she walked with them. She was still concerned that they were both weak from traveling.

Varady went to the white stallion and laid a hand on the velvet nose. Pet made a sound like a chuckle, deep in his throat.

"He's all right." Varady smiled at Stormwing. "He just told me so." He vaulted onto Pet's back. Stormwing regarded them both in wonder for a long moment, glanced west at the desert her people believed impassable, then mounted her bay without asking questions.

He thought: *She believes our sudden return of strength is another Gift of the Sunqueen. I don't know if that's bad or good.*

They rode through the night. Varady was surprised at first to find he did not miss his lost saddle or bridle. Pet bore him lightly over the moonlit grass, and he rode as though balance, muscle and reflex were the only way he had ever ridden. He reflected on the magic that had carried him so far on his journey, and on the oneness with his silver stallion.

Stormwing sat upright in her saddle with her spear laid across her thighs in readiness. Varady thought hard, as he watched her from behind.

I knew when I left Azlatan I left my known world. Though those distant mountains are my goal, I cannot ride through this abandoned land without stopping to know its people, and even their goddess, who no one names in Azlatan. If I am damned it is a choice I already made when I left Selagon.

With that burden of conscience set aside he relaxed to the ride and observed the hilly land they now traveled. Short grasses muffled their hoofbeats. Clumps of brush grew thickly as they climbed grades steadily uphill. Soon trees appeared, spaced widely at first, then in groves which Stormwing avoided in caution of the deeper shadows.

Once a pale owl drifted overhead, hunting, and Stormwing muffled a laugh at Varady's quick startle. He hoped this meant she was losing her awe of him and could accept him simply as a man and not some magic gift.

She didn't halt, but silently handed him her waterskin as they rode, and more of the dry spicy meat, until finally they reached a wall of rock rising abruptly from the steepening hillside. Varady heard the sound of water flowing as she dismounted.

"Here we rest," she told him, "and water the horses before we start the climb."

He slid to the ground, peering up at the cliff-wall. Climb? The sound of water grew louder as they walked to a stand of trees near the rock.

She halted before stepping into the shadows, glanced at her unconcerned horse, then whistled like a bird.

The whistle was answered.

She signaled Varady to follow her into the trees.

"Another Sundancer?" he asked, Pet's head bobbing at his shoulder as they walked.

"Rainsong watches us. All ways that lead to the inner land are guarded."

"Rainsong?"

"That is his name. You will meet him after the Sunqueen appears. Many of your questions will be answered then, Lord Varady, and many asked."

After the Sunqueen appears. Varady swallowed the many questions those words brought to his own mind. She had asked him, in her polite way, for patience.

They stepped into a clearing, where The Bridle swung tangled in the treetops on the other side. Stars sprinkled the small meadow with silver. A waterfall tumbled down the cliffs at the meadow's end, into a pool filled with broken ribbons of starlight.

The horses both sprang away over the grass as though still fresh after their long night's journey. Varady and Stormwing followed them more sedately and drank in their turn from the starlit pool. The water was icy, and Varady knelt at the rocky edge, awed by the beauty around him.

A light touch freed him from his reverie. He rose to follow Stormwing and the horses, surprised to see a path leading behind the waterfall. It was narrow, allowing entrance in single file to the cave hidden there.

It was dark inside. Varady halted, Pet whiffling at his bare shoulder. Stormwing took his hand in the darkness. "I will lead you." There was a smile in her voice.

Varady had a sense of immensity, as though they passed through a great cavern. Their steps echoed from distant walls. Then the walls closed in, and they began once more to climb.

Time was lost to him with sight. When they stepped at last into open air, he didn't know if it had been minutes or hours. Stormwing slipped her hand free of his, still shy of him.

They stood in a deep cleft, still not free of walls, though a paling sky was visible above. Stormwing went to her horse, stripping off both saddle and bridle which she dropped to the ground. The mare tossed her mane and trotted away from them.

"She is going home," Stormwing explained.

Pet bunted him, then snorted farewell and followed the mare.

"Come," said Stormwing. "It's almost time for the Sunqueen."

She started up the wall, walking easily. Varady was startled until he recognized the stair hewn from living rock, worn smooth by many climbers. He followed.

A horn winded, somewhere distant. One note, mellow as gold, echoing from wall to wall.

Another joined, three tones higher. Simple harmony, which his music-loving spirit rose to meet.

Light quickened about them. He stared up at the sky, listening to the horns singing up the sun, then scrambled to catch up with Stormwing.

She stood on the cliff-top, head lifted to the eastern sky. Her bare arms were down, not hanging but held down and back as though by an effort of will, her long body leaning against the air. Her hair was free now, raining down from her upflung head. The horns blew again, repeating, first and major third.

The sun came up.

With it the third horn came in, singing the perfect fifth, the harmony Varady had anticipated. It raised his hair, shivered his flesh. Stormwing's arms began to rise as though pulled by the sun.

Golden light fired the clifftop, gilded her, as she hung suspended by sunrays, her arms chained from the sky.

The horns blended, echoing. Drums began.

Stormwing began to dance. Varady's heart answered the beat of the drums, in breast and temples. Golden clifftops surrounded. Five Sundancers moved in exact precision, as though hung by sky-chains from a single point.

The sun climbed. The dance was as slow as its ascent, rimming the snow-shouldered mountains, then the fiery globe leaped free into the crystal sky of morning.

The music ended as abruptly. Silence returned to the rock walls, and sunlight ran down them to fill the inner lands.

Stormwing rejoined him, braiding her hair again as they walked.

"It seems a shame." Varady spoke without thinking. "Your hair is so beautiful, loose."

She hesitated, startled. He saw the blush beneath her dark skin.

She ducked her head and her fingers resumed their swift work.

"We only wear it free," she murmured, "for the Sundance and our mate."

He turned away, sparing them both, and noted the other dancers had vanished from their high eyries.

"There are always five," she explained from behind him, "for the five tribes of the Sundancers. We are Storm, Rain, Wind, Sky and Cloud. I think you liked our dance."

He turned back, surprised. "How could you tell?"

She tilted her head. "You are stranger than a stranger, Varady of the West. You have the body, grace, and power of a warrior of our legends. But you do not guess what is in your eyes. So, it hurts...when you look at me as you did while I danced."

Varady looked down at his Duine's hands, which had never held a warrior's weapon. *Have I changed, or does she see what exists only in her mind?* "Why does it hurt?" he ventured. "Is that one of your two-edged Gifts, Stormwing?"

She tied off her braid. "I don't know. Perhaps I will, when we go among my people." She glanced up, and he was puzzled to read the same sadness in her eyes as when she had spoken of the Shalmira leaving. "It is time, now, for you to meet them."

He followed her down the stair. For once he had not glanced at the eastern mountains, rising clear now and near, against the morning sky.

CHAPTER 20

S tormwing had picked up her saddle on the way down the ravine, and they made their way from that rocky cleft to a grassy hillside. It sloped gently to the edge of a forest, thick trees lining the banks of a wide and gentle river. The land rose again beyond it, a jumble of living green broken occasionally by golden rock, climbing to misty distance where rose the great mountains she said were called Khaibara.

"Have your people ever gone to those mountains?"

"A few. But there is nothing there for us, and there is nothing beyond but the wild sea. There are stories of a strange people who lived there once, people with hair like rusted metal, but they left a long time ago."

Varady was somehow disappointed, and felt silly for it. "We have a story in Azlatan that the world was once alive, and spoke to a woman called Prophecy's Daughter. I planned to look for her there."

Stormwing lifted her eyebrows. "The Sunqueen speaks to the world. But she lives in the sky, not in the mountains, except when she comes to walk among us."

He quit walking, touching Stormwing's arm so she stopped to meet his eyes. "She is an actual person? Have you seen her?"

"No. She has not come back to us for many years. Only the elders have seen her."

"What does she look like?"

"They say she is bright as fire."

A bright Sunqueen, he thought, and shook his head. *Of course she'd be bright. Probably just another myth.*

But he found it hard to give up his own stories. "She is a goddess, you say, and she speaks to the world."

"She is the only one who can speak to the world and receive an answer." Apparently sensing Varady's edge of disbelief, Stormwing turned away and resumed walking.

Not wanting to insult her, Varady dropped his questions and followed. Starting down the long slope to the distant trees, he took her saddle from her, resting it easily on one shoulder.

He smiled at her surprised expression. "In my land, a man would be ashamed to let a woman carry a burden while he walked unencumbered."

"Strange. Your women must be very weak."

He didn't respond, inwardly amused by her faintly superior tone. "Is that cave we came through the only entrance to the inner lands?"

"We call this place Iesse. Most passes are closed when the snow comes. There is also a southern pass. We watch it closely for the Outsiders, though they rarely come so far, this late in the year. The plains are home to us, and the deserts, but the Outsiders are cold-blooded, like their horses. They prefer the south."

He glanced across at her. He had heard contempt in her voice, and loathing.

"Thieves of children," he recalled aloud. "And murderers of souls. How?"

She shook her head grimly. "It is no discussion to ruin the bright morning. Besides, you will be meeting some of my people soon. Rainsong knows you are here, and your horse, following my Inzrah, will have convinced anyone who did not believe him. How I would have loved to see their expressions, when a strange Shal entered the herd! There, I see some of them coming now."

Varady looked ahead, took a deep breath. *Here we go.*

A grey stallion had emerged from the trees, followed shortly by a small band of riders. The grey's rider, to Varady's brief shock, was a fair-skinned man with hair as golden as the morning sun.

Varady halted, his gaze going to each rider in turn: hair of black, and gold, and brown, and several shades of skin.

Man and woman, shoulder to shoulder, all as equals.

This is not Azlatan. It was his final realization. There were no Duine, no Rioch. These were Sundancers, and this was another world.

In the horses he recognized the deerlike beauty of his own Pet. He wondered again where Danon had gotten the horse which did not belong to Azlatan.

The grey came at a gallop. Checked by his rider, he half-reared, light as laughter. Varady stared at the golden-haired man who rode him. Rainsong gazed back openly, his blue eyes wide with wonder. His hair was bound at his forehead, like Varady's, and blew free around his thick neck. He was dressed in buckskin, much like Stormwing. All the riders were.

"Your Shalmira is well," Rainsong told him, as though this were the most important fact in their world. His voice held mirth. "He introduced himself to the camp by galloping past the morning cookpots, and luring the children from their chores to run after him. He is a wonder, your Shal."

Varady only nodded, unsure what to say.

Stormwing stepped in front of him. "This is Varady. He comes from the west, beyond the sand and the grass. His land is called..." she faltered.

"Azlatan," he supplied.

"Azlatan," she repeated, as though trying to memorize it. Then she straightened. "His Shalmira is named ChanDethe."

Varady flinched, seeing the humor vanish from Rainsong's clear eyes. All the faces changed, from eager wonder to sober awe.

"We should have guessed it," said the woman who rode beside Rainsong. Her hair was of darkest gold, streaked with platinum.

"No strange Shal could there be, unless his Chosen was our promised Gift."

Varady felt an odd loneliness as their sudden respect set him apart. Stormwing was silent.

"I don't know what Gift was promised you." Varady lifted his open hands. "Stormwing can tell you I didn't even know the name of the goddess who made promises. I know only that I came on a quest commanded by my own heart, a journey not ending here. I did not know of the Sundancers, but Stormwing found me and saved my life and that of my horse, and so I would like to call the Sundancers friends..." he glanced, unsure why, at Stormwing's still figure "...before I continue on my way."

Rainsong nodded soberly. "You are welcome for as long as you wish to stay. The Sunqueen's Gifts are not always revealed, even to the Bearer. Stormwing, you have not named us to Lord Varady."

She looked abashed. "Forgive me. This is Rainsong, husband of my sister; his Shal is Elthar. Beside him is my sister, Stormdawn."

She had indicated the golden-haired woman.

"Your sister?" Varady's eyes flashed to Stormwing's dark hair and visage.

"Yes," Stormwing assured him, puzzled.

Varady collected himself, nodding at her to continue.

Beside Rainsong and his wife Stormdawn, there were Windson, Skywolf, and Cloudhost. Varady realized they represented the five tribes, and the intermarriage unknown in Azlatan had created a rainbow race.

The one called Skywolf reached down for Varady's forgotten burden. "I will take this." His blue eyes were wide as a child's. "Rainsong's Shal can bear your added weight."

Varady nodded dumbly, taking Rainsong's offered arm to swing up behind his saddle. Stormwing mounted behind her golden-haired sister, and they wheeled as one toward the trees.

The camp lay beyond the open wood, scattered along the wide bank of the shallow river. The Shalmira herd grazed on the opposite shore, bright coats shining in the morning sun. Varady sought and found Pet's white form, where he stood nose to tail with Stormwing's mare. *Content as an old carthorse*, Varady smiled to himself, and saw the white head lift in his direction.

The silent bond between them moved toward communication even at this distance. Varady felt overloaded with wonders. He turned his attention to the camp.

There were no buildings, but tents strange to his eye. They were made of tanned animal skins and bark stretched over long poles that crossed at the top, slanting wide to the earth. Each had an opening that faced east to the river. There were cooking fires before most of them, tended by men and women older than the young people Varady rode with. Children, apparently remanded to routine after Pet's interruption, carried wood or played on the sandy beach. The scene was peaceful. Varady breathed deep the smell of food in the cooking-pots, curiosity giving way to hunger.

Rainsong laughed, glancing over his shoulder. "I hear you sniffing. My mother will be glad she made plenty of food."

"So will I," Varady smiled back. He liked Rainsong, who seemed never long awed by strangers or prophecies.

The other men dropped off as they rode through the camp, waving farewell as they turned to their own dwellings. Curious children were herded away as they passed.

Stormwing's eyes were rich as summer earth, watching him. "They learn to be polite," she explained. "Children are curious, but the Sundancers live free of watchful gossip. You will be introduced to all, at the congress fires tonight. The traveler's day of rest is earned and given, free of questions."

They neared a large tent at the far end of the camp, its top poles shaded by a large tree. A smaller dwelling stood just behind.

"My lodge," Rainsong told him. "My mother, Windstar, waits for us at the fire. She shares the lodge behind with Stormwing, since my wife's mother died last winter."

Varady saw the tall woman standing beside the fire, watching them approach. Windstar's hair was threaded grey and iron, braided over both shoulders, but she was unbent beneath her buckskin. A small child peered from behind her legs.

"My granddaughter," Windstar introduced proudly, indicating the child. "Storm Wind Goldmane."

Sensing his question, Stormwing explained. "She will choose her tribe with her husband. Her children will bear only one name."

Varady slid down from Rainsong's horse and bowed, out of respect for the woman's age and for the proud eyes in her strong, lined face.

"I am Varady," he told her. He omitted the name of his horse, forestalling a change in her welcome.

She indicated a low table where plates awaited. "Food is waiting, Varady. Please join us."

The stew was succulent with meat and wild onion, and Varady could hardly stop eating long enough to compliment Windstar on her cooking. Her laughter came easily, as it seemed with all the Sundancers, and she kept the bowl filled until his stomach was as full as his spirit.

Varady looked around at friends newfound in the wilderness and wondered at himself.

He was led to the larger lodge after breakfast. It was cool inside, and the breeze whispered without. Peace, not magic. He fell asleep on a thickly woven blanket almost immediately, glad of the custom that gave this privilege to the traveler.

When he awoke something in the air and the honeyed light told him it was afternoon. Rolling over, he came face to face with the child he had glimpsed earlier.

She regarded him solemnly with her great blue eyes, rosebud mouth pursed. She was squatting at the edge of his blanket, playing with her toes. He guessed her to be about two years old.

He propped his cheek on his fist, regarding her as gravely as she seemed to require. "Storm Wind Goldmane," he said aloud. "You shall be the prettiest of all the Sundancers, in a few short years."

Her eyes remained serious. He smiled and lifted his free hand to touch her golden hair. "Then you will have to braid this lovely mane. Will you always be so sober?"

Little Goldmane leaned forward suddenly, kissed him, and scurried out of the lodge. Varady looked after her, delighted, and sat up to stretch.

The lodge darkened briefly as Stormwing ducked in. "You've bewitched the child. She hasn't left your side for a moment, even to play. I thought you must be awake, when she came out and ran to her grandmother."

He laughed. "She kissed me and ran away. The nicest awakening I've ever had."

"You like children?"

"Always."

She hesitated over something. He couldn't see her face, with the light behind her.

"Would you come with me?" she asked finally. "To meet a child?"

Puzzled, he followed her out.

It was late afternoon, the sun brassy on the curved lodge walls. The camp was quiet, either in afternoon rest or gone, busy among the Shalmira. Windstar looked up from her loom, where a bright rug was climbing under her busy hands. She nodded greeting but said nothing. Goldmane sat by her in the dirt, playing with her toes again. She blinked at Varady's wink.

Stormwing started away toward the river, walking under the trees. Sun and shadow dappled over her bare arms, and Varady noticed that she had changed into beaded white buckskin and soft white boots, and carried a bundle of the same color. He glanced down at his ragged breeches and worn boots, all that he owned, and wished mightily for a bath.

The wood ended at a small jumble of rocks, a tiny inlet where the river, briefly captured, gurgled under a leafy roof. A young girl sat on a rock, still as a hunted rabbit. Her dark hair hung in a dull curtain from her bowed head. Varady sensed a strangeness, a prickle at his scalp.

Stormwing halted short of her, where they would not be heard over the water's song.

"You asked me about the Outsiders," she said, her eyes on the lone child. "Tonight at Congress you will meet all the other Sundancers, and perhaps hear of prophecy that is bound up in our hope of destroying them, our enemies. I know you do not understand our ways or our hopes, but before a request is made...before a denial by you is given...I want you to meet this child, who is called Rainmoon."

"She looks ill," Varady frowned. "Or bewitched."

"She is both. Rainmoon was stolen, Starfall last, by the Outsiders. It is the season when the tribes separate to return to the plains, when the inner lands are cloaked by snow. The Outsiders came, as they often do in that divided time. They killed her family, all but her brother, who was away. And they took her."

"Why would they take a child?"

She looked up at him with savage brilliance in her dark eyes. "They make slaves of the dark-haired ones. They breed them like animals. Rainmoon is twelve years old."

Varady had to look away.

"Her brother," Stormwing continued, "gathered many of his tribe, and followed the thieves, thinking to rescue her before they reached their hated city of Xanthe in the south. He did, but even so it was too late. They had murdered her soul. Please, Varady...I want you to talk to her."

He didn't understand, but he couldn't ignore the pleading in her eyes. He made his way over the rocks to the girl.

Rainmoon seemed to be unaware of him. He halted, standing over her, regarding the thin hunched shoulders and the pale hands resting palms up on her closed knees.

Kneeling, he spoke her name. She didn't move. He reached up, pushing back the dull drift of her hair, looking into her face.

Jael.

But no. Jael had dreamed, eyes open. Sometimes he could be drawn from the dream, join the waking. Rainmoon did not dream. Nothing moved at all behind the open windows of her eyes. The dwelling was vacant.

Varady drew away, letting fall the merciful curtain of her hair.

Stormwing's shadow fell over him. She knelt and laid the bundle she'd brought at his feet. "Clothing for you." Her voice was soft. "And there is soap. You will want to bathe, here in the quiet place, and think on what you have just seen. I will take Rainmoon back to her aunt, who takes care of her."

Varady seized her wrist before she could leave. "Do you think I can do something about this evil? I don't know how!"

She wouldn't look at him.

"You expect too much, Stormwing. I can't defeat the Out-siders for you, just because I have a horse once named Chan-Dethe."

"Understanding has not come to you yet." Her voice was barely a whisper.

"Then tell them..." he looked from her bowed head to the child's, and released her wrist. "Tell them, please, not to ask anything of me, until I do understand. If I ever do. I can promise you nothing, Stormwing. Tell them not to ask, and then I will not have to deny them."

Stormwing took the girl's hands, pulling her to her feet. "I will tell them. Nothing will be asked of you, Lord Varady, until you can understand the request." She lifted the thin child into her arms and walked away.

When she was gone, he undressed and slipped into the moving water to swim until the last light had left the treetops and the first stars had appeared in the purple sky. He came out and found white buckskin in the bundle, soft as velvet under his water-wrin-kled fingers. It was not beaded, but there was fringe on the long sleeves, and the wide belt was woven of stiff horsehair with a buckle of heavy silver. The boots were like Stormwing's, soft white, and very high. He folded the fringed tops over just beneath his knees and tied them in place with their accompanying leather laces.

Fully dressed, he wondered at the bundle remaining on the rocks. He found himself hesitating to open it, as though fore-warned about something.

Finally, he unrolled it, and sighed.

You try to make a warrior of this Duine. Even the small knife I used to carry was frowned on, for we are supposed to be a peaceful race–children of Liethe, not Daimaine.

He picked up the knife and looked at the long silver blade, its hilt inlaid with blue stone. He remembered he was no longer in Azlatan, and he remembered Rainmoon. He slipped it into its white leather sheath and strapped it to his thigh, as he had seen Rainsong's worn.

He would discard his old breeches, his worn boots, the last remnants of his old life. For a moment he felt the loss of Danon's pack and saddle, for they had carried things which he could have gifted to his hosts. But he had to put that behind him too.

He stood up, resplendent in white to match his Shalmira, and started back to camp, surprised at the eagerness in his step.

Supper was a communal affair, held around a long pit be-tween the encircling camp and the river. Varady sat beside Rainsong and the other young men and listened to laughter and talk flow around him like music. Stormwing was somewhere on the other side of the fire. He thought sadly that it seemed she was avoiding him.

The fire burned down to coals as the food vanished. The moon built a silver road over the river and painted the sand white. Occasionally he heard the nicker of a horse borne on the soft summer air. Varady sat, half-dreaming, scarcely noticing as some stood, and voices fell away to silence.

"Congress," Rainsong whispered, leaning very near. "Do not worry, Lord Varady. Stormwing has warned them well, to ask no boon of you yet."

"Thank you."

Five Sundancers were standing, all of them elders. Varady recognized only Windstar, who turned toward him.

"We welcome a traveler," she announced solemnly. "Varady of Azlatan, in the west. His Shalmira is ChanDethe."

There was no reaction from the seated watchers. Apparently, word had already gotten around.

"Some time past," Windstar continued, "there was the passing of many Shalmira from our land. Our herds are thinned of those we kept trained for war, as the Sunqueen ordained when she gave us the sons and daughters of the first ChanDethe, in the beginning of our time. It is sad when they go from us to the destiny only the Sunqueen knows, but it is also a time of gladness, for those Shal who remain behind have their Chosen, and the herds will grow again. *Blessed is the Gift of the Sunqueen.*"

The throng repeated the mantra before she continued.

"The coming of Lord Varady and his Shal who is also Chan-Dethe has given rise to thoughts of prophecy handed down from our ancestors. These are not to be spoken of to our guest, unless he should ask, or this Congress should direct. Instead, you are all reminded of the Sunqueen's behest: that any stranger coming among us is to be treated as a friend until they are proven our enemy. Varady comes from a world beyond our understanding, and it is his need to understand ours. Answer his questions and show him our ways. We will share with him the Cup of the Sun, if the Congress now accepts."

"We accept," came the answering chorus.

"Stand to face her," Rainsong whispered to Varady, "and accept what she offers."

Varady obeyed, rising slowly to face Windstar. For the first time he heard a stir of excitement from the watchers. His face burned at the carrying whisper of a young girl: "He is as beautiful as his Shal!"

Windstar smiled, having heard it too. Varady was only sure when he saw her quick wink.

"I give to you the Cup of the Sun," she said formally. "Lift it to the Sunqueen, and she will give her blessing to this Congress."

He held out his hands and accepted the cup, seeing with surprise it was made of crystal. *To the Sunqueen? At night?*

But he lifted it, for the sky was the only offering he knew for this goddess. The sky, which held The Bridle.

As he did, The Bridle's light shot white fire against the crystal. Its contents erupted into golden sunlight between his hands.

"The Sunqueen has blessed us," Windstar said calmly, while Varady stared up into magic. He was unaware that his face was gilded like fine jewelry by the light.

Nor did he know they saw in his upraised profile that they had been brought a King.

He lowered the cup slowly, still burning golden and brighter than any fire.

"Drink," Windstar told him gently.

He obeyed, and drank the golden wine of the sun. It was cool on his throat, and more delicious than water when thirsty.

Though he drank deep, the cup was still full when he was done.

He passed it back mutely to Windstar, who lifted it to her own lips, and he wondered at the glimmer of tears in her old eyes as she regarded him.

Someone began to sing, a fine clear voice, and the others joined in. Varady listened, harmony speaking to him as strongly as words, while the Cup of the Sun was passed around, circling the throng as the sun circled the world.

We live beneath the beachless sky,
wherein all things are encompassed:
Mortal life of fate and will,
male and female, first and last.
Seasons flow, and moon and sun.
Deeds of valor, evil done.
Mortal tears and mortal blood,
mortal strife, and mortal love.

Of gods who are the gloried ones,
who walk the world beyond the sun,
alone the Sunqueen understands
the chains they craft upon our land.
Immortal they, intrepid souls,
who wander free and never know
mortal tears or mortal blood,
mortal strife, or mortal love.

Chapter 21

Varady chose to sleep under the stars instead of in a lodge. And that night, Stormwing came to him.

He was still a little drunk on the stuff in the Cup of the Sun, and the wine that flowed freely after Congress. So, when he saw her, drifting silently through the dappled moonlight, he was not sure at first if he dreamed. Her hair ran free as black water, and when she knelt beside him, she did not lean away.

Silently she came to him, and her lips were warm. Her hair was a curtain around them both, scented with clean grass and horses.

"Stormwing..." reality returned to him, and fear of hurting the innocent.

"Please." She sat back, shaking her hair free over white buckskin, her golden arms silvered by starlight. "Please," she repeated. "It was hard for me...to be so bold."

He looked up at her, sure that was true. "I wouldn't ask this of you."

"I know. You would do no dishonor to me. But you said you will travel on, and so will be gone from me. I cannot bear it."

Varady frowned and sat up. She drew away from him then, and he shook his head at her.

"I must leave here, yes...someday, probably soon. Stormwing, you are so lovely. But this is for your mate."

"You are my love." Her eyes were wide, a little afraid, and her chin trembled. "I have known it since I first looked into your eyes, before I even knew you."

"No, Stormwing. You don't know me even yet. And neither you nor your people can make me something that I am not."

She bowed her head, courage failing. He saw her gather herself to flee from him.

For the second time he seized her wrist, capturing it in both of his hands. She struggled for a moment, like a wild thing, then melted to the ground. Her quiet sobs were like a punishment.

"Damn," he whispered, and gathered her narrow body to him, hardly aware of his own strength but only of her. He held her as he would a child, cradled in his arms, her head buried against his shoulder. Her hair streamed over him, tangling in buckskin fringe. He grimaced and scooted back against a tree, settling more comfortably. She had stilled in his arms, scarcely breathing.

"Stormwing." He softly kissed the top of her head and sighed. "It's time I told you a story. Maybe I can make you understand why this...why what you want of me, cannot be."

"You are married?" she asked, muffled against his chest.

He nearly laughed. "Almost. Not to a woman, but to a way of life I find cannot be left behind so easily. Even though the Bond was broken, between me and my Rioch Lord."

He was surprised that it still hurt. After a moment he realized she was staring up at him, her eyes wide and luminous...and horrified. "You were a slave?"

"No. I am Duine, Stormwing. In Azlatan, the Duine serve the Rioch, freely and with honor, as ordered by Phaelon."

"Phaelon!" she spat the name, and he tightened his embrace to keep her from moving away.

"Phaelon." He repeated it, forcing her to listen to him. "God of Order, respected in Azlatan though he is not, here. Already you begin to see the wide gulf that lies between us."

She subsided, still staring at him, but her eyes had grown thoughtful. He smiled down at her, brushed the hair from her face.

"The Rioch Lords rule in Azlatan?" she asked.

He nodded.

"They are all dark, like me? And the Duine..."

"Fair. Like me. And your sister. The races don't mix in Azlatan. That's why I was so shocked, meeting Stormdawn."

She reached up and touched the heavy silk of his hair, silver in the starlight. "That, too, is ordered by Phaelon. We have heard of that Law, ordered by the Sunqueen's enemy. We do not honor it here. The Sunqueen tells us it is evil. It is an Outsider thing."

He raised his eyebrows, speculating about a goddess who walked among her people and told them stories. "The gulf widens."

"No! You said you would learn our ways. The Shal chose you: it is not you who are evil, but only the way you have been taught."

"It isn't an easy thing, Stormwing, to forget the ways of my people."

"I know. I will be patient, Varady. I will wait for you to learn...and to forget."

Her hand was tangled in his hair. She drew him down to her and lifted her face. He kissed her, his fair hair mingling with her dark tresses. But he would not promise more.

He met the sunrise alone, standing on the sand of the river's shore. He heard the horns blowing and watched the distant dance upon the golden clifftops. When it ended, he remained awhile, his spirit walking the sun's bright skyway. Pet brought him back to earth, touching him softly with velvet muzzle. He turned back toward the camp, Pet walking free alongside.

There were many smiles for the white-clad stranger and his silver Shal. Varady waved back politely as he walked the long length of the camp, a little alarmed at the almost reverent greetings he received. He was frowning slightly when he reached Windstar's cookfire, and she looked up from her pots with a knowing expression.

"Sit," she told him. "Eat. Things are always better on a full stomach."

He laughed and lowered himself cross-legged to the spread blankets. He saw little Goldmane peering from the lodge door and winked at her. She crept out shyly and came to him. Once assured of his permission, she snuggled against his side.

Windstar made no comment but fed them both. Varady found his appetite much diminished, and this Windstar did notice.

"The Sundance disturbs you?" she asked, taking his bowl.

He looked up in surprise. "It's beautiful. Why should it disturb me?"

"Stormwing told me about Azlatan. There would be no Sundance, where Phaelon rules."

Varady turned to Goldmane, a little embarrassed. "Your aunt," he told her, "moves quickly and has a big mouth."

Goldmane snuggled closer, uncaring.

Windstar shook her head. "Don't blame Stormwing. I am mother to her since her own is gone, and I am also Congress. She keeps no secrets from me."

Varady watched Goldmane's tiny fingers curl around his own. "I mean no disrespect to Stormwing. Either just now, or last night."

"She is young, and thinks she is in love." Windstar settled beside him with her own bowl. "She will get over it. I'm not so sure about the rest of us."

Varady threw her a pained glance. "You Sundancers set too much belief in legends. I seek only friendship among you, not..." he hesitated, thinking of the looks he had received on his way here. "Not reverence! I am just a man!"

"It has nothing to do with legends," she replied, unperturbed. "Look at the child and see your Gift."

Varady glanced down. Goldmane slept against his side, sucking a tiny thumb. He sighed, understanding nothing, and stroked the golden head while he watched the busy camp. "I realize that Phaelon is not honored here. But what of Liethe, and Daimaine? Is the Sunqueen your only deity?"

Windstar shrugged. "What have either of them to do with mortals? Liethe rules a time before the day of life, when all was pure and innocent. Its reflection can be seen in the smallest children. But life lived destroys both purity and innocence. Liethe's song of love is only an entertainment that does not last, a lovely note, but not the song. Daimaine...she takes mortal life, and her Justice is beyond the understanding of mortal beings, for many she takes are innocent victims of evil."

"And the Sunqueen?" he asked.

"She is the dual nature of all things. Neither good nor evil, like nature itself. For every joy, there is a sadness. She is bright shadow and dark flame."

"But she is Chaos. In my homeland, the fourth goddess is Chaos. There is no certainty, where Chaos walks."

"Was there certainty, in Azlatan?"

He thought of Danon and would not answer.

"We do not honor her because of certainty," Windstar continued. "She does not ask for honor, or even understanding. We have only what we find within ourselves. But there is the Gift of the Sunqueen."

"Stormwing tried to explain that. It's apparently more than just the Shalmira. What is the Gift of the Sunqueen?"

"There are many, but we wait for the last answer to that."

A horn blew.

Windstar was on her feet, her bowl rolling forgotten into the fire. She reached for Goldmane as more horns joined the first with a dissonance that set Varady's teeth on edge, even as the child was torn from him.

"What is it?" he cried.

"Outsiders!" her shout was almost lost in brass voices. "I must hide the child."

Pet was wild, striking at air with his forefeet. He dropped as Varady ran to him and swung on lowered hindquarters to offer his back. Varady vaulted from the earth and the stallion sprang into a gallop with Varady's fists clutched in his streaming mane.

Water sheeted by as Pet planed through the shallow river. Shalmira scattered as he erupted among them, flying south.

Stormwing's chestnut mare tried to run beside, but fell back, shrilling despair.

Through Pet's whipping mane Varady saw riders ahead, already racing to answer the horns sounding from the southern pass. He was stunned when Pet caught them, passing through as though his hooves flew over the earth. He glimpsed Skyson's astonished face as they winged by.

Then they were like a silver light lancing over the open grass, rising to meet the golden cliffs. Pet did not hesitate when turf ended and stone began. There were screams ahead, of men and horses. The brave horns were falling silent. Varady's hand dropped to his thigh and the silver blade gleamed free. He was aware only of Pet's hoofbeats, and the terrible sounds beyond the crest of the pass.

Pet flew over the top, strides quickening on the downhill drop. Varady saw the battle, the fallen Sundancers, and screamed anger for his friends.

His stallion leaped over fallen Shalmira and Sundancers. Those who remained upright were knotted around a single warrior, a giant out of a nightmare. He wore silver armor painted half black, and his armored horse towered over the Shalmira. Death whirled around him, a spiked mace of black iron intended to crush skulls of riders and Shal.

Varady saw the disadvantage: the enclosing cliff walls were too near for the lighter Shalmira to move freely, and at such close quarters the giant's reach and the mace on its long chain ripped through them unanswered. He knew his knife was useless even as he screamed at them to fall back, give him room.

They didn't hear him. It was Pet's shrill challenge, closing, that scattered the remaining Shalmira.

The white warrior startled the Outsider. Varady saw him check, swinging to meet him, the same moment he felt Pet gather to attempt the impossible. Varady gritted his teeth, dropping his knife to embrace Pet's neck like a lover.

The Shal leaped. The mace missed him an instant before the impact of white body against armor. Then they had cleared both horse and falling rider, and Pet came down hard. Varady's head hit the ground and he rolled clear as Pet fell, sliding down rock in a wild, screaming tangle.

Varady, crumpled on stone, was unconscious.

He awoke slowly, some worry nagging him to consciousness. Cold stone cradled his cheek. It vibrated to the steps of horses and people. The worry tugged him again, like Pet at the end of his rein.

Pet.

Hands grasped him, trying to roll him over. He shook them away, eyes opening to see his fallen silver Shalmira.

Pet, you have to be alive. The Sundancers have it all wrong. It was you that was promised to them, not me.

He began to crawl toward the horse.

Wake up, dammit! By Phaelon or Chaos, I don't care!

He reached the outstretched white head. He laid his cheek against Pet's, and almost laughed as the horses' eyelashes tickled him, fluttering.

I am here, was Pet's response. *If you remove yourself from my head, I will rise.*

Varady's life changed. He had to accept it.

He sat up while sound and reality returned around him. Pet lifted his head, neck curving, and rolled to get his legs under him.

I hurt, the stallion advised.

I think you will be fine, Varady told him. *Your Power grows, with our communication. There is some purpose here, as the Sundancers have been trying to tell me.*

Pet snorted and scrambled to his feet. Varady followed his example, swaying a little. He leaned his back a moment against his horse and saw the awed faces of the Sundancers around him.

Rainsong held the bridle of the monster horse, the dead Outsider a pile of metal at his feet.

"How many did we lose?" Varady asked him.

"Five Sundancers injured," Rainsong told him. "And one Shal killed."

There was anguish in his face. Varady looked down to see Rainsong's grey Elthar, the lovely head crushed to deformity.

"I'm sorry," was all Varady could say as his gaze turned back to Rainsong, but his heart meant it.

Rainsong seemed to see something in his eyes. His pain, his despair, disappeared.

His body straightened. "Thank you."

See your Gift. Windstar's words. Varady tugged for understanding, but it didn't come.

What he said was, "How many were there? Surely one Outsider, even that monster, couldn't have caused all this."

Skywolf spoke while others cared for their fallen brothers. "There were several. They were on foot and hidden among the rocks, to sneak past our defenses. Shal Elthar..." Skywolf glanced at the dead grey, and swiftly away again. "He warned Rainsong of their presence. The others were not armored. We slew them. Then this one came, as though he alone could get by us as the others could not." He grimaced. "He almost did. This armor and this weapon are new to us, and terrible."

Varady was scowling. "One armored rider against all of you. Surely he knew in the end he would lose, no matter how many he killed. It doesn't make sense." He looked sharply at Skywolf. "I think you'd better return to camp, and swiftly. Warn your people there may be others, who got past us while we battled this one. Search every hiding place. Hurry!"

Riders moved swiftly, in sudden understanding. Varady turned back to Rainsong, who still held the bridle of the Outsider's steed. The Sundancer was regarding the horse with distaste, as though unsure what to do with it. The giant horse was covered with armor, even its great heavy head.

"He must stand 20 hands," Varady said in wonder. "He's like a mountain."

"His rider too," Rainsong agreed. "I have never seen Outsiders so big, though none are small." He shook his head. "I don't like it, Lord Varady. It is as if...they were bred to such size, for a purpose."

"Yes. I think they are bred for war." Varady saw Cloudhost approach. "Has anyone checked beyond this pass? The others you killed here had to have horses to ride, and they must have left them somewhere. Find them, count them, and we will know how many might have slipped past us."

Cloudhost gave a slight bow and went to obey.

Varady turned back to Rainsong. "Stormwing told me they breed people like animals. Why would they need such a war machine? From what I understand, their land is in the southern steppes, which the Sundancers have never attacked. Do they have reason to fear you?"

"The Outsiders fear nothing." Rainsong scowled. "They are what they are. They want to rule the world." He faltered a moment, remembering an order of Congress, but mumbled, "Prophecy says they will try."

"Prophecy." Varady felt a stir of memory but couldn't quite hold it. "Rule the world." He repeated the phrase and thought of Azlatan. He shivered in the hot sun. He had left Azlatan through a magic border that somehow no longer existed. Perhaps the Outsiders could enter the same way. "Does your prophecy say that they will accomplish this thing...to rule the world?"

"Not if we can find the Gift of the Sunqueen."

Ten horses were found beyond the pass, heavy creatures, but none like the Beast as they referred to the giant horse. The Sundancers disdained bringing any of them near the Shal, since Varady had not commanded it. They took them, freed of leather and armor, to be released upon the steppes.

Nine unarmored Outsiders had been slain. The tenth was hunted, with Varady's order to take him alive for questioning.

All the Outsiders were blonde. Duine, Varady thought with a sense of wrongness he couldn't quite place. He ordered the bodies burned, including that of the giant he had examined.

Sunset came. The tenth Outsider had not been found.

Congress met at the community fire, but the Cup of the Sun was not passed. Varady had called for guards in the camp and among the herd, and strengthened Sundancer presence at the entrance to the inner lands. Children were kept close and guarded.

Varady's leadership had come naturally, as all but he had known it would. He reflected on this as he gazed into the dying coals and listened to the Congress of the five tribes give memorial to the Shal lost in battle. He sat with his knees drawn to his chest, arms crossed atop them with his chin resting on his wrist. Little Goldmane was curled at his boots, sleeping.

Look at the child and know your Gift.

He was Duine, never meant for war, much less leadership. But something in his nature had answered the need of these people, and he knew he would not leave them after all. There was a powerful caring in him, a sense of responsibility he couldn't deny.

The other thing, this Gift, was less easily accepted. He had believed it something attributed to him by the Sundancers, because of some legend he still did not understand. They believed in him despite himself. Or so he had thought.

Until he had looked into Rainsong's tormented eyes, and seen his pain vanish. Could simple belief accomplish that?

Perhaps.

But he remembered Skywolf telling him Elthar had warned Rainsong of the intruders. He had asked Rainsong, later, if all Shal could communicate with their Chosen.

"A few can," he was told. "It is a strong Bond, and with some, it is greater than Life itself."

"What if one of them dies?" Varady had asked.

Skywolf had looked away. "Often the other dies. They are, at the least, broken in spirit." Then, in a voice of wonder as he met Varady's eyes: "All except Rainsong."

Varady sat by the fire and knew the truth of Skywolf's words. Rainsong, beside him, looked sad as he listened to the Congress. But his wound had already begun to heal.

Varady sensed his own Shal, drowsing among the trees beyond the river. Pet was a warm presence within his mind, never intruding, but alert for his call. Varady shivered at the memory of him fallen, the panic as he thought him dead.

He realized with a start that he had been spoken to.

"I'm sorry," Varady told Windstar. "I didn't hear your question."

"No need for apology. We all retreat in memory, tonight. We have a sorrow, but by your courage it is not a greater one. You saved many lives this day, Lord Varady. I had asked if there were questions you would like to ask of us. For understanding."

Varady looked around at the expectant faces. Suddenly he missed Stormwing. He had only glimpsed her once, before the evening meal.

"I will have questions. I hope that you will understand that I am not ready yet."

Windstar nodded. "There is time. This Congress is ended, for tonight."

People began to drift away, speaking soft farewells as they passed him. Some, a few, hesitated briefly as though to say more. His silence stopped them.

At last they were gone, Rainsong gathering up his sleeping daughter. Varady sat for a time alone, till the fire was only embers. Things were coming together in his mind while The Bridle swung overhead.

His mind reached to Pet. *Have you seen Stormwing?*

She is by the river.

Varady rose stiffly. He walked across the soft shining sand and found her, a slim silhouette against the river's silver plain.

He stopped beside her, where she watched the Shalmira beyond the water.

He tried to sound stern. "It is foolish of you to be out here, alone. There is still an enemy we haven't found."

She didn't answer. He stole a sideways glance and saw twin trails of silver on her cheeks.

He turned and took her shoulders in his hands, forcing her to face him. "I've seen you cry twice now. No, three times. Your eyes glittered, as they do now, when you thought you had harmed me with water in the desert. Yet I know tears don't come easily to you women of the Sundancers. It seems I am bad for you, Stormwing."

She closed her eyes. "You belong to all of them now. Last night I tried to make you my own. Now that you have become our leader, that chance is gone forever." She ducked her head. "These are selfish tears, Varady, and foolish. I am like a child crying for the moon."

He tightened his grip on her narrow shoulders, shook her slightly. "Look at this Duine."

She obeyed, but her head was turned a little, as though to avoid the full power of his gaze. Exasperated, he shook her again. "I am what I was. Last night, I thought you understood."

"What happened today was a miracle. You were the Gift of the Sunqueen, today. No mortal man or Shal could have done what you did."

"My horse did it, not me. He was trained for war before I got him, and for all I know he could always jump like a cricket." He saw startled laughter yank at her mouth. "Now will you look at me?" he finished softly.

She obeyed, though looking sidelong. Her shoulders relaxed under his hands. "You are a strange man."

"Is that why everyone acts so odd around me?"

She shook her head. The corners of her mouth twitched. "We try to give you honor. You return irreverence."

"I know," he agreed soberly. "My Rioch thrashed me every time I told a joke." When her eyes widened, he lifted his shoulders. "He hated bad jokes."

"Oh, Varady!" Her laughter was choked with exasperation. "You are terrible!"

"That's what he said."

"Stop it." She giggled helplessly, shrugging away from him. "How can you make me laugh when my heart is broken?"

"Because it isn't broken. You're standing out here all by yourself, imagining terrible things, instead of putting things in perspective."

She crossed her arms, looking insulted. He recognized it was a barrier she placed between them, and let it pass unremarked. "Fine." She glared. "Then my heart is not broken."

"Good." He knew it hurt her, knew it might forestall a greater hurt later. Already he was gaining the broadened view of a leader. He remembered her words: *You belong to all of them now.*

He turned from her, denying that statement. *I will belong to no one, ever again.* "I need your help, Stormwing. I think I'm ready to hear about prophecies."

"The Congress would have told you."

He spun back to her. "I don't want it from the Congress. I want it from you, so I can ask foolish questions without a crowd around. You already know I'm foolish, but I don't think it's a good time for the rest of them to find out."

"You are not foolish."

"No? Well, listen to this one, Stormwing. I don't like this reverence I get around here. I don't like this Gift, that makes you avoid looking directly into my eyes. I felt less lonely out on the desert, dying of thirst."

She looked stunned. "How can such a Gift make you lonely?"

"Because it makes me different. Tell me what it is. I don't understand even that. Magic wasn't practiced by Duine in Azlatan."

She met his eyes freely then, and he saw a change come over her.

Words were caught behind her lips, trapped. She struggled with the feelings she had for him that he would not accept, with the need of her people which must replace it. He felt her pain like a knife in his own soul.

"Oh!" her hands flew to cover her eyes, then fell away, opening like flowers as they drifted down.

"Your Gift isn't like magic." The words tumbled from her now. "It isn't a binding, or a theft...not a bewitchment. It is that you care, Varady! When you look, you see. When you touch, you feel. You do not just look at a person, you see them! So, a morning greeting, a passing word, is caught before it is formed, because a person knows that their words won't be meaningless to you. You take our cares, not like a burden for your shoulders, but like a Gift you can return along with the strength to bear them. You make us.... not alone."

Her shoulders slumped. "You see pain that we think is hidden and show us our own courage. You just did that for me. Now I know why it hurt when you watched me dance."

"Why?" he asked softly.

She drew a shaky breath. "Because I saw it myself as you did...and I was beautiful."

"I am glad, if my Gift is to help you see yourself, and know that you are beautiful. Does it still hurt you?"

She shook her head, solemnly thoughtful. "No. I think I mistook my beauty for yours, and so felt myself enthralled by hopeless love. That pain is gone, now."

He had what he wanted, though it caused an ache in his heart. *So I am not immune to male pride. It was flattering, believing she wanted me.*

But he couldn't tell her that. "I'm still not sure I understand, but I do know that I will not let your people make a ritual of me, even one as beautiful as your Sundance. I'm a man, Stormwing. The same one I've always been, for all I can tell. I need friends, not servants."

Is that what Danon was trying to tell me?

Something broken in him became mended.

Danon, I am sorry I didn't understand. You didn't cast me off, but only Phaelon's Bond. It was never Phaelon's Bond that made us brothers.

The night was split by screaming.

He and Stormwing whirled as one, sprinting toward the camp which awakened with shouts.

"It's coming from Rainsong's lodge!" Stormwing cried.

Goldmane.

Varady raced, thought of the child spurring him past Sundancers already running. The cry of "Outsider!" rose ahead, and the clang of metal on metal. Men struggled in the trees behind Rainsong's lodge. Varady slowed; he had seen Goldmane, clutched safely in her grandmother's arms.

"Take him alive!" He yelled in reminder, and to Windstar, "Where were the guards I posted? He shouldn't have gotten so close."

She only shook her head and turned away with the child. Sundancers separated ahead of him, and more had come with torches to light the scene. A stranger lay face down on the ground, Rainsong kneeling on his back with a knife resting in threat below the man's ear. He looked up as Varady approached, eyes full of fury.

"He's alive," Rainsong spat. "But only because you ordered it."

Varady bent to pick up a sword with a new notch in the blade.

"You knocked this out of his hands—with a spear?"

Rainsong nodded. "You said not to kill him."

"Yes, I did. Amazing. With a spear. I guess you know how to fight." He looked around. "Who screamed?"

"It was I." Stormdawn sounded sheepish. "Rainsong thought he heard movement behind our lodge. We went to check, and when I saw the Outsider..." She shuddered. "They are monsters!"

Varady looked at the fallen enemy. He was a huge man, stretched out like a muscular lion beneath his conqueror. He wore heavy leather, studded strategically with dull metal. Soldier's garb.

Varady looked at slender Rainsong in his ordinary buckskin and simple knife, and smiled grimly. "You can let the monster up now."

Rainsong grunted, rose slowly. The soldier lifted his head, peered around through his blond fall of hair, more angry than afraid.

Varady's tenuous smile faded. No monster, but a dangerous man.

"Duine!" Varady said it coldly, saw the soldier start, then freeze.

"One wrong move and you are dead. It is not out of mercy I ordered you taken alive. Do you understand?"

The soldier nodded without looking at him. His eyes were gleaming slashes in a broad face.

Varady frowned, sensing wrongness. When he recognized it, he relaxed, only puzzled. "Rainsong, take him into your lodge, after you tie his hands. Search him. There are sure to be knives hidden in his clothing."

He turned to Stormwing. "You and your sister light the fire inside. We can't get the whole Congress in there, but Windstar can represent them. Can someone else watch Goldmane?"

"Are you afraid for the child to be near the monster?"

"Yes," he confessed. "I felt the same as Stormdawn, when I imagined Goldmane in his clutches." He sighed. "Besides, what I may have to do won't be pretty. Now light the fire. I'll be there in a minute."

"Where are you going?"

"To find out what happened to the guards," Varady said bleakly.

Others called to him through the trees.

The guard had been Cloudhost.

They turned him over gently, where he lay on the shadowed forest floor, and saw the line of black across his throat.

"Knifework," Skyson's voice was a murmur. "From behind. The Outsider had to be very quiet, to sneak up on Cloudhost."

"Was he Chosen?" Varady asked, looking at death on the young face.

"Yes," another sighed.

Varady scowled. "I think the Chosen should bring their Shal with them from now on, into the camp. Perhaps even into their lodge. The Shalmira have scent and hearing which would have prevented this."

"So we have always done, when we are separate tribes down on the plains. There has never been reason in the inner lands. I do not understand why they come among us here, in our strength."

"That's what I intend to find out," Varady said.

CHAPTER 22

Varady ducked into the lodge, white fringe swinging, feeling tension coiled in his belly. He straightened with feet braced apart, just inside. He met silence, and firelight beating back from the lodge walls.

Stormwing looked up from where she tended the fire, in the center of the white circular lodge where smoke would escape through the opening at the top. Her eyes traveled up his height and lingered on his eyes. There was no gentle understanding in them now. Their gold burned hot.

Rainsong and Skywolf sat on either side of their prisoner. Stormdawn and Windstar sat cross-legged beside them, knives unsheathed across their knees.

The Outsider was bound, wrists and ankles. He stared across the fire at Varady, dark eyes narrowed...and then suddenly looked away.

Varady circled the fire and dropped to one knee in front of him. The soldier jerked folded legs against his chest, burying his face against them.

Varady grabbed a handful of coarse yellow hair and jerked the head up.

He wasn't sure he understood the horror on the soldier's face. *I showed Stormwing her beauty. Perhaps I have shown this monster his ugliness.*

Yet the face wasn't ugly, only strange. Varady studied what he had noticed before: the broad swarthy face, and black eyebrows under yellow hair. The hair was like straw in his fingers. When he released it, the soldier continued to stare at him, frozen.

"I called you Duine," Varady told him. "I was wrong. The color of your hair has been bleached away. You are Rioch."

"No!" the soldier's voice was deep, to go with his massive body. "I am not the enemy! I am Anzihi!"

Varady froze.

Anzihi.

The word rang like a bell in his head.

He decided to let it go for now. He gestured at dark-haired Rainsong. "Then what is he?"

Following his gesture, the man's confidence seemed to return. "He is nothing. A savage. We kill them, now. Later, we may try to make Anzihi of them. When they are conquered and see the way of greatness."

Varady pointed at Stormwing. "And what is she?"

"A slave for breeding."

Varady didn't look to see Stormwing's reaction. His attention was on the Outsider, watching confidence return, a strength for which he must find the key. "But her children could be...what you call Anzihi?" he asked.

"Yes! If the father chooses, and the child is wise."

Varady lowered his arm, rested it on his upraised knee. "And what of me?" he asked softly.

The soldier wouldn't look at him.

Varady pressed on. "I am Duine, and pure. You have changed your hair, but you are not Duine. So what are you?"

The man looked confused, then seemed to swell. "I am Anzihi!" he exploded. "We are the chosen ones! We have been promised glory in the promised land!"

"What promised land?"

"In the west. There are great riches for us when we have slain those not Duine or Anzihi!"

"Who are you?"

This seemed to confuse the man. "I have told you," he said finally. "I am of the Anzihi."

"Have you no name?"

Pause. Still the Outsider had not met Varady's eyes. "Abar. My name is Abar. I weary of this questioning. Kill me and be done with it."

"I agree," Rainsong spoke for the first time. "This questioning serves no purpose."

Varady glanced at him, surprised. "Did you know all this before, about the Outsiders?"

Rainsong shrugged. "Most of it. Except that strange name you give yourself: Duine. The Outsiders always rant about being the Anzihi. The word means nothing to us."

"It is you who are Outsiders!" Abar spat, glaring at Rainsong. "You breed like wild animals, without permission or plan! You ignore the Law of Phaelon!"

"There is no law of Phaelon. The Sunqueen has spoken."

"Your belief is what makes you Outsiders. You treat the Sunqueen as a god. The Sunqueen is Chaos, and no god. Phaelon is the only god. He will make all the people of the world Anzihi, instead of savages. Phaelon will rid us of those called Rioch, and their King who claims he is a god. When we all become one race, the great race of the Anzihi, there will be no more suffering or evil in the world."

Abar ran out of breath, was drawing another to continue his tirade. Varady had heard enough of his raving, found himself shocked at the open heresy. This isn't Azlatan, he thought. But this...this is Azlatan's enemy.

He scowled. "That's enough. Are all your people fanatics?"

Black eyes blazed wide. "We are the Anzihi! We are the Chosen! We will rule, and our day is dawning!"

"Please," Stormwing begged. "Do we have to listen to any more of this?"

Varady smiled at her. "It is pretty monotonous, isn't it? But I think we're getting to the good part."

"Good?" Stormwing snorted in disbelief.

Varady's kneeling knee was getting sore. He shifted to sit on his heels.

"Abar," he said conversationally, "Have you figured out who I am yet?"

"A sorcerer," the soldier replied promptly. "You play tricks with your eyes, putting strange thoughts in my head."

"You have magicians in your land?"

"Of course. We are the Anzihi, who serve Phaelon."

Varady rose to his feet slowly, towering like a white pillar in the firelight. He was beginning to understand the ringing in his head at the dreaded word. *Anzihi. Killers of the High King. Traitors to Azlatan.* He didn't see the Sundancers shrink from him.

His Gift beat at the soldier, forcing him to look into his eyes. Abar whimpered at his gaze.

"Who sent you? And why?"

"The Anzihi," Abar whispered. "Don't look at me. It hurts."

"Why did the Anzihi send you here, where your people have never come before?"

After a long struggle, the man answered with a voice not his own, with words that came from somewhere unknown even to himself.

"We came to find you. To bring you home. Born of Duine and Rioch, in Azlatan you are known as the Forbidden Child. To us, you are the Deliverer, and your purpose is to lead us in war, where all Duine will finally know they are Anzihi, and will rise to kill the last High King and all the Rioch of Azlatan."

The Anzihi named Abar fell dead where he sat.

Varady was gone before he hit the ground.

He ran from prophecy. He ran from knowledge he hadn't known he possessed. He left behind a dead man who had never known the message he carried, the hidden reason he and his fellows had been sent on this suicide mission into the stronghold of the Sundancers.

Abar died not knowing the truth he had revealed. It didn't matter.

The Anzihi had killed before.

Varady knew he couldn't escape it by running. It was himself he needed to escape, and his destiny. It was the panicked beating of a fly's wings, tangled in the spider's web. He ran blindly, seeing only that which had been buried in his own mind, disinterred by the scream of a dying man.

He stumbled over stone, ran wading through water, like a nightmare come awake. He ran uphill until his body was a single spear of agony, and his heart was ready to burst. Still, he ran, wanting it to. Death would be easier.

Pet stopped him. His horse stood in his path, and Varady slammed into him, reeling backwards into the deep cool grass, shrieking for air. He curled into a ball. Pain subsiding, he wept.

Danon spoke again in his mind.

"Varady feels he has a lifelong claim to me because of the Bond sanctified by Phaelon. I have to reject that Bond, though I have always loved him. He is the only brother I have ever known."

"My brother," he wept. "If only I had understood then. Perhaps I would have never begun this journey that could end in your death."

He knew it would have made no difference. Varady sobbed for breath and knew nothing in his life would have made a difference. Destiny had been set before either of them were born.

He was not, as he had been told, an orphan Duine. His father was High King Allasar, as was Jael's. *I am the Forbidden Child, and I am meant to kill Danon and his beloved King and all the Rioch.*

Unless I die. I know what the prophecy says, in Azlatan. If I am allowed to live, all the Rioch of Azlatan will die.

Hoofbeats, approaching. Varady dragged himself upright, buried his face in Pet's mane. His body shook. He was too weak to mount, to ride away. He listened to the approaching horse, heard it slide to a stop, snorting.

"I came alone," Stormwing said from behind him.

"Go away." His voice was a muffled groan. He still couldn't breathe, caught between sobbing and gasping for air.

He felt her hand on his arm, wanting to comfort him. He flung it away, whirling around, and nearly collapsed. He fell back against Pet, his rock. His arms were outflung on the silver hide, his head thrown back to the sky. His chest heaved. He remembered.

"I know your prophecy," he gasped. "Too many prophecies. They can't all be true. Go away."

"That isn't why I came."

He rolled his head from side to side, where it rested on Pet's steady back. "Doesn't matter. I don't hate...the Rioch. They'll die ... anyway." His breath came in long gulps, between words.

"All the dark people?"

"Not...you. You are not Rioch. No more than...Abar was Duine. Rioch are..." one final gasp, lungs filling, pain easing. "The Lords of Azlatan," he finished.

He was still a moment, resting. He let his arms slide down to his side, lifted his head.

"All Duine are Anzihi." He spoke to Stormwing, but his eyes wandered to the west. To Azlatan. "It's no wonder the High King could not find his father's killers. It was probably High King Allasar's own Bonded Duine that murdered him, before he killed himself. If the man had given himself a little time, he probably would not have remembered what he had done. It's fixed that way. Memory closes behind them. They are not allowed to remember the truth. They call the killers the Duine Anzihi...and do not realize they speak of themselves."

He laughed bitterly. "And I am not pure of blood. I am half Duine. I am half Rioch. High King Allasar was my father." His head fell back again, resting on his horse. "You have your prophecy. Azlatan, and the Outsiders, have theirs. I am the Forbidden Child in one land, and the Deliverer in the other. I am supposed to lead all of the Anzihi, Duine and Outsiders, to kill the High King and his people who are Rioch, to conquer the world and everyone in it. All the Duine in Azlatan will rise up to help me do it."

He didn't tell her about the rest of the prophecy. He didn't tell her that his death was necessary to save the Rioch of Azlatan.

"You're scaring me," she said.

"Not as much as I'm scaring myself."

"I don't even know what you're talking about! Kings, and killing...and I don't want to know, either. I don't have to know. You don't have to be part of anyone's prophecy. You were going somewhere when I found you. You can still go and forget all of this. I could go with you."

He laughed. It was not a sound of joy. "I was going to find Prophecy's Daughter, and learn what the world had to say. That's what I told myself. To give me a goal, a purpose, I suppose. I think I was just running away...from being Duine."

He stood up, away from Pet, accepting pain and denying destiny. "I got more than I asked for. I reached for the moon, and I got it." He paused, looking down at Stormwing, who was so determined to stand with him.

He touched her braided hair almost shyly. There was sadness in his voice. "I have to go. Not to the mountains, after all. To a place I don't want to go. I have to return to Azlatan. I must warn the High King about the hidden Duine Anzihi, and stop this war. I will not be the Forbidden Child or the Deliverer leading the Anzihi to kill the Rioch."

I will die there, to be sure of it, he thought but did not say.

She captured his hand in her own. "Then I will go with you."

"You can't."

"I can, or I will follow you."

"You mustn't."

"I will."

"You're a stubborn child."

"I am a woman. I will go where you go."

"Part of your prophecy, Sundancer?"

"No. All of my heart, Varady."

He looked at her helplessly. Then she came into his arms and he held her with gentle care, hoping she didn't really love him, because he must die and so would break the heart she had too freely given.

The Sundancers were waiting for them when they returned, all of Congress sitting around the meeting-fire. Varady and Stormwing slid down from their mounts and walked into the inner circle together.

Varady scanned them. "You have given me honor I don't believe I deserve. I must test myself now to see if I am even marginally worthy. Where is the child called Rainmoon?"

A woman rose. She brought the child to him and left her standing like a puppet in front of him.

Varady kneeled to the child and cupped her chin to lift her face to his.

The girl's blue eyes were blank, as though she were blind. He lifted his free hand and held it over them for a moment.

When his hand fell, she swayed a little.

"See me," Varady whispered to her. "You are here with me, little Rainmoon. All is well. See me."

The girl blinked, and he saw the light of the living come to her eyes.

When she cried out and threw her arms around him the Sundancers gasped collectively. Varady stood, lifting the clinging girl in his arms, holding her close.

"I don't understand this Gift," Varady told them. "I don't understand how it can stop a horde of fanatics bent on destruction. But I must try. The Outsiders mean to rule the world and destroy half the people of my homeland. I must go and try to stop this madness. I'm going to ride west, to Azlatan."

"I go with him," Stormwing announced.

Rainsong stood. "I too."

Skywolf joined him. "And I."

Varady could only watch as Sundancers stood until none remained sitting.

Windstar looked around, nodded. "We ride with you. We have found the Gift of the Sunqueen. You are the Deliverer. You are meant to bring peace to the world, and we will ride with you."

PART 5: THE PROPHECY WAR

AZLATAN YEAR 995

The goddess Chaos shall not be served in Azlatan,
for she is the enemy of Order.
She has been bound for a thousand years,
and Azlatan shall know peace until she returns.
It is my prophecy that upon her return,
a Forbidden Child will come forth,
my protection of Azlatan's borders will end,
and there will come a great war.
If the Forbidden is allowed to live,
Duine will rise up to kill all Rioch.
No magic can save them.
Thereafter, all will die who disobey me.

—from The Laws of Phaelon, God of Order

CHAPTER 23

C abre gaped at the newly anchored Chaine ships. The Dominion Kings gathered in Daimaine's Temple, where they and the High Queen waited for the High King to make the declaration of war.

But Khedran wasn't there. He prowled the Temple sacristy while The Chaine sat watching him with narrowed eyes.

"So that's why Penumbra is lit up in the daytime. Marre woke her up, by taking the Star Blade from your hands...and surviving."

"Yes. Which makes me believe Daimaine has her own purposes. I'm not even sure what Marre's reasoning was."

"It's pretty obvious to me, Khedran. She was protecting you."

He stopped pacing, turned to frown at her.

She scowled in return, exasperated with him. "Dammit, Khedran, she very likely saved your life. You should never have challenged the High Tahmond to call Council when he had the Dominion Kings so thoroughly convinced the borders were secure. Phaelon trusts no one but his Tahmond. He always kills. You'd have died."

"I would have convinced them. Until Marre stepped in, facing and winning Council was my one chance to unite my people. A civil war would ensure the Outsiders would win, Shandiin. Azlatan would be destroyed."

"Well, Marre took that problem out of your hands. Did she take away your supremacy in doing so?"

"She said not. She said I remain High King, by her word and as her Consort."

She sat back, exasperation flipping to amusement. "Turned the tables on you, did she? She was raised to be your Consort, without her permission. Now you've become hers."

He settled into the chair in front of her and leaned back, his handsome face unreadable. "I told her I would not be her Consort."

Shandiin's jaw dropped. "You did *what?*"

When he simply lifted an eyebrow, she shook her head. "By all that's holy, Khedran...haven't you considered that she could be in love with you?"

"I find that doubtful. She'd already broken troth, the night she was attacked by the Outsider."

"Hurt your pride, did she?"

He looked so annoyed she had to laugh. "I'm sorry, but it is funny. And your doubt is ridiculous. You know what you have to do. Just let down your empathy barrier, Khedran. You'll see exactly how she feels about you."

He looked away. She bit her lip, understanding his aversion to the gift that caused another person's emotions to flood into his own...a twofold invasion he rarely called upon.

She was deeply glad she was immune to his magic. She had too many secrets that she couldn't share. On finding them out, he'd not forgive her for a lifetime of lies.

She also knew he was troubled, and that she was part of the reason. That had to end. As she'd told Danon, she couldn't be here for him. She could feel the Prophecy War like an incoming tide, bringing with it the end of her own mission in this world.

She wouldn't allow herself to think he wouldn't survive that war. And he deserved more than spending the rest of his life alone.

"Khedran," she began carefully, "you have no idea how many people love you. You don't even recognize that you are loved. You focus on your duty. But love comes with a price. For them. And for you."

"I can't let emotions make my decisions." He frowned, thinking of Bannon.

"That has never been your problem, Your Highness. You will always do what's right, even if your heart is elsewhere." She sighed. "Someone once told me that refusing to love is refusing to live. You have a right to live, Khedran. You have so little joy, and so many duties. Give yourself a chance to balance that."

She shook her head when he looked away again. "We are going to war," she reminded him. "It's a very great possibility we will not be coming back. I suggest you take a hard look at who you are, and what you leave behind. Starting with your Queen."

"She reeks of magic, Shandiin. She has been taken over by Daimaine."

"To be fair, she gave herself up to Daimaine. It took a lot of courage on her part. She did it for Azlatan, and...I am quite sure...for you. And then you humiliated her by refusing to be her Consort. I've never before known you to be cruel, Khedran. What are you so damned afraid of? Is it magic...or love?"

His expression went cold. When he moved to stand up, she leaned forward in her chair and held up a hand, palm out, to stop him.

"Please. I know you. Something is bothering you deeply, and you need to resolve it. Is it the magic? You've always disliked magic, Khedran. With damned good reason, and partly by my teaching. But magic is part of your world, though you try to deny it. Is that denial why you brought home the boy everyone is calling the Forbidden Child? Because you don't want to believe he is part of the prophecy? Danon told me you are protecting his mother, as well."

"Shandiin, Jael and his mother would both be dead, if the Tahmond had taken them first. He is just an innocent boy, and....my father loved his mother." He shook his head. "For more than ten years I couldn't believe he broke his vows of marriage without some magic influence, but I have had to accept that he did it out of love."

There was distress in his words. She considered, but knew there was no way to break through the inherent, horribly stringent morality that caged the High Kings. She couldn't help him understand the truth of his father's second love, even if he had accepted it.

"Alright then. That isn't the point I was trying to make anyway. Khedran, Allasar was killed because of magic's prophecy. Magic has always been around you, especially you. Yet you have denied it by taking in that boy. You think like a Chaine, Khedran, but you are not one of us. You are not immune to magic, as we are, and you are right to be afraid of it. But fear begets hate. So you need to ask yourself...is your fear of Marre's magic why you were so cruel to her? Or is it something else you are afraid of?" She paused, took a deep breath. "Do you love her, Khedran?"

He looked away.

She waited through his silence.

After a long moment, he sighed heavily. When he met her eyes she saw sadness, and refused to wonder why. "Marre is...beyond brave. I watched her kill the man who attacked her. Then she defied me, and had the perfect right to do so despite tradition or propriety. She should have had choice in who she would marry. Then...she stood up to the Dominion Kings, to her own father, to the High Tahmond. She dared to take the Star Blade from my hands. She challenged Daimaine herself."

He studied The Chaine's eyes, her face, as though waiting for some reaction from her.

She just waited.

She heard a note of sorrow when he finally continued. "I could care for her, Shandiin. Is...that what you wanted to hear?"

She stood up then, and gave him her best smile. "I believe she has earned her place as your High Queen. You should probably let her know it. But for now, I think it's time you went to the Temple, and speak to the people who are waiting for you. I'll go and be among them."

He watched her leave, his face unreadable as he had always trained it to be. But he didn't stop watching her until she was out of his sight. And he sat alone for a long time after she was gone.

The uniformed soldiers of the Black Guard rimmed the Temple where stars wheeled through walls and ceiling. The glass floor hung like a black void beneath them and the seated Dominion Kings and other authorities. The colorful finery of the citizens contrasted with the plain black of their standing guardians.

The High King, also in plain black, stopped in the doorway and looked across the expanse to the glimmering mammoth statue of Daimaine.

One person stood on either side of the statue's base. Marre, her robes webbed with Daimaine's glittering starfire, was enveloped in a silver fog from the Star Blade she held. On the other side of the statue stood Rani, now the High Tahmine, glowing with the pure white Light of Liethe. The High Tahmond, Khedran noted sardonically, was absent.

The door behind him closed. The High King strode across the room. Circling the dead Outsider, he climbed the steps to the dais, stopping to face the High Queen.

"Kneel to me." Marre's command was quiet. No one else had heard her, he knew. But he saw the warning in her eyes.

He studied her for a moment before kneeling to bow his head briefly, then stood and walked to the center of the dais, where he turned to face the room.

His voice broke the waiting silence. "War has come to us while most of Azlatan is unaware."

He paused to look around the room, seeing faces both chagrined and afraid, very few still hostile. One friendly face he sought was absent, and he wondered why Bannon wasn't there.

He pointed to the giant corpse at his feet. "This is one soldier of an unknown number of Outsiders coming to our borders. He attacked the High Queen and killed the Chaine who had been her guardian. King Bannon of Tesna has seen others just like him, who invaded his Dominion and caused the death of King Rebran of Druna. Has anyone else seen the likes of this Outsider?"

There was shuffling, and then one voice was raised. "I have." The man who spoke came forward to look at the corpse. "Yes, I have. In Talgar, my city at the eastern border. I saw him walking, but he turned when he saw me and went into the woods. I believe others were waiting there because I heard horses and movement. I thought them highwaymen and was glad they were gone."

"So have I," another came forward. "In Selagon, skulking about like the one in Talgar."

Murmurs grew louder. Khedran saw a commotion at the doorway; someone was pounding on the closed door, and soldiers moved to confront any intruder. The Chaine stepped in line with them and, drawing her sword, motioned to Danon to open the door.

When he did, Bannon appeared supporting a black-clad Guard who was obviously wounded. Others rushed forward to help him, but the injured man slapped hands away and lifted his face toward the High King.

"Tesna has fallen!" he cried.

"Bring him," Khedran ordered. Danon took the soldier's arm and he and Bannon helped him make his way across the floor to the High King, where he collapsed onto his knees and looked up with pain of many kinds written on his young face. "Tesna has fallen," he repeated. "The garrison fought bravely, but they were overridden by men, huge men, led by an armored giant. The enemy are unforgiving, cold killers, Your Highness. They leave nothing living in their wake."

Khedran looked at Bannon, who wept openly. "Commander Tyran...my nephew...he is dead. Along with all the Rioch in my realm."

Khedran's eyes glowed like an animal's by firelight. "Did the invaders look like this one?" he demanded.

The young soldier looked at the Outsider's corpse and nodded. Khedran lifted a hand for silence in the sudden outroar. "The High Queen has proclaimed the Black Guard will ride to war this day, and so we shall. The Outsiders are in Azlatan! Just as The Chaine had reported to me, as I found for myself as I traveled, our borders are no longer warded. Are there any here who still deny this?"

When there was no response from anyone present, Khedran simply nodded.

"You know I have built an army, and you must realize now it has been for the sole purpose of defending Azlatan. You call it the Black Guard, a name that will stand, for these brave soldiers from the many Dominions are the guardians of our realm. I thank The Chaine and her people, who have brought us the horses the Black Guard needs to have a chance of victory. It is my hope that our allies, the warriors of the Chaine, will ride with us to protect the Dominions from the Outsiders."

Shandiin had remained at the door on the other side of the room. With her wildfire hair and Chaine gold lacing her leather, he thought she was like a ray of sunlight in that dark Temple.

"We who are Chaine have given our oath, and we will ride with the High King," she called through the waiting silence.

Khedran gave her a nod of thanks and returned to addressing the audience. "Now we must ready for battle. The Queen's Guard, formerly my Tenth Legion, will remain to protect Cabre. The Dominion Kings may return to their Dominions if they desire, each riding with the battalion I have assigned to their Dominion."

Marre moved to stand beside him. "Daimaine rides with the High King," she proclaimed, and the throng cried out as the Star Blade lifted magically from her hand to hover before Khedran. When he took its hilt, starfire rippled up his sleeve to cover him in the silver web already blanketing the High Queen.

The new High Tahmine stepped to his other side. Liethe's pure Light bathed all three of them, battling even Daimaine's magic.

When she spoke, her voice was the blended harmony of the goddess Liethe, startling even Khedran.

"The goddess Liethe also rides with the High King. And, in reproach, she reminds the people of the Mantra within the Annals which has been sadly disregarded. *The High King is the Gift to Azlatan. He is incorruptible. He is truth. The trust and honor of Azlatan live within him.*" The beautiful voice became a thunderous chorus. "This should never again be forgotten!"

Only the soldiers remained standing. All else fell to their knees and repeated her words, the ancient Mantra for the High King.

During that reprise Khedran remembered his father's last words to him.

"You must have faith in yourself even when your own people turn against you, because your duty is to save them all.

"You must accept the homage of those who are loyal, because their faith in you is necessary to the same duty."

While he remembered, he watched his soldiers. All the young men, and the few women brave enough to stand against society's norm. All the heroes of his people, who had chosen to serve and protect.

"You must accept it all, my son, knowing they may well die for you when you call them to defend Azlatan."

Only Shandiin guessed that, insensible to the honor he was being paid, his heart was breaking.

When he looked for her again, she had left the room.

CHAPTER 24

Marre knew he was outside her door before he lifted a hand to knock. "Please come in," she called.

She was standing by the tower window, starfire still shifting around her and the robe she wore. Khedran closed the door behind him. After a moment he joined her at the window where she stood looking down over the sea and the ships of the Chaine.

"You will be leaving soon," she said.

"Yes. I wanted to thank you before I go."

She turned to look up at him, surprised.

"It's been brought to my attention," he continued formally, "that you sacrificed yourself for our realm."

"Is that what you think?"

"Daimaine has taken over your form."

"She didn't take over. I chose."

"For our realm."

For you! She thought but did not say.

"Farbet has chosen good men for you. I hope that you will not need a full Legion to defend Cabre, but you will have them."

"I want you to carry the Star Blade. You should not have given it back to me in the Temple."

He lifted an eyebrow. "As you wish."

"Oh, stop it. I'm not giving you an order, though I damn well should, you stubborn ass. You will need the Star Blade; it is your protection in battle as well as ensuring a kill." She sighed. "But of course you know that."

"Yes."

"Oh, just go. There's no reasoning with you."

"Reason I can handle. It's magic I have a problem with."

She nodded. "I know. It's why..." her voice faltered.

He watched her curiously as she turned away. "Why what?"

"It's why you won't touch me," she said, and hated herself.

"Look at me." When her back remained to him, he added, "Please."

She took a moment, but finally turned and looked up at him. Her face was defiant, but her eyes brimmed with tears.

He lifted one hand slowly to cup her chin. When he touched her, the starfire leaped to him once more. She saw him flinch, but he didn't move away.

"Why did you have me kneel to you, in the Temple?" he asked her.

"Because magic isn't enough. If I am to rule in your absence you had to acknowledge me, and show you respect me, and I didn't know how else to make you do it."

He considered. "That was wise of you. What would you have done had I refused?"

"Nothing. That's why I was quiet when I told you to do it."

"You could have used your magic."

"No. I will not use magic on you. I made that decision last night."

"When I refused to be your Consort?"

"Yes."

He judged again her defiant face, the tears she fought. He tipped her face up, studied her lovely lavender eyes.

For the first time in her presence, he carefully opened the cage that controlled his empathy, and was stunned to realize the depth of the love she had for him.

Also lust.

Love, lust...and nerves.

He closed his eyes briefly, knowing guilt because he had purposely kept himself closed off from her. Because despite being betrothed, he loved someone else, and that was wrong on so many levels.

It was also hopeless.

So he lowered his head and softly laid his lips on hers.

Her hand came up to his chest as she returned the kiss. She curved against his powerful body, and thought her bones would melt with longing, and he was shocked that...having opened to her...her desire flooded him, and he felt himself go to iron.

She was to be his wife, and Daimaine had already made her his Queen. So he looked past the magic that swarmed her, found the woman within, and gave himself to her.

He took his promised bride gently, setting aside the silent pain in his spirit. He felt tenderness for this tiny virgin with such courage, who seemed to understand his need to remain true to himself. He found his own passion in her delicate curves, in the loveliness of her, but he held back while he drenched her with sensation, caressing her with hands and lips until she fairly shimmered under him, until he saw those lavender eyes go blind. His gift of empathy swamped him as her pleasure bloomed. He had to take a moment after to ensure his own control.

And then he did it all again, until she opened for him with a soft cry of need. He filled her then at last, and they found together what was theirs alone, and left behind all the pain and loneliness that had brought them to this moment. Together they found the love that each needed so badly.

He held her close after. "I think I've been given a gift I don't deserve," he told her. "I know now what is meant by making love. I had no idea it could be like this."

"But you...you had to learn somehow...how to do what you just did."

He buried his face in her hair, saying nothing.

She stroked a hand down his cheek. "Please. I have to know. I'll ask you straight out, because I know you don't lie. Do you love The Chaine? She is very beautiful."

He turned his face to kiss her palm, then looked into her eyes. "Yes, she is beautiful as a rose, but she has a lot more thorns. And no, I have never touched her like this. She would probably behead me for the very thought of it." He propped himself on an elbow, studying her as she watched him, and brushed his thumb over her full lower lip. "I really like the fact you don't have thorns, and that you are beautiful without them."

"I am not beautiful. I was an artist once, so I know."

"Once? Why not now?"

"It was considered too childish a hobby for your bride."

He laid back to stare at the ceiling where magic still crawled in starlight. "So, even that important part of your life was taken because of me. Something neither of us asked for."

"It was Phaelon's command, and my father answered."

"It's not right. We can't change Phaelon's order for my blood-line, but we should make an end to any other arranged marriages, you and I." He sighed. "After this war. I have to go, my love." He leaned in to cup her chin. "Create your art. Take back what is yours. And keep Cabre safe while I am gone; you can have faith in Farbet. Count on Camion for your other needs. He is a good man, and you will like his daughter Tari. And....by all the gods, Marre, I don't want to leave you. I want more time with you. I have wasted so much time, and you...you have taken my heart. But I have to leave you now."

Their last kiss tasted of salt.

Only one woman had ever seen the High King's tears. Marre was the second.

The sun was setting behind Penumbra while the citizens of Cabre watched from every vantage point, pointing when they saw their High King ride out from Penumbra's garrison between columns of the Black Guard. Chaine warriors rode in separate columns on either side, except that their leader called The Chaine rode at the King's left hand.

The High King stopped at the city gate and turned Chandar, looking back at Penumbra. He lifted the Star Blade in salute to the new High Queen who watched from her distant balcony. The sword blazed against the sunset sky, and a highway of stars leaped from the Blade to her upraised hand. The deep bells of Penumbra rang across the city.

Marre stood and watched them ride out while her heart broke.

Good-bye, my Love. I am glad we had our time, short as it was. There may not be another. Daimaine, keep him safe!

There was no answer.

Danon rode on Khedran's right as they led the procession through the city. It was an honor that still astounded him, just as he had been stunned the day Khedran elevated him to Compatri, only the second in his rule. The Chaine rode to the left of the High King, her traditional place as the King's Defender, because his right was his sword-hand.

All but two of her people rode on the outside of the regiments, wearing their leather and armor of Chaine gold. Shajii and Roinn rode behind the High King. Danon had finally learned, with some surprise, that Shajii was being groomed as the next Roinn, second in command to The Chaine. That name was something like a title, handed down through the generations to the winner of the Chaine's formidable competitions which were held every two centuries. As for the current Roinn, Danon wondered again if he was *amharen* to The Chaine, and watched narrowly as the big man pulled out an ever-present flute to play as they rode. The Chaine really were an odd people, he thought.

His new bay stallion fidgeted at the bit, eying Chandar. He was of the same breed as the King's black and the horses the Chaine had brought on their golden ships. From the east, he thought. The direction we are going now.

Varady, are you alive out there?

They passed out of the city and the Dominion Kings began to move through the regiments in preparation for turning off toward their homes. Khedran signaled Danon to lead while he fell back to where Bannon rode alone.

"No words can convey how sorry I am, Bannon."

"We were all warned." Bannon looked over at the Star Blade, now sheathed and strapped to Khedran's saddle. "I couldn't forgive her. But it appears you have."

"She acted on behalf of our realm, stopping a civil war we could not afford to fight."

"And stopping you from calling Council. Which the Tahmond might have ensured you would fail, to your death."

"Perhaps."

"Why would you take such a chance, Your Highness?"

"To stop a civil war we could not afford to fight."

Bannon nodded understanding. "I would like to stay with your Black Guard. With you, Your Highness. I cannot let my people go unavenged while I hide in what's left of my castle."

"There is no question of that. I came to you now to ask that you stay at my side, as Compatri. If you would accept."

Bannon's eyes widened. "I am unworthy of such an honor! I am only a fair hand with sword or spear."

"That has little to do with my choice. I am asking you to stay near me, as you have these last many days."

"Of course I will." As he followed Khedran back to the front, Bannon thought something had changed the High King. Or someone? He had to smile.

They rode through the night, and saw villages awake and citizens with torches lining the road. Word of war had travelled quickly in some places. Danon often looked across at Khedran, but the King's mind seemed far away from the troops he led.

With the new day half of the entourage were gone to new assignments, and Khedran called halt and rest for the horses. As he dismounted, he glanced over at Danon.

"Did your stallion choose you, as the other horses chose their partner?"

Danon shook his head, easing the bay's bit and girth. "No. I think I lost that honor when I gave Pet away."

"You gave him away? I thought he was stolen."

Danon hesitated, saw Khedran's lifted eyebrow. He wouldn't lie to his King, and Khedran would know if he did. "I gave him away," he admitted. "To my Duine when the Bond was broken between us. I hope that meets with your approval."

Khedran shook his head. "A little late for that concern. Shandiin, can't you control that beast?"

The Chaine jerked Windmaker's head and teeth away from Chandar. She made no response, but stalked away with him in tow. Khedran watched her go.

"She's in a mood," Danon remarked.

"She has been, ever since we left Cabre."

Danon was surprised that Khedran seemed puzzled by her coolness. In their travel from Ordhold, he had become used to her long periods of silence. Apparently her cold shoulder was new to the High King.

They allowed a few hours for rest in morning and afternoon, then traveled again at night. When clouds obscured the stars and moon, Khedran unsheathed the Star Blade and laid it across his saddle. It brought starfire to light the riders' path.

Shandiin had fallen back to ride with Roinn, keeping an eye on the High King just ahead. Shajii swung her horse over and smiled at Danon. "How much farther?" she asked him.

"Tesna is half a day's ride yet, but I think Khedran means to continue to the border near Selagon. We found the remains of an ancient outpost there when he come there to get Jael. There is even a way down to the Plain of Admech, and I hadn't realized it though I lived there most of my life. That must be how the Outsiders came through."

"Jael is the High King's half-brother?"

"Yes."

"Those you call Tahmond believe he is an evil forewarned in a prophecy."

"Yes. But he's just a child. And I don't trust the High Tahmond. He does not support the High King, and has done a lot to undermine him."

"So, you don't believe in the prophecy?"

Danon thought of the things Shandiin had told him, but kept that to himself. "I've become very skeptical of the teachings of the Tahmond. Your leader is the main reason. Her logic is inescapable."

"Shandiin is very wise," Shajii agreed.

He looked back at The Chaine. "Who is Roinn?" he asked impulsively. "Is he her *amharen*?"

Shajii stared at Danon in shock. "That is a very personal question!"

"I'm sorry. I didn't realize those things are kept secret."

"It's a matter of respect. I am surprised that the High King was so open with his Queen in front of everyone."

"You mean their magic farewell?"

"Yes."

"I was as surprised as you. But no, I will not gossip about them either, so I see your point."

"Would it be proper for me to ask if you are matched?"

Shajii was blushing faintly and looking at her hands on the reins. Danon didn't want to lead her on. "I am not. But there is someone I care about."

Shajii looked at him then, then back at The Chaine, back at him. "I was afraid of that. For your sake."

It was his turn to be embarrassed. "Does it show?"

"Only a little. You are wise too."

"You don't think she has guessed?"

Shajii sighed. "She is very wise," she repeated. "She will always let you keep your dignity, if not your heart." With that she reined her horse away, and Danon watched her leave, feeling like a fool.

They rode through that day, and into the next night. Commotion came suddenly, in the last hours before dawn: horses running fast on the road ahead, and men shouting as they neared the front of the slow-moving column. The Star Blade lifted into full glory, and the oncoming riders reined back hard.

One man dismounted, falling to his knees in front of Chandar. Several riders waited behind him, enveloped in darkness just outside the Star Blade's light. "Your Highness!" he cried. "We need your help!"

"Name yourself," Khedran demanded.

"I am Danhar of Selagon. We have been invaded! The town has fallen to a horde of strange robbers!"

Khedran looked to Danon. "Do you know this man?"

"No." Danon looked at the heavy cap the man wore, thinking of the falsely blonde corpse in Daimaine's Temple. "He should take off his cap."

The stranger remained on his knees. "Please! You must come quickly!"

Khedran turned Chandar sideways, using the tip of the Star Blade to remove the man's cap. Blond hair fell loose.

The man's accomplices immediately sprang forward with spears and swords and a blood-curdling cry. When the man on the ground began to rise, Khedran's war-horse took him down hard, and the Star Blade rose into battle.

As did The Chaine. Her golden sword didn't wear fire, but it wheeled through reflected starlight as she and her vicious horse helped take out the remaining riders. The rest whirled to flee, but the Black Guard was on them before they had a chance.

"Stupid," Danon muttered, "trying to ambush us from the front!" Whereupon a cry arose from the rear of the column, and Khedran cursed as he spun Chandar to the real threat behind them.

The ambush would have been more successful without the Chaine's gift horses. Soldiers wielded sword and shield, but the horses were unsurpassed weapons. Danon heard one man scream "Shalmira! They have the Shal!" before he was pummeled by the forefeet of a chestnut stallion. Danon watched in amazement as their attackers were destroyed by man and horse.

The Chaine stopped next to him to watch the cleanup. "Distraction while they ambushed from the rear. They thought we wouldn't figure it out. Not much on strategy. That's a good sign."

"Didn't you use that term before...Shalmira?" Danon asked.

She didn't answer but turned as Shajii joined them. The girl was beaming as she cleaned her sword of enemy blood. "I got two! I think your High King killed several, though his soldiers were holding their own."

"Where is Roinn?"

Shajii shrugged, and Shandiin rode her big paint horse toward a knot of men and horses still milling.

"I'm sure he's fine," Shajii said, looking puzzled. Danon scowled.

Roinn was turning over an armored body as Khedran dismounted next to him.

"Another giant," the Chaine man said, "like the one who killed Jhinn."

Khedran nodded. "Yes. Jhinn fought bravely, but he was outmatched. How did you take this one?"

"With great delight." Roinn looked up as Shandiin reined in. "The armor is ill designed." He pointed at the underside of his chin. "My blade found him here."

She nodded approval. "For Jhinn. Our brother never had the chance to find out where the weakness lies."

"Burn the bodies," the High King said to the Legion Master who joined them. "Take what weapons we can use. The last of the Dominion Kings must turn off to their homeland. We need to ride hard now, to Sunhi and Selagon. The enemy is bringing the battle to us."

He mounted Chandar. The stallion sidled beneath him, and he gentled him with hand and voice. He then sat with head bowed, his dark fall of hair blowing in the night wind. "I need to alert the countryside. The enemy is coming. My people need more than rumor." He looked across at The Chaine, then frowned. His face gone cold, he lifted the dazzling Star Blade toward The Bridle as it swung above them.

"Daimaine," he called. "Goddess of Justice, hear me, and carry my words to the people. I am Khedran, seventh of the High Kings given to Azlatan. Danger is coming and my people must take up what arms they have, or retreat to Cabre where safety awaits them. Azlatan is invaded, and we are at war."

The Star Blade dimmed, then brightened, and as it did every star in the sky flared and sent a ray of light down to the world below. The land turned white as the star-beams landed and pooled. Magic sang in the air and through the very blood of everyone who lived under the stars, and the words of the High King were heard everywhere.

The magic light ignited the emerald of his eyes, and when he turned his head toward his people, Shandiin was the only one who didn't recoil in instinctive fear. She met that neon fire with fury.

"That call was heard by the enemy as well as your people," she snapped. "I thought you had quit calling on Daimaine!"

He sheathed the Star Blade, but his eyes scarcely dimmed as he regarded her in the light Daimaine had given. "It's only fitting that my enemies be aware of me. And I do not answer to you, Shandiin."

Her head jerked slightly, as though he had slapped her. Then she took a deep breath. "My apologies, Your Highness, for my disrespect. However, I now consider it necessary that I leave you for a time, to scout ahead. They may have magic in return to yours, and I will serve you best as scout, as I am immune to what they may offer."

He shook his head. "No. There is too much danger for a lone rider."

"I don't answer to you either."

He glared at her.

"Your Highness," she added snidely.

They confronted each other, tension so strong it was almost a physical presence to the frozen onlookers.

Roinn broke the silence. "I will ride with you."

"You will not." She almost snarled. "I ride alone."

She spun Windmaker and was gone at a hard gallop.

CHAPTER 25

Marre heard Khedran's call. She was in the Temple, standing at the foot of Daimaine's statue. She heard his voice as he called to Daimaine, as did all others in the world. Daimaine's statue woke with it, the beautiful face aware.

But Daimaine spoke only to Marre. *He calls my heart. But he speaks only to Justice and not my Deathqueen, and that is not enough. He is wagering his world, when he should instead leave his world and come to me. You are already with child, so his bloodline may continue when he is gone from you.*

Stunned, Marre put her hands over her belly as though to protect the child within. But her fear was for the father, and that fear swiftly merged with fury. "Why? Why would you take your King you called beloved, when he is so badly needed by his people?"

She was answered by cold laughter. "You do not ask because of your people. You think he is yours now, and you are selfish. But he has always been mine. And he knows it. He knows it very well."

Daimaine would say no more, and Marre felt sick when she finally turned to leave the Temple. She was startled to see a young boy standing by the dead Outsider, staring.

"Who is he?" the boy asked. "And where is the High King?"

"That is one of our many enemies, and your brother has gone to war, to fight all those like him."

Jael looked up at her. The magic woven around her did not seem to surprise him.

"He can't win. There is magic, a Shadow yet to come."

She felt a bolt of terror. "You can't know that!"

"I know a lot of things. I know my mother has become lost in her mind, because she can only think of my father since we came here." He looked into Marre's eyes. "You feel the same about my brother. I am sorry."

Marre went to him, knelt to take his arms in her grasp. "I am not sorry for how I feel. And I think your mother is not sorry, either, for loving your father. But I don't believe you can know the war is lost before it is begun."

Jael looked back at the Outsider. "He isn't the real danger. There is another behind him, behind all of them. That is why the High King cannot defeat them, no matter how hard he fights. There is a Shadow."

After a moment Marre stood, taking Jael's hand. "Come with me. We will go to your mother."

They left. She never looked at the dead enemy's hand, which held a symbol she would have recognized.

When Mia opened the door Jael launched himself into her arms, so she did not at first realize he had a companion. Marre saw the fear flash into Mia's eyes when she looked up and saw her.

Marre lifted a hand still netted with starfire. "Please don't be afraid. Magic was given to me when I found it necessary to protect the High King. I would not use it to harm anyone who is not an enemy."

Mia held Jael close, her face full of confusion. "You...you protected the King?"

Marre nodded. "May I come in?"

"Oh! Of course." Mia stepped back and Marre entered the room, bringing the starlight with her.

She closed the door behind her, introduced herself. "I am Marre, High Queen of Azlatan."

"I did not know there had already been a wedding."

"There was no wedding. There may never be a wedding." Marre swallowed hard. "But according to Daimaine, I already carry his child. As you carried his father's."

Mia looked into Marre's lavender eyes, and her fear ebbed. She saw horrific pain in the young woman's face and tried to set aside the terrible magic surrounding her.

"Come, sit by the fire," Mia offered. "Explain to me how a woman of Azlatan came to protect a High King. I'm sure that has never happened before."

Marre had to smile. There was warmth in Mia's eyes, and she felt an immediate kinship with this woman who had also loved a King. She took a chair, watching as Mia sat across from her and settled Jael into her lap, holding him as one would a smaller child though his legs nearly reached the floor. The mother murmured something to the son, and he burrowed his head against her shoulder. Mia didn't release her hold on him, but spoke over his dark head. "Please tell me how you came to protect Khedran?"

Marre sighed. She explained as best she could the events that led to her taking the Star Blade. Mia's eyes widened in amazement. "He forgave you for that?"

"I didn't think he would. I don't know why he did, but he came to my room, and he thanked me. He understood why I had done it. And..." she gestured helplessly, and her tears returned. "He loved me." She dropped her face into her hands and wept.

Mia watched sympathetically. "And now he has gone, and Azlatan is at war. I heard his call to Daimaine."

"The world heard his call. But she....damn her! Daimaine says he can leave this world and go to her now, because I am with child and his bloodline is secure. Why is his bloodline more important than he is, Mia? I don't understand. I don't want to understand!"

Mia looked away from Marre's tormented face, and kissed Jael's head. "The High Kings have a duty they will never set aside. Allasar was the same. But even he...he had to go to Daimaine, in the end, and he knew it. And I have dealt with Daimaine since, as she is totally involved with anyone of their bloodline. She has shadowed Jael all his life."

"How do you bear it?" Marre cried.

"You will be surprised that you can. But you will. For the child."

Marre set free the truth that burned her soul. "I would rather the child die unborn, so the father can return to me."

"Do you truly mean that?"

Marre touched her belly, where new life was beginning, and nodded miserably.

"Then you must go to the High Tahmine."

Marre blinked at her. "She would help me with this?"

"Maybe not the way you think. But you can trust her. She helped me, long ago...nearly thirty years ago, in fact."

Marre sat upright. "Thirty years!"

"Jael was our second child. Even Khedran doesn't know. I think only one person ever guessed, other than the High Tahmine. Is The Chaine still present in Penumbra?"

"The Chaine knew there was another child...thirty years ago?"

"Yes. But it became obvious, when Khedran talked to me, that she had not told him about it. Neither did I."

Marre thought of the many mysteries surrounding the High King, including not least The Chaine herself. "She rode to war with Khedran, Mia. I have not met her, but I saw her join him on the beach when the Chaine ships came...oh, you didn't know that either? She brought horses for the soldiers. From somewhere. It was like magic."

"Not just 'like' magic. Perhaps it was magic. The Chaine are immune, according to what Allasar told me, but they will take advantage of it for their own purpose. Where did these horses come from? Ordhold?"

"Ordhold is lost. The youngest Prince came to let Khedran know."

Mia fell silent for a long moment. "You need to go to the High Tahmine."

"Mia...I think the High Tahmine you knew is gone. She was very old, and sent me to find her replacement. What did she do to help you?"

Mia sighed. "She was a wise woman, and merciful. She took my baby and sent it somewhere safe. I have no idea where, or even if it lives. The Tahmine said if I knew, someone else could find out."

Marre frowned, thinking. "It seems strange that the High Tahmine would do such a thing...considering Phaelon's Law. The Prophecy War is foreshadowed by the coming of Chaos, and the Forbidden Child."

"She didn't believe the prophecy the way the High Tahmond told it. She said he twists words to his own purposes...and she suspected even Phaelon's intent. She even told me the teachings about the goddess Chaos are false."

Marre nodded thoughtfully. "I have wondered about that myself. Phaelon's Tahmonds teach that Chaos is evil because she taught mortals the sin of pride. I know Khedran is criticized for being proud, but he is very much Chaine, and the Chaine believe self-respect is critical, making pride necessary. My guardian was Chaine. He told me pride is a personal right, and only becomes wrong when you put your rights ahead of another person's."

"But how can that be?...The High King is better than others, so why should he give equal respect to others?"

"The Chaine say we're not all equally strong or smart, but we are all equally worthy of respect. Chaine beliefs require love and respect for all of nature, and people are part of the whole. It's like a law, to the Chaine. They call it amhara." She shook her head. "But they are immune to magic, and we are not. Daimaine wants Khedran to go to her, and it terrifies me."

Mia nodded in sad understanding. "All the High Kings must go to Daimaine...sooner or later."

Varady heard the call of the High King, and saw the stars bleed their light onto the earth. He stopped his horse and turned back to the Sundancers behind him. They were all immobile, frightened by this magic that had turned the steppes white with starfire.

Even Windstar looked afraid, but he went to her because he had learned to respect her deeply. "Azlatan is at war. It's really happening. The High King belongs to Daimaine, for she gave him his rule and the Star Blade. That he calls on her now means there is grave danger. The Outsiders have already invaded my land. And my people don't know the threat that already lies inside their own borders. I don't know what to do. I don't even know exactly where to ride from here."

Windstar pulled herself together, and answered gravely. "He called his goddess. You must call on the Sunqueen for guidance."

"I have no idea how to do that. How do I call on a goddess? One I know only as Chaos?"

"Call on her, just as the King called on his goddess. She will answer you with the sun." Windstar dismounted, and at her signal so did all the others.

They waited through the night, and then they all went to their knees in the deep grass, facing east when the sky began to pale with the coming day.

Varady alone remained standing. He took a deep breath as a radiant glow edged the horizon. Feeling foolish, he nevertheless believed in his Sundancers, and so followed Windstar's direction.

"I am Varady, who these people call the Deliverer and my people in Azlatan call the Forbidden Child. I call upon the goddess for guidance, she who is known as the Sunqueen. Please help me on this road to save the Rioch, to stop this war if it can be stopped."

Then he waited.

The goddess came with the dawn.

Cloaked in fire, she rose into the sky with the sun like a jewel in her flaming hair. Varady was unaware that the Sundancers put their foreheads to the ground in obeisance; he alone saw her face, the silver eyes full of sorrow on his behalf, and the tears of fire that fell from them.

There was something familiar in that face, but he didn't connect it to a moment long ago when he had met a woman he had thought was The Chaine.

The goddess lifted a hand, and released a great white bird. Then the Sunqueen vanished into a sky turned burning gold, and the Sundancers rose in that overwhelming light, talking excitedly. Then they gaped toward him.

What the Sundancers saw against a magic golden sky was their leader clothed in white light, with a great white bird aloft above him. Its wingspread was impossibly wide; a sigil like a black heart rode between its flaming eyes. Varady turned his face to it, and knew its intent as it veered west.

"We follow him. He will lead us to our enemies."

So, the Sundancers came unknowing to follow the skyborne form of ChanDethe, and Varady was the only one who knew the face of the Sunqueen.

CHAPTER 26

Purposely, Shandiin had ridden alone and ridden hard. She'd heard the call from her own end of prophecy, from the one the Sundancers called their Deliverer. She could dare to answer only while he was still outside of Azlatan. In a thousand years she had never released her goddess self, her Sunqueen, within the realm of the High Kings, because Phaelon would know...and if he recognized her presence before her time of power, his magic could stop her from freeing the people of this world from its gods.

Once away from prying eyes, she'd freed her goddess spirit to the sky outside of Azlatan. From her vantage in the sunrise, visible only over the Admech Plains, she had seen Varady and the Sundancers, the people she had lovingly watched over throughout her centuries in this world.

Her spirit knew pain, because her magic had recognized Khedran's beautiful brother, and found in him a soul as pure as any of the High Kings. She believed he was doomed by Phaelon's hated prophecy, and realized that he knew it...and that he had the courage to save the Rioch of Azlatan through his own death.

The Sundancers' belief in a Deliverer was, she knew, based on hope instead of magic. Varady would have to face the prophecy of the Forbidden Child.

Sadly, she'd sent ChanDethe to guide them.

Then, before returning to her human form, she scanned the Outsiders pouring into Azlatan, and knew despair.

She rejoined Khedran and his army on the road while the magic sky slowly returned to its normal blue, and grimly delivered her bad news. "Tesna and Druna are overrun. There are more Outsiders than I can count."

Danon felt his gut go to water. "Selagon…"

She turned to him with sympathy. "The pass nearest Selagon is what they used."

Danon thought of his father, of others he had grown up with. He had known their probable fate, but the reality hit him hard. He knew he had to find a way to put it aside, for this was truly war. The Prophecy War was upon them all.

Shandiin had brought with her a small bag filled with a sample of the dead land, the very dirt destroyed by the invading enemy. She handed it to the High King. "I am sorry to give you this, but you have to know what they are doing. This…this is all that is left when they have passed over. They have no regard for any life other than their own. We have a vicious enemy, Khedran."

He emptied the contents of the bag into his open hand. When his gaze returned to her, his eyes had gone from bright emerald to cloudy jade. She had rarely seen that deep sorrow in him, and she hurt to see it now.

As they neared Azlatan's eastern border the horizon was filled with black smoke, and when the Black Guard halted behind the High King they could see emerging from the smoke the seemingly endless numbers of their enemy. The afternoon sun glinted from metal armor worn by the giants who stood out in their ranks.

The High King set the infantry as his front line, armed with pikes set low and high, a wall of death for men and horses. Behind them were his archers. His mounted men were set ready to flank the attackers, and there they waited.

Shandiin conferred with her Chaine warriors, who gathered with the cavalry. But she commanded Roinn to lead them, and took her place on Khedran's left. She was certain that this King, unlike the leaders of her lost world of Earth, would go to war at the head of his army.

They watched the enemy advance.

One armored giant stood out, even as he rode behind the enemy's infantry. Khedran frowned at the banner he carried, half black and half white, with The Bridle constellation imposed.

That rider was the biggest man he had ever seen, on the biggest horse, and his armor reflected light like a mirror on one side. The other was painted black.

"Is he Tahmond?" Danon asked. "That looks like a thing Phaelon's Tahmond would wear. How can there be Tahmond among Outsiders?"

Shandiin watched the advance with narrowed eyes. "I've been to the outer lands, but I only know about some of it, where the goddess they call the Sunqueen is honored. Her followers are a peaceful people, but they speak of an enemy from a land called Xanthe, where they breed people like animals, to get size like that."

"Do they have Tahmond magic?" Khedran asked grimly.

"That I do not know."

They soon found out.

The infantry marched toward them, cavalry in the back, except for the mounted giant in painted armor who rode his great beast through the infantry's ranks until he had passed through them all, leaving them behind as he continued alone toward them.

Khedran lifted a hand to restrain his eager archers, waiting until the rest were within range.

Then the giant halted while the army behind him continued its advance. He raised the silver lance he had carried across his saddle, pointing it at the Black Guard.

Lightning detonated.

Mayhem shattered Khedran's ranks.

Suddenly half of his soldiers had gone insane, turning on their brothers with pike and spear and sword. The High King's own soldiers came after their King with death in their eyes.

Danon shouted warning as a nearby soldier threw his spear at the High King. Khedran swung the Star Blade and the spear shattered against it even as Danon took down the soldier.

The Chaine spun Windmaker to meet those intent on killing Khedran, and she and the High King were embroiled in a battle against their own. Danon and Roinn joined them but were soon fighting for their own lives.

The enemy fell upon them all, laughing and killing soldiers true or soldiers Shadowed. Danon saw his own death looming as a giant came at him, but Roinn swung his heavy blade, and the giant's head disappeared in a torrent of blood. Danon returned the favor a moment later as an Outsider aimed sword at Roinn's back. But he knew they were losing. Even the Star Blade's magic was not enough in this sea of enemies, both foe and once-friend.

"Fall back!" came the King's command voice.

Khedran's order was heard, but obedience was difficult. Too many of his Black Guard were overcome, and the rest were blocked by the enemy decimating their numbers.

"CHAINE NOW!" Came Shandiin's call.

And the Chaine answered their leader. Her powerful and skilled warriors, immune to magic, fought their way through the Shadowed to become a living wall between the High King's Black Guard and the enemy, making retreat possible. But as Danon wheeled his horse to follow his King, he looked back and knew even the Chaine could not hold for long.

He saw them falling, his Chaine friends. Overwhelmed by sheer numbers, they were being driven to the ground, where they were lost behind a wall, a flood, of their enemies.

Turning away from that horror, Danon was stunned to see Shandiin ride Windmaker hard against Chandar, causing the stallion to stumble as Khedran tried to turn back to the fray. Her face filled with fury and despair, she seized Chandar's bridle to force the High King to ride with her, away from the battle that was lost.

Away from the Chaine who fought and died.

Giving up her people for this world's one true hope.

Danon rode behind her vanguard in an agony of confusion. What had happened was beyond understanding.

When there was no further pursuit, they entered Athea and rode to that Dominion King's assigned garrison. Danon helped officers bring order to confusion and aided the wounded. He was surprised to see Dominion King Bannon helping as well. Bannon was covered in blood, some of it his own, and wept while holding a young soldier dying in his arms. Danon knelt by them to find there was nothing he could do.

"How could this happen?" Bannon cried. "How could they turn on us, on their own brothers?"

"Shadow."

They both looked up at the High King's voice. He stood over them, scanning grimly the aftermath of battle. Then he kneeled beside Danon and took the soldier's hand. "My thanks," he said to this one young soldier of his, who gazed raptly into those emerald eyes until the light in his own went out.

"He was barely more than a boy." Khedran grieved as blood ran down his own face.

Danon rose to his feet. "You are wounded! Let me..."

"I do not want your medicine. I need to understand how this could happen, and the only thing I can think of is the Shadow. The...thing that took the mind of Prince Brend and Rani. But why did it affect only some, and not others?"

Danon frowned. "Maybe it's because some of us can't use magic."

When his King looked at him in question, he went on. "I failed as a Temple healer," he explained. "I could not use the magic of Liethe. The others who didn't change...they must be like me."

"And the Chaine are always immune to magic," Bannon agreed.

Mention of the Chaine twisted Khedran's features, and he stood.

"She is bereft," he said starkly. "I cannot help her. They gave up their lives for us, by her order, and she is bereft."

Danon followed Khedran's gaze to see Shandiin's paint horse standing with head lowered over the woman curled at his feet. Without thinking, Danon went to her.

But there he just stood, listening to her weep, unable to speak as his eyes searched frantically through what remained of their defeated army.

No Roinn.

No Chaine warrior in sight.

Not even young Shajii.

"All of them?" he cried. "They are all gone?"

"Gone." Shandiin wept for loss beyond measure. "All of them."

The horses, along with the Chaine, had been their salvation.

Those of the Black Guard's calvary who had fallen to the Shadow had not done the damage which had surely been expected. Their bonded Shalmira had somehow understood the wrongness, and refused to fight their own, bearing their Shadowed riders in retreat with the rest.

Khedran pulled out those who had been susceptible to that terrible magic, and sent them as messengers and protectors to the garrisons he had established within the inner Dominions. It was his hope that only the giant Tahmond wielded the Shadow magic, so those particular soldiers would not have to face it again. In exchange he would receive reinforcements from those other garrisons...and he could only hope they would not be as susceptible.

"I should have assigned more exploration for border passes to the outer Dominions." He blamed himself as he paced in the home of Dominion King Ardren.

Miserable, Marre's father didn't even look up. "The outer Dominions should have done that for you instead of thwarting your attempts to protect them."

Khedran stopped to regard the man, who sat by the fire with shoulders slumped. "You would have had the border searched, had I asked you before the High Tahmond interfered with your loyalty. I had always appreciated your support, though I failed to say that to you."

Ardren looked surprised and sat up a little straighter. "Can you tell me...how my daughter fares?"

"Marre was well when I left her," Khedran reassured him. "She has a full Legion to protect her." He frowned. "Though I never truly believed the Outsiders could get as far as Cabre. I don't know anymore."

He turned away from that thought, frowning as Danon joined them. "How is she?" he asked.

"She won't talk. She's in the stable with that wicked horse of hers, and won't come out to talk, or eat, or anything. I think you should try, Khedran. She just tells me to go away."

"Is it true," Ardren asked a little timidly, "that all of the Chaine fell in the battle? All of them?"

"All except her." Khedran's grief rode through his words. "She was busy keeping me from going back to die along with them, or she would have been fighting by their side. She would have died with her people, so that the rest of us could escape that debacle." He shook his head. "I'm not sure she wants to see me, Danon."

"Marre's guardian," Ardren put in. "I never appreciated him, while he was with us. But I wish he were here now. When I think how the Chaine have been reviled, and for them to go down as they did..." Ardren shook his head. "Tragic. It's just tragic."

No one responded to the awful truth.

"She may not want to see you," Danon ventured, "but I think she needs to." He paused. "Your Highness."

Khedran regarded his Compatri grimly, and with a parting nod to Ardren left them there.

The Chaine sat in the straw at her horse's feet. Khedran leaned over the stall door to look down at her bowed head.

"I'm sorry." It was all he could say. There weren't enough words for what he felt.

She didn't look up, didn't answer.

He opened the stall door. Wary of the horse, he nevertheless sat down in the straw next to the warrior who had been his Defender his entire life.

The woman who had lost a family, a nation, to protect him.

"Tell me, Shandiin. Are there any of your people left, in the north?"

She nodded. "A very few. I will have to tell them." Her voice was hoarse. "I don't know how I'm going to do that, but I will have to go back and tell them they're all gone. All their fathers, mothers, sisters, brothers...*amharen*."

"But there are some. So, you are still The Chaine."

She tossed back her shaggy mane and glared at him. "Do you think that matters?"

"No. Any more than my title would matter to me, if there were none of my people left to my care. But since you have people left, they still need you. Even more, now."

"They would have been better off without me."

He was shocked to see her bring her hands to her face and her body tremble with sobs she couldn't control.

He didn't know what else to do but take her in his arms.

She curled against him, and he just held her until the weeping slowed and finally stilled.

She sniffed and drew herself back to calm. "I'm getting snot all over your shirt." She rested her head on his shoulder. "I don't know if I can ride with you in the next battle. I don't know if I can bear it, with all of them gone."

"I understand."

"On the other hand, if I don't go, you'll probably get yourself killed." She drew back to glare at him again. "What were you thinking, trying to go back after you had called retreat?"

"I wasn't thinking at all. They were my friends, Shandiin. I knew many of them; I grew up with them, and they always treated me as one of their own. I could be...comfortable with them."

"Which is why you chose Farbet and Danon, and now Bannon, as Compatri? Because even though they are your subjects, you are almost comfortable with them."

He nodded.

She studied his eyes, the jeweled emerald gone dull. "You've had a lonely life. I guess it goes with the title. I've seen you alone more than not...sometimes even when you are surrounded by people. I hope Marre will change that."

She saw the sadness lighten, a single window in a shuttered house. "She already has."

"I am glad for you. I have always hoped you would find happiness." Maimed by loss, temporarily unguarded, she lifted her hands to frame his handsome face and brought her lips to his. His breath stopped as they sank into the kiss, in that moment unaware of anything but each other.

She leaned back, blinking, blew out a breath. "I am so sorry. I know better. I guess I'm not immune to your personal magic, after all."

He shook his head, lifting a hand to her cheek. "Shandiin...why did you send me to Marre, if ..." but words seemed to fail him, and there was such sadness in his voice it broke her heart.

But the broken hope in his eyes was somehow worse.

She kept her voice cool. "Let it go, Khedran. You and I could never be that way. Never in the books, never in the stars. We are from different worlds, you and I."

Then she was up with her easy lioness grace. But when she reached down to give him a helping hand he didn't need, he caught her wrist to hold her in place.

"There's a message passed down from Khandor," he told her. "I don't know how he could have known, a thousand years ago, but I have always thought it was about you. He said one would come to the High Kings as an ally for the Prophecy War, one we should trust...but nevertheless, it warns, guard your heart."

She didn't try to pull away. "I had someone give me the same warning, but it was far more pointed. He told me love is the most powerful force in the universe, and it can be deadly dangerous, so I must guard my heart."

"Who gave you that warning?"

She just looked into his beautiful eyes, and saw in them the dark stranger she had told herself to forget. "You wouldn't believe me if I told you."

They were both silent as they went to rejoin the others.

Word came of the enemy advancing, and Khedran told Marre's father that he must abandon his ancestral home. "I haven't enough soldiers left to defend all of Athea. My messengers are warning your people to flee. Reinforcements from other garrisons may not arrive in time. Please take everything you can, and go to Cabre."

Next he sent the first of several missives to Cabre, to the High Queen who waited for him there. In the letter, he explained the purpose of all the building he had ordered in the expansion of that city for the seven years of his reign, and that she must open it now to the refugees who were fleeing their enemy.

And with a heavy heart, he told her that he had failed, that the land of her childhood was all but lost.

When he could find nothing of immediacy left to do, Khedran finally allowed Danon to treat his wounds. Uncharacteristically silent, Shandiin stayed nearby, but her eyes were watchful.

"Reinforcements could be here by morning," he told his Compatri. "But my scouts think the Outsiders could be here by midday. And we don't know how many of the new troops might fall under the Shadow. Losing the Chaine may have cost us the war. We need a miracle now."

Danon put down his tools, treatment finished. "What about Daimaine?"

The King wouldn't look toward Shandiin. He knew what her opinion would be. "You think I should call on the goddess for help?"

"She answered you before."

Khedran nodded, got up and left the room.

Shandiin looked at Danon, started to speak. Shook her head. And left him there.

Khedran walked away from everyone, into the lonely woods in the starlight.

He found a private grove of trees and knelt beside a pond that reflected The Bridle through overhanging limbs. He unsheathed the Star Blade and regarded its silver fire in his open palms before placing it on the grass at the pond's edge, like an offering.

He knelt there for a long time, eyes closed, head bowed. The posture was as unfamiliar to him as flying.

He had denied himself much that life had to offer, not just because of his sacred duty as High King, but because of the dread. He alone knew what the future held for him. It had seemed easier to refuse joy, so that he would not have to endure its loss.

Thinking of Marre, knowing at last the joy of love returned, he realized how foolish that had been. He had wasted so much of what time he had.

And what he must do now could end that newfound joy and take him from the world he so desperately cared for. He had been warned by his father, by The Chaine, never to bargain with Daimaine.

He knew too well that her reality did not exist in this world. If she demanded himself in return for her help...neither would he.

Unable even yet to be a supplicant, he rose to his feet and looked up at the stars sparkling through the leaves above him. He spoke softly, words meant only for the dark goddess.

"We are yours, we High Kings. We have all ruled ensuring your Justice is met. Now I am asking for your help against my enemy. If you require for that help that I am to be the last of us, I beg that you protect my people." His voice broke. "That you protect most dearly the High Queen, who has given herself to you."

There was a stirring of magic, and he closed his eyes in hatred of it, felt a night wind lifting his hair, and a coldness on his skin. He felt the Deathqueen's presence.

But when he turned to face her, it wasn't Daimaine he found.

Shandiin shook her head. "Nope. No way, Khedran. I'll fight you to my last breath before I let you give yourself to her."

"Shandiin, don't." His voice was gentle, because he knew she cared for him in her own way, and she had already suffered enough loss. "This may be the only way to fight the Outsider magic, and you know very well you can't stop me."

Her eyes were almost desperate on his. "There's something you need to know." She swallowed, knowing she was offering a glimpse of her secret, and he was too intelligent not to see it. "Haven't you ever wondered why Daimaine can't hurt anyone without permission of a High King? It's because the first High King made a deal with her. Khalen got her promise to do no harm without direction from a High King. His bargain is also the reason she can't control any of you Kings while living and aware."

She thought she saw a momentary flash of recognition at something she had said. But she also saw speculation. "His bargain? What did he bargain with, Shandiin?"

"Himself. He sacrificed himself, just like you're trying to do. He's been her living slave for a thousand years."

His eyes widened. She continued through his shock. "The fear of Daimaine is what has kept the Tahmond from challenging the rule of the High Kings. Khandor didn't want the Tahmond to realize your bloodline purposely restrained her, so he kept Khalen's sacrifice secret. The next step would be their realization that you won't use her savage powers at all."

Now he studied her narrowly. "The latest High Tahmond figured that out on his own." He lifted a warning hand before she could continue. "I have always wondered if it could be you that Khandor referred to in that ancient message. Now it seems you witnessed things that happened a thousand years ago. You don't speak like anyone else, and you sometimes use words I've never heard before. You have so many secrets, and I have no idea why you feel it's necessary to keep them from me. Who are you, Shandiin?"

Her spirit sank, because she knew his trust was moving away from her.

She could only plead. "I am the same person you have always known. I am the one you have always trusted. Please don't set aside that trust now. Your people need you alive, to lead them. To fall in battle, if destiny demands, but not to make a living sacrifice of yourself. That cannot be your legacy."

He saw tears brimming in her silver eyes. *I have never seen her weep until today. This awful day.* One tear escaped, and he denied his heart's need to brush it from her cheek.

He had always loved her. In that moment, he realized with sorrow that...despite everything...he would always love her.

But he sensed hidden magic, and he didn't trust it.

"As you wish," was all he said. "For now."

CHAPTER 27

Weeks had passed since the High King had left Cabre. The latest of his messengers rode hard into his city, to the High Queen who awaited him expectantly in her chair at the foot of Daimaine's statue, with a phalanx of her own Guards at attention near her.

He knelt, holding out a message in his two hands. "They are coming, Your Highness. The Black Guard fights valiantly, but they are being forced back yet again. They will make their stand on the ramparts of Cabre. The Outsiders.... there are too many, and they flood the land like the very sea."

She had been expecting it. Khedran had kept her apprised of the battles he fought; she knew that all of the Chaine warriors had been lost in the first battle, and that the Shadow still took loyal soldiers of the Black Guard at every engagement with the main body of the enemy.

So she took in this news without changing expression, although the part that mattered most to her had not been told.

She had dreamed once again that Khedran had gone to the Deathqueen.

"Does the High King yet lead the Black Guard?" she asked with her heart in her throat.

"Yes, Your Highness. This message is from him."

She took it with trembling fingers, breaking the seal to read with blurred vision.

She held it to her breast, then looked at the young messenger. "I thank you. Please go and take food and rest. There is no return message at this time."

He left and she saw a light at the door. It was followed by the High Tahmond. The light emanated from his bright silver staff, which warred with Daimaine's softer starlight. Marre settled back in her chair with eyes narrowed.

The Tahmond halted before her and did not kneel. "It has come to pass," he proclaimed dolefully. "The Forbidden Child has brought an end to the dark Rioch of Azlatan, unless we act immediately!"

"And what action did you have in mind?" Marre asked him coldly.

"The boy of mixed blood must die. I understand you have moved him and his sorceress mother from Penumbra into custody of the High Tahmine. She must give them to me."

"I have no power over the High Tahmine."

"She will heed your demand."

"I will not make the demand."

The Tahmond pulled himself tall and struck his staff against the floor. Thunder filled the temple. "You must! To save Azlatan!"

"The High King will save Azlatan."

The Tahmond laughed harshly. "Even if he makes a pact with the Deathqueen, it will make no difference when the hordes are at your door. Even Daimaine cannot stop the Prophecy War. Only the death of the Forbidden Child will do that!" He struck the staff again. "You must obey Phaelon!"

"I do not see Phaelon, but only an old man with a stick. Leave me now."

At her words, her phalanx of Queen's Guard stepped forward in unison. The Tahmond stared at her in wide-eyed shock. "You would not challenge the High Tahmond of Phaelon!"

She stood slowly and as she did the statue behind her moved. She felt it in her bones, when the beautiful face was turned down toward the Tahmond, and the outstretched hand became a pointing hand.

Without another word, he turned and fled.

But Marre knew the High Tahmond was not finished with her...or Khedran.

Varady looked in despair at the wasteland that had been Selagon, his former home. The Outsiders were leaving a swathe of destruction through Azlatan that proved they intended to leave no Rioch living.

The Sundancers were looking for any survivors in the charred and smoking ruins, but found only confused Duine who had turned on their Rioch, and now wept in loss and confusion.

These Duine were rounded up and brought to Varady, who sat astride his white stallion and looked down at old friends with blood on their hands, friends who had been gentle Duine or high-spirited ones, but none who had ever harmed anyone before.

"Look at me," he said to them. They did. And with his Gift, as understanding and horror filled their faces, he repeated "Look at me."

Some fell to the ground in unrestrained weeping, but had to obey his command. When they did, he gave them peace. "It is not your fault. Nothing you have done is your fault. Take that to heart. Go now and find your Rioch and bury them if that is all that can be done. You are free now from the Shadow that took you."

He turned Pet and left them looking at each other, at themselves, in disbelief at what they had done. But he had given them peace, and with it came hope, and they set themselves to doing what they could.

Varady turned to his Sundancers. "We must ride on."

The Admech's most distantly scattered Sundancer tribes had gathered to his leadership as they rode across the steppes, for they had all seen the strange sunrise and somehow understood its meaning. Varady had come to know all of them, and to admire them. He had watched them hunt as they journeyed through the steppes and was amazed at their prowess. Using a bow more compact than the familiar longbow he knew, guiding their Shalmira mounts with only their shifting weight, they never seemed to miss their mark. He saw Stormwing take down a flying pheasant while riding her mare at a dead run, but she just smiled at him shyly when he tried to compliment her.

But even with his Sundancers at full strength, as they continued to follow the trail of devastation through Azlatan, he was sure they were outnumbered by the enemy. And he did not think his Gift could change an entire army of fanatics.

Nevertheless, he rode hard because he felt the need for haste throughout his soul.

There was only silence from the Temple of Phaelon. The people of Cabre hoped that meant something good. They awaited some explanation, some official news, from any of the three Temples.

Instead, Cabre received refugees from the Dominions, who fled their homes at the High King's warning of oncoming invaders. The many empty dwellings built at the King's command began to fill, and their purpose was understood at last.

Then came the day. The sun had barely risen when the gates of Penumbra's garrison slammed open and horns rang loudly, warning that the city's main road must be cleared. Soldiers of the Queen's Guard moved people back, and watched as Farbet, Master of their Legion, rode out beside the High Queen herself.

Farbet carried the starred black banner of Azlatan, but it paled next to the Queen, who was night in the morning with darkness and stars streaming from her cloak and her hair.

The city gate of Cabre was opened as the riders neared, and everyone rushed to wall-top or roof-top to stare out at the reason for the Queen's ride.

Every garrison of Azlatan's Black Guard was coming to Cabre. They were a flood on the road and would continue arriving for days.

In the lead, also accompanied by the banner of Azlatan, rode the High King and The Chaine.

Khedran signaled Danon to take charge when he saw Cabre's gates open, then urged Chandar into a gallop to meet the High Queen.

King and Queen halted their mounts side by side, and his welcoming smile brought her heart to her eyes. In answer he simply plucked her from her horse, placing her side-saddle in front of him. "Khedran!" she exclaimed. "The whole city is watching us!"

"Let them." And he kissed her thoroughly. When he released her at last, she gazed into those emerald eyes, and meaning beyond words passed between them.

"Now put me back," she demanded primly, and with a laugh he obeyed. She gathered her reins and her dignity and did not look at the grinning Farbet.

"I had dreams." She spoke with head lowered. "Terrible dreams that you had given yourself to Daimaine to save Azlatan. Promise me that will never happen."

He saw her lowered head, saw Farbet's puzzled concern, and looked away from them both. "I cannot promise, Marre, if it becomes the only way to keep the invaders out of Cabre. They have already burned a swathe of destruction through the Dominions. If they take Cabre...then Azlatan is lost, and they intend to kill all we call Rioch."

"No. Please, no."

"It's our final stand." As Chandar sidled beneath him, Khedran watched his Legions begin to ride past them to the city's gates and the garrison he had built behind the new wall.

She swallowed hard. She knew Khedran would always put Azlatan first.

Khedran turned back to her, to Farbet. "You know that the enemy employs a Shadow that falls over many of the Guard, and causes them to turn on each other. I cannot tell you if it can reach inside the city, but it affected almost half of my troops. Danon says the only ones to escape it are those who have no talent for magic. There's no outward sign to tell who that will be. Watch your Legion, Farbet. Even the Queen's Guard may be affected."

Marre read his concern, looked to Farbet to see he understood as well. *But Khedran has enough to worry about,* she thought. "Farbet and I will take care of the City."

Khedran smiled grim approval of his High Queen.

She looked past him to The Chaine, who sat her horse out of earshot. "I was saddened to hear of her loss."

"Not just her loss. It has fair broken the back of the Guard, losing the Chaine." His expression was bleak.

She moved closer, spoke very softly. "Has she told you yet that Jael has a brother your age?"

She watched the emerald eyes go cold, and knew that she had not.

"Explain," he said.

The Guard had not finished arriving before another messenger came from the east, riding hard through the refugees who continued to flee the enemy's path. The messenger let them know the Outsiders were barely a day behind the last garrison. They had their mounted giants in the lead this time, but that wouldn't speed their progress; their heavy warhorses could never match the speed of the Shalmira.

"They are also slowed," the messenger continued, "by some great machineries they have built and bring with them." He looked toward Cabre's new walls and gates. "I believe they plan to ram through the gate, or even the walls."

Khedran only nodded, for Shandiin had warned him that could happen. He wondered, not for the first time, how she had such foreknowledge. Even her age...a thousand years...couldn't explain it all.

He had a lot of things to wonder about, he realized, and The Chaine was at the heart of much of it.

He did not return to Penumbra, but made his headquarters in the new garrison behind the outer wall, where he could plan the coming battle and meet with his Legion Masters and others as needed.

One of the others was The Chaine, who had been with him throughout the years hc had spent preparing for the war only the two of them had fully believed was coming.

The coldness between them had deepened since she had revealed part of her strange history in the starlit grove where he'd gone to bargain with Daimaine. It had turned to ice since their return to Cabre and the news Marre had shared, and when he asked her to stay back after his Legion Masters left a strategic meeting, she sat down across from him in dread.

He frowned at her lowered head. "You helped me prepare, teaching me about the need for an army, a rampart around Cabre, stockpiling the things the city needs to live through a siege. How did you know all this, Shandiin? Were there wars, in the previous land of the Chaine you do not speak about?"

She looked up at the edge in his voice. Looked away from the anger in his eyes.

"You only tell me what you think I need to hear. I am tired of it, Shandiin. You knew about Khalen and Daimaine, and finally admitted you were there as witness a thousand years ago. I have given you the respect you demanded of my father, and not asked questions about who you are or where you come from. But how can I trust someone I don't really know? You continue to be an enigma while I face the end of my world. Now I have learned there is something else you haven't told me."

He knows, she thought. *Somehow he knows.* She sighed heavily. "Yes. You have another brother. One born the same night as you. And I believe he, not Jael, is the prophecy's Forbidden Child."

She lifted her head, and met the feral eyes of the Black Wolf.

"And why haven't you told me this before?" he demanded.

When she said nothing, emerald fire ignited. "And to think I trusted you. You have lied to me. You have lied to me all my life!"

"Yes. But you can't be rid of me yet, Khedran. I can still help you."

"No. You can't. I have the Tahmond whispering in one ear and you in the other. It's time I quit listening to either of you."

"Just...don't go to Daimaine."

"I will do what I must, to save what is left of Azlatan. Now leave me. I am done with you."

When she hesitated, the Wolf's eyes told her she had no choice.

She went, but she left the door open behind her.

CHAPTER 28

Varady could hardly believe the swathe of destruction they followed. The enemy hadn't bothered to remove the dead, whether their own or the Rioch they left behind. They found no one left living. Fires burned everywhere, whole villages gone, the very earth scorched and lifeless.

So they were surprised to see walls standing and guarded as they came to the center of Lajan, the last Dominion before the broad territory dedicated to Cabre.

Since it was the enemy's army they followed, he considered riding past this outpost.

Until he saw ChanDethe.

The great white bird with fire for eyes hovered over the fortification.

"That is the bird that came from the sun," Stormwing said. "What does it mean, Varady?"

"I think it means we need to find out what is inside those walls." He turned Pet, and the tribal leaders came to him for orders.

Windstar was the most thoughtful. "It's been easy so far, just riding to war. But it seems we may have to fight now. All Sundancers are trained archers, your Stormwing being the best. We can take down the soldiers from the top of the walls, but how are you going to get through the gates?"

"Hold off on the archers," Varady decided. "Have them ready, but that's all. I am going to go knock on their door."

"No!" Stormwing cried.

He reached over to take her hand. "Stay here. Please. I don't want anyone killed. If a fight can be avoided, I will avoid it. Do you trust me?"

She looked wild-eyed at him, at Windstar.

Windstar just nodded. "You are the Gift of the Sunqueen. We do as you will."

Stormwing was silent. Varady leaned in and kissed her, this woman who had asked to be his wife while they journeyed to Azlatan. How could he have denied her? She had no way of knowing he must die before he could keep his promise to her, but it was a promise he would carry in his own heart until it quit beating. Her love had never faltered, while his had come like a slow sunrise to warm him with its light, despite his guilty sorrow that he would cause her grief she didn't deserve.

He turned Pet and rode toward the fortress.

Soldiers on the wall were alert, but apparently saw no danger in a lone horseman riding at a walk to their gate. Varady's fair hair marked him as Duine, and the bird overhead had them in awe of what magic he might bring with him...he all in white, on a white horse, with the white bird soaring above!

Varady looked up into ChanDethe's fiery golden eye and wondered about it himself. *Keep the faith. The Sundancers believe in me. I must believe too, or I dishonor them.*

He halted Pet short of the gate, looked up at the soldier who manned the great wheel that, turning, would open the huge door looming higher than his head, wider than the road where he waited.

"I seek entrance here," he called. "Will you open the gate?"

The soldier merely stared down in disbelief. "Who are you?"

His answer came from the source of his Gift. "I am the Deliverer. I come to free you and all the Anzihi. Open the gate."

There was a shout of denial from within, but the gate began to open. He sat Pet unmoving while the machinery rumbled, and men yelled in anger. The gate halted halfway, and a rider came out to meet him.

It was a giant man wearing armor. Varady looked up at him while the man stared back.

"You cannot enter," the giant growled. "What foul magic have you used on the gatekeeper?"

"I used no magic but my words, friend. I am the Deliverer. I come to free you and all the Anzihi."

After a moment of study, the giant turned his horse, and Varady followed him into the compound.

They closed the gate behind him.

The enemy took him immediately, pulling him from his horse, dragging him to a huge enclosure filled with prisoners. They used spears to warn the inhabitants back when they opened the cage door and threw him in with shouts of laughter. "He thinks he is a god," one Anzihi called, "who can have his way with words. Our leader will find out the truth about him. Until then he can rot with the rest of the heretics."

Varady ignored this, looking around at his fellow prisoners as he picked himself up from the dirt. He realized in astonishment who they were. He had heard many stories about them, and had met one once. It had been a long time ago, but it was a meeting he had never forgotten.

They were dirty and ragged and many were wounded, but he knew them by their size, their strange fiery hair, and the leather armor worked through with Chaine gold.

"You are Chaine! How did you come to be their prisoners?"

One came to him, a man with chestnut hair and intelligent grey eyes. "That's a long story, friend. It seems we don't fit into the leader's plans for vengeance, since we are neither Rioch nor Duine. Like the Tahmond, they think we are outside the order of things, like animals. And we did some bartering. They have the idea...from somewhere...that we can teach them how to overcome magic."

"From somewhere? Like from you?"

The man grinned. "From one of us who is very clever, yes. My name is Roinn. And who are you, to come riding in so boldly to the enemy's camp?"

"You won't have heard of me. I am simply...well, I thought I was Duine. No one special."

"You *thought* you were Duine?"

"Another long story, I guess. I've learned I am only half Duine."

Roinn studied him a minute, then turned to the young woman who had joined them. She looked up at Varady, back at Roinn.

"Could he be the Gift Shandiin told us to watch for?"

"Shandiin thinks we are all dead, so no longer able to watch for anything."

"Oh, stop being so gloomy, Roinn. Shandiin never gives up, and neither should we. Don't you remember the story she told, when she brought the horses from the east?" She looked back at Varady. "Did you come from the east? Did that white bird lead you here?"

"Yes."

"Then you are the one! The one they call the Gift of the Sunqueen!"

Varady blinked. "I've been called that. Do you know the Sundancers?"

"Shandiin does. She's traveled often in their lands."

"Shandiin," Varady murmured. "I have heard that name before, I think."

"She is The Chaine. Our leader. "

Varady lifted his eyebrows. "I remember now. Wait...she thinks you are all dead?"

"We were taken prisoner in battle," Roinn explained. "We thought we would be killed, as they have killed everyone they have encountered. I am sure she thinks the worst."

"Bunch of insane fanatics," Shajii snarled. "These Anzihi, as they call themselves, are marching on Cabre. They plan to kill all the Rioch and take over Azlatan. We have got to get out of here. Their leader has magic that turns the High King's soldiers against each other. They need us." She looked away. "I just hope Compatri Danon is still alive."

"Compatri Danon? Do you know Danon?"

"Do you know him?" she returned, astonished.

Varady almost laughed. "I grew up with him. I was his Bonded Duine, until he renounced me. It seems your leader convinced him it was wrong to keep me."

The two Chaine stared at each other, then back at him. "Danon rides with the High King," Shajii told him then. "He is his right sword and his friend. Our friend, as well." She tossed back her red mane and looked about the compound. Their cage, an open framework built of heavy wooden posts and rails, sat in the center where they were in full view of the watching Anzihi soldiers. "They took our weapons and our horses. Their leader is the biggest man I have ever seen, bigger than any of the giants here. He has the emerald eyes like your High King, and he's smart. He's the one who will decide what to do with us. But he left with the main body of soldiers. The jailkeeper never gets close enough for us to take him hostage or kill him."

Varady flinched. "I can't get used to the killing. It feels wrong to me."

The two Chaine just stared at him.

He shrugged. "I am...I was a simple Duine."

"But this is war," Roinn pointed out. "How did you get here? Are you alone?"

"No. The Sundancers are waiting for me out there, but they won't move without me telling them to."

"How will you get word to them?"

Varady shrugged. "I don't know how to do half the things I do. I have a Gift, but I'm still learning how to use it. Or maybe it's using me. Anyway, I wouldn't call them in now. I don't want them hurt or killed, and that would happen if they tried to storm this place. What is this, anyway?"

Roinn was regarding him with puzzled amazement. "It's a garrison. Apparently the High King had these built throughout Azlatan, to house the army he built because he saw this war coming. All his soldiers have retreated, though, to Cabre. I guess they are making a last stand there." He glanced at Shajii. "As she said, they need us. And we are trapped here."

"Will your magic get us out?" Shajii demanded.

Varady lifted his shoulders and his empty palms. She glared and walked away in disgust.

Roinn looked after her. "She is young, and very much the impatient warrior. I apologize for her rudeness."

"She's just frustrated. I don't blame her." Varady sighed, then saw something in Roinn's hand. "Is that a flute?"

Roinn nodded. "Carved from a Goldtree, in our northern home. The enemy took all the weapons but saw no use for this."

"May I borrow it?"

He took the offered flute and sat down in the dirt, his back against a cage bar. His Gift had taught him to follow his heart, and now his heart led him to do a thing which made no sense while they all sat in captivity in the middle of a war.

He lifted the flute to his lips and played.

He played the melody of the Sundancers, and closed his eyes to the peace it offered him. The sound from this special flute was like golden sunlight made into music, and while it comforted him, he was unaware of the changes that began to happen around him.

The Chaine sat down to listen, but soon began to realize the Anzihi were listening as well; they began coming to their cage like ants to honey. Some Anzihi came bodily against the cage, grasping its bars to peer in as though they were on the inside and wanted their freedom. Others knelt in the dirt outside, and to the amazement of the onlookers began to weep as though the music told a sad story.

One came through the crowd who was one of their special giants, and he stopped at the gate of the cage, his eyes wide on the white-clad stranger with the magic flute.

Shajii didn't miss her chance. Recognizing their jailkeeper, she reached through the gate and took the massive key from his hand and unlocked the cage.

The jailkeeper simply opened the door and walked in to sit down in front of Varady. Others followed him.

When Varady stopped playing, he lowered the flute and looked around at the Anzihi gathered around him, and at the Chaine who were now outside the cage, gathering their weapons and their horses. He took a breath full of amazement and tried to think.

He had spoken to...and helped...many Duine on his journey through Azlatan, but they were innocent people who had been enchanted by some awful sorcery. These Anzihi had been trained from birth to hate and kill, and were intent on killing more. He saw little chance of changing that with his Gift.

For the moment they were in his power, something he had never wanted, but it was a duty that had somehow been given to him. *What am I to do? These are the enemy. We are at war. We cannot safely leave them behind us.*

But I cannot kill while they are defenseless. Not with my Gift. And not by my order.

He reached to the jailkeeper who had fallen asleep in front of him and touched him lightly on his downturned head. "Wake up."

The man raised himself slowly to look into Varady's golden eyes and shivered visibly.

"Why are you bringing war to Azlatan?" Varady asked him.

"Because Phaelon wills it. We are his chosen people, and will replace all of those called Rioch. The Rioch make slaves of those they call Duine, who are our brothers."

"What if I told you that it was Phaelon himself who decided that the Duine would serve the Rioch? It was not a decision made by the Rioch."

The gatekeeper looked confused. "How can that be?"

"Because you have been lied to. So was I. I was told that I could not leave the borders of Azlatan, but I did. I don't think you can trust Phaelon."

"Heresy!"

"Perhaps. But does that mean it isn't true? Look at me."

Obeying, the gatekeeper cried out. "No! It is true! I cannot bear it!"

"You can. You must think for yourself, is all. It's always better to live in truth than in a lie, isn't it?"

"How can I? My brothers...my family...we all believed!"

Varady looked around at the sleeping Anzihi. "Believing something doesn't make it true. Perhaps you can help your brothers understand that."

"No! They will behead me for heresy!"

Varady flinched. "Really? Then perhaps you shouldn't tell them, but just do what is best for yourself. If you can live with that."

He looked around at those still asleep. He still didn't think he could change them all with his Gift, especially knowing the penalty for saying anything against Phaelon. He drew in a breath. He would do what he could.

"Be at peace," he told the sleeping Anzihi. He felt magic in his voice, and knew that somehow he was heard, not realizing it was a Gift of his bloodline. "What you make of your life from here forward will be yours alone. You do not have to go to war. Sleep now. When you awake you will look inside yourself and see you are free to choose. Sleep now."

With that he rose and walked through those who were, in some small possibility, no longer enemies. He walked up to Roinn to return the flute, but that was refused.

"Please keep it. As a gift from my people, with our thanks." Roinn looked toward the cage enclosure. "What have you done to them?"

"They're just asleep. I suggest locking them in and leaving a guard behind to make sure they remain here until this war is ended."

Roinn frowned. "We need every one of our warriors."

"I agree. Your people have a fierce reputation, even in the small town I came from. My friends the Sundancers are fighters, but not like yours. I will ask some to stay here as guards. Those who prefer to go on will join us as we ride to Cabre."

When his own horse was brought to him, Varady mounted to return to his adopted people.

Shajii looked after him, astonished. "What a strange man! He fights a war with sleep?"

Roinn was watching Varady ride away as well. "Shandiin said he is the Deliverer, who in Azlatan is called the Forbidden Child. I think his magic is something we have never seen before. I don't know if even she knew what he would bring."

After a long search through the garrison, Danon joined the High King on the rampart where he stood watching the enemy massing on the horizon. It was early dawn.

Danon kept looking around, finally ventured to ask. "Your Highness, where is she?"

Khedran continued gazing into the distance. "You are looking for Shandiin? I do not know where she is, Danon, and I don't care."

Danon stared at his liege in disbelief. Khedran finally turned to face him. "I sent her away. Do you have a problem with that, Compatri?"

The coldness on the King's face and in his voice would normally have sent Danon in search of somewhere else to be. But Danon had also seen the horizon, the innumerable forces that he knew they could not defeat, though they would fight to the death.

Almost certainly...to the death.

And he thought, *She should be here, beside us.*

So he gathered his courage, did the unthinkable, and challenged his liege. "Your Highness, may I ask what she has done to you, that you have sent her away? Especially now, after she's lost her people, when we are all she has left?"

He saw the change. He had seen it before, when the King's eyes became that of the Black Wolf. It made the King unreadable, and frankly terrifying.

But Danon had also seen something else before the Wolf replaced it, and remembered what Shandiin had told him about the Black Wolf, on a cold mountaintop north of Ordhold: *"He puts up a wall between himself and the world, because it can overwhelm him with sadness."*

Khedran's voice was as cold as his expression. "I don't answer to you, Compatri, and I will not. If she means so much to you, hunt her down. But she is no longer welcome where I am. She may never be welcome again. Be careful of your allegiance."

Leaving Danon stunned, Khedran walked away to talk to a nearby Legion Master.

Danon had wondered about the tension between The Chaine and the High King ever since he had returned from Ordhold. It seemed that tension had finally broken the bond between them, but Danon thought not.

Because he had just seen Khedran replace pain and guilt with the Wolf.

He went in search of Shandiin.

He found her near a sally port, sitting alone on the ground against Cabre's outer wall, at the feet of her big paint horse. She had braided her wild red hair for battle, and sword and shield were at hand.

She didn't look up at his approach. "You shouldn't have come to find me. Go now or he may not forgive you."

"What happened? What in the name of Chaos has happened?"

"He found out I am a liar. He no longer trusts me."

Danon dropped down to sit beside her, bracing his back against the wall. "What could you have lied about, Shandiin?"

"You know. I told you when I had told no one else. About the child born the same night he was."

He huffed. "So he thinks it's a lie, when you just don't tell him something? Why did you find it necessary to tell him now, with this..." he gestured in front of them at the waiting battleground.

"He found out somehow. It doesn't matter how. He's learned some other things about me, Danon, which have given him a right to mistrust me." She drew her knees to her chest, wrapped her arms around them. "He was going to barter his life with Daimaine, and I had to stop him. I had to tell him some truths I had not shared before. After that, learning I've also known he has another brother was more than he could take."

Danon looked at her helplessly. "He'll get over it. He loves you, Shandiin. I have seen it."

She hesitated, then shook her head. "If that's true, it's another reason behind his anger. No one can hurt you like someone you love."

He sighed. "So, are there any of those truths that you can tell me, while we sit here waiting for the axe to fall?"

She lifted her eyebrows and nearly smiled. "What in particular would you want to know?"

"To start with...where are you from, anyway? Your people, I mean. I know it's not from that village near Ordhold."

"No. We came from the east."

He looked over at her in disbelief. "You came from the west, in the ships."

"Haven't you ever wondered what's on the other side of the sea?"

"But that's the west."

She picked up a stick, drew a circle in the dirt between them. "The world isn't flat," she told him. "It's a globe, like the moon. You can travel around it." She dragged the stick to one side, then the other. "You can travel around it to the left...the west...and there is the other side. Then if you sail from the other side to come back..." she dragged the stick again, "...you are coming from the east."

He thought about this for a moment. "Varady...my friend told me he thought a woman lived in the east, called Prophecy's Daughter, and she could talk to the world."

She slowly lifted her eyes to his. "That's interesting."

He had more questions, but put those away as he looked out toward the enemy. It seemed more important to talk of things closer to him than history.

"Shandiin," he ventured, thinking he would be dead soon anyway, "have you ever loved anyone? A man, I mean...you know what I mean. I guess...an *amharen.* I know it's a personal..." He faltered, and bit his lip.

"No. I have never been in love in the way you mean. Is there more to your question?"

He looked at her with his heart in his eyes. "Yes."

She sighed. "I thought there might be." She lifted a gentle hand to his face, brushed back the dark fall of his hair. "You are so young. And you deserve so much. We may die very soon, and I wish I could give you what you want; I love you dearly, don't you know that? – just not in the way you want me to. So I can only give you this."

She framed his face with her hands and brought her lips to his with all the tenderness she could offer, and he felt his heart begin to heal at last. When she drew back, he imagined he saw the beauty of sunlight in her eyes, and he could only smile through his tears.

He couldn't speak for a long time. She let him be, because he was recovering from her magic. Using her magic was risky, but her time in hiding was near an end. She knew because her power was strong.

And she cared for him, so had given him the peace of a whole heart. He deserved to have someone who would return his love. *This is what I should have done for Khedran,* she thought, and refused to think why she had not.

At length he said, "I can't believe you have done anything to deserve this...this banishment, when we are all putting our lives on the line."

"Doesn't matter, Danon. His heart can be very hard. I made sure of that when I taught him my ways. Mine is pretty hard as well."

"But it's breaking right now, isn't it?"

She said nothing.

"Are you going to fight?"

"What do you think?"

He laughed bitterly. "I know you will. That's how I knew to look for you out here. When he rides to war you are going to ride in behind him, even though he doesn't want you, and defend his back until they cut you down."

Her lips curved, and her silver eyes regarded him warmly. "As will you."

"As will I."

"Look! The enemy is advancing!" Bannon cried.

Khedran lifted a gloved hand. "Hold, Bannon. It is only one rider."

One rider, one huge and familiar rider. He carried the banner that was divided: half black, half white. His bright half-black armor scattered the morning sun. He rode slowly to the halfway point between the Anzihi army and the gates of Cabre. There he stopped and planted the banner into the ground next to him. Then he waited.

Bannon looked from the giant to Khedran. "I think he wants to talk. Shall I go, Your Highness?"

"No." Khedran had come to the same conclusion. "This is for me." He looked around at the soldiers who stood with him, two of the most important missing. "Do nothing unless I signal."

"Or unless you are attacked!" Bannon exclaimed. "You should not go alone."

"Such an optimist," Khedran muttered. He climbed down to where Chandar waited, and taking the banner of his own realm, motioned for a sally port to be opened.

Like the giant Anzihi, he rode slowly across the coming battleground. Reaching the giant, he plunged the flagstaff into the earth opposite the other. Then he waited.

"We are the Anzihi, and we demand surrender of the Rioch of Azlatan," the giant rumbled. "You cannot defeat us."

"I am the High King of Azlatan. I demand you leave my realm."

The giant studied him, pushing back his helm so his face was visible.

Khedran was stunned to see the emerald eyes that marked his own bloodline. *Is this him, then? Is this my brother, the Forbidden Child?*

"We recognize no King but Phaelon," the giant said. "I am his Tahmond, and I am Commander of his army. Surrender or die."

Khedran laughed. "You want me to believe you will not kill us if we surrender?"

"We are here to kill all the Rioch, pull down the place called Penumbra and the Temples of Liethe and Daimaine, and destroy the crypts of your heretic ancestors. You and your Queen may go free, however, if you surrender your army."

Khedran's eyes blazed back at his enemy. He yanked his flagstaff from the ground and turned Chandar back to his city.

"You are a fool!" the giant called after him.

Khedran ignored him, refusing any response to the coward's choice he'd been offered. He rode slowly, head high, watching the ramparts because he knew what Bannon would do if he saw danger.

When Bannon threw an arm out to point behind him, Chandar spun at the touch of his heel, and the Star Blade blazed white fire to clove the thrown spear in two.

He waited while Chandar trembled with ears flattened, ready for battle.

The giant merely turned his horse and rode back to his own army.

"Tried to spear you in the back!" Bannon exclaimed upon his return. "What a coward!"

"I don't think we can look for honor among them," Khedran agreed wryly. "He offered to let me go in exchange for allowing everyone else to die." He frowned. "Actually, he offered to let me and my Queen go. Do you think he was guessing, or does he know about Marre? He says he is Phaelon's Tahmond."

"Then the Shadow is Phaelon's!" Bannon exclaimed.

Khedran turned to give orders to a messenger waiting nearby, flicking an angry glance past Shandiin, who had arrived to stand just within earshot. "Take a message to the High Queen. She needs to speak to the High Tahmond."

CHAPTER 29

The King's messenger found Marre in her chambers, but he came to her door with a companion on his heels.

"The High King bids you go to the Temple of Phaelon," the messenger said. "The leader of that army told him he is Tahmond to Phaelon. He needs confirmation."

Marre recognized the messenger's companion, and narrowed her eyes at the redhaired beauty.

"Your Highness," The Chaine said, "I came to warn you not to go to Phaelon's Temple."

"Khedran wants me to go and confront the High Tahmond. If he is in league with that army out there, we need to know it."

"I can tell you he is. I believe the High Tahmond has been part of this war of the Anzihi since the night Khedran was born. If you go to him now, he may do harm to you. You are safer in Penumbra."

Marre glared. "I am not here to be safe. I am here for Azlatan, and *my* King."

Shandiin considered the small woman who offered such courage, and who had asserted her sole right to Khedran with a single word of emphasis. She nodded respectfully. "Then I beg that you ask Daimaine first. Ask Daimaine if Phaelon is on the other side of this war. And ask her what can be done about it."

"Why doesn't Khedran ask? He has the Star Blade."

Shandiin frowned. "Tell me honestly: do you want Khedran going to Daimaine for anything at this point?"

Marre remembered her dreams of Khedran lost, and shivered. "No."

Shandiin nodded. "Then you are very wise. But you can seek Daimaine's counsel, as she has chosen to give her magic to you."

She glanced past Marre, and went still. Her eyes widened. "Did you paint that?"

Marre stepped aside to allow full view of her portrait of Khedran, her greatest work of love.

"You have captured him here." Shandiin's voice was thick; her gaze pinned to the painting. "Not just his male beauty, which everyone notices first. But this...this shows what is underneath. The truth behind all the High Kings. You have captured Khedran's nobility. You have captured his true spirit with a brush and some paint."

When Shandiin turned from the painting to look back at Marre, her eyes were bright with unshed tears. "I am so glad that he has you, Your Highness. I believe you are the best thing that has ever happened to him, and you have my gratitude for that."

Marre was stunned, and guessed the truth Shandiin hid even from herself. "You truly love him, don't you?"

Shandiin just looked away, toward the ramparts. "I have to go. Will you do as I ask?"

Marre nodded, thoughtful. "I will not go to Phaelon's Temple unless Daimaine is of no help."

As Shandiin turned to leave, Marre caught her sleeve. "I know you have always been his Defender. I beg of you to guard him well, in this war."

The Chaine finally met her eyes. "I will defend him for as long as I remain in this world," she promised, and Marre watched her go, wondering at the odd phrasing.

Not long after, having gathered her courage, Marre stood alone in Daimaine's Temple. She gazed up at the statue's beautiful face. *She is cruel. Does no one else see that?*

Of course, people only looked at that face for a moment because Daimaine's magic was fearful.

The magic that had been shared with her.

Does Khedran see the cruelty in her?

She walked across the glassy black floor, stopping at the foot of the dais where the two chairs waited. The statue loomed over her. Behind it, she knew, were the crypts of six High Kings...crypts that would in time hold Khedran.

Where are their souls? Unlike the rest of us, there is no peace promised to them at death. They belong to Daimaine. Where are their souls?

She forced herself into the moment, leaving old questions behind. "I come to ask about the god Phaelon," she said aloud. "Is it his power or is it some other sorcery that has attacked the soldiers of the High King?"

A ringing silence fell over the huge chamber. She felt the temperature drop.

She was afraid, but refused to let that own her. When the silence continued, she spoke again. "You have helped me. You gave me magic when I took the Star Blade to save the High King from Phaelon's Tahmond. But there will be no safety if Phaelon is our enemy. You know this. Do you stand with the High King?"

There came the chill of a night wind behind her, and a cold touch on her shoulder.

She turned to face the Deathqueen herself.

She turned slowly, fighting her trembling body, and regarded the goddess in her terrifying beauty. Daimaine's hair was incandescent darkness sweeping to the empty void upon which she stood. Living starfire chased through her form and met in her eyes, deep and cold.

"I will help the High King if he asks it of me." The voice was a dissonance of whispers, at once distant and inside her mind.

"At what price?" Marre asked.

She received only a cold smile.

Marre looked into those dreadful eyes and knew with certainty that Khedran should never ask help of Daimaine. Not while he lived. Never while he lived.

She managed to say, "Tell me then, if Phaelon is our enemy."

"Phaelon gives his strength to his Tahmonds, as I gave mine to my Kings."

"If Phaelon has his way, there would be no more High Kings. You know this!"

Daimaine smiled again. *"I have six. I will have seven. Perhaps that is enough."*

Marre put her hands against her belly, where the child within had only recently begun to stir. "You would allow Azlatan to fall? For it will, without the High King, without the help of your magic!"

"Perhaps it will be for the best. My magic has been too restricted by the High Kings."

"Why...how can that be?"

"Because I bartered with the first High King. I gave away too much authority, in exchange for... himself."

Marre couldn't speak for a long moment. "Himself? Do you mean while he lived? You took him alive?"

Daimaine only smiled again. *"Would you have me release him, in exchange for the King you think is yours?"*

Marre froze in horror. "He still lives?"

Daimaine laughed and began to fade to shadow.

"No!" Marre cried. "No! You cannot have Khedran!"

But the laughter simply faded with the shadow, and she was alone.

The messenger found Shandiin on the rampart. "The High Queen bids you meet her at the Temple of Phaelon," the nervous young woman told her.

With a curse, Shandiin was down the rampart in seconds, and on Windmaker who waited in readiness at the bottom. She let the big paint have his head, and the citizens of Cabre parted in shock as she galloped past and occasionally leaped over them.

Still, Marre got to Phaelon's Temple before she did.

The High Tahmond sat on his silver chair with his silver staff in his hand. Marre was sure his expression was smug, though it was hard to tell under the black and white paint on his face. "So, you have come to your senses. Where is the boy?"

"We can discuss that after you answer my questions. Is that your fellow Tahmond outside Cabre's walls, with the enemy Outsiders? Is it Phaelon's magic putting a spell on the Black Guard so they turn on their own?"

He sat back but did not answer.

"So. It is true."

"I do not answer to you."

Marre realized she had to do more. "Then let me talk to Phaelon."

He jerked upright. "You would dare!"

"I would. I have spoken with the goddess Daimaine. Now I wish to speak with the god Phaelon."

"That is heresy and worse! No one speaks to Phaelon but his Tahmond! I will call —"

They both heard the commotion outside the room. The door slammed open to reveal The Chaine with sword unsheathed in one hand, dragging a young Tahmond brother by the neck of his robe with the other. She stopped alongside Marre, and with a nod to the Queen dropped the young man at her feet, where he cowered.

"Who will you call?" Shandiin demanded of the High Tahmond. "It seems you have only a few of your Brothers left in this hideous Temple. They are abandoning you, aren't they? They have realized you are a madman seeking to replace the High King while he fights to defend his people. And your magic will not work on me...magic you hide behind like some rat in a hole!"

The Tahmond was on his feet, slamming his staff into the floor.

The resultant flash and thunder disturbed neither of the women in front of him.

"I told you not to come here," Shandiin said under her breath.

"I found it necessary," Marre replied just as quietly.

"I can unleash the Duine Anzihi now," the Tahmond threatened, "and destroy your High King just as I did his sire!"

Shandiin stiffened, rage surging through every part of her being.

She turned from Marre and stalked to the High Tahmond, who stumbled back onto his chair as she neared. Seizing the front of his robe, she yanked him up several inches to her eye level. He struggled, flailing and kicking at her uselessly. She just lifted him higher.

"So it was you who ordered Allasar's death," she snarled. "I should kill you here and now. I hesitate only because you are the devil I know, and Phaelon might come up with someone even worse...but I will kill you, if you dare to unleash your damned Anzihi again. Do you hear me? Keep them leashed, or I will shove your thunder-stick so far up your ass it comes out your nose."

He tried to speak, but it came out as a squeal. "Phaelon..."

"Go ahead and call on him," she sneered. "See if he comes to your aid...remembering, you fucking son of a bitch, that I am immune to magic, but you are not immune to my sword!"

As he trembled in her grasp, she looked back at Marre. "Did I hear you ask to talk to Phaelon?"

Marre swallowed. She hadn't understood some of the words Shandiin had used, but her rage and her strength were both terrifying and...she thought... quite magnificent. "Yes," she managed.

Shandiin slammed the Tahmond back onto his throne. "Take us to him, and see that no harm comes to the High Queen. On your life!"

He rose, visibly quaking, and with an old man's posture led them to an arched doorway filled with mist.

When they entered, they saw silver so brilliant it was painful, unlike Daimaine's starlight. It flashed around the room in strange and changing patterns. Marre's own magic darkness seemed to grow with it, like a living shadow glimmering with stars.

Shandiin believed her goddess identity would remain hidden from Phaelon, though she had never dared to approach the god until the prophecy was nigh, as it was now. She realized, standing in his strangely diffused presence, that he had grown erratic during the thousand years she'd hidden from him.

"Phaelon! Hear me, I beseech thee!" The Tahmond raised his arms dramatically. "These seek audience with you, to know the truth of your Order!"

Marre faced a deity for the second time that day. She saw a strange being through the mist, made of descending silver rings. While Daimaine merged darkness and starfire in her being, Phaelon's features were not even discernible, and no mouth showed when he spoke.

"Have you brought Daimaine to me?" Phaelon asked without expression. The lifeless voice issued from everywhere.

The Tahmond looked confused. Shandiin frowned curiously.

"This is the High Queen, who is now Tahmine to Daimaine." The Tahmond spoke nervously.

"Then I now address the High Queen. My Tahmond has told me there is an abomination in Liethe's Temple. Bring him to me."

Marre swallowed hard. Her mouth was dry as dust. "And what would happen then? Will the enemy leave our gates?"

"The Rioch are no longer Lords of Azlatan. A High King has broken the Law, and the end has come for his people."

"Why? And why should I bring you a boy who is innocent of doing any wrong?"

"He is not the prophesied Forbidden Child. But the sin was his father's, and he must die to wash it clean."

Marre stood in shock. "No," she whispered.

"Tell your King. Tell him to put down Daimaine's sword and lie in the dirt before my army of Anzihi. He and all Rioch must die. No magic can save them."

The High Tahmond turned to Marre victoriously. "Do you have your answer now?"

She fled. Shandiin followed thoughtfully.

Marre found Khedran in his headquarters below the rampart and ignored ceremony, walking in while he sat at the conference table with some of his leaders. "Please leave," she told them, while her eyes met those of her love from across the room. "I must speak to the High King."

He looked back at her, gave a brief nod as he stood, and everyone left quickly. Marre was surprised to see Khedran watching her coldly, and then realized his gaze was on someone behind her.

She glanced back to see Shandiin. "The Chaine can stay," she told Khedran. "She went to Phaelon's Temple to meet me, at my request."

Emerald eyes flashed back to Marre. "You saw the High Tahmond?"

Marre's face was pale behind the magic façade. "I saw Phaelon himself, Khedran. He means for all the Rioch to die. No forgiveness, no reason but disobedience by one man and one woman." She went to Khedran, placing a hand over his heart as she looked up at him. He lifted a hand to cover hers, but he was still glaring at Shandiin, and Marre was baffled by his anger.

She frowned back and forth between them. "Shandiin helped me, Khedran. You should have seen it! She picked the High Tahmond up by his robe until his feet didn't touch the floor, and threatened him with his own staff!"

He looked back at Marre in disbelief. "She did *what?*"

Shandiin crossed her arms, scowling. "He was threatening to set the Duine Anzihi on you. I told him I'd shove his damned thunder-stick up his ass."

His eyebrows went up and he snorted a shocked laugh.

When Marre added with admiration, "Until it came out his nose!" His laughter became uncontrollable.

Both women regarded him with surprise. When he finally subsided, dropping into a chair at the conference table with Marre's hand still clasped in his own, he shook his head and looked up at Shandiin while brushing tears of mirth from in his eyes.

He was no stranger to her often outrageous ways, and that somehow intimate familiarity had made him realize he could never stay angry with her. "Please. Just sit down, Shandiin. Only you could even think of such a thing...and how I wish I'd seen it!"

"He's such an asshole," she muttered, and sat down with her arms still crossed.

"I don't think I've ever seen anyone that angry," Marre put in.

"Really?" Khedran turned to his Queen with a smile. "I have. I saw you when you turned on the Dominion Kings, took the Star Blade from my hands and threatened to unleash Daimaine on them. I, for one, will be very careful about angering either of you."

He touched Marre's cheek gently. "It was brave of you to confront Phaelon himself. And I can see his words terrified you, Marre, but it is no more than I expected."

"I'm not sure it's all true." Shandiin was frowning thoughtfully. "I don't think it's Allasar's 'sinful' act that has caused Phaelon to do this. I think it's more than that. I believe Phaelon has always planned to have complete control, and logic told him that can only happen if the Rioch are gone for good. So, he produced the Forbidden Child prophecy, and added plans to make sure that the Rioch can't survive. He has Duine Anzihi hidden somewhere inside of Cabre, and his Anzihi army outside."

Khedran nodded thoughtfully. "He took down the border wards the night I was born. But the enemy in the east must have been building for far longer."

Shandiin said, "My guess? It's been building since the beginning of Azlatan. A thousand years."

Khedran nodded agreement. "I've often thought Phaelon has withdrawn from his own Temple as time passes, leaving the Tahmond free to work his own will. And now we find Phaelon has created an entire nation devoted to him alone. The God of Order probably finds the Outsiders more to his liking than the people of Azlatan. The Kings have always ruled separately from the gods, allowing people their own minds, their own rights."

He frowned and turned to The Chaine in concern. "Shandiin, the giant Anzihi Tahmond had my green eyes. The eyes of a High King. How can that be? Is he the brother I never knew about?"

"No." She shook her head in certainty. "As for the eyes, I know the realm of Xanthe has been breeding people to get the giants. That would take many generations. Some of the people in their breeding program must share the DNA..." she stopped, seeing puzzlement. "I mean the blood of your ancestors. Apparently the inbreeding among them has resulted in the green eyes showing up. You've seen inbreeding create throwbacks in your horses."

"Yes." He exhaled. "I am glad to know he is not my brother. The man's a beast." He regarded Shandiin with a lifted eyebrow. "Now explain to me why you never told me I had another brother."

She met his eyes, and he saw sadness in hers. "Because the damn Prophecy says he has to die, or all the Rioch will die. You refused to give Jael to the High Tahmond. What will you do with a brother your own age, who stands between you and your people?"

He lifted his eyebrows, surprised at her. "That would depend on the person he is, and what circumstances bring us together...if or when that should happen. I don't know enough now to make any decisions."

"You're ignoring the Prophecy. As I understand it, either he dies or all the Rioch die."

"So you didn't tell me because you believe he has to die, and you didn't think I would kill him if I knew?"

"I had hoped," she admitted, "to leave you to do what you believe is right...or at least what is necessary...without knowing he is your brother."

"So you were trying to protect me? You hoped I would act in ignorance, and so wouldn't feel the pain of his sacrifice. I'm surprised and frankly puzzled. Hiding the truth has never been your way, Shandiin. And it's based on an assumption that I would kill any innocent person, brother or not, to save others."

"Wouldn't you?"

"I would find a different path."

"I don't think there is one."

"That's very fatalistic of you."

"Dammit, Khedran...this whole damned Prophecy is fatalistic. You can't just ignore the facts."

"Can't I? It seems I have been doing just that, my entire life. I have never known who you are, why you are here. I have never known how you know the things you do. As far as facts are concerned, I don't know you at all. But I have..." he stopped mid-sentence, looked away from her to where his hand still held Marre's. Sighed, and started his sentence over. "But I have accepted you. Even though you have hidden things from me, when I get past my anger I know that I can trust you. The answers aren't always black and white, Shandiin. I will find another path. I cannot accept evil as my only alternative. I thought you understood me better than that."

When she said nothing, he asked, "Will I know him when I see him, Shandiin? Will you tell me that much?"

There was challenge, now, in those emerald eyes. *Yes*, she thought. *He knows that I am more than I appear. If...when...he learns I am the goddess called Chaos, he will hate me.*

I can't let that matter.

"My guess is yes. Just as he will know who you are. He may have some of the Gifts of your bloodline."

He nodded. "Then I will hope that both he and I will find the right path to defeat the Prophecy."

CHAPTER 30

Cabre stood against siege, and the city passed from dread into misery.

There was no way out.

Outer Azlatan, it seemed, was gone.

Many Dominion Kings were among the refugees that had come to Cabre, a fact that made life even more difficult as they realized they were now merely mortals among mortals.

They had to share their space with the livestock which, along with the stores of grain, were the only source of food as fresh foodstuffs disappeared. These stores were strictly rationed by Khedran's Duine and enforced by the Black Guard, which did not please the Dominion Kings. Some of those believed that their tributes of the past made them first in line for distribution. They were denied by order of the High King.

The High Tahmond had not been seen since the war began. The High Tahmine oversaw her own Temple, which was swollen with homeless Duine and the wounded. Penumbra alone seemed alive, it's dark beauty glittering in the day and blazing like a full moon at night.

But the High King did not go to Penumbra. He stood with the soldiers who defended Cabre against continued attacks against the ramparts. The Anzihi came with ladders to climb the walls. The walls, however, had been built out-slanting so the ladders would not hold well.

Soon the assaults became almost routine, until machinery was drawn near but too far for torched arrows to find.

Thus, safe from destruction, catapults were loaded, and their contents rained upon the city. This brought horror beyond acceptance, as dead animals crawling with disease landed within, along with the severed heads of Rioch both known and unknown.

Although removing the offal and cleaning after were made priority, disease began to ravage the city, bringing death with it. The healers of the Temple were overwhelmed. Chaine medicine was efficient, but there were not enough physicians.

Since Liethe's Temple was full, Penumbra became a hospital under Danon's command. The Sisters of Liethe, including the High Tahmine herself, came as they could, to aid and practice their healing there.

People died anyway.

And then the Anzihi brought up their giant ram, to take down Cabre's gates.

"We've known they had it," Shandiin said to Khedran as they peered across the battlefield from atop the rampart. "The messenger said it was out there, but it's taken them a long time to get it here."

"Not long enough." Khedran looked around at his weary soldiers, behind them at his devastated city. "We will have to send out a sortie to stop them before it gets to the gates. If they get through it will all be over. There are just too many of them."

Shandiin bit her lip, having heard a hint of despair in the voice of the High King. This war was wearing everyone down, but Khedran had been his usual confident self...or so everyone thought. Morale was low in the Black Guard. Phaelon's Shadow had taken half their number so that those who survived had to be locked away. The loyalists who remained and were able to fight were weary.

There seemed no way out. No way to win.

"That ram is huge! How can you destroy something so huge?" Bannon was staring toward the enemy, almost wild-eyed.

"Fire," Khedran said. "Fire will destroy anything. But I don't want that thing to get close enough for my archers, who could shoot flaming arrows. It will take..."

"Who is that?" Bannon cried, and Khedran looked sharply in the direction of his pointing finger.

A new army had appeared from nowhere, and it was attacking the ram. Khedran didn't hesitate, but called for his horse, his Guard, as he swung down from the fighting platform. He didn't know who the fighters were, but obviously—somehow—they were allies.

Shandiin was on Windmaker as soon as he mounted Chandar, and the two of them were first out a sortie gate, his Guard a column on their heels.

Even as they rode out, fire erupted from the monstrous ram. Unknown mounted archers were firing flaming arrows. But Khedran recognized the warriors who were defending the archers from the Anzihi, and his heart leaped in astounded recognition. He glanced over at Shandiin and her face told him she had seen the same thing.

The ram blazed. Two riders broke off from the scene ahead and turned toward them, riding hard.

One had red hair. The other wore white and rode a white horse. Their followers wheeled from engagement, the flaming ram surely destroyed, and raced behind their leaders toward Cabre.

The Anzihi were like an anthill, spilling around the lost ram, then pooling in confusion when they saw the Black Guard erupt from a narrow sortie gate in apparent attack.

Khedran knew the giant who was their leader would end their chaos and soon send the main body to overrun them all, but he waited and watched them scramble while his new allies thundered past on both sides of him. Smiling savagely, he held with his Guard at his back until the last new rider was safely past. Only then did he wheel Chandar to follow them into Cabre.

Cabre's big gates had swung wide to allow them all quick entrance; Bannon had thought ahead, as usual. An ovation of cheers erupted from the ramparts as they flew through to safety.

Khedran brought Chandar to a plunging halt as the gates closed, easily handling the stallion's excitement while he searched through the tumult of arrivals. He grinned at his old friend and teacher Roinn, who smiled back just as broadly. He saw a young Chaine woman slide from her horse into Shandiin's waiting arms. He didn't recognize the riders in buckskin but looked for the one he somehow knew was their leader, and found him waiting.

All in white, on a white stallion, with hair of sand and silver and eyes of gold. He seemed to be a reverse image of the High King's black on black. They stopped their mounts alongside each other, knee to knee, each measuring the other.

Khedran knew who he faced, just as his subjects always knew who he was. His heart swelled with gratitude at that recognition, because with it he found not just his bloodline, but a kindred spirit.

"Welcome, my brother. I am Khedran."

Varady's eyes were wide with the same wondrous recognition. "I am Varady, once a Duine of Azlatan...or so I thought until I ran afoul of the Outsiders who call themselves Anzihi. You are the High King."

"And you are the Forbidden Child, who is to bring the end of the Rioch." But Khedran already knew that kindred spirit was as rebellious as his own.

Varady was surprised at the complete familiarity he had also shared, and the depth of understanding that had come with it. "That is what the Anzihi want, not I. I bring a warning, and it is dire. Your enemies are not only outside your gates. All of Azlatan's Duine can be made into Anzihi at Phaelon's command. They just don't know it until Phaelon sends them to kill, and then they forget again."

Khedran was stunned. After a moment he repeated, "All of them? And they don't know?"

"That is what makes them so dangerous. They kill, and then forget, so no one can ever confess. It is why, I think, you never found the killers of the High King who was our father."

Khedran looked away, his mind racing, and then shook his head. "We can't talk here. Please come with me to my head-quarters?"

At Varady's nod Khedran swung down from Chandar. "Follow me, please. Bring who you wish." He flipped his reins to a waiting soldier, calling directions to his Legion Masters as he went, ensuring the ramparts were secured.

The scene around them was pandemonium which began to settle as the High King and his allies strode through with the assurance of command. They were soon in Khedran's war room, where he witnessed his Compatri Danon stop in front of his newfound brother and stare up at him in shock. "Varady? Is it really you?"

Varady smiled broadly. "Hello, Danon. It's good to see you alive and well. Shajii has been very worried about you."

"Shajii?" Danon looked around hopefully as a young woman he remembered very well threw herself into his arms, laughing. "Shajii!"

Khedran raised his eyebrows and went to the meeting table, waiting for the celebratory commotion to calm. He settled into a chair, his face softening as he saw the typically reserved Shandiin and Roinn in a heartfelt embrace.

Varady sat down next to him, and they watched the commotion until Khedran glanced shrewdly from Danon to Varady. "I realize now you were once Duine to my Compatri. He went through agony deciding he had to break Bond with you. It occurs to me that, having been in bondage, you could have agreed with the purpose of the Anzihi."

Varady shook his head. "I had no problem with being Duine to a Rioch I felt was like a brother. It hurt when he broke Bond, but I now understand why, and I agree with his beliefs. The bonds of service are harmful to both Rioch and Duine."

"The High Kings have never agreed with the bonds of service, but we've had no way to change it while Phaelon rules." Khedran leaned forward, hands clasped on the table. "But my immediate concern is the hidden Anzihi. It's hard to accept as possible, yet I see truth. I knew Canon...my father's loyal and Bonded Duine. Allasar's killer would have passed by him, as he always slept at Allasar's door when away from Penumbra. He was found dead in Allasar's room. Now I can guess why he had not called warning."

"He was probably Allasar's killer, and if he somehow realized it, he took his own life."

"By all the gods," Khedran swore as he sat back. "It makes sense. Horrifying sense. Varady, we will have little chance if they rise up as one."

"I have been trying to think of ways to help you with that, and perhaps I can. But first...please...I need to know what has become of Jael and Mia?"

"They are safely in the Temple of Liethe. Mia was fretful with no duties, and wanted to help with the sick and injured. Both the High Tahmine and the High Queen have been looking after them."

"Hasn't the Tahmond demanded their death?"

"Repeatedly. It has become monotonous."

Varady tilted his head. "And why did you not comply, if it could have stopped this evil war?"

Khedran lifted his eyebrows. "They are both innocents. They are not soldiers sworn to protect the people, to kill our enemies while knowing the risk to their own lives. Sacrificing innocents would be evil. Using evil to combat evil is not a solution. There must be another path, or there is no purpose to human existence."

Khedran ran his hand through his wind-tangled hair, turning his mind to more immediate concerns while Varady stared at him silently, understanding at last Danon's devotion to his liege.

"What do you suppose we can do to protect the Rioch from the hidden Duine Anzihi?" Khedran continued. "It is almost un-believable, all the Duine affected! I can't imagine trying to round them up, imprisoning them all." He laughed shortly. "Rumors of my madness would stand on firmer ground if I even suggested it. But the danger of the hidden Duine Anzihi may be greater than that horde outside the gates."

He returned his attention to Varady. "We have been under siege, with little hope, and your news is as dire as you warned. But, somehow, I believe we will find hope again...thanks to you and those you have brought with you. How did you bring the Chaine? We thought they were all lost, but you brought them back. How?"

"He played a flute!" Shajii laughed, dragging Danon with her to the table. "He played a magic flute and put all the Anzihi asleep, and we just walked out of captivity!"

"The story is a little longer than that," Varady smiled.

"I will want to hear all of it." Khedran turned courteously to the lovely young woman with long black braids who slipped into the chair next to Varady. "I am Khedran." He smiled at her, recognizing shyness.

Varady responded immediately. "My apologies, Your Highness. This is Stormwing, who is to be my wife. Stormwing, this is Khedran, the High King of Azlatan. He is also my brother."

She stared nervously into Khedran's rather terrifying emerald eyes. "I heard you, when you called on your people to warn of war."

"Where were you then?"

"On the Admech," Varady replied as Stormwing's shyness made her falter. "We have traveled a long way to bring you my bad news, following the Outsider Anzihi's path of destruction through Azlatan. They are ruthless because they all think they are fighting for a great cause."

"Yes. To destroy us."

"To destroy the Rioch of Azlatan, yes. The Anzihi have been lied to, Your Highness, and we must find a way to let them know that. I have learned there is no such thing as the 'races' of Rioch and Duine. Those are titles Phaelon created to keep Azlatan divided. We are all mortals of the same blood. The people I am with now are called the Sundancers, but..." He looked at dark Stormwing, capturing her hand in his. "Her sister has golden hair. We are all of the same blood."

Khedran leaned back, sensing it when Shandiin stopped behind his chair. "I have always suspected that. What do you think, Shandiin?"

"I think he's absolutely right." She took a deep breath and turned directly to Varady, who had seen her face in a sunrise over the Admech.

His golden eyes widened, and he shoved to his feet. "It's you!" he exclaimed.

"Please," she pleaded. "Can you put that aside for just awhile?"

After a moment Varady nodded wordlessly, and Khedran frowned. It seemed Shandiin had even more secrets, and shared one of them with his brother.

Varady looked down at Stormwing. "We have much to discuss, Your Highness, but my Sundancers are weary and need rest. Is there anywhere for them here?"

"Please. I am your brother, Varady, not your Highness. Yes, there are living quarters...enough left, even yet, for all of you, though it may be crowded." He glanced at Shandiin. "She told me to overbuild, and I did."

He turned back to Varady. "You used magic on the enemies who had the Chaine captive. Will it work on those outside the gates?"

"I don't think so. I think their leader has control of them. The giant with the green eyes like yours."

"Then we have to find a way to get to him. He's the one who has the magic that makes my people turn on each other, as well. I think it's time..."

He was interrupted by shouts outside, and shook his head in frustration. "They are attacking again. I have to go back up to the ramparts. Shandiin can take you to quarters for your people."

He left abruptly, Bannon and Danon on his heels. Shandiin remained standing while the room emptied, waiting, her eyes on Varady. She thought: *Here is another true gift to the world named Hiraeth.*

Varady's gaze held awe. "I saw you in the dawn, when we were on the Admech. Apparently my brother does not know you are the Sunqueen."

"Not yet....and he will be more than angry when he finds out. I have kept it a secret all his life, and I am very much hated in his realm, where they call me only Chaos." She shook her head, filled with sadness. "I am sorry, Varady, for your part in what is coming. I see in you the greatness of all the High Kings."

Stormwing stepped between them, having heard only the last of Shandiin's words, and looked up at Varady in concern. "What are you talking about? What is she sorry about?"

He looked down, and gently touched Stormwing's cheek. "I will try to explain later. For now, I should join the High King, to stand with him in battle."

"I'll take her to shelter," Shandiin told him. "Along with the other Sundancers. They will be fine, Varady, while you do what you must."

His lifted his eyes to hers briefly. He nodded and left.

It seemed the loss of their battering ram had angered the Anzihi, for they had renewed their attack on Cabre's walls with a vengeance, and now their ladders held steady as they had added claws to grab the top of the rampart.

And there were so many of them.

The Guard fought valiantly to destroy the ladders, to empty them, but the Anzihi came in great numbers, and many reached the top of the wall where combat came hand-to-hand. For the first time the Anzihi magic was turned on them at this last line of defense, and it was even more powerful, turning once-loyal brother against brother.

Striking down his own, Khedran was in a rage at the necessity. Wrath and sorrow met in his mind, in his eyes, and he fell on his enemies so fiercely even those who remained loyal feared to go near him. For a time only Varady and Shandiin fought alongside the High King.

But soon the Chaine warriors came to support the remaining Guard, and the Anzihi Tahmond's magic did not work on them. The Chaine sent the Anzihi screaming off the ladders. When next the Sundancers gave up needed rest to join the Guard's archers, the joined defenses began to drive the Anzihi back.

Still, it was near dark before the onslaught was over, darker yet as the sky turned to storm and brought its own warfare to that corrupted battleground, rain on mud and blood and the fallen alike. The storm shattered the night without mercy.

When the enemy finally retreated in the downpour, Khedran worked alongside the healers to save the wounded. He coldly refused Danon's concern about his own injuries until all had been done, then walked away without a word.

When Danon started to follow, Varady stopped him.

"He's mourning his lost." Varady looked sorrowfully after the brother he already loved. "His spirit is in terrible pain, greater than from the wounds to his body. He needs time. Let him be, Danon, for now. I will talk to him in the morning, and call on you if needed."

Much later Shandiin stepped out of the rain into the High King's battle headquarters, where he had lived throughout the siege. Hanging her soaked hood and cloak next to Khedran's, she saw his were still wet. She glanced around at the large and empty war room, dominated by the long table he used for meetings. There was a fireplace in one corner, next to a doorway leading to a room barely large enough for the narrow bed he rarely used.

He sat beside the fire in an overstuffed chair, which she thought he used instead of the bed. His black hair was disheveled, his striking face hollowed. His clothing hung loose now. He had fallen asleep, and her lips tightened in concern. Exhaustion was killing him.

She picked up a nearby towel and threw it at him. "It's a good thing Marre can't see you now. You look like the cat's dinner."

Waking, he used the towel to wipe his face, tossed it away. "I hope she's staying in Penumbra."

"She's not wandering the streets. She's helping with the wounded."

He looked up at her, and she saw his emerald eyes were dulled with fatigue and the edge of defeat. "You saw her?"

"Yes. She's well, Khedran." Walking to him, she noticed the blood on the towel, the terrible gash on his cheek, and swore. "That has to be sewn. That pretty face will be scarred even then, but it is bad, Khedran. Come over to the table while I get out the needle."

He obeyed slowly, then complained from the chair while Shandiin stood at work over him. "Danon is gentler."

"That's because he's still afraid of you. Hold still."

Khedran blinked as her needle came close to his eye. "We lost too many of our Black Guard. Half of them by our own hand. Shandiin, I feel like I am drowning in the blood of my own people."

She heard grief in his voice, couldn't respond, as no comfort could be given. She saw his thick black lashes lower, knew he was fighting down his pain.

After a moment he drew in a deep breath. "I like Varady. More than like, really. He is a good man with a true heart. But I think he has secrets he's not telling me...just like you."

"I know he does. He is the Forbidden Child, Khedran. The Prophecy is clear, and so is his intent. He intends to save the Rioch of Azlatan. The Prophecy says the Forbidden Child must die, or all the Rioch of Azlatan will die."

Khedran looked up at her. "I know. But...do you think he plans to die to save the people we call Rioch...the people who held him and everyone like him in bondage at Phaelon's command?"

She nudged his face back into position for stitching. "I do. And he hasn't told that pretty woman who loves him. He probably plans to die in battle, along with most of the people around here."

Khedran was silent for a long moment. "He recognized you, Shandiin. How does he know you?"

When she didn't answer he caught her hand, looked up at her again. "Why are you still keeping secrets from me?"

She pushed his hand away, tied off a knot. Then brushed his black hair from his grieving eyes, relenting. "Not for much longer. I'm sorry, Khedran, that you have had to trust me through all this without having the facts. You will know...when the time comes."

He sighed. "I'd fight you about it, but I am too tired."

"Try the bed for a change. You need to rest if you plan to keep fighting."

"Right. If I can." He got up and walked away without his usual quick stride. Stopped at his bedroom door and turned back to look at her. "He's a valiant but inept fighter. I can't just let him go out there to die."

"I don't think you have a choice."

"There's always a choice. I can't allow it, Shandiin. It's the same as killing him myself, if I don't defend him." He put a hand on the door frame as though to steady himself. "And with the news he brought, I think I only have one path left."

"Daimaine? Khedran, I'm begging you not to." When he turned his back to her, she pleaded. "At least wait until you are rested. You are distraught, and not thinking clearly."

"All right. I will wait, but not for long."

"She is evil, Khedran."

At that, he rounded to face her. "Shandiin, you don't have to tell me what she is. I know better than anyone exactly what she is." He met her eyes, and for a moment she read his truth.

She saw his torment, and his terror.

But when she moved to go to him, he slammed the door in her face.

CHAPTER 31

Khedran had never told anyone about the dreams. He never intended to.

He knew they were not just dreams, though they only happened when he lost the battle to stay awake. He had fought sleep most of his life, because when he slept Daimaine could take him to a realm that was her own.

He knew when it was going to happen because of the cold that permeated his body, and because he no longer belonged to himself.

He was helpless when she put her lips on him. Her lips on his were cold as death, and when his breath caught, she laughed and kissed him again.

And then she put her hands on him.

He was a man, and a woman's touch could have been exactly what he wanted. But not hers. Her touch was cold, and hurtful. She commanded him to do things to her. Her magic forced his obedience while his mind screamed in denial.

She stroked him magically until he grew hard, and then stroked him into torment, because she would rarely give him release, and even that was painful. Then she put him under her, and what happened then was no less than rape.

Whenever he tried to turn his head away, she fisted her hands in his hair and brought his face back to hers. She kissed him until he couldn't breathe and laughed joyfully at his struggle.

"You may be King to everyone else," she would tell him, "but here you are my plaything. My beautiful man. Mine. I should kill that stupid girl who carries your child."

He begged her not to hurt Marre, but that only made her laugh.

"We shall see," she taunted. "When you come to me...when you give up this stupid war and come to me at last...I may let her live, that she can bear another King for me. Unless we don't need one, because maybe we don't. I think you will be enough. I have waited for you for a thousand years, my love. I will own you for a thousand more. I will have all that you are. All, do you hear? Your body, your soul, your mind. Eventually, your heart. You will learn to love me and know that it is true love, not what you share with that silly mortal."

That terrified him.

Sometimes he found himself hung up in chains. She loved to torture him, and it wasn't always sex she used, though that was her favorite weapon. He writhed from the agony of blade, of fire, but he tried not to scream. Then he found it was better if he did, because she would make it worse if he didn't.

She swallowed his screams like candy.

What she sought most was his tears.

She wanted to make him weep. He would not.

He fought for that last remnant of himself with all his will.

Shandiin had warned him again and again not to go to her. He wondered if she had any idea what Daimaine wanted, what she did to him. He didn't have to go to Daimaine to know. He already knew he would live in unending torment.

This night, while thunder exploded outside the embattled walls of Cabre, Daimaine added something new. He woke to find her in his room.

At first she was a shadow, but as she took form the shadow was illumined, and the goddess became visible as she was. Her hair was a black cloak sweeping to the floor, full of stars. Her face was even more beautiful than her statue. Glittering runes outlined her cat-shaped eyes, traced her high cheekbones, and a sickle moon shone from her forehead.

"You tried to call me once." Her voice was like the night wind. *"Your Defender blocked me. I am here now, and you can come to me, and leave this war behind. Come."*

"If I did, would you then stand against Phaelon, and end this terrible war? Would you save my people? Or do you plan to let him do as he wishes?"

"I have no argument with Phaelon. My Kings have ruled for a thousand years under his Law, until his Law was broken. Phaelon's anger is righteous."

"But the High Kings have always belonged to you, My Lady. How then can you let Phaelon destroy all of us and everything we have created in your name?"

"You and all the High Kings before you are mine. Phaelon cannot destroy you."

"The Anzihi say otherwise. And they answer to Phaelon. Their stated intent is to destroy all the Rioch of Azlatan, and tear down Penumbra and your Temple. Will you endure, My Lady, if this King, this realm, your palace, your Temple, including the crypts of the High Kings...if all are destroyed by the agents of Phaelon?"

The room grew even colder. His only answer was emptiness. She was gone, taking with her his last hope of saving his people.

He sat on the side of the bed still in his war-torn bloody clothing, and knew despair.

Head in hands, he wondered what would happen in the unlikely event he ever spent a night with Marre. Would Daimaine come to him, to wake her and frighten her? Did he have to tell her, warn her?

He thought the humiliation of it would kill him.

But dying, he would go to Daimaine anyway, because she owned his soul. It wouldn't be the same as when she took him alive to her other realm, but he was sure there would be no peace in death. There was no escaping her.

Except...maybe there was. Khedran thought of what Daimaine had told him.

Your Defender blocked me.

Could Shandiin block the Deathqueen?

He remembered the night of the first battle, when he had gone to call the goddess and turned in certainty that she was behind him...and had found Shandiin there instead.

He had learned things that night. He had glimpsed pieces of Shandiin's truth, but he knew there was more. She had secrets she would not share, but this one he could not allow her.

He was at the end of his strength, and Daimaine was driving him mad.

Shandiin fought her own battles. Worried to the depths of her being about Khedran, she paced her tiny bedchamber near his headquarters.

She knew it was more than worry. It was grief. Her time here was near its end. She would soon leave this world.

She would leave *him.*

She couldn't stay to save him, and her foolish attempt to help him through his separate destiny had done more harm than good. Refusing to face her own feelings, she'd allowed them to blind her. Seeking to protect him by withholding the truth about his brother, she had hurt him. And, she realized, his anger at her had been an attempt to bury the pain of her lies.

She had hurt him, and none of it had been necessary. He was who he had been meant to be, and his destiny was his own.

She'd been warned the night of his birth, by a dark stranger she had come to recognize in his own beautiful eyes. *"Love can be deadly dangerous, Shandiin, for it is the most powerful thing in the universe. He needs your strength and your courage, but you cannot give him your love. Do not let your love bond him to you, for the sake of his world."*

She had tried to heed that warning. But she finally admitted to herself that she had fallen in love with him anyway. Now she had to go, before he guessed it...because she knew he loved her, and she knew he had gone to Marre when she rejected his last hope. Knowing the truth now would tear him apart. She didn't dare say goodbye.

Deadly dangerous.

There came a single hard knock on her door.

She froze. She knew she should disappear. She could do that; she could magically vanish this very moment and go on to accomplish what she had waited to do for a thousand years.

It was almost certainly him, and she should not open that door.

She opened the door.

He stood with his head down, which was not his way.

"What is it?" she demanded.

"Can you block Daimaine? Don't lie to me, Shandiin. Not about this."

He lifted his head slowly, and she made the mistake of looking into those emerald eyes. Her heart slammed once, hard against her ribs, as though she faced mortal danger.

"Come in." She knew it was another mistake.

He came in, shutting the door, then leaned back against it with his head rocked back and his eyes closed. He looked broken, and that was not her High King. She crossed her arms and scowled at his profile.

"Tell me why you need to know if I can block her."

"I don't want to tell you. I'm not sure I can. Just tell me if you can do it."

"I know I can't if you give yourself to her, like Khalen did. He was lost to me, just as you will be if you give in to her."

He rolled his head back and forth against the door as though in denial. He wouldn't look at her. She waited.

He finally stopped, exhaling long and hard. "I haven't given in. But she comes to me anyway. And I can't do anything to stop her." When he finally turned his head to briefly meet her eyes, the pain she glimpsed took her breath. "You told me, that night in the grove, that she made a promise to Khalen, that she could not harm a King while he was alive and aware. I understood then why she comes in my sleep. She takes me to a different reality. She uses me, Shandiin. I can't..." his voice broke, and he turned away, unable to face her, to say more.

It took her a minute to realize what he meant.

For another long moment she was too stunned to speak. Her mind spun back to a young man who had suffered similar abuse, who had begged for her silence. She realized now that her decision to be silent about evil, even to protect the innocent, had been the worst decision she'd ever made.

"How long has this gone on?" she finally managed.

He still couldn't look at her. "Since I was sixteen. She takes all the High Kings at sixteen. It used to be occasional, for "training"... forcing me to learn how to give her sexual pleasure while she inflicted pain." He drew in a deep breath. "Now it's more about pain and power, and nearly constant. There are no marks when she returns me from her reality to here, but...it's real. It's not a dream."

"Why..." she swallowed the knife in her throat, tried again. "My God, Khedran, why haven't you told me before?"

He finally looked at her, and his eyes said it all. His proud and haunted eyes, humiliated by a secret she had not known, had never guessed.

She clenched her fists in helpless fury. "I'd have found a way to stop her, if I had known."

He stared, straightening slowly. "You could *stop* it? Stop *her?* How, Shandiin? What else have you not told me?"

Seeing his rage build, she knew she would accept whatever he did to her...and felt no punishment could be enough for what he had suffered.

What all the Kings had suffered, while she only waited.

She said, "I didn't know." But she thought she should have guessed.

"I have endured this believing there was no way out, while you held back the truth that would have freed me from her magic? You have warned me about her...but you could have stopped her?"

Furious, he seized her shoulders and slammed her against the wall. With no attempt at defense, she ignored the pain, from the first and then a second slam to the wall that rocked her head.

He blinked, as though realizing what he had just done. Anger drained from him; his hands lost their iron grip.

Inches from his face, she stared into his dazed eyes. Watched his gaze drop to her parted lips. Saw his inward battle.

A battle he lost. He pulled her to him, and his lips took hers with open need...before he pushed away in broken confusion.

"I am sorry, Shandiin. That was wrong of me."

She didn't know if he meant the violence or the kiss, but it didn't matter. She crumbled to her own overwhelming necessity. She moved to fit her body against his, and returned his kiss.

He was momentarily staggered, and then his mouth was hot and avid on hers. He curved his fingers through her hair, holding her in place while he deepened the kiss until she thought she would melt. He kept that grip on her when he finally drew back, studying her face almost wildly.

"You are tearing me to pieces, Shandiin. I've loved you beyond reason while you pushed me away at every turn. If you care...if you care at all for me...why did you send me to Marre? I waited for you, I hoped for you, until you made me believe you could never love me...because you sent me to someone else."

As though suddenly remembering what that meant, he released her and stepped back. "You gave me away, Shandiin. I've loved you all my life. I have wanted you since I learned what it was to want a woman. But you sent me to someone else."

Her throat ached with unshed tears. "Do you love her?"

"I do, yes." He shook his head. "But not the way I love you. The biggest part of my soul can never be hers....because it has always belonged to you. Why did you give me away, Shandiin?"

She dared to reach up, to gently touch his wounded cheek, the heavy black silk of his hair. "Because I have to leave you, and I want you to be happy when I'm gone. To love and be loved. I'm glad you have her. You deserve so much."

He caught her hand in his, gripping it almost fiercely. "No. You can't leave me."

She was shocked to hear his command voice; he had never before used it on her. He exhaled, as though realizing that for himself, and spoke normally. "You can't convince me again that you don't care for me."

"Khedran, I am more than a thousand years old. I have loved, but I have never given myself to love. I never wanted the kind of love that would make me belong to anyone."

Unable to bear the sadness on his face, she looked down and gave in to her truth. "But it's happened anyway. I love you with every part of my being. And I'm glad for it. Because it's you."

When she then lifted her eyes to his, her voice fell to a whisper. "Oh, hey. Stop that. If your eyebrows climb any higher, they'll get tangled in your hair."

His smile dawned, but he'd been struck wordless. He wrapped his arms around her, one hand cradling her head hard against him, and buried his face in her wildfire mane. She felt his tremulous exhale, but it was a long moment before he eased that tight embrace to draw back and meet her eyes. His were so full of love it swelled the ache in her throat.

"Then why? Shandiin, why would you think you had to leave me?"

It took her a minute to regain her own purpose. "I do have to leave. And when I do, you will be free of Daimaine. So will Marre, and your unborn child. Your land will be free of all the gods. Including me."

She'd never seen him bewildered before. She'd given him the gift closest to his heart, and now must destroy it, and her own heart with it.

In despair, certain that he would hate her for her last and most terrible secret, she opened her magic to reveal who she was.

Every tear trailing down her face held a glowing drop of fire. She stood before him edged in shimmering sunlight. "I'm the one you call Chaos. The Sundancers call me the Sunqueen. I have to leave you, Khedran, to rid this world of its false gods."

He watched the magic fade, and she saw his bewilderment become understanding.

"I've never seen anything so beautiful," he whispered. He gently brushed the last tears from her face. "I've always known you are different, even from your own people. I knew you had magic when you came to me in place of Daimaine, back in the grove where I called her." He settled his warm palm against the curve of her cheek. "You are more than a goddess. You are Prophecy's Daughter. But for all that you are still my Shandiin, and I love you. Even if it means keeping all the gods, I don't want you to leave."

She blinked. "Even now? Knowing how I've lied to you?"

"Now I know why, don't I? And even before...I have tried to hate you, Shandiin. Hate and anger are much easier than heartbreak. But you are the solitary light in my life. You are the one who accepts me, even knowing I am less than human. I would still love you if you were the death of me. You can't leave me."

"I have to." She almost whispered it, because her throat had closed from the knowing. "I have to go. I was never supposed to love you, and it will hurt to leave you..." she closed her eyes, shook her head. "But now that I know what Daimaine has done to your bloodline, to you? There's not a choice in hell. I have to go, Khedran."

Her lips trembled as she gazed up at him. He kept his hand on her cheek, and shook his head in denial. "No. Not even to be my savior."

Then he tenderly gathered her tall strong body to his, and she ached for him. The love in his kiss drove the ache to the edge of torment. She'd have gone to her knees without his arms to hold her up.

And she seduced her incorruptible High King, even though he belonged to another.

He had been trained in how to please a woman by an abuser who had given him nothing in return. His only other experience had been with a virgin who knew nothing about giving. So she gave him what he'd never had, and because she was the one he trusted above all, he learned what it was to receive.

She taught him he could, without harm, tremble in glorious need, swamped helplessly by what she gave to him out of love. She did this while she savored his every touch, his taste, his very breath against her skin, until at last and finally she became helpless herself.

So he conquered his fierce warrior, the love of his life.

He had often thought of The Chaine as a lioness, but she went tame and wanting under his hands. His need for her burned beyond anything he had ever imagined. Her sweet surrender filled his soul with love. She was his light, his fire. His world.

But when those silver eyes went blind, when she arched back and moaned his name, it was he who surrendered.

Through it all he knew that he might never hold her again. His final release was bittersweet, and he buried his face in her hair while his heart ached.

She knew. Wrapped around him, stroking his back under his gloriously welcome weight, she understood. She turned her head to press her lips against his temple.

Despite everything, she felt complete for the first time in her very long life. "Thank you," she whispered.

His surprised laugh vibrated through her tight hold. He lifted his head to look into her face. "I can't believe you just thanked me."

"It seemed the polite thing to do," she smiled, "after all your hard work."

He laughed again, rolling away to stare up at the ceiling. "Only you could even think of such a thing." He closed his eyes. "Shandiin, I can't imagine life without you in it."

She turned onto her side, caught his hand to pull it to her lips, kissed his palm. "I want you to listen to me, Khedran. This is important."

He rolled his head back to look at her. "All right."

She sighed, gazing into those beautiful eyes. "You said tonight that you are less than human. You believe there is something wrong with you, and I understand why. You are different, my Highness, from the people you love so deeply. Your ancestors were created by the science of a lost world...my world...for the sole purpose of leading its survivors. Magic has magnified that purpose. I disagreed with the very idea of creating anyone for purposes not their own. I disagreed long before this world I call Hiraeth made me into a goddess."

He lifted an eyebrow. "This world did that to you?"

She shook her head. "And there it is. Out of everything I just said about your own origins, what you heard is out of concern for me, for other than yourself. Khedran, you should have a right to your own purpose, your own love, your own life. I know you will regret tonight. I beg you to fight the guilt. You deserve at least the freedom of this memory."

"I want more than memory, Shandiin. Now tell me about the rest. Why did the world make you a goddess?"

She shook her head, sighed. "The people of your world are descended from the survivors of a planet they destroyed. Hiraeth...your world...she had good reason to be afraid of us. She created four gods to control the people, but Phaelon is different than the rest. He has no heart, no understanding. The time after Phaelon's Prophecy War could end in every human being destroyed for disobedience. Hiraeth didn't want that, but couldn't change the prophecy. So...she made me different than the others. She made me immune to magic, and allowed me to hide from Phaelon until his damned prophecy is fulfilled. After that I can take all the gods away...and that has to include myself. I can't stay, Khedran. But...you are critical to what happens after."

"I am trying to understand even parts of this. Humans destroyed the world you came from. Why? And what is so different that this world would give up the control by the gods now?"

"Humans are by nature chaotic, as you well know. It's called free will. In the history of that other world, its leaders tried to chain that free will to match their own demands, and of course it never worked. It ended in Earth's destruction." She reached to touch his cheek. "Your bloodline brings wisdom. Your essential demand is that your people respect each other and their world. Your way will protect Hiraeth. She trusts you, so she will let me take the gods away."

He was silent for a long time. Finally, he said, "If you went away...where would you be, Shandiin?"

"Hiraeth told me that the ship that brought me...and your ancestors...will still be there when I take the gods away. Don't worry about me, Khedran. Take care of your people, and let me go."

He leaned in to kiss her, refusing even to acknowledge her demand.

She made sure he slept. She would leave him restored, and in his own bed. She watched him there for a time, that beloved, beautiful face of his finally at rest.

Making love to him had been the most selfish thing she had ever done. She knew his nature. He had made love to the woman he would marry, and then had been unfaithful. What a normal human might accept, even with terrible guilt, would be far worse for him. It would infect his soul, as it had his father's.

She was sorry for it, but believed Marre would help him heal.

Even though she was certain that he, being who he was, would tell his Queen the truth.

Marre would be hurt, but Khedran was worth far more than the forgiveness his Queen would surely give him.

Especially since Shandiin would be gone forever.

Not that any of that really matters, she thought. *I was unforgivably selfish.*

But she couldn't bring herself to regret it.

The realization that she would leave him, leave this world that had been her home for a thousand years, was so devastating she refused to face it at all. She would not add her sorrow to his. He had enough to shoulder, his own burden to carry. He'd carried it all his life, and by leaving she could finally lighten his load.

It was now her time to end the long waiting, to change his world forever. She wouldn't say goodbye, because she knew he wouldn't say it to her. He would never willingly let her go, especially now. So her secret departure would be just another painful lie.

She left him, and went to take leave of her people. It was no easy task, for she had grown to love those she realized were her true family.

She let Roinn know that he was to take her place as The Chaine. He didn't seem as surprised as she had anticipated. It seemed he had always considered her a goddess, even though she had never appeared as one and never used magic in his presence. He promised to give the messages she had for the others, and for the Sundancers, and gave her a goodbye kiss that left them both...very un-Chaine-like... close to tears.

She gave him a gift for Khedran, her last creation as the Sunqueen.

Then she went to finish her life on Hiraeth.

CHAPTER 32

Jael had free run of Liethe's Temple. The Sisters regarded him with a kind of credulous awe, not just because he had been called the "Forbidden Child," but because he carried a light they recognized as Liethe's.

He'd once known Liethe in his dreams. Now the goddess often walked with him, though he was the only one who could see her. He went among the Duine that Marre had seen during her time in the Temple, the displaced servants of Azlatan. Sometimes when he passed by, these lost and confused people found a kind of peace similar to what Varady brought with his Gift.

But Liethe warned him away from some of them, the ones that wore a symbol of The Bridle on their hands.

"There is danger there, young Jael. Do not go there."

"What danger?" he asked.

"When Chaos and Varady are here, those men will lead the rest to rise up against the Lords, and to destroy the High King."

"No!" he cried. "You must stop them!"

"I cannot, for the prophecy is beyond change or interpretation even by me. But, Jael....you are the wild card, never predicted, born only out of love and for your own purpose. You are the one who can do what must be done, if there is to be anyone but the Duine alive after the Prophecy War comes to pass. So...are you brave enough, young Jael, to save the man who calls you brother, who has protected you against those who would harm you? For the first time in Khedran's life, he has lost his clear path of duty, and

his heart refuses what his mind would tell him. It will take great courage on your part, to go to him, and make him understand what he must do. And what he must do will cause him hurt beyond measure."

"Why does he have to hurt? He is the High King, and he loves his people. I have seen it. He shouldn't have to be hurt!"

"But will you do it? Because it is the only thing that will save him, and those of his people called the Rioch."

Jael shivered. "The only thing?"

"Yes." Liethe was gentle with the young boy she had come to love above all others. *"It is. And you are the one who can make him understand and accept what must be."*

"Then...please tell me what I must do."

So she did.

Shandiin found the High Tahmond in his chamber, asleep. She smiled grimly and used the tip of her sword to poke his bedclothes in the approximate area of his ass. He woke shrieking...first at the pain, then at the fierce warrior standing over him.

"We need to chat," she said.

"I haven't asked Phaelon to send out the Duine Anzihi!"

"Then you're smarter than you look. Now tell me...why do you have to ask him? Why isn't he aware that the man who is the real Forbidden Child has entered Cabre?"

"He has? But I thought the boy..." he squealed as Shandiin poked him again.

"I don't care what you think. It's apparent you've been running the show without Phaelon's input. Tell me why."

"Phaelon...has withdrawn from what he calls the chaos of humanity."

That confirmed some of her suspicions about Phaelon's behavior during the brief meeting with Marre the day before. "Not from the goddess called Chaos, but all the people who don't meet his standards of order?"

The Tahmond nodded, swallowed, drawing his blankets closer to his shivering body. "He finds the other Tahmond more to his liking," he admitted miserably. "The one who commands the army of Anzihi outside Cabre's gates. Without the High King's heretic interference making people think they have personal rights, Phaelon's magic ensures his followers serve him without question."

She nodded thoughtfully, sheathed her sword. "Stay smart," she told him. "Don't call on Phaelon."

When she left he was hiding under the covers.

From Phaelon's Temple Shandiin strode into Penumbra's atrium, where the wounded were bedded in rows along the Palaces' obsidian floors. She hesitated when she saw Danon, then walked to him where he knelt next to his patient.

He looked up in surprise to find her smiling down at him. He stood to face her, and recognized something sad in her smile. "What's wrong?"

She looked around the room, her fiery mane swinging free over her sculpted shoulders. She took a deep breath when she turned back. "You know I still love you, right?"

He lifted his eyebrows. "Sure. I'm just not sure if I'm your son, your brother, or your horse."

For once she didn't joke back. "What you are is a dear friend." He looked surprised until she added, "He's going to need you soon," and he remembered their discussion atop a snowy mountain.

"You're leaving."

She only nodded.

It took him a moment to gather himself. "I see. I will keep my promise, Shandiin."

She met his eyes. Neither of them said goodbye, but both understood that's what this conversation was.

She walked away from him to where the High Queen waited, standing inside her unwanted veil of darkness and stars.

"Why aren't you on the ramparts?" Marre demanded. "Is Khedran all right?"

Shandiin regarded the small woman without a pang of guilt. She knew she would never feel guilt for her one night with her High King. If there was another emotion, it wasn't jealousy, but a strange blend of envy and gratitude surrounding Marre's future with him.

She answered with tongue in cheek. "He was fine the last time I saw him. Your Highness, I'm going to Daimaine's Temple. I'll be asking the Guards to keep anyone else out until I am done. I hope you find that acceptable?"

Marre only nodded, and she and Danon watched her walk away with some curiosity. "Better her than me," Danon murmured.

Marre frowned. "I wonder why she's going to Daimaine? She doesn't deal in magic."

She would soon learn differently.

Shandiin warned the Guardsmen to wait outside the Temple entrance, and went through the black double doors she had first entered with Allasar many years before. She had cared deeply for Allasar, sixth of her beloved green-eyed Kings, and father of the greatest of them all. His memory came with a frisson of sorrow.

She stepped into the Temple where the only light came from the stars wheeling across the walls, and from the sickle moon on the forehead of the giant statue of Daimaine.

She strode to the center of that vast room, and with the fury she'd banked since Khedran had told her his truth, she unleashed her Sunqueen.

The Temple's eternal darkness was shattered with her brilliance. Her flames overwhelmed the stars, dimming their light with her fire. Her voice roared from the depth of her own seething hell.

"Come out, you bitch, and face me!"

The statue moved. It's outstretched arm dropped; the beautiful face turned toward the fiery goddess who purposely matched the same seven-story height.

"You dare?" the cold voice echoed.

Shandiin simply pointed, and the statue exploded into a swelling shroud of darkness that fell as dust to the black glass floor.

Penumbra quaked, and everyone within its walls felt a flash of terror. Her magic's echo rang silently through the city, a tremor racing beneath the peoples' feet, then gone. Those looking toward Penumbra in that instant thought they saw its towers shift.

The Deathqueen rose from the black dust, a shadow slow to regain its glittering splendor. Her eyes were frozen starfire as she stared into the silver eyes of Chaos.

"You do not belong here!" Daimaine cried, a screaming wind over ice. *"This is my Temple, my realm!"*

"It was." Shandiin bared her teeth. "Now it's not."

True to her nature, Chaos plowed a fist into that beautiful face. With satisfaction she saw fear and pain as the dark goddess staggered back, lifting her hands as if to ward her off. The face was no longer beautiful, but crazed with fractures seeping darkness instead of blood.

"Your only real power is fear," Shandiin snarled. "You have no defense against me, because I'm damned well not afraid of you." Stepping forward to punch her again, she flinched as Daimaine screamed, a sharp high sound that hurt her ears. Daimaine began to fade, but Shandiin seized her by the throat to hold her in place.

"You made a big mistake when you hurt the High Kings. You're going to pay for that."

"They are mine!" Daimaine shrilled. Shandiin was shocked to see black tears pour down the broken face. *"They are mine, I made them! They are mine!"*

A sick hatred filled Shandiin's spirit. "You are evil. I've always known it, but now I know how deep it goes. You're going to die now."

She was distracted by a new light, a white light as brilliant as her own fire, and whirled to see Liethe standing near even as Daimaine escaped her grasp.

"A goddess cannot be killed," Liethe told her.

"I want her dead!"

"It can't be done. Neither her evil nor your anger can change that. There was hope you could take her from here, but now you cannot. You ignored the warning you were given, and ruined your High King, and the Prophecy War is upon us."

"Me?" Shandiin cried. "*Me* ruin him? Daimaine has tortured him since he was a boy! The only thing that's saved him from ruination is his courage and his determination to save his people. How can I have ruined him?"

"You were warned," Liethe repeated. *"We would have gone with you, we gods of Hiraeth's...but you cannot leave this world now. He will never let you leave this world, and without his permission you cannot go."*

When Varady stepped onto the fighting platform atop the ramparts, he knew that something had changed the High King. The terrible grief from yesterday's battle had been buried, replaced by a newer unknown burden.

Still, Khedran only shook his head when Varady offered comfort.

"You see too much." Khedran briefly laid a hand on his brother's shoulder. "You are a healer, Varady...a different kind than Liethe's Tahmine. You heal heart and mind. I watched you use your Gift when we worked on the wounded last night. Still, not all pain can be cured, not even by you. Let it go."

He turned to look over the battlefield. The rain had stopped at least momentarily, but the sky was still dark even where the dawn's early light should have shown, and thunder rumbled through the massing clouds.

Khedran frowned. "It's nothing but mud and mess down there. The enemy won't be able to move their infernal machinery to the gate, but they will come."

"You think they will attack again."

"Oh, yes." Khedran turned back, and he and Varady gazed over his City. "And we will be caught between two forces, if the Duine Anzihi awaken. I need a strategy to fight that."

"There is already a strategy." When Khedran shifted his emerald eyes to him in question, Varady added, "There is the prophecy. 'If the Forbidden Child is allowed to live, Duine will rise up to kill all Rioch.' I have to die, my brother."

"No." Khedran's voice was flat.

"Khedran..."

"I will not sacrifice you to the Anzihi."

"Perhaps that is not your choice."

Khedran sighed. "The Chaine have their own kind of prophecy. They say, 'The only thing evil requires is for good people to stand aside.' I will not stand by while you sacrifice yourself. There has to be another path."

There was a sudden break in the clouds, and the first light of dawn fired through Cabre's streets. Penumbra's black towers stood against a strangely golden sky. Both men turned to face it, and they saw the towers blur as though vibrating...an instant before that vibration rose from the ramparts through their boots.

They were both horrified to see Jael racing madly down the main thoroughfare toward them, a horde of awakened Duine Anzihi on his heels.

Climbing quickly down from the ramparts to where their horses waited, Khedran caught Varady's shoulder as they reached the bottom, turning him around to face him.

"You have to save Jael. Take this!"

Varady looked down and saw stars spinning around the bright blade Khedran offered. "I can't—"

"You are of the bloodline, and it will protect Jael, not just you!"

Varady met the emerald eyes. Without further hesitation he took the Star Blade and vaulted to Pet's back, riding onto the road where Jael's small form ran ahead of a mob of Duine.

Khedran whirled back, ordering his Legion Masters to defend the gates. "If the Duine get through, they'll open them for the Anzihi!" He could already hear the Outsiders throwing themselves against the other side of Cabre's gates.

Bannon shoved a sword into his hands, and he took it gratefully. *Chaine gold,* he thought. *It's not the Star Blade, but it's cleaner.*

He joined his Black Guard and his Chaine allies to defend the gates, and saw Jael had been outrun and thrown back into the crowd. He watched brave Varady ride his horse into that oncoming horde of crazed Duine, slashing down with the Star Blade as he fought his way through to the boy.

The Sundancers came running to stand in front of the fighters at the gates, bows at the ready.

The sun seemed to explode in the sky, and Khedran glimpsed a flaming goddess in the instant before darkness descended over everything, and a piercing scream shook the hearts of the bravest.

The Deathqueen was here.

Khedran looked up at wild Daimaine as she spread her cloak of darkness between him and the suddenly burning sky. He saw that her face was broken, all beauty gone. Her insane eyes were pinned on him as she dropped toward him, death or worse in her clawing reach.

Eyes narrowed with hatred, he raised his Chaine sword to face her. His one hope was for a clean death.

But the Sunqueen was above Daimaine. She shot a line of fire through the Deathqueen's darkness, and it set his sword aflame.

Daimaine screamed in terror. He lunged before she could escape, and the flaming sword impaled her where she should have had a heart.

Her scream this time was different, one of agony, and she seemed to dissolve into the sky.

But the miracle wasn't over. For just a moment, there appeared six tall men between him and the oncoming horde of Duine.

All in black. All with emerald eyes.

Khalen, Khandor, Khastiel, Ashtari, Mordane...and Allasar. Six High Kings.

His father smiled at him, and Khedran felt a strong wind that seemed to bear them toward him...before they all faded from sight, their spirits freed at last from the Deathqueen.

He was still catching his breath when Varady arrived, and Jael slid from the horse into his arms, almost knocking him down. "Listen!" the boy was shouting. "Liethe told me what you have to do!"

Above them, Shandiin had fired her magic into the sword of her people, and watched Khedran use it against Daimaine. She saw her flee.

"But she isn't dead yet," she muttered.

"No," said the familiar voice of the living world Hiraeth in her ear. *"But, Shandiin...he has set the Kings free, did you see? Now it is up to you to end this part of prophecy. The boy has told him what must be done. Remember one thing: should you ever find it necessary to return, you must bring me the son. Go now to your High King, Shandiin."*

Shandiin recognized a feeling, a magic transition. She had known it once before, upon her arrival on Hiraeth, when the living world had brought her to become the goddess called Chaos...Prophecy's Daughter.

"A last gift to you, for your long wait, for your courage," whispered Hiraeth.

Time stopped.

Khedran looked around in astonishment at a world and its people trapped within a single moment. Varady was stilled while lifting Jael back onto the horse; the horse was caught with head thrown up, his flying white mane painted motionless on the sky. Arrows hung in mid-air.

Realizing he was the only one who could move, Khedran stepped past Varady's stallion and saw the Duine horde just as inert, caught mid-stride in their race on the road toward him and the gates of Cabre.

He wondered if he were dreaming. Then he saw her.

In an aura of flame, the Sunqueen drifted down the sky, growing smaller until she touched down on the road that led to him. Then she walked out of the flame to come to him.

His Shandiin, just as he had known her all this life, in the simple leather worked with Chaine gold, her sculpted arms bare but for wrist-braces. She came with her long-legged stride, her hair blowing bright around her shoulders, her silver eyes on his with her typical wry amusement. Those laughing eyes clearly asked, *"How did you like that entrance?"* He imagined the question probably included some of those strange words he never understood.

He sheathed his new sword and waited for her, blinking to clear his watering vision. He knew he would always remember her like this, in this moment. He wished it would never end.

He knew, to his sorrow, that it would.

She stopped only inches away, her gaze avid on his. He was sure she felt the same sorrow under all her bravado.

"Did you do this?" He indicated the motionless world around them.

"No. This is a parting gift from your world of Hiraeth. To give us time to say goodbye."

"You were gone when I woke this morning. I thought I would never see you again."

"It was cowardly of me to do that to you, and I'm sorry. But now, it seems, I can't go anyway."

"I know. Jael told me what you were trying to explain, what I should have understood from the beginning. It seems the boy knows more than he should."

She tilted her head in amused question. "What? A little boy knows that I took the High King to my bed?"

"Not that part." He almost managed to smile. "But he knows we are in love, and we aren't supposed to be."

She took a deep breath. "The night you joined this world I was warned against allowing love to bond you to me. It appears I've broken all the rules."

"I got the same warning, I think, in that message passed down through all the High Kings. 'Nonetheless, guard your heart.' But I could never guard against you, Shandiin. I have loved you all my life, and you will always be my *amharen*, no matter where you are."

She studied those emerald eyes, so full of love and sorrow. "I don't want to leave you, or this world. But I have to, and now I can't. Your love has bound me here, Khedran. You have to let me go."

"I know. Jael made me accept what I have to do. And now I understand how literal the prophecy is. As Prophecy's Daughter, you were hidden in a single sentence, inside the prophecy itself. *'No magic can save them.'* It means the absence of magic can save the Rioch...and free the rest of the world. So...you have to go, and take the magic with you, in order to stop...all this." He lifted a hand to indicate the stillborn world around them, but his eyes never left hers. "Shandiin, I've never been able to not love you. Letting you go will be the hardest thing I have ever done."

She tried to smile. "I imagine killing Varady would have been harder. This is your other path, the one that doesn't require you to commit evil. And now you have brothers, Khedran...you have family, something no other High King has ever had. You also have Marre, who loves you very much, and soon a child who will never have to know Daimaine's cruelty. Leaving is my gift to you and your world. The last Gift of the Sunqueen."

He tried to speak, and couldn't at first, so she lifted her hands to frame his beloved face, and kissed him. "Say goodbye," she whispered against his lips.

He didn't dare put his arms around her, or reach for her when she stepped back. He was sure he wouldn't be able to let go if he did.

"Goodbye, Shandiin." His voice was soft, but strong. Because they had both always been strong, and that was important.

She started to go. But he called, "Wait," and she turned back in surprise.

"I have to know. Was it you who broke her face?"

She gave him her wicked smile. "With great pleasure. Oh, and that freaking big statue is gone. But you have a helluva mess to clean up in your basement."

Then she was just gone.

CHAPTER 33

It took him a moment. He closed his eyes and breathed, while focusing on why she was gone from him. He knew the ache behind his heart would never go; he hoped it would become less with time. Then, as was his lifelong habit, he turned away from pain to the duties still ahead of him. When he felt ready, he walked back around to where he'd been before the world stopped.

Sound and movement detonated.

"Archers hold arrows!" He used his command voice automatically, because he saw the Duine in the road were stopping, tripping over each other. The mob had become a harmless melee of confusion.

He turned as Bannon rushed up. "The gods are gone, along with their magic," Khedran told him. "Have the Legion Masters focus on the central ramparts, even if the Anzihi have quit pounding the gates. Then tell them to set free all of our imprisoned Guard who'd been changed by Anzihi magic. That magic won't work anymore. We're back to full force and more, with the addition of the Chaine and the Sundancers." He looked back at the city. "I'm leaving you in charge, Bannon, with Varady and Roinn. I have something I must take care of in Penumbra, but I'll be back as soon as I can, with a new strategy to finish this war."

Bannon, more astute than most, took this in and turned to obey. The gods and their magic might be gone, but the High King had the kind of magic necessary for leadership.

Varady had finished settling Jael onto his horse. His golden eyes were wide with amazement as he looked down at Khedran. "Your sword...the Star Blade turned into dust in my hand!"

"Good." Khedran grinned fiercely while reaching to take Jael back, gathering him into a warm hug. Then he smiled into the boy's face. "Thank you, Jael, for telling me to let her go. It's done, and the danger from the Duine is gone."

"I'm sorry if it hurt you to say goodbye to her."

"I'm not sorry, Jael. We understood, she and I." He looked up at Varady. "The gods are gone. Your people's Sunqueen gave her final gift, and took the gods and their magic away from the world. You are no longer the Forbidden Child. You should probably tell Stormwing."

He walked away then, still carrying Jael, toward the milling Duine. Camion, his own once-Bonded Duine, came running to him. Khedran looked into his old companion's confused and horrified face, and put a steadying hand on his shoulder.

"It's all right. It's over, Camion. The gods are gone. The terms Rioch and Duine no longer have meaning, for we are all one people, never again lords and servants." He smiled at Jael. "We can thank this one, who knew what had to be done, and made me see it."

Camion could only stare. "The gods are gone? How? How do you know?"

"Look for yourself." Khedran nodded toward Penumbra. "There's no magic there, no stars. It's just a palace made of stone, now. We have a lot of work to do, you and I, after I address that mob outside our gates. For now, could you help get these people back to Liethe's Temple? They can help with anyone who was hurt in the uprising. Camion, don't look so stricken. It's not their fault, or yours. It was Phaelon's, and he is gone now. Give the people something to do. It will help them."

Camion turned to help those who had been Duine. The mass of them broke ranks, stepping aside for the High King to stride through.

Khedran still carried his little brother. He needed the time to settle, to think, and Jael's weight in his arms was so precious it helped him accept what he had lost, and what came next.

He stopped when Chandar came, or he'd have walked all the way to Penumbra carrying the boy. He thought some magic must have survived, for his beloved horse to know his need. Then he rode with Jael in front of him, under a sky clearing to blue, with the sun warm on his face.

Even dreading what he must do next, the revelation that his world was free was beginning to heal his heart.

When he neared Penumbra, Marre came running down the entry stairs toward him. Khedran smiled to see her free of the dark magic she'd hated, her long black hair blowing free, wearing simple breeches and shirt like one of his soldiers. He stopped and dismounted when she neared, and laughed when she threw herself against him, crying "You're all right! I was so worried!"

"I am fine, Marre." He curled her into his arms, kissed the top of her head, then turned to lift Jael to the ground. "Is Danon inside?" he asked her.

"Yes," Marre dashed away tears of relief. "Many of the wounded are suddenly better. The Shadow that weakened them is gone. What's happened, Khedran?"

"A lot. I need to talk to you, Marre. Jael, will you go to Danon now?"

"Yes! I can help him. I want to learn to be a healer like him."

They followed Jael into the atrium, where Danon stopped work to come to his King.

"Is she gone?" he asked him, and then, "Are you all right?"

Khedran understood he meant more than the obvious.

"She is. And I think I will be. Thank you, Danon." He turned to Marre. "Can we talk?"

"In the library. I've kept it private from all this. I needed a break occasionally, and...it's yours."

He followed her in, closing the door behind them. The room had always been the family library, and he was glad to see it unchanged. There were thick rugs on the stone floor, art and weapons on the walls between the shelves of books and scrolls. There was a fire in the onyx fireplace, and lanterns made the space bright.

There were overstuffed chairs ranged by the fireplace, and he watched Marre walk around them nervously, fluffing them like it mattered.

He noticed the painting over the mantel. "Do I really look like that?" he asked in surprise.

She followed his gaze. "I think so. But if you don't like it, I will take it down."

He considered it, then turned back to her. "It's not that I don't like it. You are an amazing artist. But I think you have made me more than I am."

"That's not what Shandiin said. She said I had captured the real you, the nobility that belongs to all the High Kings. In this matter I believe her opinion above yours. What has happened, Khedran?"

"I think we should sit down. Why are you so nervous?"

"I think Shandiin fought with Daimaine. My magic is gone. The...the world feels different, Khedran, and you...you're acting strangely now, and it's all scaring me."

"The world is very different." He settled her into a chair, pulled another close to sit in front of her. Then, though aching with dread, he began telling her the truth.

All of it that had nothing to do with Daimaine. All he held in his heart.

"I didn't know," he finished. "I didn't know until last night that Shandiin loved me as I loved her. The day we left Cabre to go to war, she sent me to you because she knew you were right for me, and she understood that I cared for you. She made me believe...rightly, it turns out...that there was no chance for her and I. Marre, I am sorry that I came to you while I loved someone else, while I was trying not to love someone else. I don't expect you to forgive me for that, or for being unfaithful to you. It was wrong of me. All of it."

Marre was staring into the fire. She didn't look at him, but took a long breath before she spoke. "Did you really think that you slipped the truth past me, Khedran? I asked you about her after we made love. I asked if you loved The Chaine, and you said yes, and then added something else to convince us both it wasn't important. But I knew the truth. I also knew she loved you, even if you didn't. I knew when she saw that painting. It was in her eyes."

She turned her head and met his gaze directly. "I've always known that there was love between you. But I've told myself it can't matter. Because I love you so much."

That almost broke him. He couldn't respond for a moment. "Marre," he managed finally, "I am sorry I failed you."

"Only because you knew she was leaving."

"That's not an excuse. I begged her not to go. At the end I had no choice but to let her."

She just nodded. "I talked to the High Tahmine about you. The old one, not Rani."

"Did you? She was my foster mother. I loved her, and I realize now she knew about Varady all along, and never told me."

"Like Shandiin, I think she wanted to protect you from choosing between a brother and your people. But she also understood you. She told me you would put your people ahead of all else, including yourself. And," she went on, searching his beautiful emerald eyes, "that's exactly what you have done, isn't it?"

He blinked in surprise at her insight. But once more his duty drove him to what came next. "Marre, I can't expect you to forgive me. But I need you to remain High Queen, even if not as my wife."

"You loved a goddess. That would give me a lot to live up to, as your wife."

He scowled. "Don't do that. Don't think that, Marre. I love you for who you are, and that has nothing to do with her. I do love you. I understand I can't expect you to marry me since I was unfaithful, and I will not try to excuse the wrong I've done to you. Nevertheless...Marre, I need you to remain as High Queen."

When she began to speak, he lifted a hand to stop her. "Please. I have war still ahead of me, and no Star Blade for protection. You have to be Queen if I don't come back...and you bear the next High King. Azlatan needs you both. You must carry on, I beg of you, despite what I have done. Please tell me you will."

Unable to respond to that, she nodded, and heard his sigh of relief.

"Thank you." He ran a hand through his hair, thinking. "If I survive, I have some hope that you will nevertheless rule alongside me. There will be a lot of work to do and I need your help. But I understand if...if you can't."

"Are you finished now, Khedran?"

He nodded miserably.

"Good. Because it's my turn to speak. Of course I will be your High Queen. Moreover, you idiot, I expect you to marry me. Our child can't be born out of wedlock."

His eyes widened, and she smiled. "I also want you to marry me because I love you with all my heart. Shandiin told me she was glad that you have me. Khedran, I am more than glad to have you."

He caught her hand then, and pulled her to him. Gathered her close with wonder and gratitude for her loving heart.

He kissed her long and well.

And, once again, left her to go to war.

Much later the High King looked around his war room at the people he depended upon the most to defend Azlatan. He had explained his strategy, and now saw faces full of disbelief quickly changing to near despair. He could almost hear the words trapped behind those faces, words trapped because they feared to speak out in denial of his plan...because he was still the High King, even if he had lost his mind.

"Legion Masters," he finished, "you have your orders. Go now."

He waited while they left. Those remaining were his three Compatri, Varady...and Roinn, who was now The Chaine, leader of his people.

Roinn's manner was as blunt as his predecessor's. "Your plan is insane." Then he sighed. "But it's exactly what she expected you to do."

"Is it?" Khedran almost smiled.

Varady's golden eyes were troubled. "I understand your reasoning. If their leader accepts your challenge, many lives may be saved. But...I fear it will be at your expense."

"You think he won't accept my challenge to fight him in lieu of a battle between armies?" Khedran asked.

"Oh, he will," Bannon put in. "That...that beast won't miss a chance to kill you in front of his people."

"How can you be sure," Danon added, "that he won't order his people to cheat, and come at you all at once?"

Khedran sat back in his chair. "Because he's too proud to allow it. That beast, as Bannon correctly called him, has no soul. He is built of wrongful pride and hatred. The loss of his magic is loss of power, and that has to anger him. Losing Phaelon also removes most of the reason his people follow him."

"Even fanatics must fail without a god to believe in," Farbet agreed.

Khedran nodded, then lifted an eyebrow in Roinn's direction. "If Shandiin thought I would do this, can I assume she had a plan to address it?"

"Yes. She left special armor made for you, of Chaine gold. You will need it, without the Star Blade for protection." He studied the stitched wound on Khedran's cheek. "That protection seems to have failed you in yesterday's battle."

Khedran shrugged. "I was distracted. That's never happened before, but without magic it no longer matters."

Bannon said suddenly, "The magic is not all gone." When Khedran turned to him in surprise, he added, "You still have your command voice, Your Highness. You used it to give orders at the gate, after Daimaine disappeared. It wasn't like I heard it, but as though your voice was inside my head. So everyone knew what you said, despite all the noise."

Danon nodded. "Your gift of presence is still there, too. I felt it when you walked into Penumbra with Marre and Jael."

Varady added thoughtfully, "Stormwing said I still had some of my calming gift. Which probably saved me from her fist, when I explained to her what I had thought the prophecy meant."

"She didn't know?" Khedran asked. "Not wise, hiding that from someone you intend to marry."

"I never thought I would live long enough to marry, and didn't want her to worry when there was nothing else to be done." Varady straightened, strategizing. "The gifts we still have could be useful. I know you want to fight the giant alone, Khedran, but that doesn't mean I can't go with you. I could be of help."

"Do you plan to put them all to sleep?" Khedran smiled.

"I doubt that would work again, and never on this scale. But I met one of their kind some time back, and learned Phaelon had implanted them with a hidden secret just as he had done to the Duine Anzihi. Apparently, had I agreed to lead, they would have followed me to destroy the Rioch. If that hidden magic has also been lifted, they might recognize me as their secret leader, the one they call the Deliverer. I can help convince them that further battle is wrong."

"Or at least unnecessary," Khedran agreed, then turned back to Roinn as he stood. "Let's go so I can put on the armor."

"You're going to do this right now?" Danon's fear was obvious, and Khedran met his blue eyes in understanding.

"This war has gone on too long already. I'll be taking advantage of confusion on the other side, since they don't know everything we do." He touched his Compatri's shoulder. "They don't know the courage of my people, either. That includes you, Danon. I know you want to be there, to guard my back. This time I won't have you...or my Defender. It's a new world for all of us."

As he stepped out of the war room he was surprised to see Stormwing waiting, and he halted at her approach.

"I want to thank you," she said very carefully, "for not allowing Varady to be killed as he stupidly wanted."

"Varady is stupid?" Khedran asked. "Huh. It must be something in the bloodline. *My* promised bride called me an idiot."

Rewarded by her appreciative grin, he followed Roinn to the Chaine's own headquarters.

There he found others of the Chaine, all of them looking grim as they stepped up with armfuls of mail made of Chaine gold.

They wrapped the tightly woven links over his boots, his pants, his arms. Then they settled plate armor over his chest and back, and more over his shoulders. He looked down at his chest curiously. "What is that design?" he asked. "I've never worn insignia."

"You've never worn anything but black, either," Roinn pointed out. "For this battle you will be wearing only gold. The symbol on the breastplate is something she called an eagle, a great bird with its wings spread. I think it held some special meaning for her."

Khedran touched it, closing his eyes in thought of his lost love and her lost world. When he lifted his head again, he eyed with trepidation the helmet Roinn held. "Is that really necessary?" he asked. "I already feel like Chandar could have trouble carrying me in this armor, though it's surprisingly light and maneuverable. I don't want anything over my face. I don't know how that giant can see, with only a small slit for his eyes."

"Just put it on," Roinn ordered, and their eyes met briefly with memories of a young Prince who had learned to fight under training commands much more difficult.

So Khedran obeyed his old trainer once more, and the helmet settled into place. He turned toward the long mirror he assumed was present for this purpose, and saw his face framed by golden wings curving from the center of his forehead into wingtips at his cheekbones. A wolf's head snarled from the center, its snout protecting his nose.

His emerald eyes glittered from that golden framework as savagely as any wolf's.

He noted with satisfaction that while his head was protected, he could see and breathe, and the thing was not uncomfortable. He even smiled inwardly at the wolf, recognizing Shandiin's irony.

Roinn surveyed the armor and helmet approvingly. "Shandiin said that given the chance you would challenge their leader. You'd told her once that if your Dominion Kings ever wanted to fight each other, you would ensure they would be the ones fighting and not their citizens trapped by politics. But I don't understand why you would take such a risk, even to save many lives, when your entire realm needs you so badly."

Khedran's smile was fierce. "Saving lives is only part of my reason," he answered. "That Tahmond beast pointed his magic lance at my brave soldiers and forced them to turn on their own brothers. I hate him for that. I relish the chance to fight him, Roinn. To paraphrase the warrior we both miss...I'd like to take that lance and shove it up his ass."

Upon stepping outside, he found himself walking down a corridor of Black Guard, all standing at attention. Sunlight blazed from his golden Chaine armor as he strode between them.

The soldiers snapped salute as he stepped past. This unexpected and perfectly executed drill of homage touched his heart.

Chandar waited at the end of that corridor. The black stallion lifted his head as he approached, and Khedran was pleased to see he had also been given armor. He even wore the golden mail over his legs, and seemed not to mind as he pawed the ground eagerly.

Khedran mounted, surprised at how easily he could move in the armor, and reached for the banner Farbet held out to him. He nodded at Varady, who waited on his white stallion in readiness to follow him out at a set distance.

Varady wore only his white buckskin, as he had insisted. "I'm not there to fight," Varady had told him. "I don't want them misinterpreting. And," he had added with a smile, "Pet can outrun any horse they have, if it comes to that."

The great gates of Cabre opened. The High King rode through.

He rode across the muddy battleground, weaving through the debris of war. Because he wanted to see the faces of the enemy, he rode further from the gates than he had once before, when the giant Tahmond had come to demand his surrender. He finally stopped and planted his banner, and waited.

He'd caught them by surprise. The Anzihi frontline looked more like a rabble than soldiers, swarming around each other and, he thought with inward amusement, most pointing in his direction as though to make sure everyone knew he was there.

But it wasn't long before the giant Tahmond came on his great heavy horse. He rode through his ranks, dividing them with no apparent plan or structure, and stopped within speaking distance to plant his own banner. Khedran noted with grim pleasure that he did not carry his magic lance, but only a spear set across his saddle, and a longsword.

"Have you come to surrender?" The giant asked him. "Surely you didn't come to fight. That gold you wear may be regal, but gold is too soft for armor."

Khedran answered in the command voice he knew would be heard by everyone in his line of sight. "I have come to challenge you to a battle between leaders. You and I, and no one else."

He couldn't read expression through the giant's covering helmet, but he saw the reaction of the Anzihi soldiers. They were lining up to watch because they had heard. He would speak carefully to ensure they understood the conversation, since they could only hear him and not their leader.

The giant seemed to consider. "I see. Winner take all?" he sounded gleeful.

"No," Khedran denied him. "My realm is not at stake. Neither are your people."

The Tahmond almost snorted. "Then what use to fight?"

"There is no use for fighting. None at all. Your god is gone from the world, and he is the one who ordered this war. You would be fighting for nothing. Your people would be dying for nothing."

"We will take your city, your land, your riches, and make them our own!" the man shouted angrily.

Khedran shrugged. "You could try to take my city and my land, but my only riches are my people. If you want what belongs to them, my army isn't the only thing you would have to battle. I promise there isn't a citizen of Azlatan that won't fight if you try to take what is rightfully theirs. My people will fight you, because unlike yours, they have never known the chains of a tyrant. They will never give up anything to you, because they know what freedom is, and it is built on their own honor and respect."

Insolently, he leaned back in the saddle. "You are no longer Tahmond. You have no god. You have no chance to win. Without your corrupt magic, my soldiers and my allies can defeat yours. Particularly as they all ride the horses you call Shalmira, like this one."

He gestured behind him, because he knew Varady was riding out on his Pet, the white stallion first named ChanDethe.

The giant watched the man in white buckskin stop in line with the High King, but far to the side.

Khedran was surprised to hear his brother speak, then smiled to realize Varady shared the bloodline's command voice. It was the first time Khedran had ever heard it himself, and it did seem to come from inside his head.

"My brothers," Varady said. "You know me. I am the one your prophecies called the Deliverer. I refused to lead you into this war, for it has been neither just nor reasonable. You have been enthralled by magic, and lied to by your leaders. The magic is gone, along with the god Phaelon. Hear me, and know the truth. There is no longer magic behind the lies. All the people of this world are the same, no better and no worse than their neighbors. I promise you that the High King of this realm is both truthful and fair, and that you can walk away from this battle with honor and without fear."

Khedran thought he heard a rumble of voices from the thickening mob of Anzihi watching them, listening now to both him and Varady.

The giant heard it, too. He looked from Varady to his army, and fairly shouted in defiance. "No! It's all a lie! I do not believe you do not want vengeance for what this war has brought to your land! Do you think you can claim my army, my land of Xanthe?"

"I see no need to take vengeance on your people," Khedran answered carefully, "since they were in fact led into the misery of war by magic and the lies of a god who is gone...and by you, the ultimate liar. You don't care about your people. You want nothing more than your own power and glory. I say each of Xanthe's soldiers can either return home to live in peace, or they can remain in Azlatan in peace under my rule. You have already lost."

While he spoke, Cabre's great gates were opening. Riders of the Black Guard came through, ten wide, at an easy walk. They split in precision drill to line up before the city walls. Above, the ramparts were rimmed with allies, arrows nocked.

The giant yanked his staff from the ground, waved the banner, called for attack.

His army did not answer his command.

Khedran grinned and gave the final push. "You can always run away, if you're afraid to fight me."

The giant roared with fury, dropping his banner to hurl his spear. Chandar sprang aside, charging the other's mount even as the spear flew past.

The giant stood his ground and brought his sword up, aligned to plunge through Khedran's chest. Khedran leaned aside and the man was stunned when it glanced off the Chaine armor instead of piercing it.

In the same instant Chandar slammed hard against the other's mount. Off balance in the mud, it fell as Khedran's warhorse whirled free.

The giant was surprisingly agile, kicking free of his horse to avoid being trapped beneath it. He crouched, waiting for Khedran to use the advantage of height from horseback to cut him down.

To his shock, and to the shock of everyone watching, Khedran dismounted to face the man more than two heads taller and much, much heavier.

"You are a fool," the giant laughed, and rushed him.

A lifetime of Chaine battle training didn't fail the High King. With the giant's blows hammering his armor, he fought back fiercely, slamming the giant with his sword and with strategically well-planted boots to knees and chest, until the man was stumbling backward. When the monstrous man finally dropped his sword and went down, Khedran was breathing so hard he couldn't hear the cheering from both sides of the battlefield.

"Do you yield?" he demanded, and when the man agreed he stepped back watchfully.

The giant didn't get up. It was obvious to all that he had lost the battle. After a long moment Khedran, exhausted, turned to walk away.

But the giant had been bred and trained for war, and he knew no honor. He was on his feet like lightning; recovering his sword, he ran at Khedran and plunged the tip through the golden armor into his back. When the King fell, he yanked the sword out, raising the bloody blade high for the killing stroke through the Chaine gold finally weakened by constant pummeling.

Bruised to bleeding within the battered armor, ribs pierced by the sword, Khedran couldn't get up. He could barely roll back enough to see his enemy, that painted armor framed against the sky.

He saw the gleam of the giant's emerald eyes through the slit in his helm – a second before one of the eyes disappeared behind an arrow's feathered shaft.

Then everything went black.

When Khedran next opened his eyes he was on a litter, being carried from the battlefield. He looked up at Danon, who walked beside him looking more angry than worried. "This isn't what I call a triumphant exit," he managed to say, and Danon actually glared at him.

"You should never have fought that monster." Stormwing spoke from the other side of the litter. "Your bride was right. You are an idiot."

"Was that your arrow?" he asked her weakly.

"You told your people not to interfere." She sniffed. "I am not one of your people."

He began to smile, but passed out again.

EPILOGUE

S handiin opened her eyes to her Sunqueen's aura of flame. It faded from her vision as her reality shifted, war and flames replaced with the bridge of the starship she had left a thousand years ago.

She'd refused to think about the reality of leaving Hiraeth, for fear that she would stay and so leave the cursed gods in control. Now she relived the moment of telling her beloved High King goodbye. She had forced her best smile before she turned away from him, leaving him to his fate where war still waited.

And now she was back on the starship. She hadn't realized what a staggering change it would be to return to her prior existence, or how it would break her to pieces. She could feel the aura fade, and The Chaine with it. With that diminishment Shandiin thought her soul faded as well, and she knew despair.

She glanced into the emerald eyes of the man in front of her who looked exactly like the one she had just left behind.

With just one difference. He wasn't him.

Zion came to catch her before she sank to the floor, and she clutched his arms while panic rose.

Had it all been a dream?

"Zion...someone..." It seemed even her voice was diminished. "Please look down at the planet. Tell me what you see."

Zion seemed unable to look away from her, but Egypt turned immediately to the bank of monitors, and Shandiin heard her shocked exclamation.

"Sarnath, do you see this? There is civilization, where there was none!" Egypt spun back to Shandiin, her emerald eyes wide and almost wild. "Shandiin, where—what's happened to Khalen and Khandor?"

Sarnath also turned toward her, but his gentle face was sober with understanding that hadn't yet touched the others. "We all heard the last words the planet spoke to Shandiin before she disappeared from this ship: 'To save them, you must join them. You will then be trapped here for a thousand years.' She has done so, and come back to us changed beyond our imagination. I doubt our sons are still alive."

"Is that true?" Zion's astonishment at Shandiin's disappearance and almost immediate reappearance had become horror. His grip on her tightened. "How is that possible?"

She couldn't bring herself to look into his twice-familiar face. Not again, not yet. She didn't realize tears were coursing down her cheeks from the eyes she shut tight, sending a mental scream to the world she had left.

Hiraeth, answer me! Is he still alive? Is it over? What's happening?

But Hiraeth did not answer.

She heard instead the voice of a computer, an AI she had once known as Phil. "My operating systems have reloaded, and all systems are functional. There is a message from Roland, who has locked onto my quantum software. He says the earth-ship is in desperate need of your help. Shall I set course to return to Earth?"

THUS ENDS BOOK 2 OF THE SERIES:
PROPHECY'S DAUGHTER.
WATCH FOR BOOK 3: *PARAGON*
COMING SPRING 2025

PROTECT AND SERVE

BEFORE SHE WAS PROPHECY'S DAUGHTER, SHE WAS A COP

It might be the end of the world – it sure feels like it sometimes – but Shandiin isn't going to let that stop her from doing her job. A tough-as-nails cop, she's got a rough reputation around town but when a stray dog leads her and her rookie partner, Marcus, on the hunt for a missing kid, Shandiin proves exactly how far she's willing to go to protect the vulnerable in her city.

**Download your free copy of *Protect and Serve* at
susanlalandar.com/giveaway
for a glimpse into Shandiin's life before
the world went to shit.**

GLOSSARY

Abar, (a-BAR), an Outsider captured by the Sundancers.

Admech, (ad-MEK), the sea of grass, the plains outside the eastern border of Azlatan.

Alaura, (a-LOR-A), one of the seventy-seven dominions of Azlatan, birthplace of Rhiathe.

Allasar, (ALL-a-sir), sixth High King, father of Khedran; ruled 810-984.

Amhara, (am-HAR-a), is Chaine word combining 'love' and 'respect.' It has two meanings. In the first, it describes a relationship between people. Respect is possible without love, but love without respect is not. Love with respect is *amhara.* In the second meaning, it is a word of requirement relating to everything, and includes a note of gratitude.

Amharen, (am-HAR-an), Chaine word for the special bond created by amhara. The Chaine do not marry; this bond is as close as they get.

Anzihi, (ANZ-zi-high), the 'Outsiders' of Xanthe who follow Phaelon only; also Duine Anzihi, secret enforcers of Phaelon's aw within Azlatan.

Ardren, (AR-dram), Dominion King of Athea, father of Marre.

Ashtari, (ash-TAR-ee), the fourth High King, ruled 475-670.

Athea, (Ath-EE-ah), the Dominion of birth of the Princess Marre.

Azlatan, (AHZ-la-tawn), the nation of seventy-seven collected Dominions ruled by a single High King, created by the god

Phaelon for his chosen people. The western border is the sea. Northern border is arctic, southern tropical. The eastern border is a cliff bordering the Admech, and was guarded by magic until the night the seventh High King was born.

Bannon, (BAN-non), Dominion King of Tesna, ally to Khedran.

Black Guard, the High King's army, the first central army of Azlatan. Made up of 10 Legions, each commanded by a Legion Master.

Bond or Bonded: when the word is capitalized it represents a formalized union of individuals, Rioch (lord) and Duine (servant), usually from childhood.

Brend, (Brind), King Randmar's younger son, Prince of the Dominion of Ordhold.

Cabre, (KAW-bray), the King's City on the western sea, home to the Temples of the three gods deified in Azlatan (Phaelon, Liethe, and Daimaine.)

Camion, (CAM-mion), Duine servant to the High King.

Chaine, (Chain), a powerful anarchistic redhaired race of warriors who sailed to Azlatan from the west in the reign of the sixth High King. They are considered disruptive mercenaries by traditionalists and are immune to magic, but their metal called "Chaine gold" is sought for its strength. The Chaine's golden swords are in high demand, as well as armor of interlocking links. The Chaine people's leather armor is carved by designs in Chaine gold, but it's actually protective more than decorative.

Chandar, (CHAWN-dar), Khedran's black stallion, trained for war.

ChanDethe, (Chan-DEATH-ay), the mystic messenger of the goddess Liethe who can be cat, bird or horse; the Sundancers say the Deliverer will ride a horse by this name.

Chaos, the goddess who is not worshipped in Azlatan.

Compatri, (Com-PAW-tree), Compatri are chosen by the High King for personal reasons of trust and respect and are rare. They wear an emerald star on the collar of their uniform.

Congress, gathering of Sundancers, their version of "Council."

Consort, a title for a partner to royalty (by inference, a sexual partner.)

Council, a gathering for trial or policy purposes in Azlatan, made up of the High King, High Tahmond, High Tahmine, and selected Dominion Kings. Meetings are held in the Council Hall of Penumbra. The High King's rule is autonomous, but he generally abides by the findings of Council. By Phaelon's Law, the High King can be brought for judgement by a Council of the High Tahmond, High Tahmine, and seven Dominion Kings.

Daimaine, (Die-MANE), Goddess of Death and Justice, is under command of the High Kings. She gave the High Kings the power to rule, and several gifts for their rule. She is the power behind their throne, but she owns their souls.

Danhar (DAN-har) of Selagon, actually an Outsider posing to attack.

Danon, (DAY-nun), Physician and Compatri to the High King, formerly of Selagon.

Deliverer. The Sundancers believe that the Deliverer will come riding a horse with the name ChanDethe, and that he will bring peace to the world by stopping the enemies who have always hounded them. Those called the Outsiders, the Anzihi of Xanthe, believe the Forbidden Child is the Deliverer, and that he will lead them to destroy the Rioch and rule the world.

Deta, (DEE-ta), young friend of Marre in Athea.

Dinn, (Den), young Chaine stableboy.

Djarr, (Jar), a Chaine man.

Druna, (DREW-na), Dominion bordering Tesna on the west.

Duine, (DIN-na), the people directed by Phaelon to be servants to the Rioch, usually fair of complexion and hair. The "races" are forbidden to "lie together."

Duine Anzihi, (dinna an-zi-high), the secret enforcers of Phaelon's Law

Eleban, (El-ay-BAN), Dominion King of Lajan; High King Allasar was murdered in his castle.

Elthar, (EL-thar), Rainsong's grey Shalmira, killed in battle.

Everwhite, a range of mountains north of Ordhold.

Everwinter Pass, farthest northern pass leading out of Azlatan.

Farbet, (FAR-bet), Compatri to High King Allasar and later High King Khedran; also Master of the Tenth Legion, known as the Queen's Guard.

Farin, (Fair-in), Duine in Danon's Selagon home.

Forbidden Child. Phaelon's Law is that Rioch and Duine shall not lie together, and if a Forbidden Child of Duine and Rioch is allowed to live, the Duine will rise to destroy all Rioch, and no magic will save them.

Gods of Azlatan. Phaelon, who rules Order; Daimaine, who rules Justice and Death; Liethe, who rules Life and Healing; and Chaos, who is not deified in Azlatan because she is the enemy of Phaelon.

Goldtree, the trees of the Chaine's northern stronghold, used for building their ships and making resin for waterproofing.

High King(s), the ultimate rulers of Azlatan, created through a combination of science and magic; in addition to their special beauty and intelligence, they all have reflective emerald eyes that mark their bloodline. They are bred to be incorruptible, and they are empaths who can read the emotions of their people. They have inherent and magic gifts to reinforce their purpose, which is to serve their people through their leadership. The gifts include a 'command voice' that is heard as originating inside the listener's head; a presence that causes them to be recognized as the kingdom's ultimate authority without need of insignia; and charisma.

High Tahmond (Tah-mund), the highest priest of Phaelon.

Hiraeth, (Hi-RITH), an ancient Welsh word expressing a spiritual longing for home, a home that perhaps is real only in the heart, a home that is everywhere and nowhere; it became the name of the planet colonized by Earth's survivors, the world including Azlatan.

Iesse, (I-ESS-ay), inner mountain land of the Sundancers, between the Plain of Admech and Khaibara mountain range.

Inzrah, (In-ZRA), Shalmira belonging to Stormwing.

Jael, (Jay-EL), young son of the Duine Mia and High King Allasar, believed to be the Forbidden Child of prophecy.

Jaihann, (JIE-han), Chaine man.

Jainn, (Jane), *Amharen* of Jhinn, mother of Shajii.

Jhinn, (Jin), Chaine guardian to Marre since her birth, hired by Allasar to protect Khedran's future bride.

Jon, (John), Prince of the Dominion of Ordhold, elder son of King Randmar.

Khaibara, (Ky-BAR-a), an ancient fortress in ruins at the top of the Everwinter Pass, named after the mountains of the far eastern continent.

Khalen, (KAY-len), First High King. He never made it to Azlatan. He sacrificed himself to Daimaine in exchange for giving the High Kings the power to control her so she couldn't harm the people.

Khandor, (KON-dor), second High King, ruled years 1-250

Khastiel, (Kass-tee-ELL), third High King, ruled 250-475

Khedran, (KEY-drun), seventh High King, whose rule began in 986.

King's Way, the dangerous staircase up the seaward cliffs into the upper levels of Penumbra.

Lajan, (Lay-JAN), Dominion ruled by Eleban, where Allasar was murdered, adjacent to the territory belonging to Cabre.

Landan, (Land-ann), father of Danon, in Selagon.

Lathine, (La-THEEN), Dominion Queen of Athea, Marre's mother.

Law of Order, generally refers to Phaelon's Nine Laws.

Legion Master, commander of one of the ten Legions of the Black Guard.

Dominion King, any of the Kings of the seventy-seven Dominions within Azlatan. The High King rules over all.

Liath, (LEE-ath), Prince Brend's horse.

Liethe, (Lie-ETH-ee), goddess of Light and Love, healing; she appears with a blindfold because the blindfold is symbolic of her caring for others despite any faults they may have.

Majia, (Maj-HEE-a), giant white snowcat of Ordhold.

Marre, (MAR-ray), Princess of Athea, promised at birth to be Consort and High Queen to the High King.

Mia, (MEE-ah), mother of Jael and one other, secret love of High King Allasar.

Mikel, (Michael), a Dominion King.

Mordane, (Mor-DANE), the fifth High King, father of Allasar, ruled 670-810.

Nightstone, Penumbra is built of this magic black obsidian crystal; at night it is covered with moving stars.

Ordhold, (ORD-hold), the northernmost Dominion of Azlatan where the young Prince Khedran spent exile between 16 and 18 years of age.

Outsider, the word used in Azlatan to denote anyone living outside its borders, and by the Sundancers for anyone from Xan-the.

Penumbra, (Pen-NOOM-bruh), magic palace of the High Kings, given to them by Daimaine; Daimaine's Temple and the crypts of all of the High Kings are contained within Penumbra.

Pet, Danon's horse, given to Varady, originally named ChanDe-the.

Phaelon, (Fail-on), the God of Order.

Pharmond, (Far-mund), friend of Marre, a builder without magic who has adopted the ways of the Chaine and is disliked by the Guildmasters who have lost business to him.

Prophecy War. The God Phaelon prophesied that at the end of a thousand years Chaos will be released, Azlatan's borders will fall, and there will come a great war. A Forbidden Child of Rioch and Duine will come forward; if the Forbidden is allowed to live, Duine will rise up to kill all Rioch, and no magic can save them.

Queen's Guard, the Legion assigned to the High Queen, is also the tenth Legion of the Black Guard, which is stationed in Cabre.

They wear an emerald sickle on their collar, and their cloaks are lined with emerald satin. The Master of the Queen's Guard wears an emerald star and sickle moon on his shoulder, and has always been the Queen's choice. It is an honor for the warrior who accepts, and he serves for life.

Rainsong, a Sundancer, husband of Stormwing's sister.

Rammorth (Ram-MORTH) **Range**, mountains north of Cabre, the southern border of Ordhold.

Randmar, King of the Dominion Ordhold, ally to the High King.

Rani, (RAW-nee), young healer in the Liethe's Temple (friend of Danon), who becomes High Tahmine; she was raised with Khedran in Ordhold.

Rebran, (RE-bran), Dominion King of Druna.

Rhiathe, formerly Princess of the Dominion of Alaura, High Queen to Allasar, mother of Khedran; she died in childbirth.

Rhosa, (Rosa), novice Sister in the Temple of Liethe, assigned to Marre.

Rimon, (REE-mon), Chief of the Builder's Guild.

Rioch (REE-awk), the ruling "race" of Azlatan, usually darker in complexion and hair than the Duine who Phaelon ordered to serve them.

Roinn, (Rowan), hero of the Chaine people, is commemorated by his name being passed from one generation to the next. Second in command to The Chaine, their leader.

Sabar, (Sa-BAR), a noble woman of Athea.

Selagon, (CELL-a-gone), the border town which was home to Danon, Varady, Mia and Jael.

Shajii, (SHA-gee), young Chaine woman being mentored to become the next Roinn.

Shalmira, (Shal-MEER-ah), warhorses trained and protected by the Sundancers; they have a special bond with their riders.

Shandiin, (Shan-DEEN), The Chaine (title), leader of the Chaine people. See "The Chaine."

Star Blade, the magic sword gifted to the bloodline of the High Kings by Daimaine; it protects its wielder from harm and never fails an intent to kill. It is fired by stars and starlight when unsheathed.

Stareven, the warm season.

Starfall, the cold season, presaged by a fall of stars (meteor shower.)

Stormdawn, Stormwing's sister, blonde.

Stormwing, Sundancer woman, mate to Varady.

Sundancers, the nomads of the east, includes the tribes of Storm, Rain, Wind, Sky and Cloud.

Tahmine, (Tah-MEEN), the priestesses of the God Liethe; the High Tahmine is revered.

Tahmond, (TAH-mond), generally the priests of the god Phaelon. The High King is the only Tahmond of Daimaine.

Talgar, (TAL-gar), eastern city in Azlatan.

Tarfon, (TAR-fon), former Tahmond, living among the Chaine to study them.

Tari, (Terry), Palace Duine, Camion's daughter.

Tesna, (TES-na), Dominion on Azlatan's eastern border.

The Bridle, a constellation of stars, also used as a symbol by the Anzihi.

The Chaine, mysterious leader of the Chaine people (Shandi-in), who became the King's Defender charged with protecting the High Prince when his father Allasar was murdered. She arrived during the Allasar's reign and has never aged. See previous entry on the Chaine people.

Tyran, (TY-ran), Commander of the garrison in Tesna; Bannon's nephew.

Varady, (VERA-dee), Duine once bonded to Danon who travels outside of Azlatan and joins the Sundancers.

Windmaker, Shandinn's paint horse.

Windstar, Sundancer, Rainsong's mother, a tribal leader.

Xanthe (Zahn-thay), city of the Outsiders, who call themselves Anzihi. It is in the far south of the steppes of Admech.

Phaelon's Laws

1. I have prepared for you the land of Azlatan in the far west, a realm of seventy-seven Dominions, each ruled by a King.

2. The High King shall rule over all people in all Dominions. I shall choose the woman to become the High Queen for each High King, betrothed at her birth. The rule of the High King shall be autonomous, and he may create laws for governing the people throughout his realm, except for those I here provide.

3. There shall be two races among you. The masters are the Rioch, who shall be served with honor by the servants who are Duine.

4. The Rioch and the Duine shall not lie together. If this Law is broken, the Forbidden Child and both parents shall die. This shall be enforced without exception by those Duine I name Anzihi, whose identity shall be known only to me.

5. I give to you a High Tahmond to serve as advisor on my law, and to oversee the people's compliance with my Law. The High Tahmond may sanctify lesser Tahmonds as their service becomes necessary.

6. I am Phaelon, the God of Order. I am the only god. There exist also two goddesses, Liethe and Daimaine, who serve their own purposes in healing and judgement. Liethe

shall also sanctify a High Tahmine. The only Tahmond to Daimaine is the High King, and she owns his soul.

7. Be it known that if my High Tahmond, the High Tahmine, and the High King, should in council bring to me any person found to be in violation of my Law, I shall cast that person into the eternal void. If the High King is the person accused, council shall include seven Dominion Kings with the High Tahmond and High Tahmine.

8. The goddess Chaos shall not be served in Azlatan, for she is the enemy of Order. She has been bound for a thousand years, and Azlatan shall know peace until she returns. It is my prophecy that upon her return, my protection of Azlatan's borders will end, and a Forbidden Child will come forth.

9. If the Forbidden Child is allowed to live, Duine will rise up to kill all Rioch. There will come a great war. No magic can save them. Thereafter, all will die who disobey me.

MEET THE AUTHOR

Susan L. Alandar has written fantasy since she was a child. She grew up on Robert Heinlein and Ray Bradbury and Madeline L'Engle, discovering epic fantasy (Tolkien, of course) about the time Heinlein broke into adult work with Glory Road. But she gave up the fragile hope of a writing career when she became an abandoned mother of two and needed a stable income. In retrospect Susan would say she needed the raw experience of the real world to bring her writing to life. Now, years later, she has returned to her fantasy world of Hiraeth, ready to share The Daughter of Prophecy series with the world.

ACKNOWLEDGEMENTS

When I was left alone at the death of my husband Jim (one of those with honor and compassion), my two daughters encouraged me to return to the stories they had loved in their childhood but that I had finally put aside. So I dug out an old manuscript and started typing the words from paper into a computer. As I did, I found joy return to my spirit. I found enthusiasm, and purpose. Hiraeth and her inhabitants welcomed me home, and...because I understood more... became more.

So I thank my beloved redhaired girls, Rose and Kimberley, for their faith in me. And I thank the wonderful person I found, Keri-Rae Barnum of New Shelves, who has guided me through the practical part of writing fiction. And, most importantly, I thank all three for supporting my newfound courage to quit writing in secret.